GREG
BARRON
ROTTEN GODS

D0108160

HarperCollins_Publishers_

HarperCollins*Publishers*

First published in Australia in 2012
This edition published in 2013
by HarperCollins*Publishers* Australia Pty Limited
ABN 36 009 913 517
harpercollins.com.au

HarperCollins*Publishers*
Level 13, 201 Elizabeth Street, Sydney, NSW 2000, Australia
Unit D1, 63 Apollo Drive, Rosedale, Auckland 0632, New Zealand
A 53, Sector 57, Noida, UP, India
1 London Bridge Street, London SE1 9GF, United Kingdom
Bay Adelaide Centre, East Tower, 22 Adelaide Street West, 41st floor,
    Toronto, Ontario, M5H 4E3
195 Broadway, New York NY 10007, USA

National Library of Australia Cataloguing-in-Publication data:

Barron, Greg.
Rotten Gods.
978 0 7322 9435 9 (pbk.)
Terrorism – Fiction.
Global environmental change – Fiction.
A823.3

Cover design by Matt Stanton, HarperCollins Design Studio
Cover images: Figure by Jon Spaihts; all other images by shutterstock.com
Author image by Cliff Kent
Typeset in 10.5/14.5 ITC Garamond Std Light by Kirby Jones
Printed and bound in Australia by McPherson's Printing Group
The papers used by HarperCollins in the manufacture of this book are a natural,
recyclable product made from wood grown in sustainable plantation forests.
The fibre source and manufacturing processes meet recognised international
environmental standards, and carry certification.

Greg Barron has qualifications in education and science, and has studied terrorism at Scotland's prestigious St Andrew's University. He has lived in both North America and Australia, and has travelled widely, combining his interests in politics and current events with a passion for new horizons. His favourite places include the African savannah, the Canadian Rockies and Australia's Top End. Along with abseiling, offshore boating, skindiving and canoeing, his greatest adventure was a three-hundred-kilometre trek through the wild East Alligator region of Arnhem Land.

Greg lives on the North Coast of New South Wales with his wife and two sons. *Savage Tide* is his second novel. For more information about the author, visit gregbarron.com

See more at
gregbarron.com

 GregBarronAuthor 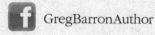 @gregorybarron

Dedicated to the memory of
David Montrose Poynten
(10/5/61–27/2/00)

The effects of global warming have spread to all continents of the world. Drought, desertification and sands are advancing on one front, while on another, torrential floods and huge storms the likes of which only used to be seen once every few decades now reoccur every few years.

The world has been kidnapped by the heads of major corporations who continue to steer it towards the abyss. The policies of the world today are not being guided by superior intellects to serve the interest of the people; but rather, with the power and greed of oil-robbers and warmongers, the beasts of predatory capitalism.

Osama bin Laden,
in an audio tape released to al-Jazeera News,
January 29 2010

THE FIRST DAY

The earth is formed and no longer empty, yet darkness rules over the surface of the deep, and the spirit of God hovers over the waters, polluted with hydrocarbons and chemical residues flowing from city drains, oil wells, and ships' ballast. These waters are devoid of fish and sea life, harvested to extinction by giant factory ships. Toxic blue-green algal blooms choke the remaining life from the sea.

Plastic shopping bags, discarded bottles, fishing line, and polystyrene cluster together to form rafts in the Pacific, Atlantic, and Indian Oceans. The largest of these floating rubbish dumps, the North Pacific Gyre, covers an area twice the size of France. Sea levels rise. Current and wind anomalies cause supertides — periodic rises of over a metre in some areas — salting arable land, destroying homes and livelihoods. Storm cells roam the earth like pillaging tribes.

Conflict flares across North Africa and the Middle East. New, free states descend into sectarian violence and disarray. In Europe and America, public anger over inequality, carbon blowouts, austerity budgets, and food prices turns to fury. A new age of protest gathers momentum.

In Aden, Yemen, Isabella Thompson, Parliamentary Under-Secretary of the British Foreign and Commonwealth

Office, sends her daughters, Hannah, 11, and Frances, 14, to the airport cafeteria with a five-hundred rial note to buy chocolates.

There was evening, and there was morning. The first day.

Rabi al-Salah Conference Centre, Residential Complex, Dubai

Day 1, 10:35

Dr Ali Khalid Abukar casts multiple shadows, dark and light, on pastel shades of walls and carpet. A white demitasse coffee cup sits on the table beside an open copy of the *Khaleej Times*. The blinds are drawn tight against the morning sun.

Sweat moistens his skin, and the lenses of his glasses fog as he moves across the room to the mirrors that make up the wardrobe doors. He removes his glasses, cleaning them with a handkerchief, and examines his image. Bloodless lips. Armani shirt, crisp with starch. Matching tie. Patent leather shoes.

Dressed in the trappings of greed and wealth ...

The telephone rings. Ali crosses the room to answer it. 'Yes?'

'Dr Abukar, security has arrived to escort you through.'

'Thank you. Please inform them that I will be ready in a few moments.' His voice is gentle, that of an educated man explaining a point of fact to his peers.

Lowering the handset, he takes a white plastic box from the bedside drawer. Examining it for a moment, recalling the instructions, he walks to the doorway, fixing it to the wall near the entry with its self-adhesive pad. He flicks a switch, and the light flashes, indicating that the infrared sensor will activate in sixty seconds.

... *I will die shahid for the glory of God.*

Counting down the time, he slips a dark jacket over his shoulders and collects the Manzoni leather briefcase from its place beside the bed. With the sensation of passing from one world to another, he leaves the room, closing the door behind him.

Moving down the corridor towards the residential wing of the conference centre, Marika Hartmann stops to adjust the black gun belt that loops around her waist, the webbing digging hard into her hips. As an afterthought she folds up the cuffs on her dark blue overalls before striding towards the elevators.

As she walks, her eyes roam through the glass and along the coastal strip — the line of international hotels beginning with the Sheraton and Royal Mirage, all the way to the thirty-nine-storey Burj al-Arab, shaped like a dhow on its artificial island. Further down: the long, sweeping Jumeirah Beach, and the City Centre, shrouded in dust borne on searing desert winds.

This is Dubai, where for generations oil dollars have come home not only to roost, but to crow. The Palm Jumeirah. Mall of the Emirates. The glass-faced skyscrapers that line Sheikh Zayed Road, dwarfed by the glorious Burj Khalifa. The minarets of private mosques, and wind towers rise from block after block of walled housing. To service this empire, hundreds of thousands of South Asian expatriates rise early each morning in the slums of Sharjah and commute to Dubai to sweep paths, clean windows, cook, and labour at one of the few remaining construction sites.

Oil revenues have fallen. Debt repayments are crippling the city. Half finished, abandoned buildings dot the skyline. Artificial islands that were planned to resemble the continents of the world lie like irregularly shaped sand bars out in the Gulf. After dark, Dubai is young and beautiful, adorned with diamonds and pearls. Under the merciless Arabian sun, however, the wrinkles are plain, and the gems are made of glass.

Marika, taking one last look as she enters the elevator, draws comfort from the complex's proximity to the water; having grown up so close to the beach in the Sydney suburb of Bondi that she would walk home barefoot, hang her towel on the Hills Hoist in the backyard, over close-cropped lawns and yellow daisies. In her mind she hears the slamming of the screen door. The drip of salt water on the linoleum floor.

Salt water. Impatient seas lapping at levees and flood barriers the world over. Heatwaves and firestorms once labelled by conservative science as ludicrous. The rise of the African Salafis, the Taliban of a new age. The collapse of national economies under the groaning weight of debt. The Secretary-General of the United Nations said it himself: 'This is a civilisation in crisis, a world on the brink. Only goodwill and honest effort can turn the tide.'

A world on the brink. A self-perpetuating reality television show, where the media spectacularises violence to such an extent that the public can no longer differentiate the latest blockbuster film from twenty-four-hour news channels. A world where personal freedom is subjugated by ever more invasive rules, yet children grow up with unfettered access to internet pornography, social networking, and the undermining influence of American underculture. A world where acts of terror, even those of marginalised amateurs, attract publicity that becomes a goal in itself.

This is a world where the United States of America spends more money on its 'defence' than the rest of the world put together spends on theirs, maintains a thousand military bases at home and seven hundred overseas. Where the nuclear club includes some of the most volatile nations on earth and a million children carry guns and fight grown-up wars in thirty different conflicts.

A world of startling inequality, where one per cent of adults own forty per cent of the world's assets. Where eighty per cent of the population lives on less than ten dollars a day, and fifty per cent lives on less than two. Where bankers and moguls draw salaries in the millions and dine with politicians who pass laws to perpetuate the system and maintain the status quo at all costs.

After school, Marika entered Duntroon Military College as an officer trainee, completing a degree in Political Science at the nearby Australian National University. She was one of the first female frontline infantry officers in the Australian Army, women who were, for the first time, permitted to kill and be killed.

Special Forces training, and a foray into Afghanistan, fuelled her need to understand why peace was so hard. She graduated top of her class in Military Intelligence, and a desire to be at the frontline saw her posted to Europe, cutting her teeth at the secret Alliance Base in Paris before volunteering for the new DRFS Directorate of Britain's MI6.

Assignments that would never make the news took her deep into Pakistan, Africa – the Maghreb, and Sahel. The world changed constantly, defying experts. The Arab Spring took even the most insightful commentators by surprise, launched when Mohamed Bouazizi set himself on fire in a Tunisian market, catching the collective imagination of a generation of tech savvy but repressed youth.

In Mali, during a freak storm, Marika saw something that would be engraved on her soul. She was stationed in the village of Yanfolila, after reports filtered through of a militant training camp in the area. A 'secret base', that turned out to be a few teenagers and old men with guns who dreamed of glory.

Waiting for a chopper pick-up in a makeshift LZ, Marika watched a man and woman build a house. They cut poles and bearers from acacia trunks, then weaved together thousands of dry branches to make up the walls. Next the woman carried wet clay from the river and, in a purpose-built pit, the man mixed it with cow dung and dry straw. They laboured to fill the spaces between the laths of sticks, packing the clay in tight to provide a weatherproof seal.

When it was done, just as they began weaving palm fronds for the thatched roof, a storm blew in from the west. Torrential rain followed. Husband and wife slapped on more fresh clay, trying to hold it together — yet they had only two hands each, and as soon as one place held, another began to subside.

The rain continued and they became distressed, hands plastering mud over the sticks while the rain washed it away. One or two neighbours, even Marika herself, came to help. More hands, but never enough, trying to keep the mud from washing away. Impossible without fresh straw, dry clay, without more hands, more hands ...

Three floors up, Marika leaves the elevator and moves along a passage carpeted in mauve, prints of famous artworks on the walls. Dwarf neanthe palms and cynerium grass grow in clusters in pots designed to resemble local bronze-age handiwork.

Dr Abukar greets her with a bow and a tap of his chest with the flat of his hand. His features are soft, almost feminine, with narrow wrists and wire-rimmed glasses. This morning, his usual nervous manner seems heightened. Dew-like sweat coats his forehead, despite the air conditioning. *He's got the shakes. Poor man is about to address a thousand people. Ambassadors. Vice presidents. Ministers of state ...*

'Follow me, please, sir. I trust you had a pleasant night?'

'Yes, yes, of course.'

Sole occupants of the elevator, they descend in tense silence. Marika says nothing about the change in him. Temperamental delegates are part of a job that has been, so far, a pleasant experience, with just the usual escort and monitoring duties. Security for the conference is provided by a partnership between the Dubai police, and international security organisations, including the DRFS.

The door slides open. Dr Abukar touches her arm. The expression on his face is strange, almost apologetic.

'The world is not a fair place, Miss Hartmann.'

The declaration increases her feeling of unease, but she says nothing, merely nodding to acknowledge his words.

'Just a short drive from here,' he continues, 'you will find shopping malls filled with designer stores. Armani, Dolce and Gabbana, Gucci, Chanel, Piaget, and many others. They tell me that you can purchase diamond-encrusted sunglasses, with a price tag of just over three hundred thousand US dollars. Sunglasses! And designer dresses can cost enough to feed a village for a year. Within a few thousand kilometres of where we stand, in Africa, fifty million people are unable to procure sufficient calories to sustain themselves. Women from twelve to forty years bear children they cannot feed. Have you ever seen a child dying of starvation, or of AIDS?' His eyes are earnest, almost pleading. 'In these last five years of drought and heat, the number of starving Africans has increased by a million people a month. Now that the rising seas — what my people call the Daad — has begun, there will be many more.'

They step together onto the carpeted walkway. Other groups pass by — UN officials, aides, and journalists. At twenty-metre intervals, Dubai Special Forces troops in grey combat fatigues stand with French-manufactured FAMAS assault rifles either slung or cradled in their arms, grey badges on their chests and dark blue berets tilted over close-shaved heads.

A checkpoint looms ahead, resembling an airport security barrier, with twin aluminium gateways and a low table. Marika takes Dr Abukar's briefcase from his hands and places it on the conveyor, watching as he steps under the arched metal detectors and body scanners. The security protocol is rigorous, foolproof.

The guard opens the case and looks perfunctorily inside: at the sheaf of papers in a manila document wallet;

paracetamol tablets, a bottle of mineral water and an apple.

'Thank you,' he says, 'enjoy the conference.'

Ali Khalid Abukar has a sense of unreality so wild it is like lysergic acid pulsing through his veins and infiltrating the frontal lobe, seeing himself through cameras on either side, imagining the security services studying each nervous pace, knowing his intention like mind readers.

An attractive woman in her mid-thirties hurries towards them. Blonde hair, stylish clothes — neat dark skirt suit, silk scarf. Left shoe scuffed, a button undone halfway down the jacket. Up close, her eye make-up seems to have been unsteadily applied. A name tag identifies her as Isabella Thompson, Parliamentary Under-Secretary of the British Foreign and Commonwealth Office. In one hand she carries a briefcase identical to his.

Thank God, she is here — just as Zhyogal promised.

Approaching him, she stands closer than would normally be considered polite. 'Dr Abukar?'

'Yes?'

'I wanted to say how much I admire your work. I just finished reading your paper in the Harvard Human Rights Journal. The one on corporate complicity in African poverty.'

'Ah, yes. You liked it?'

'Liked isn't the right word. It was horrifying.'

Watching from the corner of his eye, Ali sees the security woman's attention wander, gazing out through the glass to where, behind wire barriers, a thousand or more protesters clash with police, surging backwards and forwards like a tide, shouts just audible through the armoured glass; a moving, swelling mass of waving arms and placards.

The exchange of briefcases takes only a moment. Ali feels the weight, the power of the thing, and slippery sweat coating the handle.

Isabella Thompson prattles on. 'It affected me a great deal, and now I look forward to your address this morning.'

Ali inclines his head. 'Thank you. I'd best hurry, or I will be late.'

This is no longer a dream, but reality. He forces himself to breathe, conscious of a growing feeling of vertigo. He has the briefcase, the power to change history, and even the guard who walks beside him does not suspect.

Continuing down the corridor, the entrance to the conference room comes into view, resembling an oversized bank vault. Guards stand on either side. A backlit screen, shiny as a mirror, blinks up the day's agenda in letters two hundred millimetres high. Ali tries not to focus on his own name. It looks too solid, too respectable. At odds with what he is about to do.

At a distance of some twenty metres, he stops walking, standing with his breath burning hot in his throat. The protesters' cries sift through the glass. He stares myopically at the animal that has just caught his eye. A German shepherd — russet brown and gold, handsome and massive. The handler half kneels with one arm around the animal's neck.

Watch for kufr police dogs, Zhyogal warned him. *Despite the masking agents we have used, they may take the scent. Watch for them. Avoid them. Insha'Allah, you will get through.*

The guard walks on for a few steps before noticing that he has stopped. She turns, eyes narrowed. 'Doctor? Is something the matter? We need to hurry.'

He removes his glasses, working at a lens with his handkerchief. 'I am sorry, Miss Hartmann, but I do not like dogs. They frighten me … a great deal.' He watches the handler pat the animal around the ruff, muttering endearments, slipping something from his pocket and into the palm of his hand.

Again the security guard urges him on, brown eyes earnest, pleading. She has a nicely formed face, he notices, with cheerful lips, an upswept nose and high cheekbones. Unconsciously, he is pleased that she will not be inside the auditorium at the final moment.

'I'll walk between you and the dog,' she says. 'Please. We can't keep them waiting.'

Ali moves to her far side, takes the first step towards the entrance. The animal sits up, ears cocked, then whines and starts forwards. The handler takes a double turn of the leash around his hand and walks after them, calling out in accented English, 'Excuse me?'

Ali walks on twenty or more steps before he stops. Amplified voices from the chamber echo through the walls. He looks ahead, sees the Englishwoman again.

Thank God she is still here.

The dog handler follows, trying to control the animal. 'Excuse me. Surely the dog is mistaken, but …'

Isabella Thompson is on the spot in a moment, hands on hips. 'How dare you be so impertinent? This man is due to address the conference in a moment. Your dog is as poorly trained as you are ill-mannered.'

The animal seems to lose interest at that point, turning to look back down the walkway. The handler lowers his eyes. 'Of course, madam, please accept my apologies.' With a jerk on the leash he steers the dog away.

Marika watches Isabella Thompson escort Dr Abukar into the conference room. Disquiet narrows her eyes. Why did she react so strongly to the dog handler? Why was an FCO diplomat outside the conference room at all?

Thumbs in her pockets, Marika hovers near the entrance. Even now she is not worried. The room is secure. Hydraulically operated steel doors are hidden in the jambs, capable of isolating the room from any threat, to be opened again only with cooperation from both inside and outside. Marika has studied the specifications — manufactured by the German engineering firm Schroeder, weighing three-point-four tonnes, sealed by a chemically resistant polymer. The double-skinned 316 stainless steel face, thirty-five millimetres thick, will defeat any but the most determined, industrial strength attack.

An amplified voice echoes out through the walls. 'Please welcome Dr Ali Khalid Abukar, one of a number of silent achievers who has worked at the coal face of international aid. He holds a PhD in Human Rights and Democratisation from Debub University in Ethiopia. Dr Abukar sits on dozens of committees including the Economic and Social Council and the Committee for Climate Change in Africa. He is widely published, and speaks eight languages ...'

Swallowing her unease, telling herself that she is foolish to have misgivings about this gentle man, Marika climbs a discreet set of stairs up to the control room. This area is longer than it is wide, crammed with 3D monitor screens, and young men and women tapping at keyboards.

Marika has met more than a few of them; drunk Stella Artois at the bar with the non-Muslims, most of them delegates from various security forces from around the world. Nikulina, the Russian, lifts his eyes from the screen to give her a wave, black body hair crawling out of his cuffs and halfway down the backs of his hands.

The gaunt frame of Abdullah bin al-Rhoumi, Head of Security for Rabi al-Salah, Director of GDOIS, Dubai's General Department of Organisation, Protective Security and Emergency, dominates the room. He turns to look at her as she enters. Eyes like cameras. In just two weeks they have developed a close rapport.

'Is something wrong?' he asks.

Marika shakes her head. 'No, I don't think so.'

Various camera angles from inside the conference room are projected onto a series of screens mounted along one wall, as well as smaller monitors scattered around the room. Marika reverses a chair and sits with folded arms leaning on the back, watching the feed from a ceiling-mounted camera as it pans around the conference room — a vast space, eighty metres by one hundred and ten, an amphitheatre with eighteen concentric rings of benches, all made from the latest mycobond organic plastics.

Representatives of nations sit in rows flanked by aides and advisors, equipped with wafer-thin touch screens that allow them to call up the databases — the proportion of women dying in childbirth in Africa and Asia; AIDS deaths per capita; seismic patterns and predictions; melt rates of the polar ice caps; global temperatures; national debt for every nation — the maddening, depressing, endless statistics churned out by the committees and agencies of the United Nations.

The camera settles on Dr Abukar, reaching the dais, using a shaking forefinger to push the rim of his glasses up off the bridge of his nose, rubbing the area. So nervous. *Too nervous?*

Marika rationalises that he is about to address a television and online audience that might number in the billions. *It's OK. There's nothing wrong. Just another speech. A gabfest; a talkathon.*

The general cynicism in the control room about the conference surprises her. No one Marika has talked to believes that this latest summit will achieve anything at all. Yet surely it must — here are the leaders of every nation. The President of the United States, surrounded by a dozen aides and assistants. Britain's Prime Minister. The leaders of France, Australia, Canada, Germany, and a hundred other nations, veterans of Copenhagen, Cancún, Durban, and Rio+20. All have agreed that they must act now to prevent what has been described as the end of Western civilisation.

The camera zooms in on Dr Abukar taking a folded paper from his top pocket. Something moves in Marika's gut. *Why would he carry his speech in his pocket? Why not in the briefcase? Why did he bring the case at all?*

Turning her head, Marika sees Abdullah still hovering, eyes haunted with the same fear they all know. That something will happen.

'Sir,' she calls. Sharp and clipped.

For a man of his years, Abdullah reacts fast. She knows already that his hearing is near perfect, and that he is fit enough to run a regular ten kilometres with the rest of them, albeit at the rear of the pack.

'Yes?'

'There's something wrong.'

Dr Abukar, on the screen, clears his throat and begins to speak. *'Good day to you. My name is Ali Khalid Abukar. I have worked for the United Nations for twenty-six years.'*

The control room freezes. All eyes are on her. Marika wonders if she is about to make a fool of herself.

Abdullah's mouth sets in a single hard line. 'What do you mean?'

'The briefcase, maybe. Oh, hell … I don't know.'

'The West,' Dr Abukar continues, his voice taking on a new gravitas unmistakeable even over the speakers, *'is a gluttonous pig, wallowing in unrepayable debt and consumerism, stripping the world of resources faster than they can be replenished. Policies of intervention in order to secure these natural resources are dividing the world.'*

Marika feels her breath catch and has to force herself to resume breathing.

'The Western economic system, after many warning shocks, is on the brink of collapse. Bankers and company CEOs, whose greed has fed this unsustainable cycle, collect obscene salaries while others starve. European nations who have stripped the world to sustain lavish lifestyles, first with colonialism and now with debt, face bankruptcy and ruin. Soaring temperatures caused by industrialised countries threaten the Third World. Rising sea levels, hurricanes, floods, drought. Unprecedented seismic activity. Famine. Today, I act for my people. The dispossessed, the starving, the millions in refugee camps and on the road. I act for every child screaming out his hunger in the night, and each baby born into a family who cannot feed, clothe or educate him.

I act for the thirty million souls now fleeing famine and disaster in Africa and Asia ...'

Marika locks eyes with Abdullah. There is agreement in that gaze. Better to act now and look like fools than to ... He barks two names into the lapel transmitter. 'Shadi, Badr, get him out of there. Him and the briefcase. Now. Go.'

Marika watches the two men at extreme sides of the conference room converge on the dais, feeling herself tingling from head to toe, floating off in space, cheeks flushing — about to disrupt a speaker at the most important international conference in a decade. Rabi al-Salah. The breeze of righteousness. Eyes flick back to the screen and Dr Abukar's words continue to sear into her head.

'I come here today as the instrument of the true God. The God of Mohammed. The God of Mercy. Having realised that there is no other way but for men and women everywhere to submit to His wisdom.'

Marika's eyes lock onto the screen. She whispers, 'God no. Please, don't let it happen ...'

The two security guards approach the dais, clearly visible, but Dr Abukar opens his hand, revealing a black plastic switch, holding it high so there can be no doubt.

'Go back,' he shrieks, *'No one must come close. This briefcase contains eleven kilograms of high explosive ...'*

Pandemonium. Voices crash out through the room. Marika's lungs stop dead, as if captured by a barbed hook.

' ... the device will explode by remote control. I can close the circuit by pressing this switch. If I am attacked, or physically threatened, I will trigger the explosion. My initial instructions are for all security staff to leave the conference room, and the doors and windows sealed.

'My next requirement is for your security forces to allow a group of my comrades to enter this room. They will arrive at the Ja-noob car park by motor vehicle. Please let them through without delay.' His voice becomes hollow and empty. *'If these instructions are not followed I will kill most of the men and women in this room. For those who doubt the authenticity of this threat, I have left samples of these explosives in my room on level three at the residential complex …'*

At sixteen years of age, the East Sydney Bushwalking Club, with its close affiliation to the Wilderness Society, drew Marika in like a slow-moving vortex. Journeys into the forests and woodlands of eastern Australia became her passion. Weekend treks deep into the Blue Mountains, the Warrumbungles, the Budawangs; the trusty green Karrimor pack sweaty against her back while she negotiated steep ridges with that dry grass crunching beneath her boots.

Campfires in deep riven stone gorges, songs echoing from the cliffs. As she moved overseas for work, more opportunities presented themselves. South Africa's Drakensberg; Canada's Rockies above Banff in summer with air like cold crystal through which she could see a hundred miles of dark, snow-capped stone peaks. Once or twice it had all gone sour. A fall here and there, a twisted ankle, and once, in the rugged Gledić mountains of Serbia, a flash flood punching through the valley floor at three in the morning. A wall of water pouring through the tent, picking it up and tossing her around as if in a washing machine, leaving her bruised and battered, recuperating in a Trstenik guesthouse for days before she was able to continue the holiday.

This memory flashes across her consciousness as the speaker stands back from the lectern. The same disorientation. Images. Visions. Passing into the cortex but not responded to. The sound of hydraulic motors and moving machinery.

Dreamlike and surreal. The control room goes from order to chaos. Chairs crash sideways. Nikulina's coffee falls, droplets of brown liquid spilling up like high tide. Sunflowers in a vase on the sill. Shouts and running. The screen going blank as the man inside cuts off communications, leaving them blind.

Marika is unable to move, deep in a shocked spell she cannot break. A click as the giant door seals slide into place. A helpless cry from inside the room.

Silence from below as the protesters stop the shouting. Time passing. A cheer, stifled and high pitched from somewhere, then a crash. A burning vehicle on its side. Security forces trying to cordon off the complex, pushing the crowd away violently now. The sound of a gunshot, then another. A flush begins in her cheek and burns all the way across her neck and face.

Marika runs down the steps, head pounding, mouth dry. Dr Abukar's words ring in her ears: *I have left samples of these explosives in my room on level three at the residential complex.*

At the first checkpoint plastic chain gates have closed. An agitated security guard asks for identification, and they are forced to slow. Troops brandish automatic weapons, looking for a target. Marika gets through last, begrudging every moment of the slow examination of her ID.

Nikulina and three young Dubai policemen are ahead of her now, down the long corridor into the residential complex. Marika makes up ground on the straight, then turns into the stairwell, faster than an elevator for just a couple of floors. The steel capped shoes of the men in front ring on the marble steps.

Reaching the floor above, swinging onto the next flight of stairs, Marika recognises the danger. Dr Abukar will not wait for forensics and processing labs to test his samples. The demonstration of the efficacy of his explosives will, by necessity, be immediate. *God, how can such a gentle man do this?*

'Stop!' she screams at the others, but the sound of echoing feet drowns her out. She tries again, throat tearing with the strain, then attempts to move faster, knowing that the men ahead are as fit as she, and probably a little quicker.

What had he said that morning? Fifty million people unable to procure sufficient calories to sustain themselves. Is this his way of redressing the balance?

The sound of a door opening so hard that the handle pounds against the wall. Footsteps receding. Marika makes the third floor in time to see two figures sprint away down the carpeted corridor.

'Stop!' she tries again.

Marika comes around the corner as Nikulina opens the door to room 308. He is two paces inside when there is a roar, and a flash of light, the explosion slamming him back against the corridor wall, collecting a Dubai police sergeant on the way. Marika's ears ring, and her feet falter from the proximity to the blast. An explosive stench fills the air, mingling with the burned pork smell of Nikulina, his body and clothes smoking.

Sirens whoop through the sudden stillness. Hesitating at the door, Marika clears her head and charges inside. Blackened, cracked, sagging plaster. Shattered windows. Flames scale the curtains like rope climbers. Cotton bed sheets smoulder. No sign of human presence.

Out in the corridor men scream for medics. Others move inside. Marika backs away, eyes streaming from the gathering smoke, throat burning. Forensics will comb the room. There will be nothing to find here until they have done their work.

From deep within rises a terrible and irrepressible guilt. One man is dead. One injured. More will surely follow.

The nine mujahedin stroll through the checkpoints like celebrities. Some are pale skinned, some dark. Most wear full beards, jeans, T-shirts, and light jackets.

Marika stands back with the rest of the security staff, lining the corridors, helpless and sullen as the mujahedin pass through, pausing to pull compact automatic weapons from sports bags. Marika recognises an Uzi, and a PM63.

One walks ahead of the others, his cheeks sunken and lean, proud and watchful, with the glare and stride of a predatory animal. Marika realises that Dr Abukar is not the architect of this event. Here is the real commander, and her job is to know such people. Her mind trawls through hundreds of grainy snapshots. The leaders have histories. All of them do.

The man who walks in front of the others is known to Marika from just two file pictures. The name he goes by is Zhyogal. Hunted on three continents. Key member of the

African Salafi terror group, known as al-Muwahhidun, or Almohad. Spearhead of the new wave of terror.

Please God, not them, she pleads. *Please, why did it have to be them?*

The antechamber is almost empty of people now, but those who remain cower back from the nine men as they walk through the entrance, into the amphitheatre, down the tiers and to the front. The gunmen take up their positions around the room.

Head thrown back, face engorged with blood, veins and tendons standing proud on his neck, the leader raises his right hand, index finger pointing skywards. The others follow his lead, all shouting, 'Allahu akbar.'

Zhyogal's voice is filled with triumph and a religious fervour so visceral and powerful it might be sexual.

'In the name of God, the most gracious and merciful. Your faithful have taken possession of this room and everyone inside it. Let the overlords of taghut, of tyranny, prepare to die.'

The main doors hiss closed and Marika stands, still staring, a feeling of dread in the pit of her belly.

Faces recoil from the horror of what is coming, remembering stories and recalling images of beheadings and executions, each aware of their own mortality — that no matter how important a man or woman might be in this life, they are still no stronger nor less fallible than a beating heart and a collection of tissue and nerve endings.

The President of the United States, halfway through his term, imagines the media frenzy back home. Wonders how his media director will shape his image in the wake of this disaster. The Republican grip on power is tenuous at best, and is predicted to become even more shaky after the impending midterm elections.

How can this happen, he thinks to himself, when his country spends untold billions every year to hold back terrorism? When the sharpened point of the enemy is five hundred or, at most, a thousand, Islamists with the funds, skills and organisational backing to pose any real threat. He wonders how the little people of America will react if he is killed here. Wonders if anyone apart from his wife and three sons will give a damn.

The prime ministers of Britain and Australia tuck themselves back into their less ostentatious circles of advisors and force a phlegmatic front over the inner panic. And beneath it all is an unfounded, yet ingrained, belief that Western civilisation will always dominate.

They cannot win, because they are not like us. They cannot win because they do not have our institutions, our facilities, our industrial strength, and our veneer of invincibility.

Neither man remembers the lessons of history: that it was no industrial power, but the Goths and Vandals who reduced Rome to a smoking ruin.

Isabella Thompson, four rows back, feels the hammering of her heart, recites a prayer over and over again, the lone survivor from memories of Sunday school, the vicar's spinster daughter leading hushed voices from the front of the room, eyes closed and fingers interlocked.

Our Father, who art in Heaven,
Hallowed be Thy name ...

If You truly exist, if You love me You will bring my beautiful girls back to me now. You will remove these bastards from the face of the earth and give my girls back to me. I will do anything You want in return ... give thanks for the rest of my life if only You spare them and bring them to me alive ... and punish these men who stole them away from me ...

The mujahedin place bricks of semtex, carried in the sports bags, around the room, wired together with thin red cable to a central control box. Wired to blow from the plastic remote control Ali Khalid Abukar carries: an electronic gadget so clever it uses fine tendrils of water as conductors, tuned to explode all the charges, including those in the briefcase.

Isabella's eyes fix on Zhyogal — the lover's mask removed so that he is no longer handsome, but the face of death itself, with skin stretched tight as tissue paper over a kite frame, the sunken cheeks and the eyes recessed, showing the hatred freely now. For just an instant their eyes meet and there is no regret there, only triumph.

She feels other eyes on her. Her own people. It seems to her that they know she is the one who betrayed them. Betrayed those who employed and trusted her for so many years. Helped bring this viper into a room that holds the most powerful men and women of her generation. Of course they had not told her what was inside the briefcase, but she had known in her heart.

Head in her hands, Isabella begins to weep. Wanting it to be over, knowing she does not deserve this. She has always been so sensible.

Until she met *him* in Nairobi.

The role of British assets in protecting and ensuring the delivery of humanitarian aid to the refugee camps in Northern Kenya was politically sensitive, and it was her job to smooth the way. Hard, demanding work against bull-headed negotiators, many of whom saw the mere existence of the camps as a threat to national security.

Rami caught her at a weak moment — handsome, debonair, charming, apparently a financier. The meeting seemed to be an accident, a traveller sharing her table at the crowded Kengeles restaurant, unhurriedly engaging her in conversation.

Nairobi can be a lonely city, even dangerous when you are by yourself ...

At first she resisted, but he was persistent. Cancelling a planned engagement at the embassy, she accepted his invitation to dinner.

I'm single now. Hell, why shouldn't I have any fun?

Nightclubs frequented by Westerners in Nairobi are few, and have in the past been the target of terrorist attacks, like the grenade strike on the Mwauras Club that injured twelve people a few years earlier. Isabella hesitated when he first suggested they go dancing, but felt safe in his arms at the popular New Florida Club, the décor of which was once described by travel writer Paul Chai as looking like a spaceship crash-landed on a service station. Kelly and the children watched DVD movies back at the hotel while Isabella and Rami shared their first kiss.

On the second night she went to his charming suite at the Safari Club on University Road with its antique furniture and colonial feel, a willing subject to an intense and intelligent seduction. When she moved on to Yemen, trying to patch relations with a country devastated by the long revolution, he followed. They spent two more nights together in Aden.

'My English rose,' he joked.

'My desert stallion,' she laughed back.

The knowledge that the man who now patrols the conference room with a gun, touched her as a lover, makes her shake with anger and shame. When he catches her eyes it is with complete detachment. She glares back with all the vitriol and hatred that floods her soul, remembering that moment at Aden Airport when she realised that the girls were gone. Remembering how the luggage carousel blurred. How the man who had introduced himself as Rami gripped her arm.

'What are you doing? You're hurting me.'

'Stop drawing attention to yourself. Your daughters are safe, for the time being.'

'Where are they?'

'Safe. Listen to me. Continue your journey as planned. Tell anyone who asks that your daughters are with relatives.'

'No, please, I need them … Rami.'

'Shut up, woman, my name is not Rami. Listen to me. You will be contacted and given further instructions at Rabi al-Salah. Make arrangements to stay at the centre itself. If you alert police, or anyone at all, your children will die. Understand this. They will die a terrible death … I will personally cut their hearts from their chests.'

Isabella looked at the man who had touched her in the most intimate way. Believing his words.

'They are calling your flight. Board it. Now.'

Walking on as if in a nightmare, holding back tears …

Day 1, 12:00

Zhyogal's voice, when it comes, is the self-satisfied howl of a wild dog that brought down its victim in the night, of a cat with a mouse lying quiescent between its paws. The voice of an anti-god who promises destruction and death. That of a man who has sifted poison and hatred from a system of belief.

First he restores communications with a flick of the bank of switches, then places both hands on the dais and glares out at the cameras and the delegations in their rows. 'On behalf of our brothers in all lands, we make the following demands. First, the United States must withdraw its troops from Saudi Arabia, home of the two most sacred Islamic sites, Maccah and Medina. If they do not, every person in this room will die.

'The United States must disband its AFRICOM military command, and remove all troops from the continent: Somalia; Mauritania; Nigeria. States moving to Sharia law will do so without interference. Foreign journalists will leave these countries without delay, or every person in this room will die.

'All Western troops, military advisors and security firms will abandon their crusade against the nations of Islam: Iraq; Libya; Afghanistan; Somalia; Pakistan; Yemen. They must withdraw immediately. Or every person in this room will die.

'Catastrophic global warming is killing Africa and Asia. Coal-fired power stations will be shut down. Immediately. Coal mining will cease. Immediately. High-emissions industries will stop production. All major cities must provide free public transport ... the manufacture of luxury goods must cease … the production of immoral products such as Western music and fiction books …

'The governments of the West have seven days to act. If they do not, at the moment of Maghrib — sunset — on the seventh day, this room and everyone inside it will be destroyed.

'I make the following arrangements for the physical needs of the people in this room. There will be no tea, no coffee, no cakes, no biscuits. At sixteen hundred hours this afternoon I will allow the main doors to open while supplies are brought in. The only allowable food will be United Nations-issue emergency humanitarian ration packs.' His voice rises. 'Let the leaders of nations eat what refugees eat, what the luckiest of those dispossessed by their policies subsist on. You are free to use the toilets but no cubicle door will be closed. You will know what it is like to lack privacy.

'Finally, I warn that war criminals present in this room will be tried under Sharia law. Those found guilty will be executed, beginning one hour from now.'

The mujahedin appear at the ends of the rows, weapons gripped tight, waiting with that same hunting-dog eagerness, barely controlled savagery on their faces.

Zhyogal's face twists with rage as he goes on. 'These are the war criminals. Bring them to me. President Martin Bourque of France; President Edward Purcell of the United States; President Eitam Yedidyah of Israel …'

The mujahedin move in pairs, identifying the targets and sliding down along the rows, grasping men under the arms and dragging them back to the aisles and down the carpeted steps. One or two fight back, and their attackers respond violently, swinging rifle butts onto the sides of heads, depositing victims in a row on the carpet on the dais, pushing them down, and all the time shouting, 'Kneel, kneel!' Blood flows from nostrils and lips onto the carpet.

The voice drones on: 'Hussein Malik of Pakistan; Wasef Ansari of the Afghanistan Transitional Government ...'

Muslim leaders are treated more savagely than the Westerners, suffering hammer-like blows from pistol butt and boot, as if a special breed of hatred is reserved for them.

Someone shouts, 'For the love of God, leave them alone.'

The speaker is identified and a lone mujahedin leaves the pack, drags the man from his seat and beats him about the head until he slumps to the floor, a groaning, bloodied, mess.

The war criminals kneel in a row that extends across the dais, some shaking, others weeping openly.

Day 1, 12:35

Simon Thompson has flown everything from a Piper Aztec to a Boeing Y3, working his way up through the British Airways hierarchy from trainee pilot to first officer, and finally captain, four gold bars on his epaulettes. He has seen it all — force eight storms over Greece; flying through black, fortress-like cumulonimbus cloud formations with St Elmo's fire dancing on the wingtips; visited every major country on earth; and been propositioned in both the sexual and the criminal sense.

Still, after ten years in the cockpit he loves his job, loves the rush as the full-bellied 747-8 rises up through thirty thousand feet, loves to see the Gulf from the air, set against the brown desert landscape of the Emirates.

Beginning the initial adjustments that will see them land in some thirty minutes, he smiles to himself. With Dubai the scheduled stopover on the way to Singapore, he has two hours at the airport. Isabella will be busy at the conference, but Kelly has promised to bring the girls out from the Towers Rotana on Sheikh Zayed Road to see him. They'll have lunch, and talk a bit before he has to board. If he has time, he will choose a gift for each of the girls at the airport shops — a book perhaps. Frances, the eldest, reads teen romance novels that stop short of sex with vampires but make up for it with plenty of suggestive neck puncturing. Simon smiles when he thinks of her — a pretty girl, so attractive that one of Isabella's brothers mumbled once: *Boys are gonna slash their wrists over that girl, you just wait and see.*

Hannah, two years younger, likes fairy tales and spooky stories, when she can sit still for long enough to read more than a page or two. Her preference, of course, would be a new charm for her Pandora bracelet. Already she has six sterling silver charms, one gold, purchased from gift shops and jewellers around the world.

Isabella might get away from the conference and bring the girls out herself. A little jolt of electricity sparks through his chest. Three months have passed since the separation, and still he wishes she did not look so perfect, that she would not smile at him in quite *that* way …

Lost in his thoughts, he looks up as Penny Maynard opens the bulkhead door and enters the cockpit, immaculate in her red scarf and dark blue British Airways blazer.

'You wanted me, sir?'

'Just thought I'd let you know that there might be some moderate turbulence on the way down — thermals off the desert. Could be a bit uncomfortable. Let the passengers know it's nothing serious, will you?'

'Sure. Is that all?'

'That's it, thanks.'

The door closes behind her, leaving a lingering and expensive scent. Simon half smiles to himself, enjoying the fragrance, while returning to the series of manoeuvres that will soon see the giant craft taxiing down Runway 12L at Dubai International.

The SELCAL light on the aircraft communications addressing and reporting system lights up, and a beep sounds, signalling a ground-to-air voice communication. Vince, the first officer, pushes the VHF-R microphone selector switch on the ACP.

Simon assumes the call is routine, but Vince's forehead creases into a frown. Something is wrong. Vince is prone to the occasional overreaction, but not so obvious as this. A knot forms in Simon's stomach while he waits for the call to conclude. 'What's going on?'

Vince turns, shifting the mike to one side. 'Just had a message from ATC. The Rabi al-Salah conference. Isabella's a delegate, isn't she?'

'Yes. She's there.'

'There's been some kind of terrorist attack. The conference centre's locked down.'

Simon's hands freeze on the controls. 'Jesus. They said the damn thing was impregnable.'

'Apparently not.'

'What happened?'

'They don't know at this stage.'

Isabella. Christ. Are you OK?

Simon's next thought is for the girls. Kelly, the nanny, will be with them, but at best they will be worried. Panicked even. Intense pain, searing hot, comes out of the blue and settles in his chest. He takes the wheel, scarcely breathing, barely in control.

When the plane stops rolling, Simon conducts the post-flight checks without thinking, waiting for the final straggler to leave his seat and get his hand luggage from the overhead locker, cursing how some passengers seem to think that lingering until last is a hallmark of experience. Finally, he takes his bag from a nook on the flight deck and hurries down the passenger tube.

One of the stewards calls after him. 'Sir, why are you taking your bag? Aren't you coming back?'

Simon hurries into the terminal, where a crowd has gathered below a wall-mounted LCD screen. Al-Jazeera news footage shows the Rabi al-Salah complex from the air; the heavy beat of a chopper and the voice of a journalist, who cannot hide a note of triumph coming through the speakers.

The capitalist leaders of the West ... forced to listen. Forced to eat the rations of the dispossessed; to live like refugees ...'

Watching for long enough to ascertain that so far there have been no deaths among the delegates, Simon moves on, through the colossal extravagance of Terminal Two, where silver columns and mirrored ceilings rear to impossible heights. With one hand he digs into his bag for his passport, opening it for the customs officers in their shemagh head cloths and spotlessly white kandoura, enduring their distracted, unsmiling gaze. Green uniformed police stand in tight little groups and passengers hurry past.

Approaching the bank of monitors where they had planned to meet, he sees that Kelly and the girls are not there. Swearing under his breath, he takes his phone from his pocket, one of the new credit card-thin Ubiks with IMS, holographic screen, and videophone capability. The icons change as he switches to the voicephone app and selects Isabella's number from the address book. Her image appears on the screen in high-definition colour. There is no dial tone, only the message. 'This is Isabella Thompson, Parliamentary Under-Secretary of the British Foreign and Commonwealth Office. I am unable to take your call at the moment, but please leave a message ...'

'Call me, it's Simon,' he says, then slips the phone into his jacket pocket. He finds it hard to leave the meeting place, lingering in case they arrive at the last minute, Hannah laughing, everything normal again. Each passing minute increases the worry that gnaws at him. He is on his way to the doors when he sees Vince and a steward hurrying towards him.

'Hey, Simon, what the hell are you doing? You can't leave a flight halfway through. Think of the passengers, man ...'

Simon ignores him, moving out through the automatic doors. Beyond the pavement, and four lanes of bitumen, water cascades down stone, fringed with green vegetation. This is the shaded lower parking level, yet Dubai's heat hits him like a hot towel over the face. Choosing one of the ubiquitous white and yellow Toyota taxis, he throws his flight bag into the back, sinking down into the seat, and closing the door.

Vince is just behind him. 'Stop, Simon! We'll be grounded, for fuck's sake. There's nothing you can do here anyway ...'

Ignoring him, Simon presses the switch to close the window. The co-pilot's lips move but there is no longer any sound. 'The Rotana, please,' Simon tells the driver, then takes out his phone and tries Isabella's number, again getting her voicemail, swearing, putting the phone away in time to watch the Pakistani driver speed out of the rank and dart in front of an approaching SUV.

'Have you heard what has happened, sah?' the man says, swinging through the roundabout and onto Airport Road.

'Yes, thank you.' The prospect of pointless small talk appals him. To fend off any further attempt at conversation he stares out the window at the constant overpasses, green banners and billboards.

The traffic is dense but moving at breakneck speed as they pass al-Fatten plaza and red tiled residential villas. Simon scarcely sees the rows of palm trees, nor the water of Dubai Creek as they cross al-Garhoud Bridge and merge onto Sheikh Zayed Road, one of the fastest moving yet busiest thoroughfares in the world, twelve lanes of mayhem, lined with skyscrapers, airconditioned bus shelters and the elevated metro train line on the western side.

Craning his neck, Simon sees the Rotana ahead, competing for attention among the cluster of towers around and behind. The driver goes past, then swerves into a service road. As the taxi pulls up, Simon studies the meter, makes a rough calculation then pulls out his wallet. 'Euros OK?'

The driver rolls his eyes, as if exchanging the money will ruin his day. 'OK. One hundred Euro.'

This is extortion, but Simon is in no mood to care, handing him five twenties. He grips his bag and leaves the cab, waiting at the hotel's revolving door while a European couple comes through. The woman, at least twenty years younger than the man, wears pearls like bantam eggs on a string around her neck.

Inside, Simon hurries past the restaurant on his right, and on to the curved, marble topped reception desk, dominated by that red hued landscape painting that Isabella has always loved. The concierge finishes tapping at a keyboard then smiles up at him, dressed in an immaculate cream suit, a pink kerchief in the top pocket, hair slicked back. Almost too clean to be human.

'Good morning, my name is Simon Thompson. My wife, Isabella, is a guest here.' *Ex-wife, you mean*, the voice in his head says. 'She will have left a message for me.'

The concierge taps on a keypad, eyes fixed on a sleek computer screen. 'I'm sorry, sir, we did indeed have a booking for your wife but she has not arrived. The car despatched to collect her from the airport returned without her, so I imagine that she arrived on a later flight and chose to stay elsewhere ...'

Turning away from the desk, Simon's heart feels as if there is a monster inside, doing its best to claw its way out through his rib cage. He walks like an automaton, blundering out through the revolving door, back into the heat, past cigarette-smoking pedestrians, moving around the building and into an adjacent vacant lot of bare earth, where the traffic is not deafening. Taking out his phone he checks Isabella's accounts on Facebook, Tumblr, and Twitter, then the RSS feed for news of the Rabi al-Salah attack just starting to filter through.

The sun, radiating off the earth, increases the heat to unbearable levels. Dubai is dotted with these inexplicable bare areas, so much, it seems to Simon, that it looks more like a desert with buildings rather than a city.

The phone rings. Private. He clamps it to his ear.

'Simon Thompson speaking.'

'Simon. This is Tom Mossel.'

'Excuse me, but am I supposed to know you?'

'I work for the British government. We've been trying to track you down ...'

'Where is Isabella?'

'You haven't heard?'

'I've heard what happened, but I don't know if she's inside or not. She never turned up at the hotel.'

'She's inside the centre, Simon. Sorry. No one can get in or out. Security have sealed it off for a kilometre or so around the complex.'

'How can you be sure that she's in there?'

'Believe me. I'm sure.'

'Who the hell are you again?'

'My name is Tom Mossel. I run a Directorate of British Intelligence called the DRFS. We are jointly responsible for security at the conference.'

Simon frowns, dredging up what he knows of the organisation. From what he can recall the DRFS is some kind of spy agency; it does a pretty good job of keeping out of the public eye, but rumours abound that it is funded by industry levies, and operates what amounts to a private army of Special Forces operatives under the umbrella of MI6.

'Why are you calling me?'

'Your wife has been doing some analytical work for us on the side. We are concerned for her.'

Simon finds that he has been holding his breath. 'Where are my girls?'

A pause. 'Simon, you're going to have to be strong here. We think something might have happened.'

'Like what?'

'We've just learned that Isabella spent some time in Nairobi, then Yemen, with a man.'

'That's the last thing I need to know right now, and it's none of your business. Or mine.'

'Simon. She was with one of the terrorists now in the centre. The Algerian. One of *them*.'

Simon tries to say something, but no sound comes.

'She's been involved with him.' A pause. 'She helped Dr Abukar into the centre and may have brought in the explosive charges.'

Silence builds like compressed air into a tyre. 'That's not true.'

'Listen, she checked into the Mercure Hotel in Aden, four nights ago. We have first-hand confirmation that the Algerian was with her for two nights. Staff saw them walking hand in hand on the beach. They kissed. They shared a bed, Simon.'

'Where are the kids?'

'We don't know.'

'What the hell do you mean?' Sweat, not just from the heat, begins to trickle down his forehead and sting his eyes. His hand is slippery on the phone.

'The children were in Yemen with her at that stage and then she came on alone. We're investigating.'

Fucking hell. It's not possible. 'Are you saying the kids have been taken by someone?'

'We don't know what the hell happened. What hotel are you at?'

'The Towers Rotana.'

'Stay there. I'm sending someone to pick you up. We need to ask you some questions. Don't move. We'll find the girls. They are British citizens and we do not abandon British citizens. I won't let anything happen to them. Fifty men are on it …'

Down on the kerb an airport shuttle bus has just pulled up. Almost empty. Simon terminates the call and hurries towards it, still gripping his flight bag. He climbs aboard the bus, pays, and settles into the seat.

As soon as he has done so, he again phones Isabella. The recorded message seems even more impersonal. It takes all his self-control not to smash the useless instrument down on the stainless steel seat frame in front of him.

Day 1, 16:00

Al-Muwahhidun burst onto the international scene in the wake of the Egyptian and Syrian revolutions, the death of Osama bin Laden, and the Libyan civil war, with the militarily inexperienced rebels and NATO air power forcing that terrible and bloody endgame, culminating with Muammar Gaddafi being dragged from a sewer pipe, beaten and ultimately shot by a crowd screaming, shooting, and firing into the air.

One thousand years after al-Muwahhidun's first conquests, the movement was revived by a Moroccan cleric, Yaqub Yusuf, a pale, bespectacled Moroccan Salafi. Yaqub was just twenty-nine years old when he became a student of Osama bin Laden, spending a month with the Lion Sheikh in his Abbotabad compound before SEAL Team Six arrived in their choppers.

Osama was then almost sixty years old, yet appeared older. He was very tall, towering six feet five inches from the limewashed floor. Never far from his side was a battered Kalashnikov with a scarred wooden stock. Yaqub knew the folklore; that this was the weapon he took from a Russian infantryman he killed, some thirty-five years earlier.

Nearby, at all times, stood the bodyguard, whose Tokarev pistol, according to legend, was loaded with just two bullets. These were intended to martyr Osama rather than let him be captured by the kufr. The rumours that followed the Lion Sheikh were many, and Yaqub believed that truth lay behind all of them.

Yes, he is rich, Yaqub thought to himself, *yet he does not flaunt wealth. He has the ears of the world, yet he chooses to speak only when necessary. He is pious, for the singda is plain to see on his forehead. He is a military commander, yet he chooses his battles, knowing that the time has not yet come, that the mujahedin of the world are still building strength and self-belief, that soon the forces of righteousness will no longer be contained …*

Osama touched the crown of Yaqub's head with the tips of his fingers. 'My time is passing, Yaqub. The world has changed. Al-Qa'ida is watched and hunted ceaselessly by the security organisations of the world. You and the others must carry on the work.'

'How, sayyid?'

'Look to the past. To the time when the ummah conquered Spain and made our empire so strong and rich that the rest of Europe seemed like a pale shadow. Use the weapons of mass communication to teach the ummah to hate the Americans and the West. Use the tools of the enemy. The ummah need to understand that the industrialised West and their greedy corporations will destroy the earth. Climate change, accompanied by lack of food and water, will bring fear to our people. Frightened people hate. Frightened people will fight. Use that fear.'

Yaqub learned from the Lion Sheikh of the thousand-year-old brotherhood of the al-Muwahhidun, led by the Moroccan Ibn Tumart. Puny in body, and sharp-tongued, Ibn was a cripple with a chip on his shoulder, yet pious in faith. He was destined to influence the world far beyond that of his father, Cheraghchi, lamplighter for the local mosque. He made the hajj to Maccah, when still a youth, and was expelled from the city for trying to instil his own extreme beliefs on the other pilgrims.

In Baghdad, he fell under the spell of both the learned physician al-Ash'ari and the demented mystic Ghazali. Then, as a young man, under the tutelage of the latter, his zeal and knowledge combined into a new and twisted system of belief, a hatred for the lax and impious practices then common across the Arab world. He came to realise that change was not possible using mere pedagogy and charm. On a dark night outside al-Jisr, he and his mystic teacher used ancient rituals borrowed from the Shia to have dialogue with God. By the end of that night, Ibn believed himself authorised to use any means at his disposal to force others to practise his own rigorous interpretation of the one true religion.

Attempts to browbeat others into following his methods saw Ibn ejected from town after town across Persia and North Africa. While these setbacks did not deter his efforts, he was forced to return to his own Masmuda people, in the Atlas mountains of Morocco.

Perversely, his beliefs, while puritanical in the extreme, gave him the justification to publicly rape the sister of a local emir who had dared to set forth in public without a veil. His reputation was growing now, and even the emir dared not punish him.

Chief among his followers was the Algerian Abd al-Mu'min al-Kumi, a soldier and statesman, everything Ibn would never be. Together building an army, al-Muwahhidun, as they became known, conquered all of North Africa within thirty years, then most of southern Spain and Portugal.

In all countries al-Muwahhidun killed or converted Jews and Christians, and forced the most puritanical beliefs on Muslims. The enemies of God, they believed, could be defeated using any means at their disposal: death; trickery; evil. There were no rules in the war against the unbeliever.

Osama bin Laden reinforced this latter belief: 'The West will not listen without massive bloodletting. They heed only fear and death. Revive the methods of al-Muwahhidun. Use past and present together as a sword to bring the kufr to their knees.'

Yaqub left bin Laden's compound the day before the fatal attack, and when he heard the news of Osama's martyrdom from a safe house in Islamabad, he wept and swore vengeance, declaring a revival of the cult of al-Muwahhidun, with himself as leader.

Followers, disoriented by the death of bin Laden, then a string of Islamist leaders, flocked to the cause. Yaqub studied the methods of the superstar Muslim televangelists such as Amr Khaled, Ahmad al-Shugairi and Moez Masoud who were then using mass media to preach a moderate Islam, geared to the modern world, gathering hundreds of millions of followers and partially inspiring the spreading fight for reform and freedom across the Middle East. Yaqub understood Osama's wisdom in seeking to link modern issues with Salafism and archaic fundamentals.

The Middle East remained a complicated place. In Egypt, for example, supposedly delivered from tyranny by revolution, the populace found themselves little better off under SCAF, the transitional government. New powers, however, were rising. One of the biggest beneficiaries of the Egyptian revolt was the Muslim Brotherhood, or Ikhwan. The Ikhwan fought for freedom alongside their moderate co-believers, Coptic Christians and the liberal youth who drove the revolution, using social media to coordinate and plan their uprising.

'We use Facebook to schedule the protests, Twitter to coordinate, and YouTube to tell the world,' one Egyptian activist put it.

With the fall of Hosni Mubarak, however, the once banned Ikhwan became a fully fledged and open political organisation, calling their new legitimate wing the Freedom and Justice Party. They sponsored the rise of a new, five-thousand-member Salafi political party, whose leader said, 'We oppose anything that contradicts Islamic Sharia, even if it is accepted by the majority.'

Together the Brotherhood and Salafi groups, including the developing al-Muwahhidun, incited violence against the Copts and other Christians, promoting a new era of sectarian unrest. Followers of one god against followers of another. So on and over again.

Water shortages fuelled conflict, and the still unresolved Palestinian situation remained an open, bleeding sore. Tanks rolled into Gaza. Palestinians responded with suicide bombers and Grad rockets.

In Africa, desperately poor nations slipped into deep unrest or civil war. South Sudan, formed in 2011, was by 2012 a failed state, fighting seven different militia armies; tribal warfare tearing its social fabric apart. Somalia remained impenetrable and lawless, much of her territory ruled by Shabaab al-Mujahedin and allied Islamist groups. Security issues exacerbated the worst famine in decades, the country's starving people filing into refugee camps in Mogadishu and over the border into Kenya and Ethiopia.

Yaqub declared himself the Mahdi reborn. After continuing to inspire followers through modern mass media, he appointed a ten member council, making fear of climate change and starvation caused by the industrial West the centrepoint of this new jihad. As real terrors came — rising sea levels and a procession of natural disasters — the flock grew into a phenomenon of which the spearhead was a couple of thousand freedom fighters backed by five hundred million sympathisers.

The ummah were all too ready to believe that the West was defiling God's gift of the bountiful earth with their pollution. The evidence was clear before their eyes.

The world is not fair became a catchcry shouted on YouTube videos sent viral by Muslims looking for answers. *The West grows rich and fat at the expense of our future.*

Tumblr, Twitter and Facebook sites gathered countless likes and follows.

At the perfect moment, Yaqub died a martyr also, torn apart by a drone-launched Hellfire missile at a coffee shop in Shabwa, Yemen. His death was applauded by Western leaders and mourned by millions. His funeral, in the Moroccan village of Tahanaout, was filmed in HD video and posted on websites across the world. Fundamentalists from Mogadishu to Sana'a shook their fists and loaded their weapons, one thing on their minds.

Reprisal.

Opening the door presents a risk, but an unavoidable one, and just one among many that the planning team had to consider. Another is the sheer number of hostages, increasing the potential for collusion and a concerted attempt on the mujahedin. A third possible danger is the small, armoured glass window on the northern wall, with its view across to the sea. The nearest structure, however, a power station smokestack, is almost a kilometre away, too far for all but specialised small arms fire.

The transfer of rations is quickly achieved, and the three men wheel their trolleys back through the entrance, risking a wary look behind them as they go. The door closes and the sense of relief among the mujahedin is obvious — smiles and nervous laughter; slinging guns over shoulders; a whispered comment and a brief embrace. Zhyogal struts across to the stacked rations, directing two of the men to open the nearest carton with a knife.

Zhyogal lifts a shrink-wrapped package: 'This is a United Nations standard ration pack, referred to by the

American enemy as an MRE. It is made by any of three firms in the United States, stockpiled at around five million units. It contains two thousand two hundred calories, and is designed to keep an adult human alive indefinitely. This is less than half the calories greedy Western males consume each day. Inside, you will find crackers, flat bread, a fruit bar, raisins, and a protein ration of meat or beans. In addition, each contains salt, pepper and a paper towel. Each pack must last twenty-four hours.'

Zhyogal takes in the room with a sweep of his eyes. 'Eat,' he cries. 'Learn what the by-products of imperialism and greed eat to survive — the fortunate ones in the camps, those who do not lie dead on the desert sands of Africa and the Middle East.'

One of the men kneeling at the dais stands, tall and grey headed, yet handsome for his age. The French President Martin Bourque. 'That is enough,' he shouts, 'enough of your rhetoric and lies. Lay down your weapons and you may survive this day. My country will not deal with terror, a fact you will learn soon enough.' The bristles of his moustache stand out like quills, and his eyes are rounded, glaring.

Zhyogal says nothing, but works his way towards the Frenchman, face betraying little, stopping just a few paces away. 'You have been told to kneel, old man.'

The French President folds his arms and shakes his head. His suit and tie are still perfectly arranged, a red poppy pinned to his lapel. 'Kill me if you like, but it will only delay the end for you. You cannot do what you have done and live.'

Zhyogal moves with the speed and grace of a leopard, gripping the older man's hair at the back where it is thickest, dragging him down with what must be tremendous strength. The Frenchman attempts to fight back, but his tormentor, having manhandled him down to the carpet, leaves him teetering for a moment then smashes his weapon into the temple. Blood trickles down into his eyes and lips.

Twice more Zhyogal strikes, once on the point of the chin, once into the eye socket, leaving Bourque on his knees, holding his face with both hands. The mujahedin leader reverses the gun, pointing the muzzle at his victim's head. 'Go back to your place or I will shoot you now.'

At first Bourque ignores the command, but Zhyogal's face contorts in fury, again grasping the man's hair and twisting the gun muzzle into his temple. 'Move, or you die.'

The Frenchman half-crawls, half-staggers back to his place in the row.

'Is there anyone else?' Zhyogal shrieks. 'Anyone who wishes to prove his courage, and trade insults with me?'

Silence.

'Then let it be known that cellular telephones, computers and tablets are now outlawed. The mujahedin will move around the room collecting them. Delegates withholding a telephone will be shot.'

One of the militants empties the contents of a plastic tub onto the floor and Isabella resents even this minor callousness, staring at the scattered documents. *The work of hundreds of people, for months.*

Holding the tub, a pair of mujahedin move around the room. Phones, dropped from nervous hands, clatter inside. iPhone. Ubik. Nokia. Samsung. When someone is slow to produce, the collector becomes agitated, shouting and haranguing.

When the tub pauses in front of Isabella she lifts the tiny Siemens from an inside suit pocket. She hesitates for a moment — deep in her handbag is another, an old iPhone that was once Simon's, now used by the girls if they travel unaccompanied. It is turned off, but ...

'Is that all?' the man grunts.

Up close she can smell his body odour, heavy and rank, and the expression on his face frightens her — staring right through her, so that she feels naked and vulnerable. He is a big man, heavy in the face, dark beard curling from his chin.

His eyes fall on her and he grins lasciviously. Isabella realises that Zhyogal has told the other men what he did to her. Surely couched in religious reasoning about how it was necessary and was therefore not sinful, but yes, he has told them.

The shuttle bus pulls up outside Dubai International Airport's Terminal One, and moving in through the doors, Simon studies the latest flight information on the monitors. The quarter-hour journey has given him time to think. He has one lead. Aden, Yemen.

He sets off down past the airline desks — African Express, Royal Jordanian, Saudi Arabian Airways, and Yemenia. The counter is not busy and he has just a short wait before a young man looks up and smiles the gap-toothed, stained, Yemenia version of the famous airline smile.

Simon takes his clip-on British Airways ID from his pocket and holds it up. 'There's a flight to Aden, Yemen, in forty minutes. Do you have a seat available?'

'Certainly, sir. Holiday or work?'

'Holiday.'

'Lucky you. Aden is a very beautiful city — and very safe now. Looks like we can accommodate you in business class — that flight's almost empty.'

'Thank you very much.' Simon feels the tension relax a notch. Producing a credit card, he waits while the man processes his booking and prints a boarding pass.

After passing through security, and a long walk down white corridors with arched, high windows on either side, past prayer rooms, crowded duty-free shops, and even artificial palm trees, Simon settles into the departure lounge to wait. The phone display shows no new messages. On impulse he punches out a new text and sends it to Isabella's regular number, along with an older phone that she often carries around, the spare that Frances sometimes uses. No reply comes through, even when he watches the display, waiting for the tone to sound, a snippet from a pop song that Frances programmed for him last time they were together. Was it two weeks ago? A few days snatched in Paris while Isabella flew to Helsinki.

Sitting there on the soft upholstery, Simon holds the images of the girls in his mind, studying them like dolls in his hands. They are polite kids. Sweet. So much like their mother but with elements of his own DNA that both frighten and thrill him. So different: Frances with her placid, sweet face and blonde hair almost to her waist; Hannah tall for her age, thinner, more spontaneous. Aching deep in his heart, he tries not to think of the various scenarios that might have overwhelmed one grown nanny and two smart kids. At how something must have forced Isabella to leave them.

The boarding announcement comes over the loudspeakers in Arabic, then English. Simon joins the fifty or so passengers streaming down through the tube and into the aircraft.

Simon dozes on the flight, head lolling, waking often, gasping for breath; a heavy acidic sweat on his neck and cheeks.

If only I could talk to her ... to them.

He has told and embellished the story of his and Isabella's first meeting so many times that he can no longer distinguish the facts from the frills.

He *does* know that they met at his Great Aunt Delilah's funeral, crammed into the pews at Ewhurst Parish Church in Surrey. To Simon, a senior at nearby Cranleigh School, the lucky seating coincidence was the only bright spot on a day that saw him miss opening the batting with the First XI, the elite school cricket team he had been trying to crack for two years.

When Isabella settled into the pew beside him, she turned and smiled, leaving him too stunned to respond. Her eyes, he decided, were as green as summer grass, her body slim but full in the right places. During the entrance hymn and the homily they shared a number of stolen glances. After the return from communion she was just a little closer. Their thighs touched.

This brief contact was a charge of high voltage current that widened Simon's eyes and caused a twinge in his groin that necessitated an adjustment, achieved under cover of the funeral program produced and printed by his mother on the family Apple Mac.

As the service scudded to its conclusion, Simon dropped his arm on the seat beside him, and the backs of his knuckles were close enough to brush her leg. Again that flash of excitement. As the pall bearers carried their burden down the aisle, Simon was able to study her for the first time, blonde hair pulled back tight, a few tantalising wisps still free. Her skin was as smooth and perfect as a petal, her face structured like that of a model, or an actress. Breasts too. *Oh God, what breasts.* By leaning forwards he could see patches of white bra and skin between the buttons of her blouse. It seemed to Simon that he had *never* seen a girl as pretty as her. He almost sighed aloud when she, catching him staring, turned again and smiled.

Exiting the church, he loitered among the post-funeral chatterers and tried to get past Uncle Alan and his dull jokes to the patch of concrete where she stood with her parents. By the time he emerged from the crowd, ready with a smile and a line, she was already walking away.

The wake was held at a family friend's country house, a solid old residence built of Bargate stone, apparently once constructed as a woodsman's cottage, with white-framed windows and doors, surrounded by an acre of hedges, ponds and garden beds. Silver trays lined the dining room table. Scones with cream, devilled eggs, and cucumber sandwiches occupied Simon for a good twenty minutes, and he had just emptied his plate for the third time when she came in. Again he felt that shock in his chest. Their eyes met for a moment before an elderly relative collared her, and he lost sight of her. He turned to Mabel, the sixty-something spinster aunt who, rumour had it, was either a lesbian or sexual predator — or both.

'Who's that girl?' he asked, inclining his head towards her.

Mabel threw back her head and cackled, brown teeth sharp as files in her upper jaw. 'That one caught your eye, didn't she, boy?' She slapped his knee, then lowered her voice. 'That's Isabella Wilkes-Tower. Her grandmother, Augustine, was Delilah's friend, for many years. They went to school together.'

Simon felt a lightening of the spirit. 'So I am not related to her?'

Another guffaw. 'Oh no, dear boy, so rest assured, if you and she should happen to rub nasties, your offspring are unlikely to be born with two heads.'

Simon felt his face burning. 'Aunt Mabel, you're disgusting.'

The criticism added to the old lady's mirth, and she held her chest as if to prevent her laughter from spilling out from between her bony cleavage.

An hour passed in which Simon attempted to hustle Isabella away from the henhouse of aunts, uncles and grandparents. People were leaving, cars crunching off down the gravel drive, and he had almost given up hope when he saw her out in the garden, kneeling at a bed of roses to inhale the scent of a blossom. He was too young and inexperienced to recognise a deliberate pose. He almost tripped in his hurry to get out there, but now that he was crossing the lawn towards her he felt as clumsy as a puppy in the shadow of her self-assured poise. He stopped five paces from her, thrust his hands in his pockets and said, 'I missed out on a darn good cricket game for this funeral.'

Isabella turned, then looked away. 'I loathe cricket. So boring.'

It was spring. Sunny. Bright. Bees over the flowers. A heady scent of blossoms in the air.

Simon grinned and took another step. 'Lots of people say that, but it's not, you know. It's quite fun, smashing the ball, and there's an awful lot of skill involved. Hook shot, cover drive, leg glance and all that ...' His voice fell away.

She was staring at him, lips tilting into a smile. 'What's your name?'

'Simon.' He wished she would stay still but instead she began walking along the edge of the garden.

'Aren't you going to ask mine?'

'I already know. You're Isabella.' He skipped a step or two to catch up. 'I asked my auntie Mabel.'

'The old dyke.' Isabella smiled. 'Mum says that she's had her hand up more skirts than a French dressmaker.'

'I like her. Well, she's a bit different — not so square, you know.'

The garden was set on an incline, roses giving way to less labour-intensive blooms — pansies and snapdragons, crowded and colourful. Down in the lower garden they were out of sight of the house, the bank above retained by a stone wall. Beyond was a valley of fields, and the village of Ellens Green in the distance.

Isabella stopped and turned, then twirled once. 'I had two glasses of Champagne, and now I feel silly.'

Without warning, she gripped his arms and pressed her lips against his. At first it seemed like a joke — a careless gesture — but her mouth opened like a hot clam and her arms encircled his back. The kiss went on for a long time, and then she drew back.

He stared, eyes wide, shoulders heaving with each breath.

They kissed again. Isabella changed, her eyes huge and misty, her body becoming limp, as if she would fall if he didn't support her. Then, abruptly, she stopped for a second time. 'I'm sorry, that was naughty of me. I don't usually do things like that.'

From above came the sound of a sliding door opening and a voice, calling, 'Isabella, we're going.'

'Oh shit. Dad's calling me. Is my lipstick OK?'

Simon used his finger to wipe a smear away. 'Looks awfully good to me. Can I see you again?'

'If you like. Ring me. We're in the book.'

With that she turned and took the slope at a run.

When she had gone, Simon sat on the springy grass and smiled to himself.

There was no first date in a traditional sense. Simon ran into her at the counter of David Mann's department store the next day on his way to net practice. Everyone in Cranleigh seemed to meet up there. Since the shelves contained almost everything worth buying, there always seemed to be a reason to visit the place.

'I got another chance with the firsts on Saturday,' he enthused.

There was no trace of the giddy Isabella of the previous day. Mystified silence, then: 'What the hell are you on about?'

'Cricket.'

'Oh.'

The shop assistant placed her hands on her hips and coughed.

'So sorry,' Simon said, slipping a five pound note from his wallet and passing it across, before turning his attention back to Isabella. 'Do you want to come and watch?' He remembered what she had said about the game, and looked away, accepting his change. 'You might not think it's the most exciting thing in the world, but you can bring a book and we'll have a bite to eat afterwards.'

Isabella shrugged, then lifted one bare shoulder to scratch the side of her neck. 'I guess. If you really want me to.'

At Shamley Green a brown pole topped with a white duck and set of wickets marked the cricket ground, surrounded on all sides by sealed roads. Simon loved to play here: the soft, green turf; the trees; the red and brown brick houses with their picket fences and white framed windows, often with nets hung over glass panes in case of an errant six. Horse riders, practising golfers and even the local mobile library often turned up on the fringes of the game.

With Isabella watching demurely from a borrowed deckchair, novel closed and resting in her lap, Simon strode out to face the Godalming bowling attack, led by a six-foot-six streak of lightning known across the county as Chicken Leg Harris.

The first ball, a bouncer, Simon hooked into the car park of Arbuthnot Hall to scattered applause. The second he nicked clean to second slip and found himself walking, embarrassed, back to the bleachers.

After the game, he took Isabella across the road to the Red Lion, a square, whitewashed building that sported twin white chimneys and a gabled doorway. Showered, a pint of London Pride on his breath and team songs ringing in his ears he bought her dinner, while his victorious teammates played pool in the adjacent room, making lewd gestures behind her back as they passed on their way to the gents.

Later, Simon drove her home. Parked outside her house, he wasn't sure what to expect. Her kiss, however, was feverish, and he slid one hand down under the coarse fabric of her dress.

She groaned. 'I'm not sure what it is, but you seem to have a strange effect on me.'

Her words inflamed him further, and he reached for her.

She pushed him away. 'I don't think I'll fall in love with you, though.'

'Why not?'

'You're too nice. I think I've got a thing for rogues.'

'I can be a rogue too.'

'Can you?' Her tongue was just visible behind the parted lips.

'Yes, I can.'

'There's a quiet place down by the old canal. We could go there if you like.'

Simon remembered how it felt, that first time, how she lay back in his arms in the reclined seat afterwards and confessed her virginity.

'Really? I thought you must have …'

'Because I was so forward. Sorry, but you just happened to come along at the right time. I was ready.'

Simon hugged her tight. 'It was my first time too.'

'Was it good?'

Simon's voice took on a languorous tone. 'I rather think it was.' A pause then, 'Do you think we might try it again?'

The relationship sustained them through his pilot training and Isabella's Bachelor of Political Science. Marriage followed. Children. Fatherhood. Simon came to understand that to be a parent is to live not one, but two, three or four lives. That you share every fall, every success, every tear; every disgrace. That you feel each more keenly than your own.

A blur of years followed. Soon there were bad memories, too. Fights. Sullen silences that went on for days. Unbridgeable gaps.

More than anything now, Simon wants the wasted time back again. How could he have let it happen? He shudders to himself. If there is ever another chance … If she survives this. If the girls survive this. Simon steels himself. It is up to him to make sure that they come through, but first he has to find the girls. Without them there is no future worth living.

CNN runs the story dispassionately, while FOX presents Dr Abukar as a once loyal servant, now deranged, having teetered off into extremism. SKY News labels him as a complex villain; a fundamentalist on a mission to save the world. Acting presidents and prime ministers promise that they will not cave in to terrorism, not even for the life of their own leader.

Men and women all over the world gather information, draw their conclusions, perpetuate their prejudices, air their opinions over backyard fences, and on Quora, Scribd, Tumblr, Facebook, Twitter, Diaspora and Namesake. Amateur news gatherers use Twitter to disseminate information hours ahead of traditional news services.

The general opinion is that Dr Abukar will be content to make his point then walk away. The demands are unworkable, and he must realise this. Zhyogal is another matter. The word evil is bandied about by people who should know better. Clever journalists uncover evidence of his earlier exploits, including footage of a massacre in an Algerian village, and predict dire results this time around.

In student unions, East and West, young men and women cheer and raise their glasses, while working-class strollers, polled by rough-and-tumble street journalists, click their tongues at such a treacherous lack of patriotism. 'After all,' fifty-three-year-old Isaac Stanton of Bethany, Pennsylvania, tells FOX and the world, 'he's our president. Even if I never voted for him myself I wouldn't like to see him blown into little pieces.'

The name Zhyogal takes on the media-fuelled proportions of a Saddam Hussein, Idi Amin or Slobodan Milošević, an uncomplicated vision even Isaac Stanton of Bethany, Pennsylvania, can understand. Dr Ali Khalid Abukar, however, is condemned as a traitor to the world that once gave him his living. Reports that a substantial UN salary is still being paid into a bank account in his name outrages the moral majority, leading to a rapid and comprehensive freezing of his assets.

The team behind Inspire, the al-Qa'ida magazine launched and originally edited by the American born martyr, Anwar al-Awlaki, rushes to upload a special edition. This ten-page feature praises the brave mujahedin at Rabi al-Salah, and takes pains to link al-Muwahhidun with their own organisation, devoting half a page to details of the original association between Osama bin Laden and Yaqub Yusuf.

Financial markets, never secure in these troubled times, reflect the possibility of a world without leadership. The Dow Jones dives, and the Hang Seng suffers its worst one-day loss since a wave of water destroyed the Miyagi prefecture's coastal strip and an ageing nuclear power station went into meltdown years earlier. The index creeps back when the *Tokyo Times* reports a possible negotiated end to the crisis. This report proves to be false, and another round of selling begins, cut short by the close of trade.

Day 1, 20:00

As stars appear in the darkened sky, visible through the single high window, the conference room lights remain on. Isabella sees eyes close and sleep arrive for many of the delegates. Of course, she has scarcely dozed in seventy-two hours, and for at least an hour, she too sleeps. When she wakes it is with an unpleasant jolt. Someone has dimmed the lights.

The man who once introduced himself as a suave and urbane businessman called Rami — now revealed as terrorist and murderer Zhyogal — prowls the room, scarcely glancing at her now.

At least one of the hijackers is asleep far across the room, lying on the carpet beside the wall. The mujahedin, she decides, must be taking turns to rest, sleeping in relays.

Rather than enlivening her, the short sleep fills Isabella with despair at what has happened to Hannah and Frances, at the memory of what she has done — that she is to blame, in part, for this. Her eyes fall on the shoulder bag near her feet, remembering the spare phone still inside. Using one foot she hooks the bag closer, waiting until she is sure Zhyogal and the others are not watching.

Trying not to think of what they will do to her if she is caught, she leans over, delves into the bag, and brings out the phone in its blue silicone case. She covers it with both hands and waits again.

Delegates withholding a telephone will be shot.

Isabella presses the power button; there is a soft electronic beep. Again she hides the machine and looks around before choosing the 'silent' option and looking at the screen. Three missed calls flagged in red. She checks the numbers — Simon. She almost sobs with frustration. Then, seeing that an SMS has come through, she opens it up, reading the words in their light grey LCD bubble, fighting to keep the tears from her eyes.

What have you done? Frantic. Looking for girls. Where? Simon.

Isabella looks around again. The mujahedin have not stirred, but she meets the eyes of another delegate a row behind. She is certain that he has seen her with the phone. He is pleasant looking, with a clean jawline and athletic shoulders, his brown hair longer than that of most of the other males in the room, and his smile open and honest.

They exchange what she decides is understanding. Is he part of the large American delegation?

Looking up between letters, Isabella uses her thumb on the virtual keypad to reply.

Simon. Forgive me. Girls taken from Aden airport. My heart is with you, along with all my hopes and trust.

She pauses, wanting to say more. Everything seems so petty now. At that moment she feels closer to him than to any human being alive — the man who held her hand while she screamed in pain and brought forth the children they conceived together. She could never doubt his love for his children and thinking of him warms her heart. Still, it is all too complicated — the wounds so fresh. What can she say that will not undo all that was so hard to do? Moving her thumb back to the keypad she picks out the final word — Isabella.

Sitting in the dull light, she gathers courage. Now she has the means to explain herself, then to help; to pay back some of what she owes. She composes a text in her mind. It has to be short, and to the point. The next question is who to address the message to.

Isabella's immediate superior is a genuine Dame — the honour bestowed because of her charity work — Shelley Chandler. She is a capable woman with a busy social life of openings and exhibitions, but can be a little vague, and might sit on the message until she decides what to do with it.

Almost a year earlier Isabella was approached by a Director at MI6 to provide intelligence on the East African and Middle Eastern region — just incidental stuff — and since then she has passed on bits and pieces as they cropped up, nothing serious or consequential. In this way she has met Tom Mossel half a dozen times. She freezes inside when she thinks of him. He is just one of many people who must feel let down by what she did. They would all know by now — of course they would.

Again she holds the phone low between her knees. Mossel is both smart and discrete — she will not need to spell things out.

How can I explain? Was tricked and used. Girls abducted Aden airport, acted under duress. Please find them, heart is breaking. One m'tant asleep. AKA awake and Zhyogal. How can I help? IJT

Without stopping to think too hard she thumbs the 'send' tab.

Looking around, she moves her hand inside the waistband of her skirt and all the way to her knickers, slipping the phone underneath. Out of despair, worry and fear, a new determination is rising.

Day 1, 20:30

Abdullah bin al-Rhoumi, head of GDOIS division, Dubai police, sits in his office with his head in his hands. He is a tall man, sixty-seven years of age, with faint crow's feet in the corners of his eyes. His nose has a prominent dorsal hump falling away just above the nostrils. He wears the white kandoura robe at home and when going about the city, but at work he prefers a grey, off-the-peg Western suit, coupled with a shemagh head cloth, tied with the black woollen aqal rope. A city engineer has just briefed him on the possibility of building a tunnel from Interchange Number Seven to the fortified bunker that lies deep beneath the Rabi al-Salah Centre.

This is *his* Dubai. *His* world. That makes it hard to believe that al-Muwahhidun have brought their abhorrent brand of terror to the city that he has loved from its beginnings.

In the earliest years of Abdullah's childhood, Dubai was a nondescript, local port centred around Dubai Creek, a silted, disturbed channel of water. Pearl diving and the trading of dates and copra were the main economic activities. Oil had recently been discovered in the area and, while men whispered of its potential, nothing changed until hired barges came and dredged the creek. The biggest oil discoveries were a hundred and fifty kilometres to the north, and it seemed that little would change here.

Like most of his peers, Abdullah lived in a thatched hut without running water or electricity, and received a basic schooling in the local madrasah. His family were of the merchant al-Tujjar class, and thus wealthy. They ate yoghurt and flat bread each day for breakfast, washed down with dark coffee. Lunch, the main meal of the day, was a happy, chatty event with the brothers sitting with their father. The women ate in the kitchen. All dined on fish or meat, rice and vegetables, supplemented at times with dates or olives.

When he was ten, the British, long-term rulers in this part of the world, packed up and left. The United Arab Emirates were formed in 1971, from a rabble of Sheikhdoms. To Abdullah, this changed his life only a little. The Sheikh of Dubai, Mohammed, once titular ruler for the British, was now de facto head of the greater Emirates government. Abdullah's father moved from trading pearls to importing Western consumer goods for a growing market.

Abdullah's passion was his horse, a roan gelding called Mulham, the inspired one. Like the other children, he rode bareback, yet with a skill that amazed his contemporaries: moulded to the back of his mount; becoming one organism; swifter than the wind; gliding over the desert sands. Arab horses are among the most beautiful of all living creatures, and over thousands of years of Bedouin life only those of good temperament and manners were permitted to breed. Prized specimens were stabled inside the family tent, and interacted with their owners like few other species. Such horses are easy to love.

In his teens, Abdullah discovered endurance horse riding — the sport of a million steps, as it was called, conducted over desert courses of one or even two hundred kilometres, in the most forbidding terrain. These were dirty, difficult affairs where riders and horses were fortunate to finish, and even more fortunate to do so without injury.

Sheikh Mohammed, meanwhile, planned to inspire Dubai's growth via massive investment in infrastructure. An ambitious new port and airport went from drawing board to mortar and steel. Both facilities, however, remained lightly used until the strategic thinker Ahmed bin Sulayem suggested to Sheikh Mohammed that they should set up a free-trade zone, where international companies could trade without income tax, tariffs, or duties to trouble them.

This was the spark that would ignite the phenomenon of Dubai.

Abdullah, at twenty-three, returned from London with a degree in economics, placed it in his bottom drawer and went straight to the stables, disinterested in work as many young men can be.

A few weeks later, however, competing in a Djibouti endurance race, he saw Ahmed bin Sulayem, who had been a few years above him at school, and was now the official in charge of the free trade zone. Ahmed rode a beautiful stallion, fifteen hands high, with all the hallmarks of the best Arabian breeding: wide nostrils, a slight jibbah-bulge between large, inquisitive eyes, and a broad, strong back. The horse carried his tail high, almost arrogantly.

In the closing stages of the race, Mulham, then eighteen years of age, lost his wind and Abdullah was forced to walk. He was surprised when Ahmed slid off his own mount and walked with him.

'What are you going to do with your life, Abdullah?'

'I don't know.'

'You have a degree in economics.'

'Yes.'

'Would you like to work in that field?'

Abdullah moved his eyes from Mulham to his companion, then lowered them. 'No, I don't think so.' In truth, a life of ledgers and profit statements left him cold. That career path had been his father's idea, a way of making him useful to the family business.

Ahmed went on, 'There are many foreigners here now, and you are a man of action, not of numbers and account books. Sheikh Mohammed is struggling to put together a police force able to cope. You have spent time overseas. You understand the challenges. I could suggest you to him?'

Abdullah shrugged, scarcely listening. 'Thank you, I would like that.'

* * *

A strange and unexpected thing happened. Abdullah found that he cared about police work. He discovered a belief in the importance of the values he had grown up with. That people should feel safe to enjoy the burgeoning night life of the city. That within a few minutes of a crime being committed, a patrol car cruised out to investigate.

When Abdullah was twenty-six, still living at home, his father divorced his mother with the traditional, *I divorce thee, I divorce thee, I divorce thee*. Being past the age of ten, Abdullah had entered the male realm of his father, but their relationship had soured since he refused the career path chosen for him, and entered the police force. He accepted his mother's pleas for him to go with her. Life for a divorcee is difficult without a male relative close at hand for escort duties and dealing with the outside world. Even calling a tradesman for a lone Muslim woman is difficult.

Mother and son went to live in one of the new apartments above the sands of Jumeirah Beach, just a short walk from the mosque. They had always been close, but now they became closer still. In the evenings after work he would buy her a flower, or some Swiss chocolate. Perhaps a small gift of jewellery.

Still, the grief of being spurned by the man she had supported all her life weighed upon her. She smiled only rarely, and spent hours staring out through the window at the world of men that she could not join.

Abdullah, meanwhile, rose through the ranks of a force that expanded almost daily, until from a ragtag band of just forty men he commanded a division of five hundred. The keys to his leadership were high expectations, supreme personal standards and a willingness to try new techniques, often gleaned from overseas forces: London, New York, and Paris.

Into his thirties he remained at home with his mother, refusing social invitations. Apart from riding weekly, he had few engagements outside work and home. With no father to plan his marriage, he made no efforts in that direction, and he lavished attention on his mother, even as she became devout — mindful of a thousand tiny superstitions, many of which revolved around the Holy Qur'an itself. The book, for example, could never touch the ground. Abdullah's mother insisted on using stands purchased to hold the book at eye level. It must never be left open or the Devil would come and read it, assimilating the wisdom inside. When not in use it must be wrapped and placed on the highest shelf in the house.

Like much of the population of the Arab world, she burned bakhoor — incense — in the belief that it discouraged devils, or jinn, from inhabiting the house. After cutting her own or Abdullah's hair, she collected every fallen strand, wrapped it in newspaper and hid it in a closet. It was well known that Jews and other potential enemies might use discarded hairs or nails to cause sickness and death to good Muslims.

Each morning mother and son would together recite the thirty-sixth Surah, the Ya Sin, with its powers of healing, protection of property, defence against the jinn and an eventual easy passage to Paradise.

You, O Muhammad, are one of the Messengers, on a Straight Path. This is a Revelation sent down by the Almighty, the Most Merciful, in order that you may

warn a people whose forefathers were not warned, so
they are heedless. The Word has proved true against
most of them, so they will not believe. We have put
on their necks iron collars reaching to chins, so that
their heads are forced up. And we have put a barrier
before them, and a barrier behind them, and we
have covered them up, so that they cannot see. It is
the same to them whether you warn them or you
warn them not; they will not believe.

Saddam Hussein's invasion of Kuwait, and the resulting
First Gulf War, when half-a-million American servicemen
flooded the region, rattled Dubai's economy, but still it
rebounded. Further concessions brought more foreign
companies into the trade zones, and money flowed into
an economy boosted by ambitious local infrastructure
projects.

Abdullah's mother sank into a depression no doctor
could comprehend or cure. One morning he woke to
silence. No sound of activity in the kitchen where she had
prepared his morning meal for fifteen years.

They found her in Dubai Creek, between the pylons of
al-Maktoum Bridge, yellow nightshirt wound tight around
her body. She had, according to the coroner, been dead for
three hours. Abdullah used his position to have the details
suppressed, and a short press release issued, explaining
that his mother had drowned while swimming. He sold the
apartment and took a smaller one.

He remained friends with Ahmed, who went on to head
Dubai World, a government-backed corporation worth a
hundred billion dollars in assets at its peak. He watched

the building of the Palms, towering hotel after towering hotel, then some of the most extravagant shopping malls in existence. Countless thousands of Pakistanis crossed the Arabian Sea to slave for this empire of money.

Finally, he watched the economic ravages of the first and second Global Financial Crises, then the slow rising of the sea so that the Palms and the unfinished World were threatened by water, ravaged by supertides. Billions of dollars worth of man-made real estate, threatened by the changing planet. Itinerant workers were trapped without employment, housed in their slum estates, unable to afford the fares home. Crime rates soared. The world of Abdullah's childhood cracked and crumbled.

Now past any likelihood of marriage, Abdullah is experienced in sexual intercourse only with Russian and Chinese prostitutes, who solicit in certain streets and nightclubs of Dubai. Technically no virgin, spiritually he has never been touched. Modern Dubai courtship, much of which centres on passing business cards to members of the opposite sex you find attractive, is repugnant to him.

His home is visited only by Lualhati, the Filipino maid who has, for twenty years, parked her Corolla in his underground parking space at 11:00am, cleaned the unit, and prepared an evening meal. Rarely laying eyes on her, Abdullah mails her a cheque every second Thursday, with a small bonus on the holiday of Eid, at the conclusion of Ramadan.

A long-standing member of the Equestrian Club, he competes in three or four races a year, and maintains four hardy Arabs, agisted through the club and stabled by professionals. On weekends he still rides, finding pleasure in companionship with the finest horses money can buy.

The job of coordinating security at Rabi al-Salah is the culmination of a lifetime's work, a task at which he has already failed. The overall plan was simple: a core of GDOIS and British DRFS, supplemented by representatives from other nations, backed up by the elite Dubai Fifth Air Battalion.

It should have been enough. Would normally have been enough. But there is always the imponderable — the gentle man who has gone to the other side. Something that defies even the most rigorous security checks.

Abdullah prays, inviting his God to prepare for Dr Ali Khalid Abukar the hottest fires at His disposal.

Despite his job, Simon hasn't been to Aden for years, a city that remains impoverished and relatively lawless. It did, however, escape the mass killings seen in Taiz and Sana'a, during the vigorous protest movement that resulted in such severe wounds to the dictator Saleh that he was forced to leave the country to seek treatment. The violence worsened on his return, and thousands died in the pursuit of freedom. Even now, Yemen teeters on the edge of civil war.

Reputedly the site where Noah built his ark and invited the animals aboard two by two, the peninsula is shaped like a dragon's head, divided by the crater of a long dead volcano, the industrial city of Sheikh Othman on the opposite shore to the sprawling port complex. Ripples of rock make up the ridges of the mountain — the backbone of the dragon.

The airport was once a RAF base, and those hangars of 1950s corrugated iron remain. It boasts long and serviceable runways; the only hazard on take-off and landing being the volcano itself.

As the plane comes to rest, Simon is already moving, lifting down his bag and leading a line of passengers to the door, waiting while the stairway is clipped into place. Inside the terminal, he switches on his phone and reads Isabella's text message.

Simon. Forgive me. Girls taken from Aden airport. My heart is with you, along with all my hopes and trust.

For a moment he cannot move, instead running her words through his mind.

Forgive you for what? What did you do, Isabella? Is it true that you had sex with him? That you screwed an Algerian terrorist? That while our girls slept you rutted with a killer, a planter of bombs? That you let the bastards take the one beautiful thing in our lives. The daughters we both love, whatever our own failings ...

Entering a grimy bathroom of pale linoleum and ceramic, rust-stained sinks, Simon wrinkles his nose at the smell of urine and worse. He washes and shaves, changing his shirt for a lightly soiled one from his bag, losing some travel sweat in the process. Finally he combs his hair, pins his BA identification card to his top pocket and walks towards the security gate where other visitors have queued up to display their documentation.

Simon feels the first trepidation at what he is about to do, opening his passport with its flight crew stamp. A pair of dark eyes fix on his, and he wonders if he is about to be questioned, but then he is through and there is no shout behind him. He passes on, pleased that bluff is still possible in a world of suspicion, body scans and iris readers.

At first he is content to wander the concourse, aware of the obvious differences between this airport and the showpiece at Dubai — this is older, more workmanlike than ostentatious. Aden, he decides, is a perfect place to abduct the children of a high-ranking official — one not so important as to attract her own security detail, but senior enough to serve their purposes.

Workers and travellers pass by in twos and threes, talking loudly as is common in the local culture. The bulk of the speech is in Gulf Arabic or, occasionally, Farsi. Simon has a working knowledge of both, gleaned over years of travel, and dealing often with staff from Middle Eastern airports. He deciphers what he can. Snippets, statements, questions, the clutter of everyday life.

'No, that is not the way to lift a box, let me show you ...'

A man in a long, white thoub says to the man beside him, 'When I am finished this evening I will go to al-Rayyan restaurant in Crater, with my brothers, if it pleases God ...'

'I and my sons will go to the cinema ...'

Simon remembers his and Isabella's visit to the open air cinema here, years earlier on their long honeymoon, travelling virtually free by nature of his profession. Back then he was the established wage earner and she fresh out of university, starting with the FCO as an administrative assistant.

The women he sees, almost without exception, wear the niqab face covering, along with an abaya robe to the ankles, sometimes studded with beads or tiny faux diamonds, or worn with sunglasses and discreet jewellery.

These women live in one of the most gender divided societies on earth — where even in a court of law the testimony of two women is required to equal that of one man — yet Simon has discovered, over the years, that these women are not as timid or powerless as Westerners might believe. Now and then one will turn her eyes brazenly on him as he passes, while he is simultaneously trying to avoid looking at them. Just for an instant, dark eyes swing towards him, promise unimaginable delights, then turn away demurely as if it had never happened, and by then they are gone down the concourse.

As he passes through the main corridor, Simon continues to scan. Workers on breaks chew qat — the narcotic leaf popular in the region — noticeable via one bulging cheek. Though Simon should be tired, he feels distraught but energised — every sense wide and receptive, soaking up each nuance, not ceasing to explore until he reaches the main doors, walking outside to look at the taxis: dusty Toyotas, Fiats, Renaults and Nissans competing for space with elongated white buses with Arabic lettering on the sides. He inhales the night air, stares out towards the lights of a city as foreign as any on earth, with jagged hills as a backdrop.

Simon has to fight a sense of despair. Once the children and their abductors left this airport they could have gone anywhere in the Middle East or Africa without trace. The Western mania for record keeping, Simon knows, is not de rigueur here. There will be few, if any, clues to their whereabouts. He has just one lead and this is it. With that thought he turns and walks back inside the building.

Day 1, 21:30

Marika's eyelids are rimmed with red, and if she allows herself the luxury of closing her eyes, even at the computer, she finds herself drifting away from the world of shrill telephones and chattering keyboards into something more appealing.

With Abdullah bin al-Rhoumi's name opening doors, she has an FBI team from the Tactical Support Branch of the CIRG on their way into a New York apartment, managed by radio waves beamed halfway across the world. The sense of power is dizzying, and dangerous. Marika frowns with concentration so intense it gives her a headache. There can be no mistakes. Lives hang on her decisions, her instincts, and reactions.

Abdullah appears beside Marika's chair, accompanied by a tall and lean figure. He wears a goatee beard trimmed close to his face, and the same blue overalls as the other members of the security team. She has seen him around the centre, one of many hundreds, yet has not exchanged a word with him.

'Miss Hartmann. Have you met Madoowbe?'

Marika stands, shaking the man's hand. 'No, not yet.'

The grip is dry and firm. Long fingers. His voice is deep, and smooth as honey. 'Pleased to meet you.'

'Madoowbe is a very experienced operative indeed, so he may be of help up here,' Abdullah explains. 'He is Somalia's Transitional Federal Government's contribution to the security force. I'm assigning him to you for the moment.'

Madoowbe's eyes are black, owl like, glistening with curiosity and intelligence. Marika hands him a spare pair of headphones from the desk, and plugs them in. 'You better listen in,' she tells him. 'We might need help if the woman we are chasing is at the apartment.'

'Who is she?' he asks.

Marika tries to sum up the situation in as few words as possible. 'The woman in question is the wife of Dr Abukar. We are unsure of her whereabouts.'

'What is her name?'

'Sufia Haweeya. She might have played some part in the plot, or if not, might be used as leverage. In either case, she is worth finding.'

An electronic voice crackles through the headphones and Marika slips them over her head, the frame so light she can scarcely feel it.

'This is Rabi al-Salah control, go ahead HRT.'

'Reading you, Rabi al-Salah. Position outside apartment building in question. We have identified unit nineteen. Ground floor.' The voice is male, east coast American.

Ground floor. A passage from a well known al-Qa'ida terror manual comes to mind, a publication named *Declaration of Jihad against the Country's Tyrants – Military Series.* According to this tract, *It is preferable to rent apartments on the ground floor to facilitate escape and digging of trenches ...*

Marika forms a mental image of what is happening in New York. Despite the name, Hostage Rescue Team, this group has a wide variety of responsibilities, including high-risk searches, counter-terrorism, manhunts and personnel protection. The team will be dressed in black, equipped with Springfield 1911 automatic handguns in side holsters. Many will carry M16 rifles while others sport Remington 870 shotguns or even a 7.62mm sniper rifle. One or two operatives will be explosives experts, equipped to locate and disarm anti-personnel weapons encountered in the course of the job. Each man or woman is wired up for hands-free communications. It is just past noon over there now. They will deal politely but firmly with members of the public who come to gawk or obstruct.

'Does the apartment show any signs of occupancy, HRT?'

'Negative.'

'Then please approach and seal building. Detain any personnel trying to enter or leave. When area is secure I want you to penetrate apartment.'

'Understood, please stand by.'

Ten minutes of nothing passes. Marika taps her pen on the desk and waits. The inactivity irks her; she is a physical woman, and would rather be there on the ground. The headphones crackle back to life.

'Building secure.'

'There is a possibility of claymore-type mines or other set hazards in apartment. Proceed with caution.'

'Understood.' A longer pause. The sound of booted feet on tiles. 'We are outside apartment door. Confirm that no lights show from inside. Listening devices detect no sound from the interior.'

'Ring the bell.'

'No response.'

'Try it again.'

'No response. Door swept for attachments. No set hazards.'

'Proceed to force entry.'

Even across thousands of miles, Marika hears heavy blows from a Zak ram on the door. For the first time she hears her contact breathing. 'The apartment is dark. Light switch does not work, moving to personal lighting.'

'General impressions?' Marika glances across at Madoowbe, who is also listening, making no sound.

'Room is tidy. Musty but clean.' Nothing for thirty or forty seconds. 'Table surfaces free of clutter. I am now entering the kitchen. The refrigerator door is open, turned off, and it is empty. Linoleum floor clean.'

'Secure the other rooms and start checking drawers and cupboards.'

'What are we looking for?'

'Travel plans, brochures, maps. Anything. Have you come across any computer equipment?'

'Not yet.'

'Tell me if you do.'

Marika reaches for a tissue from the half-empty box beside her workstation. Blowing her nose, she waits for the operative to recommence communications. Beside her, Madoowbe shifts in his seat. For a few more seconds she allows herself the indulgence of watching him. He is an attractive man: tall, with Nilotic features. Lean, but wiry. It is the smouldering eyes, however, that hold her attention.

'How long have you been in Dubai?' she asks, taking advantage of the break in radio traffic.

'A little over a month.'

'Do you like it here?'

The expression on his face is comical, as if he finds her question amusing. 'Strangely, no.'

Aware that she is still holding the used tissue in her hand Marika stands up and drops it in the nearest bin. 'A little too hectic for you?'

'Not exactly.'

Again that expression, and Marika finds herself growing angry. *You patronising bastard. Wish I'd never asked*.

The earphones crackle into life. 'The apartment is clear. I've got men combing it now, and forensics on site.'

'Good, can we find out if the neighbours know anything?'

'Affirmative.'

Marika glances again at Madoowbe, who has found something interesting to look at on the far side of the room. Dismissing him from her thoughts, she finds herself thinking of home, imagining a good clean southerly swell rolling up the coast to Bondi. There are dolphins cruising just behind the break, and cormorants diving. Quite often, these days, the microbe count is so high swimming is not recommended, but with all her heart she wishes she was there — soaking up the winter sun in her favourite spot just down from the RSL club walkway.

This is a great time of year in the mountains, too — freezing at night, so she'd pack her treasured Black Wolf sleeping bag, rated for ten below, and the Salewa tent. Yet it rains less in July than most other months, and there are few people on the trails. A great time to sit on the boulder-strewn banks of the Shoalhaven, deep in the gorge where only the tough and well-prepared penetrate, and watch the platypus at play. Her mind roams, planning a solo trip — no one else to get in the way, particularly not a man. That kind of complication, she muses, sneaking another glance at Madoowbe, she doesn't need.

The voice over the radio brings her back to reality. 'The apartment is clean. No computers. No toothbrushes. Even the bed sheets look brand new. Forensics are beginning to think that there's not a fingerprint in the whole damn place — and that's not possible unless it's been swept clean, and by someone who knows what they're doing.'

'That alone tells us something. Look at the curtains,

and the paintings on the walls, the books on the shelves. What kind of people are they?'

There is a long pause. 'Intellectual types.'

Marika endures thirty minutes of waiting — risking a visit to the female bathrooms outside the massive hydraulic doors, acknowledging, on the way back, security staff swarming like bull ants around a nest. Hurrying back to Madoowbe, who shakes his head to indicate that no transmissions have come through. She makes notes and waits.

Finally, the headphones come to life again. 'We have some information, Rabi al-Salah. The male occupant, Dr Abukar, left three weeks ago, followed by the female, Sufia Haweeya, seven days later. One of the neighbours spoke to the woman before she left and asked her where she was going.'

Marika is almost frightened to ask the question. 'Where?'

'Home. The woman said that she was going home. That's all.'

'Great,' Marika says, 'just great.' She turns to Madoowbe. 'What should we do?'

'The woman, Sufia, must be very important to Dr Abukar. He has placed her out of danger.'

Marika taps at the keyboard and brings up all the information she has collected on Sufia. Her home village is the same as that of her husband. She turns to Madoowbe. 'Are you familiar with the village of Bacaadweyn?'

'Very much so. My mother's cousins are from there. Many times when I was young I visited them.'

'Any idea on the political situation in the area?' The question seems almost redundant. All Somalia is dangerous. A graveyard for foreign armies.

'Technically it's part of Puntland — governed by the Harti and Tanade clans — but in practice it's lawless, with a few local subclans and their warlords vying for power.'

Marika turns to Abdullah, hovering a few yards away. 'We've got a lead on the location of the woman.'

The gaunt face stares back at her. 'Deep in Somalia?'

'Yes.'

'Then she is inaccessible. We will have to think of something else — other angles.'

'Perhaps,' Marika says, 'it is worth a try. To pick her up, I mean.' Her heart beats hard against her chest. *What the hell am I proposing here?*

'No, Miss Hartmann. There is nothing to say that Sufia Haweeya's presence here will change the situation one iota. Besides, even a battalion of troops could not fight their way out of trouble in the Somali interior. I cannot throw lives away.'

'No, but what about sending just me?'

'Do you understand how much of a risk you'd be taking? You cannot speak the language.'

'I speak pretty good Arabic — it'll get me out of trouble, and ...' She turns to the tall Somali. 'Perhaps Madoowbe would come with me?'

The dark eyes settle on her for a moment, then a nod. 'I would be pleased to.'

'Can you parachute?'

'I was trained by the British SAS many years ago.'

'You were SAS?'

'Yes, for a time.'

Abdullah sighs. 'Miss Hartmann. You are a good agent, and you are under my care. The answer is no.'

Marika stands up, almost as tall as Abdullah. Despite having worked under the man for less than a month she feels a strong connection with him — his methods are as efficient and up-to-date as any in the world, yet his leadership is compassionate and thoughtful. 'Sir, with all due respect, I have a feeling that this woman may be the key. I feel responsible for what happened. I should have acted on my gut — just one minute earlier and none of this would have happened. You must give me the opportunity to make amends.'

'I think, with my help, we would have a strong chance of success,' Madoowbe adds.

Abdullah's face changes little. If anything he looks even older and more tired than usual. 'You are a brave young woman,' he says, then turning to Madoowbe, 'and you are a credit to your people. May God go with both of you. Give me details of what you need. Rest assured that Dubai's armed forces will be at your disposal.'

When Abdullah has gone Marika turns to Madoowbe and shrugs. 'I kind of dropped you in it, there. Thanks for the support.'

He gives no visible sign of displeasure at his involvement in the mission. 'I am happy to be of service to you.'

Marika is about to turn back to the desk when she again catches that sardonic twinkle in his eye, gone again so fast she might have imagined it.

Day 1, 23:50

The pub is as dark as a cave, subdued now as it winds down into the early hours. The barman, drying wine glasses on a chequered tea towel, glares around the room as if to say, *When are you people gonna piss off?*

A middle-aged man and woman are kissing, pressed together like wax statues against the wall near the toilet doors. A quartet of young travellers guffaw. One stands, gripping a chair for balance, and makes for the gents.

PJ Johnson takes a sip of his whisky, the raw liquid stinging where he has been chewing his lips — he always chews his lips when drinking, which is one of the reasons he doesn't imbibe too often. Don Lockyer lays a hand on his shoulder.

'Come on, it's two in the morning. We'll be in the shit for sure.'

PJ shrinks away. 'One more, OK?'

'The bar's closed.'

'Just let me finish this one.'

Two other men occupy the table. Tourists. Both hold cards in their hands. One is short and squat, and the other so tall his hair, when standing, almost touches the ceiling.

'Come on. Captain Pennington will get the shits — we'll be on a charge for sure.'

PJ stands, swaying on his feet like a tree in the wind. 'He doesn't like me, does he?'

'Who?'

'Captain Bloody Pennington.'

Don shakes his head. 'He's young. Trying too hard. Officers can be like that. He'll relax after a while, you'll see.'

PJ thinks about what Don just said. The previous Troop Commander had been a man in his forties, veteran of Bosnia, Kosovo, and Iraq, and a harder nut than any of them. PJ had hero worshipped the man, and his retirement from the forces had come as a blow.

Don grips the meat of PJ's shoulder. 'Come on, stop arsing about, it's time to go.'

PJ drains his glass, slams it down, takes the first step, pauses to regain his balance, then strides to the doorway, where he steadies himself on the frame. From that vantage point he turns back to look at Don. 'Well come on, you said you wanted to get going.'

'Smart bastard.'

Few people are about as they walk down the street to the Land Rover. Gibraltar never really closes down, with its combination of naval base, garrulous locals, and tourists, yet tonight the atmosphere is quiet, even subdued. For three weeks, M Squadron, Special Boat Service, has been posted here, ready for God alone knows what.

PJ opens the passenger door, collapses inside and waits for Don, conscious of the engine starting, half dozing on the short drive. They cruise along Winston Churchill Avenue, with its airport and stadium, then turn downhill, past tightly packed houses with their balconies and Georgian charm. Now the darkened port area spreads out before them, straddled by the sea on two sides — a British naval base since before the time of Nelson, sitting on the entrance to the Mediterranean, and one key reason why the British became such an important sea power. A few people, such as PJ himself, know that it is also a SIGINT listening post and a staging point for Special Forces units heading into the various and ever-changing war zones of the Middle East and Africa. A few more know about the nuclear submarines in their Z berths, but that fact is omitted from the tourist brochures.

Gibraltar, it seems to PJ, is a brooding outpost, with its views across the strait to Morocco, the cliffs of Jebel

Musa, and of the fleet of patrolling warships attempting to stop the dozens of ancient boats that each night run the ten-mile gauntlet, fleeing desperate Africa for what they see as the halcyon life of Europe, decks piled with families and their possessions. Families who have pawned their last valuables for the chance of a better life. Many of the boats sink under the strain, and bodies wash up on the shore like driftwood. The hopeless and dispossessed, giving their lives for a dream.

Beside the guard house, as Don changes down a gear and brakes, PJ sees a tall, slim figure waiting. At first the sight does not register, but then a sickening awareness descends, slowed by the alcohol in his veins.

Don reaches the same conclusion. 'Uh oh, looks like we're busted.'

PJ groans. 'Doesn't he ever sleep?'

'Obviously not. But just let me do the talking, OK? You open that gob of yours and we're both on a charge for sure.'

As the jeep slides to a halt, Captain Pennington's face appears in the window, narrow and angular. 'Where the hell have you two been? Your leave pass expired at twenty-three-hundred.' PJ opens his mouth to speak, but Pennington hasn't finished. 'Pull over and get out.'

As Don pulls over to the road verge PJ hisses, 'What the hell is he up to?'

'Don't know, but I doubt it's pleasant.'

They walk towards Pennington, who snaps, 'Take off those jackets and leave them in the jeep. You don't need them.' Standing in front of them he begins to stretch. 'Now copy me.'

'What the hell are we doing?'

'You mean what the hell are we doing, *sir*?'

PJ mumbles the correction.

'We're warming up,' Pennington continues. 'You should know that; you're the fittest man in the troop.'

For a minute or two, PJ attempts the bends and stretches, losing his balance more than once. 'Why are we warming up, *sir*?'

Pennington begins to jog on the spot. 'Because we're going for a run. The Rock.'

PJ groans aloud. 'The Rock? At night? You've got to be joking. It'll kill us.' He sees Don from the corner of his eyes, reads his expression — *It's your fault we're so late.*

'Follow me,' Pennington shouts.

First Don, then PJ, lumbers drunkenly after him.

'Why?' PJ gasps. 'Why this? Why now?'

'Because you're drunk, and in two hours you're going to war.'

THE SECOND DAY

And God said, 'Let there be an expanse between the waters to separate water from water. So God made the expanse and divided the waters. God called the expanse 'Sky'. Yet carbon from the cars, fires and machines of the world poisons the firmament. Toxic gas forms a blanket over the planet, locking in heat.

Trees and other plants that might absorb the deadly gases are removed at unprecedented rates. In the world's largest cities, fog mingled with a soup of chemical aerosols and smoke settles on windless days, forcing the inhabitants to wear masks. In some places the haze never lifts, and Homo sapiens lose touch with the stars and the moon. The sun is forever aflame, tinged with orange fire.

There was evening and morning. The second day.

Day 2, 05:00

Even now, with the power of life and death over a thousand men and women, surrounded by comrades with guns, Dr Ali Khalid Abukar's rage burns as brightly as ever.

He is angry at how the Western media machine seeks to stamp the label 'terrorist' on every Muslim; at how the truths of history can be glossed over by men and women

with short memories and a vested interest, the media
forgetting that violent Christian militancy predates that of
·Muslims in the twentieth century. How in Lebanon such
groups as the Maronites launched a reign of terror as the
country descended into a bloody fifteen-year civil war
back in the 1980s. A time when gangs belonging to both
religions struck and retaliated with atrocity after atrocity.

When the Twin Towers fell in New York, mosques
were firebombed and Muslims assaulted from Sydney to
London, and the Western man on the street was happy
to tar one billion human beings with the same brush.
When young, dispossessed Muslims responded in kind,
it served to fuel the futile cycle of violence while the
real struggle, that of survival, continued in the majority
world. Westerners seemed unable to understand that there
are as many different kinds of Muslims as there are fish
in the sea. The reverse was also true, Ali knew. Not all
Westerners are thoughtless and bigoted.

The US-led attack on Afghanistan, Ali decided, could
be justified. But the second invasion of Iraq confused and
enraged him. So many wrongs. One million deaths. Five
million displaced civilians. Half the population living in
utter poverty even ten years after the invasion. A nation of
orphans and widows.

Abu Ghraib. Seven thousand prisoners guarded by
three hundred and fifty reservists who had orders to
'soften' the prisoners up. Ali would never forget images
of Lynndie England and her Iraqi prisoner on a chain.
America as overlord. Muslim as dog.

The murder of Baha Mousa, and the abuse of ten
others at the hands of troops from Britain's Lancashire
Regiment, led to compensation payouts in the millions of

pounds, and a realisation that so-called higher civilisation does not preclude cruelty. Ali felt a terrible, powerless rage as he followed the trial of the soldiers responsible. One man was jailed for a year, the others suspended from duty. He wondered how much more harshly the perpetrators of homicide and torture would have been treated if the victims were Western civilians.

In March 2011, Reverend Terry Jones of the Dove World Outreach Center, Gainsville, Florida, burned a Qur'an in front of his congregation. Afghan media whipped the public into a frenzy of outrage about the incident, forming a mob that marched from the central suburb of Chowk Saheedan to the UN compound in Kandahar, burning schools, tipping vehicles, chanting 'Death to America'. The violence spread to other regions. Ten people died in the chaos, almost a hundred were injured.

Meanwhile, in Uganda, a Christian militia gang, the Lord's Resistance Army, developed recruitment tactics that included setting fire to a school, ringing it with gunmen, and press-ganging any boy who managed to escape the flames. These new recruits were then introduced to the arts of rape and murder in the name of God.

Dozens of ex-Guantanamo Bay detainees took up arms for al-Qa'ida in the Arabian Peninsula, fighting security forces in Yemen. US officials expressed surprise. This reaction confused Ali. *Are they really so blind? Why can they not see that hate breeds hate?* At this time he read Abdullah Azzam's *The Love and Hour of the Martyrs*, a work that both frightened and compelled him, calling on all Muslims to fight jihad in the name of God.

Swathes of Africa were purchased by foreign interests and planted to the new wonder crop, the South Americasourced jatropha, grown to produce biodiesel for a Western world unable to conceive of life without the emissions-belching engines that power it. Subsistence farmers were evicted from land formerly useless to serious monoculture, now made possible by the amazing resilience of jatropha.

The focus of oil production moved to Africa, and the environmentally destructive and poisonous tar sands of Canada and Asia. The melting ice caps of the polar regions opened up ninety billion barrels of potential reserves, at huge environmental cost. Oil companies spent more on political lobbying than Gabon or the Ivory Coast spend on health and education combined. Fracking techniques used for extracting coal seam gas set off seismic waves around the globe. Earthquakes shook cities and filled mortuaries with the bodies of the dead.

Meanwhile, in the Congo, children and teenagers laboured from dusk to dawn, working knee-deep in water, using long rakes to scrape the mud from the river bed, then dig a basin in which gravel is swirled so that the precious mineral coltan — vital ingredient of smartphones, video game consoles and computers — could be extracted.

Armed guards of the FDLR, the Democratic Forces for the Liberation of Rwanda, stood nearby with assault rifles and whips. They checked the extracted ore and placed it in chests, ready for collection. The profits from the illegal theft of these Congolese resources bought guns and ammunition for this Hutu army in exile, the same men who once shocked the world with the genocide of the Tutsi people, one of the blackest chapters in human history that saw almost a million humans shot or hacked to death.

Accelerated climate change saw the ice caps melt at a pace beyond any forecasts. No one predicted just how quickly it would happen. The permafrost melt accelerated, quadrupling the rate of carbon absorption into the atmosphere. One of the first manifestations of catastrophic climate change was the invasion of salt into freshwater rivers. The Mekong, in Vietnam, relied on by seventeen million subsistence farmers, became saline up to eighty kilometres from the mouth. Families watched their crops fail to emerge, or wilt and die.

First, second, and even third generation refugees, born on the long hard flight to safety and freedom, filled internment camps in Germany, Great Britain, Poland, the Czech Republic, Malaysia, Indonesia, and Australia's offshore islands. Public opinion swayed governments into dealing harshly with asylum seekers, often in defiance of their human rights obligations.

Sea levels continued to rise, and supertides wrought havoc on low lying villages, drinking water supplies and arable land. The Daad. Drought and famine in the Horn of Africa. Refugees poured out of Somalia's rural areas and into the camps. Religious and clan warfare made effective aid distribution impossible.

When climate change became an awakening humanitarian disaster the West vacillated — sent token aid and expressed regret — but coal power station smokestacks bellowed because no one could afford to stop them. The Fukushima nuclear accident in Japan provoked a wholesale movement back to the dirtier-fuelled plants. There was no money to spend on clean alternatives. Governments had borrowed hundreds of billions that they could not afford to repay.

Hard decisions had to be made. Steps taken that would mean privation and difficulty for the citizens of developed nations. For Western governments, however, already fighting public anger over austerity budgets aimed at cutting unsustainable public sector and welfare spending, the required measures were political suicide and they knew it. They must be forced. There was no alternative.

Ali Khalid Abukar watched his mother die in the Somali famine. Held her hand in those last moments. Learned how an aid agency had, in good faith, installed a petrol-powered pump in the wells of Durukh, providing gushing water where previously there had been just a trickle. Millennia-old channels overflowed, and precious water evaporated. Wells that had proved faithful for two thousand years ran dry in six months. The fields failed. No rain came, and the people starved.

Ali made no secret of his feelings, joined with secret talk at the mosque and cafe. Flying to Algeria under a pretext, he met with the new wave of mujahedin. Under heavy guard, he travelled south on ancient, and often secret, trade routes deep into the Sahel, that ocean of semi-arid sand and stone that belts Africa at its widest. US strategists call this the 'Terrorist Corridor', lapping against Mali, Algeria and Nigeria.

The convoy was a daisy chain of stolen vehicles — dusty Opel Fronteras, Land Rovers, Toyota Land Cruisers — manned by silent, bearded men with guns that never left their hands, climbing dusty, dry mountains that average less than one inch of rain each year. Ali rode in the back seat, flanked by the mujahedin, many of them blooded through years in AQIM — al-Qa'ida in the Islamic Maghreb — or the GSPC, both organisations famous for hijackings going back to the turn of the new century.

The journey ended at a sandstone gorge, with hollowed entrances honeycombed into the rock, the Tora Bora of Africa. This cave complex, now home to al-Muwahhidun, might have been in use for ten or even fifty thousand years. Inside were storehouses, sleeping places, and meeting rooms. Ali was summoned to a separate chamber, alone.

On the wall someone had scrawled the infamous words of the Egyptian Sheikh Omar Abdel Rahman. Words that had found a home on thousands of placards, terror manuals, and even bookmarks across the Muslim world:

> *Divide their nation, tear them to shreds, destroy their economy, burn their companies, ruin their welfare, sink their ships and kill them on land, sea and air ... may God torture them at your hands.*

Ali Khalid Abukar — forty-five years old, yet shaking like a child — looked across at the sweating faces, lit by a fire that smouldered in a stone crevice. The man who introduced himself as Zhyogal leaned close, cradling an assault rifle, tendons bunched like cables beneath the olive skin of his neck and shoulders. He, like the others, was dressed in camouflage fatigues, with the chequered shemagh wound around head and shoulders, his eyes just a slit in the opening. His voice was strong and persuasive, rising and falling poetically, each word enunciated with that rounded accent common to educated Africans, echoing in the vaulted darkness of the cavern.

'You have told me of your anger, doctor, at how it is a choking vine that twists and twines through the vessels of blood that feed your heart. You are a believer in the true God, praise and glory be to Him. You have seen the Muslim tribes of Africa — the Bambara, the Tuareg, the Hutu, the Fulani, the Hausa, and the Mandinka — die in their hundreds of thousands from the policies and procrastination of the Zionists and Americans. You have seen the new terror that comes from the sea and the sky.'

One of the men across the fire lit a cigarette, the tip flaring red as he inhaled. Pungent tobacco smoke drifted through the cavern, mingling with the underlying odours of bat excreta and decaying stone.

'Your people are dying — screaming for help that never comes. North Africa is a well of poverty and corruption that the kufr fills with the waters of indifference and exploitation.'

A helpless ache burned up from Ali's throat, flooding into the back of his mouth. 'That is true.'

Another of the militants stood, his face furious. His eyes burned like coals in the pit of his skull. A man of unusual physical presence. His name was Saif al-Din, now growing in stature across the Muslim world. A wraith who broadcast fear and terror like a jinn, inflaming the faithful, putting steel in the core of the most fainthearted of believers. His face was as dark as the blackest reaches of the cave. The illusion of madness resided behind his eyes. His resolute spirit was as obvious as that of Zhyogal. In fact, the two might have been brothers. They looked at each other often, as if for approval. Two warriors. Kindred souls.

'I have just returned from the Niger Delta,' Saif said. 'The American oil companies continue their plunder, and the seas are rising — seas polluted with oil. We must fight with more resolve even than those who came before us.

Swear a bayat of allegiance to us and join your brothers in the struggle.'

Tears welled in the corner of Ali's eyes, burning as they rolled down the plane of his cheek. His throat ached. 'I will do so without reservation. The leaders of the Western world will not listen. They seek to prolong the financial empire owned by a rich elite — unchanged. They send their young men and their missiles and their bombs to kill and maim our people. They have caused the world itself to alter and threaten my people. I have come to believe that Muslim countries must be ruled by the Sharia, not by foreigners and alien political systems.'

Zhyogal kissed Ali first on one cheek, and then the other. 'You are indeed welcome. You and I, from this moment, are brothers.'

Day 2, 06:00

The Hercules is Lockheed's C130J stretched version, the latest manifestation of the giant transport aircraft that has flown everything from armoured personnel carriers to emergency aid into the world's trouble spots for more than half a century. Marika finds the throbbing turboprops comforting — perhaps a throwback to her training days. Cables run along the starboard side, along with bench seats that would normally be lined with paratroopers making last-minute checks. Madoowbe sits beside her, occupied with adjusting a buckle on his harness, sinewy black arms shining with nervous sweat in the half light.

Marika can smell him. Wonders if she emits the same scent. There is no Rexona in her underarms today. Smells can be as dangerous as sounds. Either can mean discovery and death on clandestine ops like this one.

The logistics of this headlong rush through perilous airspace occupies Marika's mind. On her back is a bulky Special Forces-issue parachute. A smaller pack, strapped to her ammo belt, contains clothes and food. Her Glock 9mm automatic is clipped tight into a canvas holster at her side.

In less than thirty minutes they will drop into Somalia, the problem child of Africa — a land torn apart by feuding warlords and their followers. The Transitional Federal Government, backed by the West, and bolstered by troops from the African Union, cannot unite a land where law issues from the barrel of an assault rifle, a place of famine, disarray, and disunity; bleeding and torn.

Even so, Marika is determined, even in that failed state, to find Sufia Haweeya and take her back to Dubai. From the top pocket of her jacket she removes her personal CVCID, nicknamed 'Sid', the military version of the civilian smartphone that has proved indispensable in modern intelligence work. She punches in her PIN, then brings up a photograph of the woman on the screen: tall and willowy, high, sloping forehead and defined cheekbones lending her a regal beauty that Marika finds appealing yet intimidating. The sadness of her eyes suggests that life has not always been easy, yet the lips make a half-moon smile, as if she is ready to laugh. There is something familiar about her, also, something troubling that Marika cannot quite place.

Can this woman make a difference? Marika isn't sure, but it is one possibility in a situation devoid of options. It may not be possible to find her, in any case. *I hope you're ready*, she says to the image, *because I'm coming to get you.*

Putting the Sid unit back in its place she settles into the seat. She has always found parachuting into strange territory nerve-racking. Low-light drops are an order of magnitude worse. Now, scarcely dawn — ten thousand feet above the Somali desert, with God alone knows what down below — she feels close to terror. Slipping out of her harness, she staggers aft to the head and uses it, determined that it will be a long time before she needs to avail herself again. Back at her seat, she looks at her watch, knowing they must be close, regretting taking the mission on herself. She could have brought in any elite fighting force in the region. It was she, however, who insisted that one or two personnel would be less obvious, able to get in, assess the situation and call for backup if necessary. Madoowbe's language skills and local knowledge will be invaluable.

If possible, they will bring Sufia Haweeya out themselves, utilising a chopper from the heavy cruiser USS *Chicago* in the Red Sea. Of course, Marika tells herself, the exercise is academic if Sufia has *not* gone home. It is, after all, mere hearsay — the word of a neighbour. There are a million other places she could be.

The pilot's voice crackles over the headphones: 'Eight minutes to target. Weather conditions clear, but moderate to fresh surface winds and thick airborne dust. Do we abort?'

'Negative. Proceed.' Marika knows that the wind will make things difficult for them, but it is not enough to delay. They have so little time. They need to bring Sufia out well in advance of the deadline in order to use her as leverage.

'Five minutes to target.'

Clipping her line to the rail, she watches Madoowbe do the same. She has only his word that he is experienced, but notes that he seems to know what he is doing. Being ex-SAS, she reminds herself, of course he would.

'Is your Sid turned on?' she shouts.

'Yes.'

She nods in approval, knowing that the electronic devices might be their sole means of locating each other when they hit the ground.

'Two minutes.'

The door opens. Fear dries her lips. Her hands shake. Talking becomes impossible in the slipstream. Looking down, she cannot see the ground, only a shroud of brown dust, moving like a living organism.

'Twenty seconds.'

Just as Marika is about to jump, the giant aircraft hits a pocket of turbulence, throwing her back into the fuselage and onto her side. Her elbow strikes the deck hard at the nerve point. The pain is sharp but fades, and she struggles to her feet.

The pilot's accented English comes through the intercom: 'Very sorry.'

The plane rocks a few more times, and Marika clenches her teeth and grips her arm. *Yeah, I bet you are.*

'Are you OK?' The pilot again.

'Yes. Fine. Proceeding with jump.'

'Do you want us to circle back?'

'No.' Meeting a surface-to-air missile in Somali airspace is always a chance, and the more circling that goes on, the greater the risk.

As if the pain of her elbow helps steel her, Marika finds that she is no longer afraid. Moving back to the open doorway, she holds her breath and slides out and away into the silent dawn.

The queue at the toilets suggests to Isabella that daylight is approaching. She joins the half-dozen women waiting against the wall, too frightened to exchange more than a few monosyllables; drawn, tired and anxious.

The fat, light-skinned terrorist drifts closer. Isabella has heard the others call him Jafar. As far as she knows he has not slept at all, but once she saw him take a pill from a vial in his pocket and wash it down with bottled water. Is it caffeine, or something stronger; Benzedrine, perhaps? Either way, a man cannot stay functional without sleep indefinitely. Thirty hours? Fifty? A hundred? Some of the mujahedin take turns to sleep in an alcove, yet even so, the tablets must assist them to stay alert.

Reptilian eyes rove down over her body. She glares back. Jafar drifts away, yet not too far. The line moves on, for it is a large bathroom, with multiple cubicles and a long sink. As Isabella steps inside she sees women washing their faces. She walks into a cubicle and closes the door in defiance of instructions, then takes the phone from her underwear before dropping them to her knees and sitting on the seat.

The message received flag is up. *Understand circumstances. Will pass on any intel. Keep it coming when safe. Tom. PS Will bring as much pressure as possible to bear re your girls.*

Isabella deletes the message, then fires back a quick one mentioning the pills she has seen the mujahedin take. Breathing quickly, she clicks on the second message — from Simon.

The bathroom door opens. These footfalls sound different on the tiles. Flat-footed. Male. Isabella freezes. Her bladder opens without conscious direction.

'Hurry up. What are you doing in here? Hatching plans? Who has shut the door? It is forbidden to shut the door.' The voice is not that of Zhyogal, but the fat one, Jafar. The hair on the back of her neck stands erect. *Did he follow her in here?*

Isabella slips the phone into her right bra cup. The footsteps echo. Her body tenses, even as her water streams into the bowl. Mouth open, she searches for air. Finally she is able to pull up her underwear, moving the phone back to her knickers and flushing the toilet. Opening the door she steps back out into the bathroom.

The other women have hurried from the room. She is alone with him. This man knows where her girls are. She faces him, shoulders squared, chin high. 'I have done what you people asked of me,' she says. 'I have sold out my country and my honour. I want my daughters returned to my husband. Now.'

The smile comes slowly to his face. 'More powerful men than I have decided that it is best for us to keep the little girls until this is over. They will ensure your cooperation. We may need your services again. After that, I know not what my brothers will do with them. Perhaps they will kill them. Perhaps not.'

Isabella raises one hand to strike him, but he moves out of reach, laughing. 'When we go back inside, I will tell your colleagues that it is you who betrayed them — that you handed a leather case filled with explosives to the gentle Dr Abukar. Would you like that?'

'No.'

'Then shut up about your brats. I do not care if they live or die.' His eyes move from her face down the curve of her throat to her breasts. Following his gaze she sees that the top two buttons of her blouse are undone. His face reddens, and his breathing quickens.

Oh God, he's aroused.

'You disgust me,' she cries. Before he can react she opens the door and hurries out into the auditorium.

The rising sun is red, as if hewn from stone, illuminating the air itself and, far below, an unseen landscape cloaked in brown. Marika feels relief as her chute opens, yet calculates that the delay in her jump might have set them off course by up to ten kilometres.

Looking ahead and above, she sees Madoowbe's chute, an uncertain distance to the south. She manipulates the steering toggles so as to move closer.

The rectangular folds hang above her, cells taut with air. This is one of the new ATPS ram-air chutes designed for experts to reach the ground before they attract enemy fire. Marika smells the dust first, then passes into it, the wind tearing at the chute and the air so thick she pushes her collar against her lips with her shoulder and breathes through the heavy cotton.

The parachute billows and flaps. The light that seemed so benign is blotted out as if shrouded by cloth. The comforting sight of the other chute disappears also, and the wind howls through the strings.

The dust becomes a gritty mess between her fingers, and each breath a struggle. Worst of all is the feeling of disorientation. Like the time she fell from an old plywood dinghy into a farm dam, where the suspended clay made it impossible to see which way was up. For twenty or thirty frightening seconds she drove herself deeper into the cold depths, until confusion stopped her, and down there the gas in her lungs was more buoyant. Controlling her panic, she began to rise.

Now, high above the ground, the slipstream tells her which way is down. This is the parachutist's second-worst nightmare: unable to prepare for impact; or to steer away from obstacles. All she can do is lift her legs and tense, ready for an impact that might be seconds away.

The whistling of air in her ears and the constant need to depressurise becomes an ache deep into her head. Mucus runs from both nostrils, and just when the stress on her body becomes too much, the earth pounds into her legs, driving her knees into her chest so the air leaves her lungs in a rush.

Instinct tells her to roll, but rolling can be dangerous in unknown terrain. Instead she folds her upper body and legs, absorbing the impact with the flexibility of muscle and bone, finishing the manoeuvre in a squatting position, weight balanced like that of a cat, pain from the impact already subsiding. Still in that position, she listens for any sound that might be a threat to her, but hears just the moan of wind and sand.

Satisfied, Marika begins to gather the parachute, sand filling the folds as fast as she can work. Finished, she takes

Sid from her pocket and switches between apps until the GPS chart of the area comes up, her own location a steady green sphere. She increases the view 'altitude' with a deft pincer movement of thumb and forefinger, searching for Madoowbe's signal.

Sid tracks satellites very fast, but in the sandstorm minutes pass before it acquires enough satellites for a fix. It is comforting to see the village of Bacaadweyn on the screen thirty-five kilometres away — further than they had planned yet still not an insurmountable distance, even on foot. At first she cannot locate Madoowbe's signal, but by increasing the range control it becomes clear: two thousand three hundred metres on a bearing of seventy degrees. Less than half an hour over good terrain.

Picking herself up, Marika moves towards the signal. At first she is cautious, but relaxes when she comes across nothing but sand interspersed with flat-topped acacias and the occasional baobab tree. This is wilderness — Somali style. With visibility restricted to just a few metres, she does not hurry.

At one stage the ground becomes rocky, and as she navigates this more difficult terrain, she finds herself at the lip of a precipice so deep that the bottom is hidden in swirls of shifting sand and dust. Recovering her balance with difficulty, she moves back, turning northwards until she is able to resume her heading.

Marika is as fit as an athlete, yet the constant soft sand makes her calves ache, and the dust storm forces her to wear goggles. Even so, the distance between her and Madoowbe shortens rapidly. His blip is almost superimposed on hers when she stops and calls.

There is no answer but the wind and the sigh of shifting sand.

Again she calls and nothing happens.

Shaking her head in frustration she removes her goggles. He must be close, surely?

Marika feels her legs collapse. Something grips her arms. Even as she falls, her training takes over, and she pulls away, using gravity to multiply her own strength. Her attacker responds, anticipating her, until, still standing, he takes her neck in the crook of his arm. Twisting sideways, from a distance of just a few centimetres, she looks into Madoowbe's eyes. In his hand he holds a Browning Hi-Power pistol. The muzzle moves to the side of her head, and she sees his teeth as he smiles.

At first the sense of betrayal is so great that her limbs freeze, but then anger takes over, and her reaction is physical, bringing her arm back ready to strike, slamming the heel of her hand against the gun, pushing it away from her. The move unbalances the Somali, who is slow on the counterattack. She punches him hard on the centre of his broad nose. Anyone, struck in such a manner, cannot help raising one hand to soothe the injured extremity, and Madoowbe is no exception.

Using this momentary advantage, she turns to run, aiming to disappear into the shroud of windblown sand, when the toe of his boot smashes into her shin, and she hurtles face-first towards the ground, tripped with the skill of a top-level football player, forced to use both arms to cushion her fall.

Madoowbe is on her in a moment, giving her no time to roll. Sitting on her back, the muzzle of his handgun boring into the back of her head. 'Do not move, or your unborn children will perish here on the sand with you.'

Marika has seen footage of Islamist executions. A line of men on their knees, mujahedin with handguns shooting each in the back of the head, bodies tumbling, dying while the killers shout Allahu akbar — God is great. Ronald Schultz, the American security consultant, hands tied, shot with twenty or more 7.62mm rounds from a Kalashnikov, the death so violent that his kneeling body performed a near cartwheel before coming to rest on his side. The beheadings were perhaps the worst: Eugene Armstrong; Jack Hensley; Durmus Kumdereli, the Turkish driver. Marika wonders if her own face has the same numbed fear.

'I trusted you,' she spits, trying to turn her head. *Worse. Fuck it. I liked you.*

Engine noise cuts through the shrieking wind. Into the clearing roars two of the vehicles referred to in this part of the world as 'technicals' — four-wheel-drive utilities with a machine gun mounted on the tray, belts of shiny brass cartridges drooping from the chambers. Three men, shemagh head cloths about the neck and head, armed with assault rifles, jump down from the tray even before the vehicles stop, covering her with their weapons.

A fourth man, bandolier of ammunition across his chest, steps from the passenger seat of the second vehicle. He is lighter-skinned than many of the others, wearing just a keffiiyeh cap on his head. He is very lean, with a pencil-thin moustache that emphasises that fact. His more military dress and bearing, along with an obvious swagger, mark him as a leader. A ring in his left earlobe is startlingly bright — real gold.

'*Sheel qasnaan*,' he shouts at Madoowbe, and they carry on a brief conversation. Marika's Arabic is good, and many words cross over into the Somali language, yet still she understands almost nothing of what they are saying.

Two men drag her to her feet, and the leader pats along her sides and legs, grinning as he removes her sidearm, and a knife in a holster. Sid catches his eye. He takes the unit and passes it to a comrade, who fools with it for a moment before shoving it into a pocket.

Marika watches the man's eyes rest on the chain that hangs around her neck, with the tiny silver scapular — a confirmation present from her parents. She raises a hand to protect it but the man restrains her while another lifts it over her head, then holds it up like a trophy.

More talk with Madoowbe. This lasts for perhaps a minute before the gunmen again take her arms and lead her towards the nearest vehicle, ushering her into a back seat. The sweat smell of them is intense, and they make no effort to keep their distance, sandwiching her between them. Craning her neck, she sees Madoowbe step up into the back seat of the other vehicle.

Treacherous bastard, she thinks. Yet she is more hurt than angry; hurt that he made a fool of her. Her anger she reserves for herself, for the ease with which he overpowered her. *Tripped, for God's sake.* Her face burns. *If ever there's a round two, you won't be so lucky.*

The engine roars into life and the vehicle lurches forwards, tyres spinning in the sand before finding purchase. The other technical takes the lead. The wheels kick up a fountain of sand as the driver accelerates down the track. Marika finds herself swaying, her knees touching the rifles that lie across the men's laps.

With a professional eye, she appraises the weapons —
Czech-made Samopal VZ58 assault rifles, not in generic
use in this part of the world. This suggests that money is
behind them. One man holds a stubby grenade launcher
of Chinese manufacture.

In addition to the guns, each man carries a curved
dagger in a leather scabbard, the bone handle carved with
intricate images and wound with copper wire.

The dark-faced men chew qat, or miraa, constantly,
the leaf imported from Kenya and distributed by Somali
warlords as a means of both making money and ensuring
the loyalty of their troops. Nothing good, Marika knows,
can come of being captured by this lot.

'I am an Australian citizen,' she declares. 'You have
detained me without permission and are therefore in
breach of international law. I will see that you are caught
and punished.'

If anyone understands her speech they say, nothing
coherent in reply, but her threat sparks a round of rich,
deep-voiced laughter. Marika ignores it, instead staring out
the window, the landscape revealed and snatched away as
the dust thins and thickens in waves. Once or twice they
pass through settlements. The smell of camel and goat wafts
inside, overpowering the livestock stench of the armed men.

They turn onto a main road, where, on the verge, men
and women, bone thin and obviously starving, pass by.
Many walk in pathetic family groups, carrying firewood,
filthy plastic water cans or bundled possessions on their
heads. None look at the armed vehicles, as if frightened
to present any challenge, imagined or real, to the armed
men. Many carry infants. Most have a defeated, haunted
look. These are the dispossessed. The phenomenon

that is inadequately summed up by such a simple word as refugee. Marika remains silent, watching the passing parade, her heart and belly aching with helplessness.

As the journey progresses, Marika finds a hand on her upper arm, fingers curling over her bicep. The sensation is no less alarming than a spider crawling over her bare flesh. Fingertips brush the side of her breast. Her reaction is instinctive, and she spits, 'Don't touch me. Don't you bloody dare!'

The man withdraws his hand as the moustached leader in the front turns and barks an order. Marika senses that he is telling the man not to touch her but cannot be sure. Either way, nothing happens for some time, until the convoy slows to a stop, engines running. A man from the lead technical opens a chain mesh gate.

With the vehicles now motionless, visibility deepens to a couple of hundred metres. The wire-protected compound looks to be at least two hectares, with dishevelled white-painted buildings standing in clusters. Men with firearms who have been lounging against a wall walk out to meet the vehicles as they skid to a halt.

Dark faces peer inside, teeth exposed, laughing when they see her. One of her captors winds down the window and chats with his comrade outside. Another photographs her on his cell phone from the window, then stands back, fiddling with the device, probably, she decides, sending the image to his friends.

The doors open, and a man on the outside seizes her arm, dragging her off the seat and onto the ground. Coughing, choking, sprawled in the dust, trying to crawl. Others lift her to her feet — too many to resist — leading her, half dazed, into the nearest building.

Passing through the door and into the darkness inside, the smell strikes her: unwashed bodies, curry, and rotten food scraps. A series of openings loom ahead, and Marika is propelled through the nearest one. A heavy iron door slams behind her, and she shrinks back against the far wall, sucking air like a turbine, staring back at the faces that peer through the barred cell door, laughing and making comments she imagines are crude.

Marika's eyes flick around the cell, a surprisingly large space designed for many more prisoners. An uncovered, half-full latrine bucket sits at one corner, attended by a cloud of green and metallic blue flies. The concrete floor is littered with detritus — chewed animal bones and discarded packaging — so that it resembles the cave of a predator. The smell of urine and faeces, uneaten food, and decay combine into a miasma that numbs the senses.

A stone bench sits against the far wall, a filthy blanket crumpled into a heap at one end. The cell is divided from its neighbours by bars, and the occupants stare in at her also. Bony knuckled hands and gaunt faces.

Marika stands, hands on hips. 'You have no right to lock me in here. I demand that you release me.' The crowd at the door laugh, as if the angry woman is the funniest sight of their lives. She crosses her arms in front of her chest. 'Piss off, why don't you?'

The answer is another round of laughter followed by silence, then more footsteps. Shouted orders, a commotion. The watchers melt away.

The cell door opens and three men enter. One is the senior man from the vehicle, with that thin moustache and cruel twist to his lips. He saunters up to her, stops, and examines her from head to toe. Abruptly, he lifts one hand

and slaps her face so hard that she reels, registering the whiplash effect on her spine as her head flies sideways with the impact of the blow.

Marika is more shocked than hurt at the sudden assault. But she holds her hand to the affected area, swaying, trying to regain her balance. The man who struck her whispers something harsh, and sneers, nostrils flaring. She picks out the word 'American' from the torrent he aims at her.

Finding her balance, she steps back, just out of range of another unprovoked blow. 'I am not an American. Australian, OK?'

Again without changing expression, the man cocks his arm and his fist flies out. Marika ducks, rolling her head sideways, avoiding much of the force of the punch. Even so, bony knuckles ring against her skull.

Marika feels the anger build. One, two, three. Creeping like fire into her veins. *OK, you want to fight? I'm not going to lose out twice to you bastards.* She backs away, lifting both hands, weight on her right foot, crouched, lips set in a grim line.

At one hundred and eighty centimetres in height, and lithe rather than bulky, Marika knows she can handle herself against all but the most skilled and strongest of men. Years earlier, at a month-long hand-to-hand combat course at Australia's SAS barracks near Perth, she was forced to spar with one man after another who could not believe that a woman, albeit a fourth dan black belt, could beat them on the mats.

The Somali smiles and lifts his own fists in a boxing stance, feet even and widely spaced. Marika sums up his approach, noting that he has left his groin vulnerable. He feints once, watching her respond, then turns to laugh with the other men, but cuts this short and goes on the attack. He moves in fast, launching a strike to her kidneys that never lands.

Marika's foot connects like a pile-driver into the apex of his legs, feeling the soft crunch of his testicles beneath the blow. He goes down into a crouch with a shriek of pain, clutching at his damaged balls with both hands.

The sight of the guards cocking their assault rifles prevents her from going in for the kill — a stiffened hand to the base of the neck would finish the man, but instinct tells her that they will shoot if she does so. Instead, she backs up and hovers, still poised to defend herself.

The Samopal rifles are levelled at her, the gunmen growling ominously, talking each other up, shouting warnings. More men appear at the cell door. The injured man is recovering, standing, yet his face is still twisted in pain and anger. He gives an order, then stands, glaring at her, teeth clamped together, lips drawn back.

Nothing happens for perhaps a minute. Marika holds her stance, watchful, every nerve and muscle strained to snapping point. Footsteps sound in the corridor. Running men. She wonders what they are doing. More men perhaps — enough to overcome her with numbers and strength.

The cell door opens and another man enters. In his right hand he carries a weapon that she recognises as a Taser X3. She backs against the wall, trying to prepare herself, but there is no time. The tiny darts, powered by nitrogen, strike her chest and the shock turns her muscles to jelly. She wavers, almost falling.

They give her no time to recover, rushing in at her. A rifle butt strikes the point of her elbow and another crashes into the side of her head. Now she goes down, getting her hands out just in time to break her fall.

A boot strikes her nose and she feels the blood well and drip from the end of her nose. She rolls, covering her face as best she can as the blows rain down on her. Three men at once. Boots connecting all over her body. The abuse stops then, and the leader, face glowing with anger, goes down to one knee and screams at her.

Up close, her tormentor's face is terrifying, and the smell of an unwashed male body overpowering. More of the same diatribe; again she picks up the word 'American'.

Marika spits out the words, 'Sorry, mate, but I don't know what the hell you're on about.'

The face twists with rage, and a palm, held flat, connects with the side of her head, and her hearing goes, becoming a high-pitched hiss, like the sound of a seashell held to the ear. For the first time she considers the prospect of long-term damage at the hands of these thugs.

Now the leader lifts her by her shirt. His mouth opens and closes, but she can no longer hear him. She feels her eyes roll back in her head. Only the pain breaks through as he grips her tighter. She feels as if she is about to suffocate. Blood drips over her lips and down along her neck.

'Fuck you ...'

He drops her, and she falls like a sack of fertiliser. Lying on her back she tries to gather her wits while the officer pulls a knife from a sheath at his side and squats down, sitting on her abdomen, holding the knife close to her face.

This is not the traditional knife some of the others carry, but a large fighting blade of the type Marika has seen for sale in mail-order catalogues and gun shops, an inch-wide blade, viciously serrated on the top; known as Rambo knives after a decades-old movie of the same name. He moves the blade close to her neck and at that moment she believes that she is about to die.

Just before slitting her windpipe, however, the officer grins, changes grip and brings the razor edge up to her face, making as if to cut off her nose. Marika squeals and the other men in the cell, along with spectators at the door, laugh as though this is the funniest sight of their lives. Her tormentor's eyes move to her breasts. Again he brings the knife blade down and pretends to cut. Again they laugh.

Finally, as if tired of the game, the man stands, sheathes the knife and says something to her, followed by a hawking sound deep in his throat. He spits into her face so that she can feel the loathsome excretion on her cheek and lips.

The cell door opens and the three men leave. When they have gone she picks herself up off the floor and wipes her face, aching in a dozen places, uncaring of the crowd who regather at the doorway.

Day 2, 11:00

Faruq Nabighah has been at work since before dawn, yet down here sun and moon are irrelevant. The roar of the tunnel boring machine is continuous. He is a big man, with long, shaggy hair over his neck and broad shoulders. His most noticeable feature, however, is a set of porcelain-white false teeth, legacy of a blasting accident as a young man that left him with a broken jaw and a mouthful of

fragmented molars and incisors. A full beard hides the
scar that stretches down from his lower lip and across his
chin. Even now he remembers the six months he needed
to conquer his new fear of the underground. Months
when he trembled with each step into that nether region
of artificial light and earthy, unfamiliar scents.

That, however, was long ago, and now he is more at
home down here than on any city street. He turns to Kamal.

'Go, get the geo reports. Run.'

Faruq watches him move — good workers are hard
to find, and just when he has them trained to perfection,
they leave, worn down by the dust and the noise. In the
heavy engineering industry, even in these tough times,
there is still work in Dubai and the wider Emirates. The
days of wealthy Sheikhs vying with each other to perform
miracles are over, but there are still road tunnels and
underground walkways to build. Faruq is a rich man. He
has an apartment that overlooks al-Mamzar beach, and a
red car with an Italian name, yet still he loves his work,
drilling tunnels so perfect he could, if he chose, start at
either end, two kilometres apart, and join them up to
within a metre. This is the environment he thrives on; his
office and his passion.

Faruq walks to the cage, opens the door and steps
inside, pressing a buzzer on a brushed aluminium console.
The door rattles closed, and moments later he hears the
whine of an electric motor. The cage hurtles up towards
the surface. The sun is bright and hot as he steps out. He
slips a pair of dark sunglasses from his pocket, walking
towards the transportable shed that makes up his office.

Almost there, he stops and squints at a pair of
unfamiliar cars that sit in the dusty car park, both neat

little Nissan hybrids, both new, and both dark silver. He crinkles his nose and sniffs the air like an animal sensing ... not danger, but something unusual that might threaten his routine.

Continuing to walk, he sees men waiting, and the smell of officialdom becomes as strong as that of offal. Faruq dislikes rules and red tape. They cost money and time, and he values both.

The group walks towards him, led by a tall man with hair greying at the sides. 'My name is Abdullah bin al-Rhoumi, may peace be upon you.'

They fill the site office to capacity, the air-conditioner rattling away on the wall. For a minute or two, as custom dictates, they make conversation, including polite inquiry as to the health of each man.

Faruq has heard of Abdullah, for his name features occasionally in the *al-Bayan* newspaper he reads each day. 'I am honoured by your visit,' he says at last, 'yet remain at a loss as to how I can help you.'

The visitor unrolls a chart on the desk. 'This is the Rabi al-Salah Centre near the port. You do, of course, know what has happened there?'

Faruq glances at his watch. 'God has blessed me with sufficient intelligence to grasp the affairs of the world.'

'We want to dig a tunnel from here, near the Interchange Number Seven, to beneath the centre itself. How do you assess the feasibility of such a plan?'

Faruq studies the map for a full minute. The work would entail burrowing under built-up streets and even industrial sites. Dredging up what he knows of the area he leans back in his chair, understanding at last why they have come to see him. 'Everything is possible, but how do you intend to dig the tunnel?'

'That is a question I will address to you. How will *you* dig the tunnel?'

'No, not me. Impossible. It would take several days just to move my machines and equipment. By the time it is done your crisis will be over.'

'Can you move your operation in twelve hours?'

Faruq mulls through the machinery, the consumables, the portable toilets, and the low loaders necessary. Then he considers the distance from here to the new site. The region of greater Dubai exists in his head as a grid of one-kilometre squares. Eighteen kilometres as the crow flies, he calculates. 'No. I am sorry. Perhaps seventy-two hours if we work like ants ... But this is academic. I am committed to a project. We are running on time. I will not abort it — a contract is my law, and these days they are hard to come by.'

Again the tall man seems not to have heard this last comment, instead mumbling to himself. 'Seventy-two hours. That is too long, and we could move heavy gear only at night. Many eyes will be watching.'

Faruq folds his arms. 'I will not do it. There is no use in discussing the logistics.'

'You *have* to do it.'

'I will not.' Standing, he brushes down the crease in his cotton work trousers. 'Thank you, gentlemen, but I have work to do.'

Still Abdullah makes no effort to move, but produces a cell phone and punches a few buttons. 'This is Abdullah bin al-Rhoumi. Head of GDOIS. Put me through to Sheikh

Mohammed al-Rashid, Vice President of the UAE and Prime Minister of Dubai.'

Faruq sits down, feeling like a gambler who is about to lose to a card cheat. His visitor, it seems, has contacts.

'Hello. Abdullah here. It is necessary to requisition the assets of a company. Yes; yes; good.' He puts the phone down and turns to the young Frenchman beside him. 'We can take all the machinery. You have researched some men who can direct the work for us, haven't you, Léon?'

'Certainly — Pierre Dauphin, in Paris, and James Lloyd in London. Both are happy to fly across at a moment's notice.'

Faruq glares at the young man, bristling at his obscene good looks and obvious arrogance. He explodes with anger. 'You think I would let Dauphin place one filthy hand on my TBM? Or James Lloyd, the philanderer? Never, may God curse them both. Neither man could ever do what you want — they are like bulls rushing in and making noise and blasting when they do not have to blast. They do not know the soils here in Dubai and I will not let them near al-Moler. You will have to kill me first.'

The Frenchman continues as if he has not heard. 'Dauphin said he could get the gear on site and ready to roll in eighteen hours.'

Faruq scowls. 'I could do it in sixteen if I had to ...'

Abdullah smiles, seizing the chance he has orchestrated. 'Then *you* will need to do it for us. You will be paid, of course. Paid well.'

Gritting his teeth, Faruq places both hairy arms on the table, callused palms open. 'I would want a thirty per cent bonus over my usual rates — I will have to placate my client, and pay the men overtime.'

'That is acceptable. I will have someone make contact, and you can work out the financial details with them.'

Faruq heaves a sigh in his throat and leans over the map, eyebrows beetling as he studies it. 'This tunnel, what is the point? We cannot bore our way up through the floor of your conference room. That is ludicrous.'

'No. There is a bunker, twenty metres beneath Rabi al-Salah, designed to shelter the leaders of the world from war and,' Abdullah clears his throat, 'terrorist action. Even from a nuclear blast. That is where we must drill to. The most practical access point.'

'Then we should start the tunnel here, at the base of the hill of Ut-la. You know the one? It has many satellite dishes on the top, beside the new housing development?'

Abdullah nods. 'I know it.'

'The hill will shield us from view and the subsoil is sand all the way to the centre. We will be able to drill very quickly — I realise that you are ignorant of the mechanics of this business, but al-Moler is a double-shielded machine, and therefore fast. Yet because we are passing under an urban area it is important that there is no surface subsidence. Our system uses the latest bentonite slurry techniques to negate such problems.'

'The details we leave to you, but if you need anything, just pick up the phone and ask.'

Faruq points at the site. 'This is public land. Anyone could wander in.'

'No longer. We'll have it fenced off by dusk.'

'Good. Please leave now, I have many things to do.'

'Sixteen hours, are you sure?'

Faruq grins so that his false teeth shine white in the fluorescent light. 'I am a man of my word. By dawn tomorrow al-Moler, the mole, will be diving below the earth, eating soil like the subterranean beast she is.'

Even as the car doors slam, Faruq presses a switch on the intercom set.

'Hello, Rahul?'

'Yes.'

'Call the men in and get al-Moler out of the tunnel.'

Silence, then: 'Truly? But that will cause delays, cost much time. I mean no disrespect in asking, but why?'

'We have another job to do — one week. It is worth it, trust me.'

His next act is to pick up the phone. Other men need to be mobilised, some of them outside contractors: truck drivers, road escort services. The TBM is carried on a custom-built low loader, but there are many other items to be moved: a site office, earthmoving machinery. Within an hour, the calls are made, the orders issued. Now Faruq steps outside. The first task is the safe loading of al-Moler.

With a flash of his security card, Simon moves through the gate and into the staff cafeteria. It is past noon and the tables are full. The room smells of spicy meat and starchy rice.

Buying a meal, he takes the plate back to a table, its peeling laminex surface in need of hot water and detergent. The meat is fatty and stringy — old mutton or goat — and the rice grains congealed as if with glue. Even so, he eats, watching and listening to everyone who comes and goes, hearing snatches of conversation, all of it innocuous, mundane, most of it from an adjacent table where four men are eating together, obvious friends.

For countless hours, Simon has walked the corridors, listened outside doors and passed in and out of the security area, using his British Airways ID like a skeleton key, surprised at how invisible it is possible to become when you hide behind an official badge. For an hour, perhaps two, he slept on a toilet seat in the men's bathroom, woken by a pair of cleaners whose loud banter announced their arrival.

The group of diners beside him laugh together. The moon-faced individual in the centre appears to be the butt of some teasing, and Simon chews slowly, listening to the theatrical whine of a thinner man, who uses widened eyes and head lolling to accentuate his words. 'So now,' he says, 'our friend Mu'ayyad is boastful that he is rich, merely for making certain that one item of luggage went on the carousel without incident.'

Simon stops chewing. Turns in time to see Mu'ayyad's frown of annoyance, then a finger held lightly over his lips.

'I wish they had asked me,' the other says, ignoring the warning. 'I spent last month's wages by yesterday.'

Strange things happen at airports, Simon is well aware, much of it related to the importation of drugs. Baggage handlers of all nationalities are involved in the trade. He is interested enough, however, after the meal, to follow the group from the cafeteria and outside. Here they disperse, moving off to different parts of the terminal. Mu'ayyad and two others walk through a door near the carousels.

Simon pushes through before the lock clicks shut. The group turns and looks at him, but without real interest. Airports, even regional ones, are big places with many employees, often from different nations.

As he walks through the area, not yet convinced that the conversation he heard is of interest, he approaches Mu'ayyad, who has just returned to work, lifting bags onto a trolley. 'Assalam alaikum,' he greets the man. 'I'm Simon Thompson, from British Airways. We've been sent over to see how you chaps do things over here. Help you out with efficiency ... you know what bosses are like.' He smiles, hoping to develop a feeling of camaraderie.

The man continues his task, not making eye contact. 'I'm sorry. You will have to speak to my supervisor.'

Without missing a beat, Simon follows up on what he heard in the cafeteria. 'The other men were telling me that you had some good luck last week, that you made some easy money.'

Mu'ayyad's eyes focus on his, wide and suspicious. 'Are you police? Security?'

'Security? Hah. No, I am just crew. I do what I am told like everyone else.'

The man stops working, a scowl deepening across his face, eyes narrowing. 'There is no money, now why don't you leave me alone, eh? I do not like being questioned.'

The man is hiding something, Simon is sure. 'Now come, talk to me. I am curious, and no harm will come from the telling. What happened last week that helped make you some money?'

'Neek rasi,' the man hisses.

Simon is familiar with the insult, translating into English as, literally, fuck my skull. 'You have a way with words, but you have not yet answered my question.'

'Move on — foreskin of a goat — or I will call my friends and we will help you to move on.'

Simon stops, deflated, turning to the sound of footsteps. Another baggage handler, yet not one who was in the cafeteria, walks towards them.

'Mu'ayyad,' he says, 'Abu Sherid says that we must ...'

Seeing Simon, he stops. He too, is a tall man, and thin, with a bony nose and cheeks. A patterned shemagh hangs loosely over his shoulders, clashing with his workmanlike overalls, but this is not what catches Simon's attention. Around his neck he wears a chain, and nestled in the hair of his chest is a charm — a St George's cross. Simon has seen it before — threaded onto Hannah's charm bracelet. He remembers the day he made the purchase, at a stall on the Campo de Fiori markets in Rome.

'Where did you get that charm?'

The man stops, eyes wide. 'What?'

Mu'ayyad speaks from behind. 'Do not mind this Englishman, Hisham, he is crazy, and very rude.'

Simon seizes the necklace, ripping it from the man's neck. He holds the prize aloft, hand shaking, certain now. It is Hannah's. He knows it well. He feels breathless, angry, and excited.

Mu'ayyad pushes him hard in the upper back with the flat of both hands. 'You have no manners, Englishman. Give it back to him or I'll be forced to teach you a lesson.'

Simon ignores him. 'This charm belongs to my daughter. Where did you get it?'

The man says nothing, and Simon loses control, going for the throat with a two-handed grip, feeling the soft skin, the sharp sinews and the hard tube of the windpipe. Then, hearing a stifled battle cry behind him, he turns to see Mu'ayyad go on the attack.

Simon has never had a serious fight in his life, but he is big in the shoulders, and, though cricket was his first love, he locked the scrum for the second XV at Cranleigh, wading into enough on-field scuffles to know how to swing his fist. As if by instinct, he clenches his fingers hard together and drives them into the side of Mu'ayyad's chin.

Not waiting to see the him fall, he leaps after the other, now trying to flee. He catches him in a couple of strides and grips the back of his shirt.

'Tell me, where did you get the charm?' Again he cocks his fist, knowing that he will gladly pulverise that frightened face.

'I found it, sir, really. Take it, I don't want it. Just give me back the chain.'

'Where did you find it?'

'Near the luggage carousel. It is pretty, so I kept it.'

'When?'

'Tuesday. No, Wednesday. In the morning.'

'Did you see anything? Did you see two girls?'

'No, I saw nothing. Let me go. Keep the chain as well. In the sight of God, I saw nothing and know nothing.'

Mu'ayyad has left the area, but two other men saunter past. Simon steps back, still fingering the charm. 'I did not mean to hurt you, but my children are gone. Someone has taken them.'

'Taken? You mean kidnapped?'

'Yes.'

The baggage handler's eyes droop in sympathy. 'I too have children.'

'Good, then you understand how I feel.'

'I will help you, because I feel bad about taking the … what did you call it? Charm?'

There is a commotion behind them. Mu'ayyad is returning with a pair of security guards. 'That's the Englishman,' he says. 'He is violent.'

The baggage handler whispers, 'I will ask the door security. Insha'Allah, one of them might have seen something.'

'Where can I meet you?'

'Outside the main doors at the end of my shift. Eight o'clock tonight.'

Simon studies the man's face, wondering if he can trust him. He has no reason to lie. 'I will see you there,' he says, then turns to face security.

'Hey, ferenghi,' one calls, 'you do not have clearance for this area.'

'I am sorry, there was a misunderstanding but it is resolved now. I am leaving.' He begins to walk back towards the doors, ignoring them.

'Stop, ferenghi. Show me your identification.'

Simon's pace does not falter. 'There is no need. As you can see, I am leaving the area and will cause no further problems. I am an employee of British Airways.' He does not want a formal interrogation — he would be deported without delay.

The security guards look at each other, confused, and Simon takes the opportunity to run the last dozen yards, open the door and close it behind him. Out on the concourse a group of disembarked passengers are moving towards the doors. He runs deep into the pack, mingling, using the crowd to cover his retreat into the car park, running through a press of buses and turning into the maze of small hangars that make up the commercial fleet.

The cell phone croaks in his pocket, and Simon fumbles for it so fast he almost drops it. 'Hello.'

'Simon?' The voice is male — Tom Mossel. 'Where the hell are you?'

Simon stops walking. 'At my hotel.'

'That's not true, and you know it. Now, listen to me — don't you dare go off on some kind of half-cocked crusade. We've got people on this; professionals. Isabella is already in a heap of trouble. Don't make it worse.'

'Come on. Shagging a terrorist isn't a capital offence.'

'No, but smuggling explosives into a meeting of world leaders is.'

The darkness seems to press in on him from all sides. The rows of multi-storeyed dwellings in the distance are a honeycomb of misery and evil, part of a world that is taking everything he knows and loves.

'Now you're making things up.'

'Sorry, Simon, but I'm not. Even if she gets out of there alive, she could be charged with some serious offences. Treason, perhaps.'

'Isabella isn't capable of treason. She's the most patriotic person I know.'

'Let's forget about all that for a moment. The main thing is that she's OK. I've been in contact with her.'

'So have I.'

'Where are you?'

'Cairo.'

'Don't take me for a fool. At worst you're going to get yourself killed, and at best you'll get in the bloody way. Your employers, British Airways, are furious. Four hundred passengers stranded at Dubai until they flew another pilot in.'

'Three hundred and eighty-six.'

'Whatever. You better talk to them soon or you won't have a job.'

'My girls are more important.'

'OK, but there's nothing you can do. Nothing. We will find the kids for you, trust me. I've got a bloody task force convening as we speak.'

'Why is this so important? Why are you even looking for them? I wouldn't have thought a couple of children would be a priority with so much going on.'

'They're British citizens, Simon, we look after our own.'

'Bullshit.'

A long silence, then, 'All right. We had a report of two senior Almohad operatives in Aden the same day as your girls disappeared — one was Zhyogal, as you know, the other a Nigerian who calls himself Saif al-Din. Part of the same cell. We're certain he's involved, and there's a good chance that if we find your girls we'll find him, too.'

'So how important will the lives of my kids be if you decide the easiest way to kill this Saif al-Din is to send a cruise missile in to take him out?'

'We won't do that.'

'I wish I could believe you, but I don't.'

'Please, Simon, just come in.'

'I'll think about it.'

'Really?'

'Would I lie to you?'

Simon ends the call, trying not to look at the digital clock on the screen. Finding Hannah and Frances before anyone else just became even more critical. His hand moves to the cold silver charm in his pocket as he stares back towards the terminal, angry at himself. Now he is shut out of the airport, and at the mercy of a man, possibly a thief, who may or may not meet him as promised.

As he watches the main terminal doors, however, a black vehicle pulls up. Three men in suits step out, and appear to confer with the security guards near the entrance. MI6 has tentacles everywhere, it seems, even Yemen.

Tom Mossel, you bugger, he says to himself. *You traced me pretty damn quick, didn't you?*

There is no way back inside. Not without losing both freedom and hope. He has no choice but to wait.

Day 2, 15:00

Occupants of the adjoining cells squat in silent, defeated groups, and the men who gathered to look at her have grown bored and wandered away. The heat of the day shows no sign of abating, yet finally Marika can move unobserved.

First she tends to her wounds, using a handkerchief to wipe the blood from her face. Her fingers probe specific injuries. Most of the blood flow has come from her nose, yet despite some tenderness, it is not broken. Her teeth she examines one by one, finding nothing loose, just a dull pain from a lower molar. Her lower lip has a single fat swelling to one side. Satisfied, she examines her surroundings in detail. Three metres up the wall is a barred opening among heavy stone blocks. This is, she decides, worthy of investigation.

Marika kicks the tin latrine bucket over, watching weeks-old refuse flood the cell floor, the stench multiplying ten-fold so that even her neighbour utters an exclamation of disgust. Standing on the upturned pot, however, gives her enough height to reach up and touch the window. She tries the bars, attempting to bend the stiff iron — hoping, with her slim profile, to squeeze through. At length, out of breath and despondent, she drops down, sinks to her haunches just out of the puddle of filth.

Footsteps sound in the corridor and a hatch in the door slides open. A man in a grubby camo shirt with green qat-stained teeth passes in an earthenware bowl filled with rice and vegetables, along with a coke bottle full of water.

There is no question of eating the food, and Marika lays it aside, more interested in quenching her thirst. Holding the bottle up towards the light, however, she sees the swirling particles inside. She puts it down, knowing that she cannot stay here — that somehow she has to find a way out.

Possibilities play through her mind — injuring herself badly enough that they have to take her for help. Would they bother? Even if they did, are there hospitals in Somalia? She is pretty sure there aren't many, and besides, she has heard stories of Third World medical facilities and the antibiotic resistant bacteria that thrive there. Is it worth the risk? Does the risk matter, considering what is at stake? Her mind turns to methods — is it possible to break a bone by wedging an arm in the bars?

Even as she entertains that thought, a familiar face appears at the door, a finger held to his lips to indicate the need for silence. Marika turns, shocked to recognise Madoowbe. She stands, crosses her arms and walks to the door, standing just a pace back from the opening.

'You dirty bloody traitor. Have you come here to gloat, or what?'

His eyes darken. 'Don't waste time venting your emotions. None of the guards nearby know English, but others might come.'

'Why is that important?'

'Listen. I am on your side. They are suspicious of me, but for now I still have my freedom. Unfortunately they are checking out the story I told them and when they have done so my position will not be so secure.'

Marika tries to laugh, but the sound becomes a cough. 'Oh, you're on my side. Right. That's funny, people who are on my side don't usually attack me without warning and hold a gun to my head.'

Madoowbe's face, however, has the pallor of a frightened man. Marika can see the pores on his nose, and smell the dry sweat on his body even over the stench of the cell.

'There is blood in your hair,' he says.

'Yes. Does that bother you?'

'I am sorry that they hurt you, but this is the territory of the warlord Dalmar Asad. We could not have moved through without his knowledge. It was better for me to establish my bona fides by capturing you.'

'Why didn't you warn me of this so-called plan?'

'It had to be real — these men know fear. It cannot be faked.'

'I don't trust you as far as I could kick you.'

'That is not important, but please understand that there is no way out of here without my help. This prison was part of a British outpost in the nineteen twenties. If there is one thing the British do well it is build prisons. Dalmar Asad has many enemies and the lucky ones end up here. The unlucky? Let us just say that he has enough earthmoving equipment to ensure they are buried deep.'

Marika hisses in frustration. 'Who the hell are these people? Are they Almohad too?'

'No. As I just said, Dalmar Asad is a warlord and a clan leader. These are his men. He rules this part of Somalia.'

'So where is this Dalmar Asad now?'

'In the town of Gaalkacyo. He has been informed of your capture and is looking forward to making your acquaintance when he returns tomorrow. I doubt they will kill you before then.'

'OK, you bastard. If you are on my side, prove it. Get me the hell out of here.'

'I am trying. Trust me.'

'Trust you? What a laugh. I'd rather trust a snake.'

The sound of footsteps reverberates from down the corridor. Someone is coming. Madoowbe lifts a finger to his lips once more, then slinks away.

Marika knows from her training that sleep deprivation can be a killer in the field. A dozen instructors, over the years, have drummed into her the importance of taking every opportunity to curl up. The benefits to reasoning power and observation skills are significant.

Using her arm as a pillow, she is not too uncomfortable on the bench, above the foetid floor. Most of all, she is safe — being alone in the cell, no one can approach without the racket inherent in opening the iron door.

Before long, she sleeps — an exhausted nothingness that lasts more than an hour. She wakes calmer, and sitting up, fully alert, she turns to look into the neighbouring cell where the young, wire-thin Somali is staring at her, grinning.

Holding out a grubby finger he points towards the filthy latrine bucket.

'Get stuffed,' she snarls at him. 'So that's what you're waiting for — you want to watch me squat, eh? You filthy bastard.'

The dark eyes continue to stare.

'Oh piss off,' she says. 'I can hold on all day when I have to, and I will if it saves me from putting on a show for you.'

The man blows his nose on his fingers, inspects the result, then grins back at her, showing a cavernous mouth. Like the guards, his teeth are green from qat.

A face only a mother could love, Marika thinks.

Her attention is diverted by the sound of low and purposeful voices, then the clang of iron as they unlock her cell. She stands and backs against the far wall, keeping her hands at her sides.

Three men enter the cell. The first is the taser-equipped guard, the second is a civilian, dressed in keffiyeh and long, flowing cloak. The other, the moustached officer who delivered her earlier beating, takes one step into the room, sees the contents of the chamber pot on the floor and makes an exclamation of disgust. After a series of harsh orders, two men appear with mops and clean the mess, to the continued scrutiny and direction from the officer. When they are done the cell door closes behind them, the guard still covering her with the taser.

The civilian inclines his head in greeting. He too wears a moustache, thick and bristled as a shoebrush. His eyes are dull brown, the left one bloodshot and staring above and to one side. He strikes her as a businessman, or small-time politician. 'Good evening,' he says, 'my name is Walid Aqbar, and this is Captain Wanami.'

Marika comes no closer, yet stares at the officer, lower lip jutting in anger. 'Don't worry,' she says, 'I've already met the arsehole.'

Walid Aqbar ignores her. 'Captain Wanami has asked me to act as interpreter. Is that acceptable to you?'

'Tell him that I am an Australian citizen. I am being wrongfully detained, and physically abused and mistreated.'

The interpreter translates, waiting for a response before addressing Marika again. 'The captain says that you deserved punishment for an unprovoked attack on him. Yet he is willing to put that behind him, in the interests of obtaining your full confession before his commander Dalmar Asad gets back tomorrow. Mr Asad will not treat you so kindly.'

Wanami does not attempt to hide his contempt for her, and Marika knows that it will take little to provoke him. She shrugs and holds her palms out, a gesture she intends to indicate that she is hiding nothing.

'Please tell Captain Wanami that I am happy to answer his questions.'

This seems to please the officer. He turns back to converse with the guard at the door. Both smile widely.

The interpreter turns his eyes on Marika. 'The captain wishes to inquire as to what your American masters intend by sending you into a country that does not belong to you.'

'Please tell him that I am not American, but Australian, and that I work for the United Nations.'

The captain's face changes as the interpreter translates, and the interpreter turns back to Marika, shaking his head, and clicking his tongue as if remonstrating with a wicked child. 'The captain says that you are being silly. Lies are an offence to God and you are obviously lying, since you carried guns and other military equipment. He asks you to tell the truth. Who do you work for and why did you come here?'

Marika swallows hard, and glares at Wanami. 'My name is Marika Hartmann, I am an Australian citizen, and I work for the United Nations. The details of my mission do not concern you.'

The last sentence, once translated, infuriates Captain Wanami — his face turning purple and a series of veins standing out on his forehead. The interpreter's voice rises with shared authority, like the school bully's best friend.

'The captain says that you are a very pretty young woman, but that you will not be so much if he has to extract the information from you. He says that you have tonight to think. He will be back in the morning equipped to take steps to find out what Dalmar Asad has demanded to know. Then, when the warlord himself returns, you can be truly afraid.'

As abruptly as they arrived the cell door closes behind them. Marika sits back on the bench and closes her eyes, wondering what Abdullah bin al-Rhoumi would think of the mess she was in.

Day 2, 17:00

Alek Chastakorlenka, Vice President of the Russian Republic, kneels on the carpet. Sweat flows in a channel from brow to ear and along his neck. He will be next to die. Already the Almohad have killed two: the Presidents of South Sudan and Pakistan. Their bodies lie, bloodied and limp, against the front wall.

Zhyogal stands over him, reading from a typewritten sheaf of paper. 'In the year two thousand and three, General Chastakorlenka, then commander of the kontraktniki forty-sixth Motor Rifle Division of the Russian Army, did order the use of a heavy flamethrower weapon on the inhabitants of the Muslim village Beroznya, Chechnya. In spite of pleas from these unarmed civilians, many died in agony. For this atrocity, for this crime, in the name of God, the prescribed penalty is death.'

The kneeling man wails a long stream of Russian, tears spilling down his face, jowls wobbling like jelly. The words are accompanied by violent shakes of the head. Then, 'No, no.'

Two men seize a shoulder each and lift, trying to make Chastakorlenka walk but, whether in sheer fright or defiance, his body sags and will not support his weight. They half drag, half carry him to the bloodstained patch of carpet from which the body of the previous victim was only recently removed.

Zhyogal stands over the Russian Vice President, draws his pistol and fires. The first shot, despite passing through the head, does not kill him, leaving him kicking his legs and calling out in an inhuman, howling moan. Zhyogal fires again. Alek Chastakorlenka lies still.

Staying in the shadows, Simon rounds the corner towards the taxi stand. Pink fluorescent tubes on the arched facade of the terminal building spell out the abbreviated ADEN INT'L AIRPORT, followed by the same in Arabic. A huddle of drivers laugh and smoke together but, despite a slow and careful examination of the area, there is no sign of security, or British secret service men in their suits.

A sound makes him turn, an amplified voice in Arabic, a distant mosque calling believers to prayer, drifting out across the city, haunting and beautiful. He waits until the normal sounds of life resume before walking towards the terminal.

Passing the taxis he scans ahead for the baggage handler, half expecting him not to show, or to find himself surrounded by men with guns. To his relief Simon sees the familiar face up ahead, smoking like the others, looking nervously in all directions.

Simon hurries towards him, and shakes his hand. 'Thank you for meeting me.'

The man drops his butt and grinds it under the toe of his shoe, holding a pack of Gitane cigarettes in one hand. 'As I said, I feel shame that I took something that belongs to your daughter.'

'Did you find anything out?'

'I think so.'

'Yes?'

'One of the door guards, a friend called Ishaq, told me that *his* friend Malik mentioned that he saw a man, a woman and two children behaving strangely on Tuesday.'

'In what way?'

'The woman and children appeared to be upset. The man walked very close beside one of the children, who was weeping. The woman and children were Westerners. That is all I know.'

'Where is this Malik — can I see him?'

'He is not at work right now, but I can take you to his house.'

Simon feels the first stirring of suspicion. Could this man be planning to take him somewhere secluded and have him shot? 'How far away?'

'Not far. I have a car, I can take you.'

Simon wants to believe him — all his considerable experience with human nature tells him to trust this man. Besides, he is no longer able to move freely in the terminal, and this is his sole lead. 'Let's go then.'

The baggage handler offers his hand for a second time. 'My name is Hisham al-Fahdi. What's yours?'

'Simon Thompson.'

'Come this way, Simon. My car is in the parking lot there.'

'Thanks very much. I appreciate your efforts.'

The car is a compact Toyota. The console is filled with the usual paraphernalia of family life — a pen; a folded copy of *al-Ayyam*, the local paper; an open packet of mints. An electric bakhoor burner is plugged into the cigarette lighter, and the car smells of stale yet aromatic smoke.

'If you don't mind,' Hisham says, 'I will call first.'

'Of course. Go ahead.'

Cel phone in one hand, the Yemeni consults a folded scrap of paper from his top pocket and dials a number. Simon listens to the conversation. If this is a plot to get him alone it is an elaborate one. Why would they go to such lengths?

The conversation over, Hisham slips the phone back in his pocket and starts the car. 'Malik is happy for us to come over.'

'Thank you. You are going to a lot of trouble for me.'

Hisham nods and backs the car out of the parking space.

Their route takes them along a four-lane motorway, then into the thick of the city, a place of narrow, chaotic streets, buildings crammed together with their teardrop arched windows. Mosques stand on corners every few blocks, narrow minaret towers pointing to the sky, elegant arches, screens, and whitewashed walls.

The streets are alive with people. Homeless families with sleeping children on beds of discarded cardboard. Beggars. Groups of young men wearing a pastiche of Western and Eastern clothing. Hawkers. Hotels are surrounded by chain-wire barriers. Uniformed security guards with assault rifles stand watch over the entrances.

The termite colony complexity of the city reinforces to Simon that anything and anyone could disappear into this maze. No one would ever know. Traffic is light and moves at speed. Hisham turns the car into a side street.

'You said you had children,' Simon asks, 'how old are they?'

'My boy, Ghali, is twelve, and Ramona is eight. Nuriyah is just three.' The Yemeni smiles. 'They are the suns and moons of my life. Even the girls bring me much joy.' The words cut deep into Simon's heart. Hisham appears to notice. 'I'm sorry.'

'No, it's fine. Really.'

They pass a wide market square with a mosque to one side and date palms in clusters.

'This is the district of Maalla,' Hisham says. 'Here was the worst of the fighting in the revolution. My cousin was killed here, and I, too, fought for freedom. Back then I was a student at the university. I had dreams of becoming a lawyer.'

Simon glances across and sees regret, but remembrance of past glory, in the Yemeni's eyes.

'We, the youth, stood as brothers, shoulder to shoulder and chanted, "Allahu akbar." Soldiers fired on us, and we did not fight back, but trusted in God. And then Saleh was, praise God, struck by a shell in his mosque, and shrapnel pierced his chest. That was God's warning to him. He came back, but we continued to fight, and eventually we had our freedom.'

The car turns several times more before pulling up outside a block of three-storey buildings, resembling cave entrances in a cliff. Simon follows his new friend up a flight of steps, with smells and sounds wafting through open windows: curry and saffron-tinged air; the sound of crying babies; raised voices and *al-Jazeera* Arabic language news from Doha, Qatar.

Finally, Hisham stops at a door and knocks. The man who opens it looks as unthreatening as a Surrey grocer. He is slim, with prominent front teeth, holding a male child of around two years in his arms — the child's wide brown eyes rest on Simon's with a curiosity common to children everywhere, the soaking up of sights and sounds; the undeniable need to learn.

Hisham says, 'Malik, this is the Englishman I told you about. The one who seeks his daughters.'

'Yes. Come in, please.'

Hisham bends to remove his shoes. Simon follows that example, leaving his socks on and stepping onto the clean swept floor inside. Still carrying the child, Malik leads them past a side table with framed portraits of family members into a sitting room decked out with red patterned cushions and a low dark-grained table, set with a copper sugar bowl and glass salt and pepper shakers. A face-down newspaper sits beside them, stained with bread crumbs and yoghurt. Bakhoor smoke wafts from a ceramic udd burner on a shelf. Long use has left a blackened smudge on the ceiling above.

Malik calls his wife with a sharp order. She appears in the doorway into what must be the kitchen — short in stature, all but her eyes, nose and lips hidden by the balto. Her hands and wrists are covered with intricate henna tattoos, something that must have taken many hours to complete. Despite the apparent freedom with which she shows herself, Simon is careful not to look at her face, and she too keeps her eyes averted. Talking to her directly could be fraught with danger — a single incorrect word might offend her husband.

'Make coffee, Lutfiyah, please,' Malik commands, then points to his guests to take a cushion. Malik, himself, is the last to sit, his son settling onto his lap, still looking at Simon in obvious fascination.

The coffee comes in half full demitasse cups, light in colour and with a layer of froth. Simon sips the steaming liquid, enjoying the spicy cardamom taste, waiting while Malik fusses with his little son, helping him with a mug of milk the woman brings. When his wife has left the room, Malik pours fresh coffee from the brass pot.

'Your wife and children have been kidnapped?'

'My two girls, yes, and their nanny — the woman who looks after them. Did you see them?'

'Perhaps. I saw two men leave the terminal, with a European woman and two girls. One of the girls was crying — the younger one ...'

'Did she have long blonde hair?'

'Yes.'

Simon makes a fist, only uncurling his fingers when his nails bite deep into his palm. 'And the woman. Was she about nineteen; short dark hair in a bob?'

'Bob?'

'Like this.' Simon fashions imaginary hair with his hands.

'Yes, I think so.'

'Where did they go?'

'Ordinarily I would not have looked, but they went through the doors and into a car at the kerb.'

'A taxi?' A policeman friend of Simon's, chief inspector at Shoreditch Police Station had once told him that few people remember precisely what they have seen until a specific question is put to them.

'No.'

'What colour?'

'White. A Chinese car.'

'Was there anything distinctive about it?'

Malik strokes his beard. 'I noticed rust in the corners of the doors.'

'Did the men who were with them get into the car?'

'Yes. One was the driver.'

'Were there any other identifying marks?'

'There was a decal on the vehicle, on the back window. Those stick-on numbers you can buy at a stationery shop.'

'Do you remember what the number was?'

'No, sorry. I think there was maybe a three and a two, but I cannot be sure.'

'What about the licence plate?'

'Sorry. I did not look. I was curious, but not that curious.'

Simon lowers his eyes, frustrated. 'Tell me about the men.'

'One was very dark — African. The other had lighter skin.' He hesitates. 'I … er, think I have seen him again, but I am not sure.'

'Where?'

Malik picks up the newspaper that was face down on the table. Like all Arabic tabloids the front page is what would be the back in the West. Two grainy photographs dominate the cover. One is Dr Abukar, scholarly and, to all appearances, incapable of violence. To his right is a sharply featured face. The word underneath is in English script: Zhyogal.

'I am insane,' Malik says, 'but he looked so much like that one there. The more I look, the more I am certain. Yes. I recognise him as I would the devil. He was … a frightening man.'

Simon stares down at that face with a swelling hatred that he knows he will never control.

Marika wakes once during the night. The cell is dark, and strange shadows move across the walls. Huddled in one corner she hears the moaning howl of a man in agony, the sound of voices, then moaning again. Fighting the ache in face and abdomen where she was hit, she sits up, aware that the hairs on the back of her neck and her forearms are standing erect, as if in a reaction to something primordial and terrible out there in the darkness of this hellhole in the wilderness.

The sound becomes a shriek, and then low sobbing. There is something familiar in that voice, and a terrible, sickening awareness settles upon her.

Now it is his turn.

As if in sympathy, Marika holds both hands against her face and weeps until tears coat her cheeks, and her throat aches with the acid gall of shared suffering.

THE THIRD DAY

And God said, 'Let the water under the sky be gathered to one place, and let dry ground appear.' And it was so. God called the dry ground 'land'. And it was good.

Yet the land has been disturbed and tunnelled through to find gold and oil, and poisoned with radioactive waste, sewers, and heavy metals that fall in the ash from the sky. The earth has been so denuded of nutrients that farmers pile seabird droppings on the fields, but now even the guano is running out.

God said, 'Let the land produce vegetation: seed-bearing plants and trees on the land that bear fruit with seed in it, according to their various kinds.'

Biotech companies engineer plant genomes to make them resistant to disease and herbicides; to grow faster; to bear more fruit. The number of species under cultivation dwindles. Engineered species 'infect' their wild cousins, and the gene pool narrows. When drought comes, engineered plants wilt — all of them, for there is no longer the genetic diversity required to cope with change.

Diverse ecosystems such as rainforests are cleared at a rate of one hundred thousand acres every week. Soils planted to monoculture are leached of all fertility

*by unseasonable flooding rains, or blown away by the
powder-dry winds of drought.*

*And there was evening and there was morning. The
third day.*

Day 3, 04:55

In Karachi, Pakistan, sixteen-year-old Sehba Hamid
reads *The Way of Jihad* by Hassan al-Banna, founder of
the Muslim Brotherhood. He sits on a hand-embroidered
cushion in a one-room house thick with the smell of
incense and the open sewer on the street. The tract sets
out the case for war, why all Muslims must fight. He reads
the words:

*My brothers! The ummah that knows how to die a noble
and honourable death is granted an exalted life in this world
and eternal felicity in the next. Degradation and dishonour
are the results of the love of this world and the fear of death.
Therefore prepare for jihad and be the lovers of death ...*

New meaning awakens and grows; a sense that Sehba's
life may have purpose, that he too can be a warrior. That
he can rise above the squalor of his surroundings and
bring glory to God.

At the madrasah an older man makes contact with him,
one who keeps himself apart. A man known for silent
purity and intolerance of vice. The others whisper that
he belongs to the al-Muwahhidun. Over several days the
recruiter sounds Sehba out, then invites him to a meeting.

Sehba listens to what they have to say, then decides
that he will join with them, and if he is required to die in
the name of God, he will do it willingly. A sense of joy
pervades his soul.

Zhyogal, warrior for Islam, beloved of the Prophet, has been known by many names over the years, moving across borders like a phantom, new passports just an encrypted email and a dead letter drop away.

He was born Sami Kazaati, in Illizi, Algeria, in 1983, between the desert of Issaouane Irarraren and the mountains of Tassili-n-Ajjer. He was still a student at the village school when friction between Islamist protesters and the government reached a peak with the slaughter of more than forty civilians at the Place des Martyrs, Algiers, by security forces.

As if knowing that control was slipping from his grasp, the President, Colonel Chadli Bendjedid, announced major reforms, including free speech, the right to form and join political parties, and ultimately, democratic elections. The most powerful new party was the Front Islamique du Salut, the FIS, led by Abassi Madani, a university professor.

The 1990 elections were won by the FIS over the hated Chadli regime. The second stage, the parliamentary elections of a year later, would have finished with the same result had not the army stepped in, annulled the elections, and suspended the second stage of voting, effectively taking control of the country. The FIS and the general populace were enraged. Algeria embarked on a civil war that became known as La Sale Guerre — The Dirty War.

The path to extremism and violence was inevitable for Sami. His three brothers fought for the FIS, and he was thirteen when they carried the eldest home on a broken door, his left arm hanging from the bloody shoulder muscle by a thread. He lived for three hours before loss of blood took his life. This was the day that Sami learned to hate. The day he picked up a weapon for himself.

As a teenager, Sami fought the dirty war like a hardened adult, blowing up electricity installations, burning churches, ambushing foreign workers, and beheading captured members of the security forces. He developed a talent for killing, but also political awareness, learning from events in the rest of the Muslim world; from the Shi'ites who were then pioneering suicide-bombing techniques in Lebanon, with devastating effect.

By the end of the war, he was a trusted lieutenant to the GSPC's Hassan Khattab, and was chosen to attend an al-Qa'ida-sponsored training camp in Sudan. Here, the training was fifty per cent martial, fifty per cent spiritual. He learned to fire, strip and clean a dozen different handguns, assault rifles and submachine guns. He learned to aim and fire an Igla 9K38 shoulder-mounted anti-aircraft rocket launcher, to manufacture explosives and Molotov cocktails. He learned to control and inspire men but most of all, to use his faith to break down barriers. His spiritual cup was filled by days of instruction by Salman al-Awdah, an advisor to bin Laden himself.

Sami learned that saving Africa and the tenets of his religion were intertwined. That the only possible future was under Sharia law.

There, at the camp, mingling with men of twenty nationalities, he was no longer Sami Kazaati, becoming instead Zhyogal — so named by a Chechen member of the mujahedin, for his stealth, his endless cunning, and his way of moving silently, looking in all directions as if sniffing for danger. Urged on by men of Iran, Nigeria, Afghanistan, Egypt, and Saudi Arabia, he adopted the rigorous interpretation of the Sharia as practised by the men around him.

Books such as *Teaching to Pray*, by Dr Abdullah bin-Ahmad al-Zayd, called for all Muslims of purity to unite, preaching that it was not a sin to execute those who followed what the author regarded as impure forms of Islam. Zhyogal was also taken with the works of Syed Qutb, a revisionist thinker, and inspiration to modern Sunni activists.

It was through a man of about his own age, however, a Nigerian called Saif al-Din, that Zhyogal came to al-Muwahhidun. The initiation was complex. Under the pale light of the shawwal moon, the sign that marks the end of Ramadan and advent of Eid al-Fitr, Saif slit the throat of a living goat and removed the jugular like a hose, using it to fill a bowl with dark, sticky blood, warm as sunshine.

Their hands joined in the bowl while Saif led Zhyogal through an oath, accepting the sacred entrustment that authorised the use of evil in dire circumstances, as a necessity to defeat His enemies. And what time could be more dire than now? When only God's law could save the people of North Africa and Arabia from the West, who have raped the earth and her people to the point of destruction.

Almohadism was a drug to fill the empty places of his soul — the soul of a true warrior. Saif al-Din became more friend than teacher. He was like no one Zhyogal had ever met, with eyes like beacons. The two were inseparable: learning together; sleeping huddled for warmth on desert exercises.

Zhyogal became what he had always thirsted to be: ghazi, an Islamic warrior in the tradition of the fabled janissary, yet so much more. In Nigeria's Delta Region, he and Saif al-Din commanded their own force of elite mujahedin, joining a wave of terror fighting, attacking government soldiers wherever they could be found, slaughtering any man wearing a uniform; stopping vehicles and killing; breaking down doors and killing; on and on until the smell of death became the smell of life. A dozen times they blew up oil pipelines, once making world headlines with the severing of Chevron's main pipeline south-west of Warri.

A few years later, Zhyogal, now a seasoned freedom fighter, leader and strategic planner — met with two high ranking men at a Somali version of the Khalid bin Waleed training camp, a facility of the same name once having been located in Afghanistan on the road to Khost.

One of these men was called Abdel Bakhi and the other Mounir Khalaf. 'It is time,' they declared, 'for you to join al-Jama'a al-Ashara, the council. It is time to show the West that Muslim lands can no longer be ravaged at will. That we will not permit them to poison the earth indefinitely.'

That moment changed Zhyogal's life. No longer was he merely a man waging jihad, but a leader of a semi-mystical movement that would save the world and bring all God's lands back into His fold. His heart felt as if it would burst with emotion, and that year he made the hajj for the second time to show his gratitude and increasing piety.

Zhyogal took on this new role with unsleeping fervour, slipping across borders, meeting in halls and forest clearings with leaders of fifty disparate tribes, people united by their passion for God and His Prophet. Recruiting. Spreading the faith. Showing these people that the storms and droughts that ravaged their crops were the direct result of the industrial powers of the West. That tampering with the earth's core through deep drilling and fracking was causing seismic unrest on an unprecedented scale.

With Saif, he organised and outfitted an Algerian cell of al-Muwahhidun which parked a school bus loaded with two and a half tonnes of nitrate fertiliser outside the United States Embassy in Algiers, blowing the eastern wing of the building into dust and rubble. Eight Americans and forty-two Algerians were killed.

The organisation, funded by donations from all around the world, sent technicians and money through a clearing house and communications centre in Sana'a, Yemen. From his position on al-Jama'a al-Ashara, Zhyogal became privy to information just a handful of men around the world shared.

Always he remembered the words of the Lion Sheikh, Osama bin Laden, as passed on by Yaqub Yusuf.

The West will not listen without massive bloodletting. They heed only fear and death.

Al-Moler, the TBM, weighs just under sixty tonnes, with a diameter of four-point-seven metres and a length of twelve. The business end is a cutting wheel, and behind it, a conveyor system that carries earth away from the face. An array of hydraulic jacks both support and move the mechanism as it bites into the earth.

Faruq watches the unloading like a Western father might watch his wife give birth. The ten-tonne Hitachi excavator scrapes out the initial bed for al-Moler, filling a procession of dump trucks with yellow soil in the predawn light.

Contractors have been at work during the night, fencing off the site. Signwriters have affixed massive blue signs announcing that a hotel will be built. People are used to that here. It will raise few eyebrows and, if God wills it, before traffic starts moving on the roads, al-Moler will be deep underground doing what she does best: eating the earth like a beast.

Faruq knows from the sting in his eyes and ache in his shoulders that he is tired, yet mentally he feels alert. It has been interesting to see what he can do, working outside the world of permits and regulations — just picking up the phone and saying, 'Go, go, go.' No environmental assessments, no cultural impact statements. Watching doors open. Taking phone calls at three o'clock in the morning from suppliers of everything from prefab concrete ballast to water tankers that will be required as work in the tunnel progresses.

The purpose-designed crane that supports al-Moler in its slings is not tall but squat, the body covering a massive area, with thirty-two lugged, solid rubber tyres and floor stands to keep it from tipping.

Faruq lifts the radio handset and presses the transmit button. 'Idiot! Slower. Hold her still. Do you want to keep your job? Would you rather shovel goat shit for a living?'

Al-Moler stops, swinging in its slings.

Faruq lifts the radio again. 'Now, move.' He turns to look at the excavator in the pit, its bucket arm locking and unlocking with the dexterity of a human wrist, dumping a car-sized load of earth with each scoop, filling one truck before the next moves into line.

Faruq strides ahead of the crawling crane, the smell of raw earth thick in his nostrils — a smell that to him is as intoxicating as any drug. The pit is twice as wide as al-Moler and one and a half times as long. In depth it is perhaps six metres, and the floor has a five to one gradient in order to give the machine an angle to work with, aiming her down to the planned operating depth of thirty-five metres.

Faruq himself shot the laser levels they used to get the pit right, but he trusts his eyes more. He lifts the handset again. 'Kamal, take the skin off the back rear. There is a hump there.'

In just a few scoops it is done. The last truck rolls away, and the excavator tucks the bucket up and rumbles backwards.

Now the crane positions al-Moler above the pit.

'That is well done, Salamah. You have learned to drive, praise God. Now, nice and slow.'

Lifting his eyes over the pit, Faruq sees the waiting concrete trucks, snail-like rotating tanks turning, mixing the wet aggregate inside. Flat bed trucks are stacked high with steel reinforcing, for as soon as al-Moler moves off, the pit will be poured with quick-setting cement before the business of shoring up the tunnel begins.

Now, however, al-Moler settles to the ground and Faruq is first into the pit, thick yet agile fingers lifting off the hooks that fasten the straps. Then the crane arm drifts away and Faruq looks up to see the sun almost ready to peep over the horizon. He grins to himself. Hadn't he promised that al-Moler would be operating by dawn? And that he would be at the controls?

Other men swarm over the machine, ready for the series of checks that precede al-Moler entering operational status. Faruq works his way towards the hatch. This will be the pinnacle of his career. His name might soon be famous. It is worth a week of diversion to be that way.

Abdullah bin al-Rhoumi wakes on a chair, back creaking and eyes gummed with fatigue. Rising without a word, he hurries past the men and women at their workstations, heading for the bathrooms, carrying a small leather case.

Finding an empty corner on the smooth ceramic bench he opens the case, removing a toothbrush and toothpaste. He cleans upper and lower teeth — backs, sides, and fronts. When this is done he washes his face and hands, combs his hair and then, with a sharp pair of scissors, trims his beard.

Finished, he stares back at his image in the mirror, eyes sunken into deep pits, red with veins. Wiping his face with a paper towel, Abdullah picks up the shattered pieces of his psyche, rolls them together and grits his teeth.

Don't let me fall apart now, please God, he says to himself, then walks through the doors and back into the control room. On the other side of the door an assistant is waiting.

'Coffee,' Abdullah tells him, 'and toast, please.' The latter is a Western habit but a useful way to eat in a hurry. 'Then I want a briefing — assemble the team leaders in my office ...' Abdullah smiles to himself. This is it, back in control, keep the momentum, never let them relax, never let them know you are tired, or that your back hurts. Don't let them know that you are human; that you have needs like everyone else.

The coffee goes down like honey, and he eats as they talk — situation reports, succinct, factual. The Frenchman,

Léon Benardt, speaks first. 'The engineer, Faruq Nabighah, has started drilling ...'

Next is one of his managers from GDOIS. 'We have lost contact with our two operatives in Somalia ...'

Abdullah feels a twinge of remorse — the Australian, Marika Hartmann, was a good agent despite her failure to recognise the impending attempt on the centre. He had liked her a lot. Even so, he puts his personal feelings aside. 'That line of inquiry is finished. There is no time to get someone else in there. What else?'

'We have had contact from two of the hostages. Both via MMS.'

'Didn't the militants collect all the phones?'

'They did. Just not those two.'

'Who are they?'

'One is a British analyst: Isabella Thompson. Her contact is Tom Mossel, Director of the DRFS. He's passed her on to us. She is prepared to send further information when possible.'

Abdullah recognises the name. 'Isabella Thompson is the one the British are investigating in regard to aiding and abetting the terrorists. Yet it seems that she acted under duress.'

The Islamists have taken her children, he thinks to himself, *yet she is prepared to do this. The woman has courage. They will kill her if they find her with a phone. Yet why not let her atone for what she did? It may help her when this is over, and we are all still alive to answer for our crimes and inadequacies.* 'Who is the other one?'

'Raphael Perreira, one of the Brazilian President's bodyguards, brought in as an advisor. He contacted his embassy here in Dubai, and we've sent through a direct number for him to use.'

The meeting ends with a short prayer, and as he watches them go, Abdullah wonders at the risk these people inside are taking. He wonders if this will mean death for a wife and mother.

Marika wakes not long after dawn, her body so bruised that she takes time to come to a sitting position. Outside, at some distance, a rooster crows. Her headache is an organic, living thing, moving from room to room and kicking the furniture to bits in the doll's house rooms of her mind.

There is a new sound, yet distant. At first it reminds her of the sea. It has the same power. That irrepressible force.

As she comes awake, Marika realises that it is not just one sound, but many. The movement of feet, voices, wailing infants. Then singing, starting off softly, but growing, taking over from the other noises, overwhelming them.

The singing is unique, African, full of anger and pain. Shouts, raised voices, yet still at a distance. Like a swell rising with a storm front, the sound reaches a crescendo. The crack of a gunshot echoes out across the stillness of dawn. Another follows.

Again inverting the mercifully empty latrine, she reaches for the bars of the high window, gripping them with two hands. Arms trembling with the strain, she eases her body and head upwards so that she can see outside between the bars, over a makuti thatched rooftop and down across the compound.

A crowd has gathered outside the main gate. Perhaps two thousand, three thousand souls — women in brightly coloured kanga and kikoi; men and children in everything from football shirts to kanzu robes and keffiyeh — press against the chain-mesh fence. Men with guns stand shoulder to shoulder before the gates, firing over the crowd, smoke puffing from the barrels of the assault rifles, staccato bursts of sound following microseconds later.

The singing stops, replaced by screams and shouts of fear, and the tramp of running feet. This is loud at first, then recedes. The crowd is in full retreat, and Marika wants and needs to keep watching but the strain on her arms is insufferable, and she is too high for the latrine bucket to support her. She lowers herself to a height from which she can drop to the ground and sits with her head in her hands, trying to cope with her own pain and what she has just seen and heard.

The cell door opens and an earthenware bowl of porridge appears. After what she has just seen she lacks appetite, but eats because of a determination to keep up her strength, without putting herself through the angst of examining the meal too closely. It is made from an unidentifiable grain, glutinous and thick. The taste is neutral, and the smell is of rank milk. It is, however, filling.

When she has eaten, she reaches for the coke bottle of water she was given the previous day. She screws her eyes shut and swallows it in a few long pulls. The liquid seems to help her headache, and the food provides a new energy. More for something to do than anything else, she removes her headband, brushes her hair with her fingers and ties it back.

Just as she begins to feel somewhat human there is a tramp of feet and the shadow of men behind the grate. The door swings open. Three men enter the cell. The captain, the interpreter and the Taser-equipped guard. A fourth man arrives, burdened with an automotive lead acid battery, a bundle of wire and a black electronic device. After a single glance at her, he places the battery on the floor and begins connecting wires from battery to machine. Marika watches the activity, then turns to the interpreter. 'You bastards better not be planning on connecting that thing up to me. No one does that kind of thing these days.'

'Unfortunately for you, the captain intends to extract the required information before Dalmar Asad returns. It would give him stature, and therefore he seeks your cooperation in telling him what he needs to know now. If not, he will be forced to use these archaic and brutal means to make you speak.'

Marika feels her breakfast as a bitter lump at the base of her throat. She turns to look at Wanami. There is a bloodstain on his lapel that was not there the previous day. A big one — surely connected to the screams and moans in the night.

'You bastard,' she says. 'Why don't you just let me go? This has nothing to do with you.'

The interpreter's voice is gentle. 'That is not possible. You have come to our country to spy on us and Dalmar Asad wants to know why. The captain is being a loyal servant and taking steps to extract the correct information from you.'

At that moment, Marika makes the decision that she will not allow these men to place those sharp-toothed little alligator clips on her body without a struggle. She knows the theory: the little black box is a transformer, designed to multiply the current from the battery. The charge will be highly painful. Not only that but she knows that the shock will be greatest when attached to the moister membranes of her body: lips, tongue, eyelids, vagina, anus …

The captain grins, and takes a step towards her.

Marika lunges, swinging hard at his head but he weaves, leaving only air. Again she strikes with her left arm and this time finds the sternum. He leaps back, almost tripping over the battery and other paraphernalia, avoiding the worst of the blow, but still she hears breath leave his lungs.

The guard with the Taser fires, and again she reels with the shock. The captain moves in before she can recover, a flurry of blows and a side kick that connects with her midriff, then a punch to the side of the head that feels like it's delivered with a sledgehammer.

Somehow recovering her balance and her wits, she tries to strike back, but he is too quick for her, again punching to the head. Disoriented, she falls to the concrete floor. He gives her no breathing room, but straddles her, producing oversized plastic cable ties from his shirt pocket. These he uses to bind her wrists and ankles, leaving her moaning, doubled up. With more cable ties he secures her feet to the bars between her cell and the adjoining one.

When he speaks she can see the excitement on his face.

You bastard. You're enjoying every minute of this.

The interpreter smiles. 'This is your last chance to speak. The captain wants to know which American spy organisation you work for, and why they sent you here.'

'I work for the United Nations. That is all.'

As soon as the words are out, Wanami moves back and lets his underling work, attaching one alligator clip to her lower lip and the other to her left nostril. The clips are themselves a small agony and she thrashes from side to side in an attempt to rid herself of them.

'You have five seconds,' the interpreter drones. 'What spy organisation sent you here and what is your mission?' A pause, then. 'One, two, three ...'

Marika discovers a world of pain that she had, to that point, never imagined. It has many forms: an overall jolting ache that begins in her spine and spreads like a mushroom cloud through her sinuses and the bones of her skull. There are also precise, dentist drill-fine agonies. Her teeth, her nose and lips. Behind her eyes. The base of her head.

There is no time to scream. No ability to suck in the necessary air. Only a roaring in her ears and a strange awareness of her own mortality, at how fragile her grip on life.

Mercifully, it is soon over, and she finds that she has sagged back onto the concrete cell floor, having bitten her tongue, without remembering how and when she did so. When the pain becomes manageable she opens her eyes, and Wanami pushes her torso up so that she is in the sitting position.

The interpreter leans close. 'The pain was very bad, was it not? The captain says that as soon as you tell him the truth he will leave and have you brought good food, and perhaps let you stroll outside.'

Marika shakes her head, trying to steel herself for the next surge of current. Before it can happen, however, a man appears at the cell door. He is subservient to the captain, lowering his eyes respectfully. A conversation ensues before the man disappears. As soon as he is gone, Wanami issues an instruction to his assistant, who begins packing up the battery.

The captain himself produces a Swiss Army knife and cuts Marika's cable ties. The interpreter smiles down at her.

'Do not think for a moment that you have escaped. This is a short reprieve only. Dalmar Asad has called and asked that the questioning waits until he returns, some time in the afternoon. A delay, nothing more.'

'What will he do to me?'

'I imagine that first he will want to rape you. He likes Western women, and you are, if you will allow me to say so, rather nubile.'

The interpreter leaves the cell, then the guard and his equipment. Captain Wanami lingers until last, his face clouded by apparent disappointment as he closes the door behind him. Finally he, too, is gone, and Marika wipes at the sweat that coats every square millimetre of her skin.

Day 3, 09:10

Approaching the al-Tawahi port area, Simon watches the crowded streets from the car window — women in balto or intricately patterned sitara veils in groups of twos and threes, escorted by their maharams, male chaperones, hurrying past men lounging outside coffee shops. Political posters adorn brick walls, moustached men staring imperiously at the artist, bold Arabic type above and below. The red, black and white Yemeni flag is everywhere, whether from nationalistic fervour or an attempt to appear so, Simon is not sure.

'Here, too, climate change has taken its toll,' Hisham explains. 'Sea levels have risen enough to inundate the lowest docks at high tide. Many have been extended and rebuilt, and some lower slopes of the volcano that were once exposed are now under water.'

Simon looks down and sees the low-lying areas that have flooded, the shadowy shapes of old jetties under shallow water. He is no stranger to the phenomenon. The London City Council has, over the last five years, spent hundreds of millions of pounds on strengthening the famous Thames Barrier and other flood defence works. Even now no one is able to predict just how high sea and estuary levels will rise. The only consensus is that they will go higher, much higher.

'I am sorry I cannot do more,' Hisham says. 'If I did not have to work I would walk the streets with you today.'

'You have given me a bed, and some hope,' Simon says, grateful for the chance to wash and shave, change his clothes and sleep.

'I pray to God that you find your girls. Fathers are the same everywhere, no matter what their religion.'

Simon leaves the car with the feeling that he has made a friend, but walks down along the road without a backwards glance. Shops on both sides of the street are opening, their keepers out on the footpath, engrossed in that quaint ritual of praising God and asking Him for a day of good sales and profits to bank at the end of it.

At another time, Simon might have enjoyed the magic of the scene, but today he hurries on. Homeless children, huge brown eyes staring as he passes, sit on the flattened cardboard beds where they have slept. One or two approach, begging, and his small supply of coins is soon exhausted. This is the tragedy of war and political unrest — the orphans, the abandoned, the flotsam of chaos that a broken system has no way of supporting.

There is nothing further he can do, and his mind turns to the task at hand. Over a breakfast of tea, flatbread and yoghurt, he and Hisham together perused the city telephone directory, finding dozens of hire car firms, yet few with yards close enough to the sea to produce rust on the body of a late model car.

They found three businesses here in the port area, and Simon now approaches the yard of the first. The cars are lined up in rows — Fiats, Renaults and an archaic American Lincoln with bright chrome side mirrors and door handles. Each vehicle has a prominent sign on the passenger door, painted in bright orange. Malik did not mention such a thing so Simon walks on, taking the map from his pocket and scanning it, identifying the next place that Hisham has marked with a pencil.

This prospect is down a side road. On impulse Simon decides to skip it. Another firm on the list is much closer to corrosive salt water, located beside the main road into the port. Putting the map away he increases his pace to a brisk walk, passing a vacant yard where a man, with blood to his elbows, has just slaughtered a goat, an act that appears to attract no comment from other pedestrians. Nearby, two men squat in the characteristic local posture, feet close together, knees spread, talking in low voices.

At the base of the hill the salt air thickens, along with the odour of diesel and paint. Aden was once the world's third busiest port, and even now it receives as much boat traffic as New York City. Consulting the map again he sets off, seeing the car hire yard loom up on the right, protected by a chain-mesh fence topped with three strands of barbed wire.

Hire cars are parked with the front bumper to the fence, but when Simon walks around the corner and inside the yard he sees that each has a number in gold and black adhesive letters on the back window. Two high-voltage wires join in his chest. More than one of the cars is afflicted with surface rust, others show evidence of having been bogged with fibreglass and painted over.

The office is a corrugated iron structure with a low skillion roof. Simon steps inside, closing the door behind him, and fronting up to a counter, looking around while he waits. Ughniyah — the ubiquitous Arabic pop music cranked out of Cairo and Beirut recording studios — emanates from a transistor radio on a shelf. A bead curtain parts and a man of perhaps fifty appears, a curling goatee beard on his chin, rubbing his hands together as if pleased at the prospect of a customer.

'Peace be upon you, sir.' He smiles. 'A beautiful day, isn't it? A good day for driving, perhaps. A good day to rent a reliable, clean motor car.'

'Peace be to you, also. It is indeed a beautiful day.' Simon decides that while the proprietor speaks standard Gulf Arabic, he does so with an unusual inflection for this part of the world. An Egyptian, perhaps, or even a Libyan. His clothes seem, at first glance, expensive, but there are patches where his suit has been mended.

'You are a man who wishes to travel our beautiful country, brave enough to venture where his government says he is at peril. Yemen is, now that Saleh has gone, safer than London or New York, but one or two extremists, always foreigners, must give us a bad name. You are a man who looks past such things and will go where the urge compels you. Do you travel alone, or is there a companion, a wife, perhaps?'

Simon shakes his head, wondering if his assessment of the man's origin is correct — his patriotism seems to verge on the jingoistic.

The salesman thrusts out a wide-fingered hand joined to a solid, hairy wrist. 'My name is Ahmed, a name famous for fair dealing and the supply of humble yet reliable motor vehicles. I am honoured that a man such as you would patronise my business.'

'Sorry, but I don't wish to hire a car.'

The man's eyebrows rise as if pulled by a string. 'No? Then I fear you have come to the wrong place. If you want rice, you go to Mustafah's grocery down the road; if you want meat, go to Wali the halal butcher. People come to me, Ahmed, when they wish to hire a motor vehicle.'

Simon flashes his British Airways ID, watching Ahmed's eyes widen as he studies it. 'I am with airline security. My job is to investigate a crime committed at the airport last week.'

The effect is dramatic. The smile disappears, and the previously smooth forehead becomes a roadmap of wrinkles. 'One of my cars is involved?'

'I fear so.'

'That is a terrible thing, yet what my customers do is beyond my control, I cannot be held responsible for their actions.'

'No one will hold you responsible. We want to find the perpetrator.'

Tension leaves the man's shoulders. 'Of course. I will do my best to help you.'

Simon takes a folded square of newspaper from his pocket and lays it out on the table. 'Have you seen this man?'

Ahmed studies the picture. His face turns angry, as if at a bitter memory. 'Yes, he hired a car last Monday — I remember because he did not bring it back, may God curse him. A friend of mine spotted it abandoned at the port and I went down to fetch it myself.'

'Are you sure it was this man?'

'Of course.' Ahmed taps his forefinger just above one eye socket. 'I never forget the face of an untrustworthy customer. I saw him on the television last night and I said to my wife that I had seen him before and she did not believe me. She called me an old fool.'

'Can you show me the car?'

'Of course.'

Halfway out the door the telephone rings and while Ahmed excuses himself, Simon wanders the rows unaccompanied, finding a white sedan with rust just as Malik had described. When he opens the door and looks inside, Ahmed wanders out, an exaggerated expression of surprise on his face. 'This is the one. How did you know?'

Simon's eyes move to the corroded patch in the body. 'There was a description given. An eyewitness. They told of rust in that panel.'

'Yes. There is a price to pay for being the closest hire car firm to the port,' Ahmed explains. 'As well as salt air, the mains water is sometimes contaminated with salt. That does not help when we must wash the vehicles down.'

Simon looks at the number on the back window: one-four-three. 'Why are the numbers so high when you have just a dozen cars?'

'Does it not seem more impressive, to hire car number one-four-three than number seven, eight or nine?'

'I guess so.' Simon steps back, thinking of the charm that led him this far. The Pandora bracelet, as far as he remembers from the intermittent interest he has paid to it, is quite secure. It seems strange that one charm detached itself at the airport. If the bracelet had torn they would have all been scattered.

Hannah, he remembers, as a little girl, was enamoured of the story of Hansel and Gretel, fascinated at how the boy left a trail of little white pebbles. She even renamed the fable 'Hannah and Gretel', acting the story out with little girl inventiveness, using dominos or marbles as pebbles, leaving them through the house for him to follow and find her hiding place.

Have you left me a trail, my darling? Did you release the charm on purpose?

He turns back to Ahmed. 'Are the cars cleaned after each hire?'

'Not all the time — there is little point if the customer has kept them tidy.'

'This one?'

'No. It was clean. I did not need to touch it.'

'Do you mind if I have a look inside?'

'Of course not.'

Simon slips into the front seat, feeling underneath the mats and looking through the glove box, then the console. There is only the usual paraphernalia — candy wrappers and registration papers. A screwdriver.

Moving out and into the back seat, Simon delves under the seats and then, frustration growing, slips his hand under the upholstery. The object is so small he almost misses it, yet his fingers close around a hard sliver of metal.

When he brings it out he sees the shine of sterling silver, smiling with recognition. This is the sword he bought in New York; the charm that so entranced Hannah when he gave it to her.

'Hannah,' he whispers, 'you smart, smart girl.'

'What is it?' Ahmed asks.

'Nothing, and everything. Can you show me where the car was abandoned?'

Ahmed's eyes drop. 'I'm very sorry, but I cannot leave my business. My wife and children will starve if I ignore my customers. Already, Wafiyah complains that there is not enough money for us to live like her sister Nuzhah, and her brother-in-law Aswad ...'

Simon all but rolls his eyes — business hardly seems to be booming. 'I have some Euro dollars to recompense you for your time. Is that acceptable?'

Ahmed nods. 'It is not far, but still I might miss a customer. Shall we say seventy Euro?'

'I was thinking fifty.'

'That is fair. Fifty it is.'

Ahmed drives him deep into the port of Aden, away from cranes, containers and modern ships, into a place of wooden dhows interspersed with pleasure vessels — white cruising catamarans and ageing gin palaces. Smaller fishing boats are painted white, with iron reels for hauling in nets and Arabic dedications rendered in blue or red near sweeping, graceful bows.

This area is a throwback to the days before shipping containers destroyed the charm of the world's merchant navies. Here, beside the multicoloured dhows rising and falling at their berths, the docks are crowded with bales, crates, discarded ballast, and loose cardboard boxes with Chinese or Arabic lettering. The occasional heavily burdened donkey supplements an eclectic collection of vehicles.

Ahmed slides number one-four-seven to a halt alongside an empty berth. 'My car, number one-four-three, was here — keys in the ignition. Lucky she wasn't stolen.' He points to the berth with one manicured finger. 'There was a boat there, if I remember.'

'What kind?'

'If she were a car I could tell you everything. I am in the motor business, and therefore know nothing of boats and sailing ships.' He shrugs. 'It was big, rusty, with faded paint.'

Simon opens the door, then his wallet, passing across a note. 'Did she have a name?'

'Sorry, not that I saw.'

The man is genuine, and Simon sees no sense in wasting time pressing him. 'Thank you. I appreciate your cooperation.'

Ahmed crinkles the money as if testing it for authenticity. 'That is all? You do not wish to have a lift somewhere else?'

'No, thank you.'

'You will come back to me if you wish to hire a car?'

'You can count on it. Your cars are very nice.' Simon closes the door and watches Ahmed accelerate away, honking the horn at a man carrying a bamboo cage of live chickens across his path.

Alone at last, Simon stares at the empty berth. The charms in his pocket tell him that he is on the right trail, yet once, on the BBC news, he heard an expert on such things state that time is critical with kidnappings; that every passing hour makes a successful recovery less likely.

His phone rings. Simon plucks it out of his shirt pocket with his right hand, lifting it to his ear.

'Good morning, Simon.' Tom Mossel sounds tired, yet the air of polite boredom — that unflappable veneer — never falters.

'Glad to know you haven't forgotten me. Have you found my girls?'

'No. But you're not helping. You're in the way, actually.'

'I can't see how.'

'Don't make this hard. I'll have you picked up by force, and I must warn you that it is getting to the point where charges might be laid against you.'

'What for?'

'We'll think of something, I can assure you.'

'How is Isabella?'

'Same as the rest of them — frightened out of her wits.' A pause, then, 'Simon, they're killing people in there.'

Simon feels himself swoon, the growing heat off the concrete dock becoming a malevolent force. 'But she is OK, isn't she? I had one text message from her, but nothing since.'

'We are in contact with her. She is in a position to help us out.'

Simon feels his breath catch, then a growing anger. 'Don't you dare put her at risk.'

'No risk, she's just passing on some information.'

'You're using her. That has to stop. Right now.'

'Simon, your wife can help save a thousand lives, and do I need to remind you what she has done? Let her vindicate herself, for Christ's sake. We all have to be able to live with ourselves.'

'They are holding her children,' he flared. 'How dare you —'

Mossel's voice is as low and cold as a whisper. 'I hear what you're saying. But I have no choice. No more choice than she did.'

Still holding the phone to his ear, Simon walks closer to the empty berth, hollow and afraid. Squatting down and reaching out with his free hand, he touches a bollard worn to shiny smooth metal by years of heavy lines looped over the rusty iron.

'The boat was called *Sa-baah*,' Mossel says.

'What?'

'The boat they took your daughters on. *Sa-baah* means "Morning", I'm told. A Danish-built tug retired from a thirty-year career towing Saudi offshore rigs. Purchased by a Yemeni company five months ago. I must congratulate you on getting this far. Nice detective work. You look tired, though. Bet you'd love clean clothes. You can't keep recycling the same ones forever.'

'You bastard, can you see me?'

'Had an idea you'd get here sooner or later. The company that now owns the vessel lists its sole director and shareholder as one Da'ud Iqbal, a Saudi lawyer with links to several terror organisations, including the Algerian AQIM and these Almohad bastards. We found him on holiday, pretty sure he was laying low. Had him picked up in the resort city of Taif. He hasn't talked yet, but we're hoping he might.'

'You didn't answer my question. Can you see me?'

'Of course. Turn around. You'll see a man in a white shirt and sunglasses; he's holding up a cell phone.'

Simon turns.

'Now walk over there. His name is Juwain, he will take you back to the airport, get you through customs and on a plane.'

'Where to?'

'Here. London.'

When Juwain takes a stride towards him, Simon feels the first stirring of panic. 'My girls are on board the boat you're talking about?'

'We think so.'

'Where are they headed?'

'That we can't be sure about, but we suspect Socotra.'

The name hammers away in Simon's head. Socotra. The pirate capital of the Indian Ocean. Inaccessible and unapproachable, in the news for all the wrong reasons. 'Why are you telling me all this?'

'Because I want to impress on you that we are way ahead. We have resources that you cannot compete with. Go with Juwain now, Simon, work with us — I'll keep you in the loop, I promise. We can do so much that you can't: aerial surveillance, a network of informers. Navy. Air Force. We'll find them.'

Simon takes three steps towards the man with the camera then terminates the call, slipping the phone into his pocket. Turning his back, he begins to run, almost colliding with a labourer pushing a trolley of industrial equipment along the concrete dock, swerving just in time.

Ahead, a crowd disembarks from a tourist catamaran, and Simon joins the throng, finding himself carried along. Most are Arabic, and have, he assumes, just concluded a sea tour of the famous Sirah Fort that lies just off the coast.

The layout of the port makes little sense, and Simon uses this to his advantage, turning in to a side street and running. Across the road is a souk, and he moves into the jungle of tables, basket sellers and carpet weavers, spruikers singing their musical invitations.

At the other side, when he looks back, the man with the cell phone is gone.

Day 3, 13:00

When Jafar Zartosht, steady of hand and eye, first learned to shoot, his instructors, veterans of the Afghan jihad, could hardly credit that a newcomer could shoot so straight. He was given a Russian Dragunov SVD sniper rifle and trained until, he joked, he could shoot the wings from a fly at a hundred paces.

Jafar's family made up part of Tehran's one-million-strong Sunni minority, scarcely tolerated by the Shi'ite Ayatollah, who would not allow them a single mosque for their worship. Jafar left this restrictive environment as soon as he was old enough to do so, after a short stint in the Jundullah terrorist group. The Komiteh — Iranian Secret Police — were, by that time, hot on his heels.

Of just average intelligence, he was able to grasp and follow orders, and did not mind killing when told to do so. One instructor described him as the perfect soldier for a jihad hungry for coffin fodder. In Iraq he joined al-Muqawama al-Iraqiya, the Sunni freedom fighters based to

the north of Baghdad; the remnants of the private army
once commanded by the deceased Abu Musab al-Zarqawi.

In the capital itself, Jafar was able to mingle with
the local population. There he saw Western women
up close for the first time. One was a foreign reporter
fronting the cameras at the site of a suicide attack on the
packed Kazimain Mosque, in the suburb of Doura. Shia
worshippers had been attending Friday prayers when
the martyr triggered his explosives, killing fifteen and
wounding many more.

Jafar stopped and stared at the reporter — the
slacks, the blouse that showed the shape of her breasts
and creamy white skin under the open top button. The
immorality of her display was breathtaking. How could a
woman stand not only in front of a crowd, but cameras
also, and flaunt herself like a whore? He knew that he
should have been disgusted, but instead felt an immediate
sexual excitement that left his mouth dry, skin tingling,
and heart beating fast.

Islamist militants, in general, are recruited as young
men, and suffer the usual hyper sexual drive of youth. They
are, however, taught that physical love outside of sanctified
marriage is an offence to the Prophet and to God. Sexual
thoughts must be repressed and, to Jafar and his teachers,
American sexual innuendo and flaunting of female bodies
is a disgrace, and symbolic of cultural weakness.

Knowing that it was wrong to do so, he continued to
stare. She was closer to naked than any woman he had
ever seen and, for a twenty-three-year-old virgin who
had boxed up every sexual urge within the tight confines
of Mohammedan strictures, it was enough to leave him
aching and depressed, outraged and aroused.

Jafar never saw that particular woman again, but he sought out these whores of the West whenever possible — savouring and hating each experience; staring and watching, removing the few clothes they wore with his eyes; imagining what it might be like to touch them. Later he would pay for the pleasure with hours on his knees seeking al-istighfar — forgiveness.

My Lord forgive me and accept my repentance, verily you are the acceptor of repentance ...

Jafar acted from compulsion. He had no way of stopping the dreams and fantasies conjured by these visions of whoredom and immorality. He wanted sexual freedom but was afraid of it. Seeing Arab women with uncovered faces made him so angry that, one day in Rabat, he beat one such abomination with his fists until she lay bloodied and senseless on the footpath.

As elements of the first, second and third infantry divisions, along with the second brigade, 82nd Airborne, prepared for George W Bush's 'surge', Jafar was sent in with a crack terror squad to capture a team of Red Cross workers who had set up shop outside Mosul, patching up victims from istishhad operations and helping Shia refugees through to safer havens.

Jafar and his team waited for the dead of night, when their targets were asleep. Their knives sliced through tent canvas, rounding up the doctors and administrators still in their pyjamas, lashing out with boot and rifle butt; smelling the vomit-fear smell on their victims' lips. They killed one who caused trouble, two rounds in the gut so that he squirmed in his own entrails like a fish in slime. Blood from the shots spattered Jafar's shoes.

There is no god but God and Mohammed is His Messenger.

Cramming the prisoners into a van, driving out into the desert and into the abandoned village honeycombed with tunnels that hid their base, Jafar could not keep his eyes off a young American prisoner. She was around twenty-five years of age, blonde and fair skinned, with blue eyes, like those of a doll.

Deep underground, the prisoners were locked in separate chambers. Jafar watched the woman for an hour before falling to his knees in the prayer room.

Afterwards, he approached the guard assigned to the woman. 'You may sleep now, Kamal, I will take over.'

'Are you certain?'

'Of course.'

Jafar watched her for a minute or two, giddy with desire. Sex for pleasure was forbidden, yet surely it was allowable to punish the woman?

He gagged her with a strip of cloth, looking down to watch her buttocks beneath the material of her trousers. Already he was in a state of arousal so strong that he felt dizzy.

Jafar unslung his rifle and leaned it against the wall. He touched her right shoulder and pressured her to turn. Her scent filled his nostrils.

Even then she tried to fight him, lashing out with her hands, forcing him to grip her tight and use his weight to drag her down, whispering endearments in Farsi as they slid to the floor together, snatches of love poetry he had read as a teenager. *Oh, my beautiful darling, you are a flower, waiting for the bee with his pollen.*

Jafar felt as tall as a mountain, as hard as iron, his spear as sharp and ready as that of a fabled warrior of the janissary.

Even now, years later, Jafar becomes aroused with the memory. He looks around, checking if Zhyogal has noticed his daydreaming. It seems not. He relaxes, grateful to God for the opportunity to be part of this team. Should martyrdom come he will welcome it with open arms. Death as part of an operation is unique to the jihad; a powerful symbol, proving a depth of commitment that the kufr cannot match.

Here at Rabi al-Salah, there is one who draws his eye most. The one from the British delegation — not as young as some, but voluptuous, with large breasts. The one who Zhyogal seduced as part of the cause. Isabella. The cell leader had told of his reluctance to perform the duty, of her fat white breasts and the repugnant smell of her sex when aroused. He told them how much she had wanted to be violated, how she had begged him to enter her, and how he had closed his eyes and thought only of God while he did his duty so that the mission might succeed.

Jafar's encounter with the woman in the bathroom inflamed him, and now his desire reaches fever pitch. He wants her as much as he has ever wanted anything in his life. He dreams of parting the petals of her womanhood and delving deep inside. He feels guilt at this thought and prays for forgiveness.

Day 3, 19:00

Footsteps in the corridor. The door opens. Marika looks up, expecting Captain Wanami and his interpreter. Instead, a pair of armed Somalis open the door, saying nothing. The closest of the two, a short man with a paunch, crooks one finger in an unspoken order to get up.

'Polite bastards, aren't you,' Marika comments, but stands and allows them to escort her down the corridor. Once outside, they lead her past the gate that a thousand hands had pressed against that morning, towards the largest of the buildings. Like the jail, this edifice is built of stone, and some attempt at a garden has been made — rock-bordered beds outside the veranda. A row of withered flower stems adorn the dry soil.

Inside, combat boots thump on timber floors, and Marika finds herself in a room furnished as a dining hall, yet might once have been a courthouse, an impression heightened by heavy timbers and vaulted ceiling. Men occupy a number of tables.

As she approaches, a giant of a man stands from his place at the head of one table. He is perhaps the largest human Marika has ever seen — at least seven feet in height and with powerful shoulders and arms. Even his neck is packed tight with muscle and sinew. Moving closer, she sees that his pigmentation is not uniformly black, but varies in swathes across his face and neck: white in places; jet black in others. The effect, coupled with his size and musculature, is startling.

'Good gracious,' he says in a cultivated voice. 'They did not tell me that you are beautiful. Merhika, isn't it?'

'Marika.'

'Apologies, my men are not very literate, and have a poor ear for foreign words.'

'That's fine.' Marika has already decided that being pleasant and cooperative might be her best chance of not going straight back to the cell. 'Your English is very good.'

'Of course it is. I have worked hard on it over a number of years. It is useful for us to share a language, don't you think? There is no need for us to communicate with signs like monkeys.' He leans down to take her right hand in his, making it look small and white. Delicately, he raises the hand to his bulbous lips and kisses it just above the middle knuckle. 'My name is Dalmar Asad. It is a pleasure to meet you — we have few, er, uninvited guests in this part of the country and, as you can imagine, it is very refreshing when it happens.'

'Thank you.' Marika finds herself reluctant to break the touch. His voice and the feel of his skin are compelling.

'Now we will go to where we can talk in private.'

Dalmar Asad leading the way, they leave the room, accompanied by the two guards who collected her from the cell. Halfway down the corridor the big Somali opens a door. The office behind it is furnished in the kind of old-fashioned elegance Marika remembers from Sunday night period serials. The desk is of dark timber but covered with leather to within a hand-span of the edge. The books on the shelves are beautifully bound, with the names of classic authors on the spines. The visitor's chairs are upholstered in washed-out royal blue.

'Sit down, please,' Asad says.

The guards take up position beside the door, and Captain Wanami enters last, choosing a seat under the bookcase, lolling back, chewing qat like a cricketer chews gum, eyes invisible behind reflective dark sunglasses. Marika feels a knot of fear and pain in the pit of her belly at the sight of him. She sits, her legs weak and powerless.

After snapping an instruction to one of the guards in Somali, Asad turns back to her. 'The man who brought you in — Madoowbe — will be here in a moment, but in the meantime, tell me about yourself.'

'I am an Australian. I work for the United Nations.'

'Oh come, we are both adults. Employees of the UN hardly go parachuting into faraway nations under the cover of night. You are some kind of spy or Special Forces operative, and you are here for some specific reason. I'd like to know what that reason is.'

The door opens and the guard returns. Marika gasps in shock as a badly beaten man is propelled into the room. Dried blood covers his face and one eye is puffed almost closed.

Seconds pass before Marika recognises Madoowbe. She slides from her seat, kneeling beside him. 'What have you done to him?'

Asad shows no surprise, looking at the bleeding figure without remorse or even much interest. 'I thought you would be pleased, since he is the man who handed you over to us.'

'Violence never pleases me.'

'Then I suggest that you are in the wrong line of work. Let us cut to the chase. I have followed developments at Rabi al-Salah with interest. I know you are involved. This man has admitted your involvement, but unfortunately our questioning has revealed nothing more. Perhaps you will tell us instead.'

Marika says nothing while Asad stands up and walks to her side, reaching down to cup her chin between thumb and forefinger, twisting her face to look at him. 'I need to know what you are looking for. This is my domain and nothing happens here without my knowledge. Cooperate, and I'm sure we can work together for our mutual benefit.' He turns to the guard. 'This man is bleeding on my floor. Get rid of him.'

The guard drags Madoowbe away by the legs, a mournful groan emanating from his lips.

'Let us have the facts, for a start,' Asad says. 'What is your name?'

'Marika Hartmann.'

'Who is your employer?'

'UNESCO.'

'Don't toy with me, Miss Hartmann. The equipment you carry is MI6 issue. You are here on a political mission and we know it has something to do with Rabi al-Salah. I am in a position to help, provided you inform me of your purpose.'

'And if I don't?'

'I will consider you a threat to the stability and peace of my domains and take steps to extract the information from you.'

Her eyes move to the silent Captain Wanami, then flick away. 'Your friend here will be pleased — he seems to enjoy torturing people.'

'It is not a matter of enjoyment,' Dalmar Asad snarls, 'but of necessity.'

'You,' Marika says, 'have no understanding of human rights.'

'And you are a Western brat with no experience of life in Africa.' He takes a pistol, a nickel-plated Colt automatic, from the holster at his belt. Marika wonders how many times it has been fired in anger. How many times it has killed.

'In Somalia,' he says, 'the gun rules, and the weak do not survive. There is neither time nor reason to feel sorry for them. Do you understand?'

She says nothing, unable to tear her eyes away from the gun.

'You have a choice: either I hand you over to Wanami, or — ' he twirls the gun, grinning, ' — you accept my help and come with me.'

'Where to?'

Dalmar Asad laughs. 'Fairyland.' The other men join in the general mirth.

Marika frowns, thinking. This is a brutal man, with few morals, yet he takes pains to cultivate the veneer of a gentleman. The choice between a twelve-volt battery and alligator clips or the unknown is not a choice.

'I am at your mercy,' Marika says, wondering what the hell she is letting herself in for.

Humid sea air lies heavily over the port area. Simon hovers in the shadows beside a street light, where flying ants circle the humming globe, tiny shadows rising and falling. Checking his watch, he swears to himself, impatient.

'You are ready?'

Simon turns to see Ishmael, a Yemeni seaman he met through a series of referrals earlier in the day, hovering on the fringe of the light. 'Yes. Has the vessel we discussed reached port?'

'Not an hour ago my brother docked here at Aden. I have spoken to him and he is happy to accept a charter, as soon as he refuels and takes on provisions. You have no luggage?'

'Just a small bag.'

Ishmael grunts. 'What about money? My brother will want to see it.'

'Yes.'

Arranging a substantial transfer from an investment account into the Queen Arwa branch of the al-Ahli Bank of Yemen, has taken time and some frustration, yet now the wad of US dollars — the seagoing brothers' preferred currency — in his pocket is thick enough to be noticeable. Ishmael's eyes flick towards it. The avarice is unmistakeable and unsubtle.

'The full amount necessary?'

'Of course.'

'Then follow me.'

Simon ponders the chances of being knifed for the cash in his pocket. This man does not inspire trust, his eyes dark and secretive, resembling one of the starved port rats, visible at the periphery of the light since nightfall. Rats or not, Simon has no choice. He follows in silence down narrow and dark walkways between containers and crates, boats to the left, masts black against the starlight, always that creaking sound of vessels at rest, fenders squealing, grinding against iron and concrete, the slap of water on ageing piles and the distant rumble of pumps and compressors.

They stop beside a vessel of around fifteen metres in length, of fibreglass construction, unlike most of the timber or iron boats surrounding her. Her hull is streamlined, with a fine entry at the bow. A boat built for speed. A man lounges nearby, smoking a cigarette. He and Ishmael exchange a few words in Arabic before the latter turns back to Simon. 'You like her? Her name is the *Jameela*. She is nice, eh? Her name means "beautiful". As I told you, she is the fastest boat of her size to work out of Aden. Come aboard, meet my brother.'

Still wary, yet impressed with the vessel, Simon follows; stepping up from the jetty, over the gunwale, and onto the non-slip moulded surface of the deck. From there, past coiled ropes and a life ring hanging against a bulkhead, they pass through a hinged door into a saloon area, controls and instrument panel up forward.

The saloon is dominated by a dinette table and galley. The cherrywood surface of the table is strewn with books and an open notepad. An unfired coffee mug, half full, sits to one side. A very old woman, head and body cloaked in a red, blue, green and yellow, coarse woven setarrah, occupies one end of the table, eyes staring glassily.

The air in here, Simon decides, has a tinge of something once familiar — an aromatic, burned smell. At first he thinks it might be roasting coffee beans. A studious-looking man of about thirty occupies the helm chair. Like his brother he sports a white kandoura robe and a shemagh. He wears a short black beard and gold rings on the middle fingers of both hands. He stands and comes aft, bony hand extended, regarding Simon intently, saying nothing.

Ishmael acknowledges his brother with that distinctive Yemeni greeting, raising both hands above his head, fists clenched. Then he turns back to Simon. 'I am happy to introduce my brother, Lubayd. His intellect is considerable. He is a genius.'

Lubayd nods, as if to grudgingly accept the praise. 'My brother is too effusive. Peace be upon you.'

'Peace to you also. My name is Simon.'

Ishmael, however, has not finished. 'Do you know, Lubayd has solved Professor Archimedes's puzzle every week for one hundred and twenty-two consecutive weeks? No man alive can boast of such a feat.'

Simon raises his eyebrows. 'I am sure that is a great achievement, yet forgive my ignorance. Who is Professor Archimedes?'

'Professor Archimedes,' the younger brother announces, 'has a puzzle in the *al-Ayyam* newspaper every Saturday.'

'That is enough, Ishmael,' Lubayd chides him. 'My intellect is no greater than that of a cockroach when compared to God, may praise and glory be to Him.' He turns to Simon. 'Will you refresh yourself with us?'

'If you don't mind.'

'Would you like coffee, or mint tea perhaps?'

'Coffee, please.'

'Dear brother, will you make coffee for our guest?'

While Ishmael rattles cups and plates, spooning coffee from a tin of instant Nescafe, the elder sibling goes on, 'Sit please, Simon.' A smile crosses his face, in the manner of a man having a very pleasant thought. '*Ah*, what a name. I am pleased to host a man with such a wonderful name, so much history — Simon the Zealot, the Canaanite beloved of your Jesus, or the Jewish hero Simon Wiesenthal, the Nazi hunter. Paul Simon the American singer. Illustrious men have borne your name.'

'Ishmael is right, you are knowledgeable.'

'Thanks be to God. I spend each day improving my mind. What other worthwhile pursuits are there?'

They move to the dinette, where the old woman remains, saying nothing, just continuing to stare. Lubayd moves his face close to hers. 'Do you want coffee, Mama?'

A shake of the head. Eyes unfocused, directionless.

Turning his attention back to Simon, Lubayd apologises for her. 'I am sorry about my mother. She is old and, if not for Ishmael and I, she would be alone. I do not think it is

right for a man to abandon his mother, and she loves the
sea. Our father sailed a dhow, and she has travelled all
over the Red Sea, the Persian Gulf and the ports of East
Africa.'

The old woman continues her silence, yet it seems to
Simon that something changes in her face, as if with the
memory of blue seas, sunsets and the love of a young
husband. There is something beautiful in her now,
something that a woman never loses.

The coffee comes in enamel mugs. Simon sips the
dark, hot drink, then turns to Lubayd. 'Ishmael tells me
that your boat is very fast.'

'Oh, she is. We can call on two and a half thousand
horsepower. Thirty-six knots in a smooth sea. No one can
catch us. My brother tells me that you are interested in
chartering her.'

'That's true. I am.'

'She will be very kind to you. No man has ever been
seasick aboard the *Jameela*.'

'The boat I wish to follow left here two days ago, but
she is a slow vessel — a tug, I am told.'

'Bound for where?'

'The Isles of Socotra, I believe.'

'At full throttle we can be there not long after dawn,
but at such a speed we would use almost every drop of
fuel on board. At a more prudent rate we will reach the
area by mid-afternoon tomorrow.'

Simon brightens. 'Can we make a deal?'

'There is a problem.'

'What is that?'

'I will not go there. Despite the indescribable
and famous beauty of those islands, even the most

inexperienced sailor knows to avoid the area, for all charts warn of the perils.'

'Then we will find our target on the open sea.'

'What then? You expect me to fight another boat? My brother and I are not fighters. We are men of peace.'

Simon bites his lip. The effort is starting to tell — there is no time to find another boat, not one as sleek and fast as this. He glares at Lubayd. 'I want you to take me there. I am not a wealthy man, but I can pay you very well.'

Lubayd sighs, placing both elbows on the table, his chin in his palms, flattening his beard like steel wool. 'I have no understanding of what you want. You speak of a boat you must find, but why?'

Simon tells him everything, seeing no point in anything but honesty. Beginning with the terrifying announcement high over the Gulf, then the search for clues. By the time it is done he has to wipe his eyes with his sleeve.

'I am sorry,' Lubayd says, 'but there are forces in this world that it is best not to contend with. The Almohad are one such force. Their hands pull the strings of terror and intimidation from Kabul to Jakarta, Gaza to Baghdad. They are masterful exploiters of men, and they plan nothing short of political and religious domination of the world. I am sorry, but I cannot take you out there against them, not even to find your two daughters.'

Simon looks around, as if seeking an outlet for his frustration. 'What do you and your brother do with this boat, Lubayd?'

'I beg your pardon?'

'Vessels like this do not pay for themselves. What do you do with a thirty-six-knot cruiser?'

'That is *our* business.'

'It is mine also if I am going to associate myself with you.'

Lubayd's eyes glow darkly. 'There are many things that need to pass between the coasts of Arabia and Africa — unmarked crates; silent men in suits. I have a reputation for the utmost discretion and trustworthiness, attributes that are priceless in this world.'

'If you are so well regarded and busy with lucrative work, why did your brother think you might be interested in my charter?'

'Because I have a week now without prospect of employment of our services. The business of the region has been postponed. Rabi al-Salah is the cause. The Middle East will wait, mid breath, while events unfold. The world may change beyond recognition by the time it is over.'

'You think so?'

'I am certain of it. History hinges on the leaders of the nations of the world. Any student of the past knows that. Who can predict what will happen? Instability, even war.'

'Take me to Socotra. Leave me there. I will swim ashore if I have to. That is all I ask of you. Surely you can outrun any pirate boat in the sea.'

'Socotran and Somali pirates have machine guns, heavy weapons; I cannot risk damage to my beautiful boat.'

'If you are as fast as you say, they will not get close enough to do so. Name your price, any price, but I need to leave now, this minute. Each tick of the clock may be the death knell for my children. Can you imagine how that feels for me?'

'Just say I agree to take you. Please understand that my fuel burn at fast cruise may exceed two hundred dollars an hour. My costs will number in the thousands. You tell me, Simon of England, how much this is worth to you. Put a figure on the love of a father for his daughters.'

'I have five thousand dollars cash in my pocket. It is yours if you take me.' Of course, there is another roll in his sock, but he does not want to use it now — there will be other obstacles, and nothing removes obstacles like money.

Lubayd shows some emotion. 'One thousand now.'

'That is reasonable.'

'Ishmael,' Lubayd calls.

The brother arrives from down below. 'Yes?'

'Prepare for sea. I am setting a course for Socotra.'

'Socotra? Brother, we have not been there for many years, and my memories of the last time are unpleasant. Is this something we have to do?'

'Yes, Ishmael. This is a lot of money, and we have nothing else to do.' He turns back to Simon. 'I will not go against al-Muwahhidun, nor pirates, but I will take you to Socotra. The main island. From there you will have to make your own way.'

Simon inclines his head. 'You are a kind man. Can we leave now?'

'It will take an hour or more to inform the harbourmaster and make last-minute preparations.'

'Half an hour?'

'I will try.'

When Simon extracts the required deposit and hands it across, Lubayd opens a drawer in the chart table and slips the notes inside. Simon has time to see the dark outline of an automatic pistol inside, and wonders why men of peace feel the need to have a gun so close at hand.

*

A veteran of several hostage grabs, Zhyogal is aware that the situation is at its most dangerous when the initial shock has worn off, when braver souls start assessing the odds of playing hero. One or more of his men might, at any time, be overpowered and disarmed.

He never tires of scanning the long tiers of men and women. Most of the crowd have settled into groups based on the country of origin. They talk among themselves, yet with a watchful eye on the mujahedin. No one has yet tried anything, but it is always a possibility.

The auditorium layout is unusual and, in some ways, difficult to defend, partly because in order to see everything Zhyogal must stand at the bottom, giving any potential attacker the benefit of high ground.

The pulse of movement in the satellite telephone in his top pocket cuts these thoughts short. Several messages appear every day, not always relevant; information routed from all around the world through a clearing house in Sana'a, Yemen. It has always amused Zhyogal that Western intelligence services do not appear to know that they are being observed by the people they themselves spend so much time and money keeping under surveillance.

In just a few years, al-Muwahhidun have developed one of the most powerful clandestine networks in the world, not least because of the utmost loyalty of its operatives. Leaks are unheard of, mistakes are few. Sympathisers exist in media organisations and political groups around the world.

Zhyogal does not hurry to read his messages, but waits until he has finished the patrol from the top of the most northerly aisle to the bottom, feet dragging on the carpet the only sign of his fatigue, knowing by heart the gaps between steps on the tiered surface. *Three paces flat, three down. Three paces flat, three steps down.* Men and women alike avoid his eyes, and their obvious fear pleases him. Fear means that he has done his job.

Near the dais he removes the phone and waves a hand across the tinted face to power it up. Scrolling to the message app he begins to read, flicking his eyes from the screen to the crowd, not daring to leave them unobserved for too long.

The email begins with movements of US navy ships. The USS *Atlanta* to the Red Sea. The USS *George Bush* to Valetta Harbour, Malta. The next section covers the fortuitous escape, assisted by God, of three trusted mujahedin who were under pressure from security forces in Bonn, Germany.

Then, Zhyogal freezes, reading the next message over and over.

Rabi al-Salah: *Kufr plan tunnel into bunker underneath centre.*

Following this is a series of details. Names. Places.

When he has finished reading, Zhyogal gives the matter some thought. The idea of a tunnel had occurred to the planning team but was dismissed as not viable in the allotted time. Now it seems that the kufr are pursuing this option, however unlikely it might seem.

Countering this distant threat is now important. First Zhyogal studies the number of men at his disposal, then calls one across, a wiry little man, Algerian like himself. 'Khalil,' he says, 'there is a possible threat to the bunker below. I would like you to occupy it and listen for unexpected sounds.'

'Yes, sayyid.'

'But you will report to me each hour.'

That requirement, of course, will ensure that the chosen guard will not spend his time sleeping.

'Yes, sayyid.'

Zhyogal again takes out the phone. It was a good thing that as part of the mission plan they decided to keep Saif al-Din on the outside to coordinate the support teams and carry out general troubleshooting.

Last time they spoke, Saif al-Din was in the city, in a safe house in the al-Satwa district. Zhyogal types out a brief, encrypted text. Saif will ensure that no tunnel will ever be finished.

The Mercedes 350 SE sits in a concrete garage that smells of grease, wax and polish. Even in the darkness it glows. The interior is luxurious and clean. Marika slides into the back seat and Dalmar Asad slips in beside her. The driver starts the engine, an unobtrusive hum.

Marika feels nervous again, thinking of what the interpreter said earlier about Dalmar Asad wanting to rape her. Is it possible that the civilised veneer hides a man who will force her sexually? She doesn't think so, but this is a worrying train of thought that has her shifting in her seat. Is she on her way to some sophisticated torture chamber from which she will never emerge? Anything is possible. All she can do is look for an opportunity to get away, and back to the mission that may yet be so critical.

The gate opens and the Mercedes floats like a magic carpet over the desert roads. She wonders at the possibility of opening the door and rolling out — no mean feat against the slipstream, and besides, what then? The driver carries a pistol in the holster at his side, as does Dalmar Asad. Even if she does get away, she will be alone in the middle of the desert. No map, no guide, no weapons and little prospect of obtaining any one of the three.

Always she sees the shadow people, the refugees, tramping down the sides of the road. The slow and hopeless walk of the dispossessed. Some fall to their knees and beg as the Mercedes flies past, necessitating the occasional cold blast on the horn from the driver, who scarcely slows, forcing them to clear the road or be run down. There are glowing dung or charcoal fires out in the darkness from those who have settled down for the night.

'Where are they all from?' Marika asks, whispering.

'Them? They are a nuisance. Refugees from the coast. Not only drought, but now the sea has risen, flooding their villages and crops.'

Marika frowns. 'Their villages are flooded? I didn't realise that sea levels had risen so high here.'

'They are not flooded all the time, but on the spring tides. Supertides they are called now. Together with sea level rises and the ocean currents, rises of more than a metre over the old marks have salted hundreds of thousands of hectares of once arable lands. Nothing will grow. The seas have also polluted wells and lakes with salt. There is no drinking water. The refugees move inland, where drought and famine have ravaged the land. Hardly a stalk of corn has not wilted in the heat. They come here and find nothing. They come here and die.'

'What about the UN? And the NGOs?'

'They cannot penetrate far beyond Mogadishu — it is not safe for their people. We are not the most moderate of peoples, and have never liked outsiders.'

'But there must be tens of thousands of refugees on the road.'

'More, many more.'

'This is a humanitarian disaster on a terrible scale.'

'Somalia has been a humanitarian disaster for almost thirty years. This is just the latest manifestation of it.'

Marika's sense of outrage grows. 'This morning when refugees came to the gate of your compound I watched from the cell window. Your men fired shots to keep them away. You have money, power, and therefore a responsibility to help. You could at least offer them a meal.'

'You want me, Dalmar Asad, to open a soup kitchen for the wandering vermin of the world?' He laughs, turning to the driver, who guffaws with sycophantic vigour. 'No. Like it or not, here life is hard, and you must, if need be, fight tooth and nail for every meal. When I was a child I would fight my own brothers for food. That is the way of the land. That is how we live here. The life expectancy for a male is forty-six years, and that was before this drought and the rising sea. Women die in childbirth in staggering numbers.' He strikes his own chest with an audible thump. 'I am above such statistics, yet now that I have everything I could ever want there are many who seek to take it away from me. Always I am looking behind, searching the eyes of those who serve me, asking myself, can I trust this man or woman? Even when I believe I can trust him, I make it difficult for him to betray me. Make Man A believe that Man B is watching him — set up suspicions to ensure that no man feels safe.'

Marika does not comment, continuing to stare out at the wraiths in the night. *This is the result of two centuries of an industrialised West. The pursuit of labour-saving machines, of gadgets that save us from working. Give us pleasure. Entertain us. In the process we are killing ourselves, starting with the most vulnerable.*

The vehicle hits a pothole at speed, and even the Mercedes' suspension is unable to smother the sharp jolt. Marika clutches at the seat while Asad remonstrates with the driver for his carelessness. She ignores the exchange, filled with a powerless rage at what she has seen, staring ahead at a guard post surrounded by another high cyclone fence, illuminated in the yellow glare of the headlights. Two armed men salute as the vehicle moves through.

Ahead looms a building complex, illuminated by lights of varied colours. The sight, Marika decides, would be more at home in the city than here in the desert. The construction is set on a small hill, two or three storeys high, with marble steps leading to the first level. White pillars frame the entrance. Hues of blue and green light the walls, and the Mercedes circles a fountain with water cascading down a statue carved also of marble: a pair of elephants, massive and angry, trunks raised and tusks curling in the artificial light.

'Look,' Marika says, 'this is all very nice but I am in a hurry. You are a civilised man and I have to remind you that I am being held against my will.'

Dalmar Asad does not answer, but holds a hand up as if to say, 'Stop,' while the driver hurries around to open first Asad's door, then hers.

* * *

When Marika leaves the car she is both surprised and horrified. The comparison between this opulence and the dispossessed families on the road is breathtaking. She warns herself: *Remember. You have a job to do. Pissing this man off will not help.* She turns to Dalmar Asad. 'You're kidding. You live here?'

'This is my home. Fifty men laboured for two years to build it for me. The finest craftsmen — stonemasons, carpenters, decorators from all over the Middle East: Syria, Saudi Arabia, Egypt, even Israel.' He chuckles. 'But don't tell anyone about that.'

'And who lives here? Just you?'

'Not quite. My staff numbers nineteen in total, including guards. More than enough to keep me diverted. I am a busy and intensely religious man, and thus have little time for entertaining.' He lowers his voice. 'Except, of course, when a beautiful young woman like yourself comes my way.'

'You flatter me.' Marika forces herself to play the game, even allowing Dalmar Asad to take her hand for the gentle ascent up the stairs. She hears soft music from inside, making her wonder at the instructions he has called ahead.

At the top of the stairs there is a courtyard similar to those she has seen in the lobbies of expensive hotels, with a long, raised garden, and intricate patterns in the paving stones. The entrance columns, she realises, are so thick that her arms would not encircle them. Another blue-tinged fountain is surrounded by a fishpond. Marika walks close and stares down into the water. Orange and black shapes flutter decorative tail fins near green water plants as if expecting her to feed them.

'A unique variety of koi,' Dalmar Asad says, 'imported from China. They are good feng shui; the very best, I am told.'

'Beautiful. But they do seem hungry.'

'Ah, but does a prudent nurse give a child her breast the first time it bleats of hunger? No. My servants are instructed to feed them sparingly. That keeps the water healthy and the fish also. Wanting will not hurt them, and makes them more disposed to eat the mosquito larvae that would soon make evenings in the courtyard unpleasant.'

Marika looks through the glass windows. There she sees pale leather lounge chairs, plush and inviting, arranged under soft lighting — a room straight from the pages of *Vogue Living*.

'Would you like to come inside?' he asks.

'Yes, of course.'

A dapper servant opens the glass door and admits Marika first, then Asad. The servant's eyes are light brown, wide with hero worship, whether feigned or real, Marika cannot tell. 'Good evening, Aaba, and madam.'

When he moves away again, Marika asks, 'What did he call you just then?'

'Aaba. Father. All my staff call me that. I consider it a mark of respect. The men and women here are of my own subclan, so there is no question of their loyalty.'

'Your own clan? You enslave your own people?'

'They live a thousand times better than their less fortunate brothers and cousins, I can assure you. Not one would hesitate to lay down his life for me.' He rubs his hands together. 'Now I expect that you would like to shower and change.'

No, I want to find a woman called Sufia Haweeya and get the hell out of here, she wants to say. Instead she nods. 'Sounds good.'

Dalmar Asad places one giant hand on her shoulder. 'Ghedi will show you to your room.'

The second-floor bedroom has views across the moonlit desert through glass sliding doors that open onto a balcony. Ghedi, crossing the floor with a rapid flutter of his short legs, opens a wardrobe door, made, like the others, of cowhide stretched over timber frames. 'There is clothing in here, madam, everything from bathing costumes to evening wear.' His eyes circle her body like a shark then appraise it from shoulders to ankles. 'I'm certain that some will be in your size.'

'Thank you.'

Marika waits while he steps back out into the corridor, the door closing behind him. She goes to the bed and lifts a pillow, feeling the sheets with the palm of her hand. Soft, closely weaved with shining threads — real silk. That will be an experience in itself, she decides, as will the feather quilt that covers them. She sits on the bed and stares at the wall, trying to make sense of her current situation — whether it is any less of a prison than the filthy cell back at the compound.

Scanning the ceiling she notes tiny, almost imperceptible holes where hidden cameras must be. Of course Dalmar Asad will have his guests under surveillance, and with the realisation comes self-consciousness. Even so, the lure of a hot shower is too strong to resist.

Walking into the bathroom, she closes the door behind her, studying the ceiling and walls. Yes, there is a concealed camera here also. *Let 'em look*, she decides. The lack of privacy is fair exchange for hot water.

Still, determined to protect as much of her modesty as possible, she steps into the shower cubicle and closes the curtain around her before she undresses. With the taps turned on hard, she opens a plastic package of soap and massages the suds over her abdomen, breasts, upper arms and neck. The water is soft and steaming hot. A pump pack of shampoo sits at the edge of the cubicle and she extracts a handful before lathering up her scalp.

Where the hell does he get these things?

After rinsing herself off she opens the curtain to take a towel off the rail before drying herself and wrapping it around her body. Moving back into the bedroom, she opens the wardrobe, choosing from a stock of underwear still in the packet. After a quick study of the clothes on offer, she unfolds an East African kikoi, dyed with one bright primary colour and a patterned border. Tassels hang from the lower hem.

Retreating into the toilet cubicle, where there are no cameras, she dresses, knotting the bright fabric around her chest. On the way through she studies herself in the mirror, tousles her hair, then turns and opens the door.

The bar is the kind of tasteful, elegant establishment that, had it been a commercial venture, Marika would have avoided. Pubs that smell of beer and echo to arguments over the pool table are more her style. Ghedi is waiting for her, opening the door, bowing his head respectfully.

'Aaba has not yet returned from his ablutions. May I bring you a drink?'

'No thank you, I will wait for him, if that is OK.'

Ghedi inclines his head and goes back to cleaning glasses at the bar, yet, she suspects, watching her movements at the same time. Walking casually she approaches a large fish tank built into the wall. This does not contain more of the gaudy carp, but a recreation of a tropical sea, with painted crayfish hiding in the coral, and fish darting in iridescent schools. A clownfish. A striped mado. A dramatic wrasse half burrowed into the gravel. Urchins and sea stars. Most of the others are unfamiliar to her, though exquisitely coloured and formed, fins thin as silk waving in the current generated by the filter return.

The tank, beautiful though it is, holds her attention for just a few seconds before her eyes roam around the room and beyond. The windows are thick, double-glazed.

Flicking her eyes to the door, Marika sees motion sensors on either side, and automatic locking bars recessed into the floor. Yes, she decides, this palace could become a prison, or a fortress, with the flick of a switch.

A cowhide door opens and closes, and Dalmar Asad comes through, dressed in a white thoub shirt, buttoned at the front and an embroidered keffiyeh cap — the work of months by someone skilled in needlework.

'Ah, you are admiring my pets,' he says, 'are they not brilliant? Most come from Koyaama off our southern coast, collected by a rather eccentric enthusiast — a great friend of mine.'

'They are beautiful.'

'Of course. Now come, let us drink. I hope you don't mind my dress. It must seem unusual to you, but in my leisure time I like to return to my faith. Ghedi,' he calls, 'come here, please.' The servant pads over and waits. 'The lady would like a cocktail. Have you any suggestions?'

The man nods, never looking at her face, voice formal and polite. 'Madam, we have today taken delivery of fresh mangos from Marerey, on the Webi Jubba. I can prepare a most excellent mango daiquiri.'

'That sounds lovely,' she says, 'but half the rum and vodka, please. I'm tired and the alcohol will go straight to my head.'

'As you wish, madam.'

'Aren't you drinking?' she asks her host.

'No, I am Muslim.' He pronounces the word *Moos-lem.* 'I do not drink alcohol. Ghedi will prepare a mixture of fruit juices that I find refreshing.'

The servant nods and withdraws. Marika is dismayed to find herself relaxing when there is no time for such luxuries. Dalmar Asad, while cruel and unscrupulous, is a charming companion, his deep voice and general presence somewhat intoxicating.

As they settle back at the table Ghedi brings the drinks, along with a plate of tiny red chilli peppers dusted with coarse salt, and fried in olive oil. Marika raises her cocktail glass, hesitating at the last moment. There are many substances that might have been added to the drink. Rohypnol and GHB spring to mind. Dalmar Asad appears to notice her hesitation, raising one long forefinger like a barrister about to introduce a point of fact. 'There is nothing in that drink but clean, fresh ingredients. You have my word on that. If I am to seduce a woman I will do so on my merits rather than with a chemical.'

Marika shudders. *Seduce her?* The idea is ludicrous. She lifts the glass and takes a sip. The taste is mango rich, reminding her of Queensland summer holidays, when the Kensington Prides hang heavy and orange-yellow from among the broad green leaves, the air sweet with their scent. Having eaten little for so long, however, the alcohol has an immediate effect, clearing her head to the purity of crystal.

Lifting one smaller chilli between thumb and forefinger she takes a cautious nibble at one end. The heat is immediate, but the piquant mingling of salt and garlic arouses the senses. A close inspection reveals that the pepper has been split and the seeds removed. She works her way through the morsel then washes much of the heat away with her drink. 'Don't you get bored?' She asks the question to fill the silence, yet she is curious. She waves a hand at the bar. 'Do you sit here by yourself every night?'

'I drink my juice, then eat a fine meal. As I have said, I come from a poor background, poorer than you can imagine, and I cannot express how much pleasure I draw from my home. I look at the fine timbers and remember how my father and I gathered sticks into bundles and carried them mile after mile for a few coins. I see the marble and think of the stones richer boys would throw at me as I laboured.'

'Sounds hard.'

'Indeed, yes. Shall we go through for dinner now?'

'I'd like that, thank you.'

It seems prudent to let him take her arm and lead her through to an adjoining room. While the centrepiece of the bar was the fish tank, here it is indoor plants, with lush foliage that freshens the air and gives the area the impression of being unenclosed.

'You have surprised me again,' Marika says, 'this is amazing.'

'I'm glad you think so.'

The central table is large enough to seat a party of at least twenty, but Dalmar Asad leads her past that massive timber slab, so close to plants bursting from their pots that she has to turn sideways to avoid the fronds.

'Tiger palms,' he explains, 'native to New Caledonia. Wonderful tolerance to air conditioning.'

They sit at a table against the window that might have been set in a clearing of some tropical jungle. Ghedi appears with a magician's timing and pulls Marika's chair back for her.

'Thank you.'

'Champagne, madam?'

'Why not?'

The servant returns with a bottle of Dom Perignon, peeling the foil from around the cork. Marika recognises the famous name and clutches one hand to her chest, eyes on her host. 'No, please, don't open that on my account. You don't even drink. I feel terrible.'

'Oh but I insist. It is very important to me that you have — how shall I say — the time of your life.' Dalmar Asad's face is as impassive as the granite face of a mountain, but his eyes are alive, twinkling darkly.

'Really?'

'Really. Drink and enjoy.'

Marika watches Ghedi pour the effervescent liquid and smiles. 'I've never tasted this stuff, so it's all new to me.'

'Why would you go through life with second best when

you can have the ultimate in everything?'

Because like most people in the world, I can't afford it, Marika wants to say, but instead she takes a sip from the glass, the bubbles tickling her nose, almost afraid to swallow the liquid. At first she thinks she might be disappointed, but the aftertaste is as fresh as the bubbles in her nose. She realises then that this is not just a drink, but an experience.

A moment later, however, her hand freezes on the glass stem, and she can feel herself stare out into space.

'What is wrong?' Dalmar Asad asks. 'Is the Champagne not to your taste?'

'No, it's lovely, of course. I just feel so guilty. I'm supposed to be working. Instead I'm sitting here drinking Dom bloody Perignon like a princess ...' She wants to express her disgust at how she is being indulged while lines of starving men, women and children trudge the roads into a drought-ravaged and bare interior. Feels guilty because the price of one stinking bottle of French Champagne would feed a hundred of those refugees for a week ...

'Kill two birds with one stone. Let us have dinner, and when it is over we will talk of your work. As you have seen, I am a powerful man. I can help you.'

Marika says nothing, but is surprised to see Ghedi walk across carrying two dishes. The experience has been so much like that of a restaurant she feels she should have ordered first.

Dalmar Asad hastens to explain: 'I hope you don't mind. I took the liberty of discussing the menu with my chef earlier — it makes things much easier for him to have prior warning.'

'I don't mind at all. Smells delicious, in fact.' The plate Ghedi places on the table contains a deliciously aromatic concoction, tinged with saffron; reminiscent of desert mountains and dust and a warm Arabian Sea.

'The meat is camel — halal, of course. You will enjoy it.'

The identification of the animal troubles Marika little — she has eaten kangaroo mince in her bolognaise since birth and her Special Forces training included field survival courses, eating everything from lizard meat to stringy desert birds.

The taste is sensational — so many individual flavours seeming to stand alone, then blend into something far greater than the parts. For two weeks she has suffered catered food — curries and rice; mass produced and bland.

'This is great,' she says, waving her fork, 'it really is.'

'I'm glad you like it.'

The main meal is a seafood feast — the centrepiece a spiny crayfish, cooked to deep orange and smelling of the sea. The tail has been cracked and the meat removed, cooked in a mornay sauce then replaced. On each side of the crayfish lie tiger prawns and spanner crabs with spindly legs and broad carapaces. The oysters are as large as Marika's cupped hands, and painted with a tangy sauce. Beside them, hairy-shelled mussels sit back to back.

'I hope you like seafood?'

'I'm an Australian, mate. I would have been raised on the stuff if it wasn't so bloody expensive. Do you mind if I use my fingers?'

'That, as they say, is the way to do it.'

Attacking the array of seafood is a task she approaches with tenacity, twisting a leg off the spanner crab, snapping the brittle cylinder to reveal a tube of white meat inside. She sucks it out, eyes half closed, and washes it down with a sip of Champagne. The oysters she scoops out of their shells with a splade.

Dalmar Asad also eats with appetite, yet more thoroughly than Marika has ever seen — opening the crab and wiping the body meat in the entrails, devouring every scrap of edible matter from inside.

'You know,' Marika observes, 'I've never seen anyone eat seafood so *completely*.'

'It's amazing how a childhood of want makes one abhor waste.'

'That's very commendable.'

Marika cannot remember ever feeling satiated from a meal of such quality. Yet by the time the crustaceans are mere piles of hollow, cracked carapace, and the mollusc shells bare of all but the toughest portions, her belly has that uncomfortable fullness born of a period of abstention then indulgence. Dalmar Asad lifts the bottle and refills her glass.

'I hope you've left room for dessert, my dear.'

Marika's eyes widen, then crinkle in amused thought. 'I guess I'll find space somewhere.' She lifts the nut cracker she has been using on the crabs' nippers, squeezes the arms together, then lays it on the plate.

Dessert is a rich mousse topped with flaked chocolate that has Marika's senses stirring. If there is any food in the world that she might consider herself a connoisseur of, it is chocolate. This is the real thing, dark and rich, melt-in-the-mouth stuff. Yet guilt and revulsion swells inside her like a tumour — with so little time remaining she has somehow been duped into indulging herself all evening. There are questions she has not even begun to ask. Madoowbe's whereabouts, for a start. Traitor or not, he didn't deserve to get beaten into a pulp and dumped.

'I shouldn't be enjoying this,' she says.

'No? As I have said, together you and I can achieve what you came here to do, quickly, and without fuss. In fact, I feel confident that I already know why you are here in my country.'

Marika plants one elbow on the table, then her chin on her knuckles. 'Oh yes?'

'If we accept that you are working for the multinational security forces at Rabi al-Salah, then it follows that you seek to help resolve the situation that has developed there. The Somali humanitarian turned militant, Ali Khalid Abukar, is a loner, but we know that he has a wife. She is of a desert tribe. That is why you came to this area — to find her. To see what she knows and if she can help. Perhaps you hope she might be used to coerce her husband. Am I correct?'

Marika is intrigued; this man has a network that must span a large chunk of Somalia. She would be a fool to spurn his help. 'Let's just say, for a moment, that you are right. What can you do for me?'

'If I give the order, a thousand men will go out to the villages of my tribal lands. We will find her, I promise you. When she is located we will either bring her to you, or you may accompany us to her.'

'That is a generous offer, but I can't help wondering what you will get out of it.'

'Several things. One is that I gain a bargaining chip with your masters, and their good regard. Let me tell you that soon I will make a play for all of this area of Puntland and will need the support of the United Nations to do so.'

'An Islamic state?'

'No, no, dear girl. I am a good Muslim, but to me politics and religion are separate entities. My rule would be secular. There are times, I admit, when it suits my purposes to work with al-Shabaab, or Hizb al-Islam, or even, once or twice, the Almohad, but these people are fanatical and suicidal. I am neither of those things. I want the support of the West to bring stability to this region, and beyond. I am an ambitious man.'

Marika considers the reasoning. It makes sense, yet she still cannot quite fathom his enthusiasm. 'What else?'

Dalmar Asad moves his hand to her upper arm, curling around her bicep. Black and white on white. 'You, my dear girl. One night together. One night of passion in return for my help.'

Marika's face screws up in confusion. Surely this man, master of all he surveys, would not initiate such an important cooperative effort in order to secure a sexual partner. 'You're kidding me?'

'Not at all. I am a man of voracious appetites, as you have seen. That extends to the sexual also. I find you very attractive indeed, and … I have never made love to a woman from your part of the world. Let's say that I am sensually curious.'

Marika looks back at the strongly featured face, with its powerful jawline and broad nose. The atmosphere becomes charged. 'You said before that you like to seduce a woman on your merits.'

'True, yet I sense that you will be a, er, tough nut to crack in the limited time that is available to me. Do I have your agreement?'

'When we find Sufia and our bargain is fulfilled you will allow me to call in an aircraft and take her out without hindrance?'

'Of course, provided I get the credit for locating her.'

'Then I don't see that I have any choice.' She looks down at the shape of her breasts through the kikoi, accentuated by the tight wrap of the material. 'I suppose you want your "payment" in advance.'

Dalmar Asad's face softens. 'Not at all. I am a man of honour and you have made me very pleased. I will find this Sufia first, and then I will take my prize — I am skilled in the art of love, I can assure you.' He points down at his lap. 'You will also find that my unusual colouring extends to all parts of my body. When I was a child my brothers had a name for my male appendage because of its pigmentation and unusual size.'

Marika bristles. 'Listen. I appreciate the dinner, and the wine, and I'm desperate enough to accept your so-called deal. But I will not sit here and talk about your donger, multicoloured or otherwise.'

Dalmar Asad's eyes barely flicker, yet she can see that her words have stung him. Already rising, he pauses to speak. 'I now have some work to do. Ghedi will take you to your room while I get things underway. Perhaps we can meet at the pool in thirty minutes? I habitually swim after supper.'

Marika watches him go, feeling relief, guilt, and fear in equal measure. Ghedi pads across and waits while she gets up, and follows him back up to her room. There she changes into modest one-piece bathers, again using the toilet cubicle.

After a moment of sitting on the bed, running the events of the previous hour through her head, she opens the glass doors and walks out onto a spacious balcony. The swimming pool below is lit deep under the water, and so clear that it glows iridescent blue. This area is lined with banana chairs and tables with umbrellas. Exotic palms and ferns grow from pots and garden beds.

Again her anger flares at how, in a land ravaged by drought, this man has the audacity to fill a swimming pool when others die of thirst. How much water must it take to keep it full in an area where evaporation far exceeds rainfall?

Oblivious to the unfairness of his lifestyle, Dalmar Asad strokes backwards and forwards along the length of the pool, in an economical freestyle. One mottled, muscled arm, then the other rises from the water to propel him onward, breathing every third stroke and using a four-beat flutter kick as good as any up-and-comer on the Bondi squad team. Marika stares at the unusual colouring on his back and arms, then, making a decision, descends the steps from the balcony to the pool. There, on the softly lit verge she removes the kikoi now looped around her waist and walks to the water's edge, watching him through another half-dozen laps. Finally, he stops at the shallow end and leans on the edge, turning to look at her.

'I'm glad you decided to join me.'

Marika nods back at him, then lifts her arms and dives in, shimmying her hips to keep her body driving underwater. She surfaces near the other side of the pool, then turns, completing half a lap in a lazy breaststroke then striking out for the other end. Her desire to swim is unclear to her — perhaps to show Dalmar Asad that she too is a strong swimmer, or just for the sheer pleasure of feeling her arms and legs work in a way they have not for many days.

Four laps later she changes to butterfly, enjoying the warmth in her arms and shoulders as she charges up and down at a competitive speed, finally stopping and standing in waist-deep water alongside her host.

'That is impressive,' he says. 'Not many people can swim the butterfly.'

'Practice makes perfect. I had a bit of talent so they pushed me. Got to state level and when I realised that I'd never make the Olympics, I quit and got interested in other things. I still swim for fitness, though.'

'It shows.'

Marika looks around. 'Not bad for a private pool.'

Dalmar Asad grins, his teeth white in the eerie glow of the lights and water. 'I like that expression. *Not bad*. You Australians are like us. We have a saying in our country, *diep maleh*. It means "no problem". A bit like your "no worries".'

He takes a breath and disappears under the water, surfacing again at the other end, before returning in the same manner. When he stands again he is much closer, and Marika sees his chest and upper arms revealed for the first time. He has one of the most highly developed musculatures she has ever seen, ballooning biceps and flat pads of muscle across the expanse of his chest, tapering to a narrow belly — a boxer's physique. The colouring on his torso is startling — a stripe of livid white across his sternum and smaller patches lower down. She has always been attracted to physical power, and finds it hard not to stare. 'You are an exceptionally fit man,' she says at last.

'Yes, physical fitness is a mania for me. I will show you the gymnasium later, if you are interested.' He runs a hand over his short hair, water slicking out as it might from a water rat. 'I believe that a man's physical state is aligned with that of his mind, and I intend to keep both as finely tuned as possible. I believe that a man is born to be a man in all ways.'

'Mmm, interesting. So how come there is no Mrs Dalmar Asad? You are attractive. Rich. Intelligent. Powerful. Where are the women in your life?'

'There are women, yes, but it is very difficult, in Somalia, to find a female who is my equal. Few have had more than a basic education. Most who have, go overseas. Sexual partners I can find, but to be honest, there has been little satisfaction for me in recent times.'

Marika swims a lazy lap, breaststroke, then resurfaces beside him. 'You are very frank.'

'Yes, and perhaps you might return the favour. What about you? Are there men in your life?'

'No one special at the moment, but yes, there are men.' Smart, articulate men, often in almost as excellent physical condition as the one who stands before her. 'I am no virgin, if that is what you are asking.'

'Have you ever been in love?'

'I can only answer that by saying, I think so. Is that enough?'

'Of course. That is enough.'

Marika wonders if he will advance on her, take her in his arms — try to pre-empt the agreement that stands between them. Instead he places both hands on the concrete sill of the pool and eases himself from the water — polished, chiselled torso shining like wet ebony. 'Tomorrow will be a big day for us,' he says. 'I will retire now, and wake you if there is any need. We will find this Sufia by morning, you can be assured of that.'

'I hope you are right,' Marika says, watching him stand and dry himself off with brisk strokes of the towel. Then, with a strange, knowing twist to his lips, he turns and walks down the path and back into the building.

THE FOURTH DAY

God said, Let there be lights in the expanse of the sky to separate the day from the night, and let them serve as signs to mark seasons and days and years. And it was so. God made two lights — the greater light to govern the day and the lesser light to govern the night. He also made the stars. God set them in the expanse of the sky to give light on the earth, to govern the day and the night, and to separate light from darkness.

The human species, however, creates artificial lights that run on electricity, the generation of which requires the burning of coal and gas. More carbon enters the air, hundreds of millions of tonnes until the heat of the earth cannot escape. Because there is money to be made, power companies will not stop the burning, and the world grows hotter.

Ice melts, waters rise, and still the carbon is pumped from the exhaust pipes and smokestacks of the world. Dirty industries spend millions lobbying and bankrolling political parties so they can keep doing what they have always done — making money for shareholders by poisoning the earth.

And there was evening, and there was morning. The fourth day.

Day 4, 04:45

In the suburb of Everton Hills, Brisbane, twenty-three-year-old Adam McDonald arrives home at his flat from a night of clubbing with friends. He flicks a switch: electrons bump each other along a copper wire; filaments at either end of a glass tube excite the mercury vapour present inside, producing a fluorescent effect from the phosphor-coated glass. Night becomes day.

One hundred and eighty kilometres northwest of the city, at Tarong Power Station, coal tumbles along a massive conveyor from the open pit scar of Kunioon Mine. The black fuel empties into fire pits that heat four boilers, each as big as a mid-sized office building. Superheated steam from the boilers is fed through pipes, turning giant turbines, and this energy spins the generators. Despite electrostatic precipitators and bag filter particulate control, Tarong produces nine-point-eight million tonnes of greenhouse gases each year, as much as two million petrol-powered passenger cars. There are twenty-four comparably sized coal-fired power stations in Australia alone. Together they produce one-third of that country's carbon emissions.

Adam McDonald turns on the oven to heat a packaged dinner, flicks on the television, and plugs his phone into the charger. That afternoon he will join a march down Roma Street to protest the government's inadequate response to climate change.

When he sleeps, he dreams of a better world for his unborn children.

* * *

Faruq Nabighah has few rituals apart from work. One is to observe the five daily prayers, beginning with the Salat-ul-fajr early in the morning and concluding with the Salat-ul-'isha in the night. Today, even though he arrived home at 1:00 am, having not slept for thirty-two hours, he wakes at 4:45 am, showers, dresses, kisses his sleeping children on the forehead, and walks outside to the practical little Renault he drives to work.

First stop is the magnificent Jumeirah Mosque, set just back from the beach with its pale yellow stone sides, parallel towers and central dome. This is Faruq's favourite time of day, the call to prayer echoing in his ears, the air cooler and invigorating.

The Salat-ul-fajr completed, he drives to the Hassan al-Bacha cafe for breakfast. Most of the faces at the tables are nodding acquaintances. Faruq has no interest in talking, taking his seat while a waiter hurries over. Smoke from a stub of bakhoor in an etched copper burner wafts up his nose and he moves it further away across the table.

'Peace be upon you, Faruq,' says the waiter. 'Will you have your usual?'

'Yes, thank you, Nu'aim.'

Placing his Samsung tablet on the table, swiping a finger across the screen to power it up, Faruq watches the latest edition of the *al-Bayan* daily newspaper load and display across the screen. The animated main picture frame alternates from Rabi al-Salah to images of other trouble spots across the globe.

Before he has read to the bottom of the front page update on the Rabi al-Salah debacle, he has a mug of cardamom and clove scented Arabic coffee within reach and a plate of flat bread with labaneh. He works his way through the newspaper, digesting everything, even the classifieds, birth and death announcements, paying close attention to the government tender and contract sections at the back. Having done so, he wipes the last smear of sour yoghurt from his plate, drains his coffee to the gritty last, and rises.

He pays the tab, and walks back through the tables and outside, turning towards his car, parked halfway down the block. His mind is already on the job, assessing metres per hour, and how to deal with the large rock 'floaters' known to be in the area. Opening his door he gets in and slips the key into the ignition. Before he can turn the key he feels the hard steel of a gun barrel against his neck.

Air, sharply drawn, hisses through his throat as he turns to look into a dark and bearded face. A wiry arm, snaked with veins, holds the gun steady, and the eyes are dark and unblinking.

'Who are you?' Faruq croaks.

'Never mind. Start the engine, then drive. I will direct.'

'You want money? I have five hundred dirhams in my wallet, more perhaps. It is yours. Just let me go to work.'

'Soon, brother. But first, start your engine and drive. This will not take long, but if you do not do as I say, I will leave your corpse on the side of the road.'

Faruq's lips tighten as he turns the key, releases the handbrake and directs the Renault out into the awakening traffic of al-Wasl Road. 'Which way now?'

'Just drive, I will tell you when to turn.'

Faruq nods, deciding that he should speak as little as possible, lessening the chance of offending this man.

They are past the Iranian Hospital before the man with the gun speaks again.

'Turn right here.'

Faruq does as he is told, followed by another series of rapid turns into a district of wall-to-wall residential high-rise, many with air-conditioning units on the rooftops, gardens on some of the more modern complexes. Now he begins to worry. What if there are more of these gunmen at their destination? What if he is about to be killed? Surely this has something to do with the tunnel.

They enter narrow streets of low-rise slums in the suburb of al-Satwa. Laundry hangs from building fronts, and men sit listlessly in pairs outside the houses.

'Pull up here,' the gunman directs. 'And get out of the car.'

Faruq thinks of running, but two men appear out of nowhere, both bearded like the other. One slams him face down against the car and frisks him. The original gunman appears, tucking a dull black revolver into his waistband, exchanging a few quick, congratulatory words with his comrades. They walk through a narrow space between adobe walls and into a courtyard filthy with old rubbish. The smell of shisha smoke and decay fills his nostrils. They move through a door and into the interior. Faruq looks in all directions like a captured animal, seeking assurance that he is not about to get a bullet in the head.

The room they enter is dominated by a stained wooden table, an open hearth beside it. Benches run along one side. Dried herbs occupy an unfired clay vase, their fragrance long ago exhausted.

Another man squats beside the table, rising as they enter. Faruq's eyes are drawn to him, for he is of impressive physical bearing: narrow across the shoulders yet with eyes that mesmerise. Darker skinned than the others; blacker than any Arab. Something about him makes Faruq want to fall to his knees in obeisance.

'Faruq Nabighah,' the man says, taking both his hands. 'Beloved of the Prophet, peace be upon you.' He pauses. 'You are a devout and godly man. Is that not true?'

'It is true.' Now Faruq understands: this is an imam, a scholar priest — the signs are unmistakeable. He falls to his knees, overcome by the man's aura, the overwhelming presence.

'Rise, my brother. Sit with me.'

Faruq looks around him. The three armed men remain, leaning back against the wall. Is this some kind of test? He takes a chair and sits, looking at the dark face with its compelling eyes.

'My name is Saif al-Din,' the man says, 'and I would like to talk with you.'

'It will be an honour,' Faruq replies. The other man's name means 'Sword of the Prophet', a name that resonates deep in the bones of his soul.

Those hypnotic eyes settle on his. 'Do you believe that there is no God but Allah, and that Mohammed is His Messenger?'

'Of course. I so believe.'

'Do you practise Zakat? Do you set aside a portion of your earnings for the poor and needy in order to eliminate inequality among people of the one true religion?'

Faruq coughs, wondering if such questions might be asked at the bridge to Jannah. He is ready, and proud to have done the right thing for so long. 'Each week, sayyid, two hundred and fifty dirhams are transferred from my account to the Muslim Hands aid organisation.'

The man nods. 'And during Ramadan, do you observe the sawm?'

'Yes, and I break my fast with a date, just as Mohammed did himself.'

'What about the Hajj? Have you performed this most sacred of duties?'

Faruq's chest, already proud, swells further. 'Yes, sayyid, I have journeyed to Maccah, I have worn the Ihram, and walked seven times around the Kaaba. I have stoned the devil with my own two hands.'

'You observe Salat?'

'Always, sayyid.' Faruq holds his head high, displaying the singda in the middle of his forehead. The callus proves his devotion, caused by a lifetime of observing the five daily prayers, his head touching the earth each time.

'You are a good Muslim, Faruq.'

'Yes, I believe I am.'

The black man changes, seeming to rise in the seat, his eyes burning with fire. 'Then why,' he shouts, 'have you chosen to help the kufr, the Americans and their filthy pig allies, to dig towards Rabi al-Salah, where your brothers risk their lives to bring glory to God?'

Faruq swallows, wondering how they found out. It is just a job, he wants to say, but his lips make no sound.

'You are an affront to your religion. Your piety means nothing in the face of such an insult to your God and your people.'

Faruq's eyes widen. 'I am sorry, but ...'

'The Americans will always lie, and their lies are like honey. Let me draw your attention to the word of God: "Such companions will divert them from the path, yet make them believe that they are guided."'

Faruq's voice takes on a note of pleading, like a man arguing with his bank manager for a loan. 'I am familiar with that surah. I am devout, as I have told you.'

'Yes, you are devout, yet now you help the infidel against your own brothers for the shiny dollar — of which you already have a plentiful supply.' Saif al-Din's voice lowers. 'They will use you like a dog, and cast you aside when they have extracted the last puff of benefit from you.'

'I am sorry, I did not think ...'

'That's right, you did not think.' The black man opens a leather folder on the table. The first photograph shows a high-rise apartment building and the second, a woman and child entering a car on the street outside. Faruq feels his breath catch in his throat and a prickle of pure terror begin at the base of his spine and spread upwards.

'You know who those people are?'

'Yes, sayyid.'

'Who are they?'

'That is my wife, Hamidah, and my daughter, Akilah.'

'And the building?'

'It is my home.'

'Then you understand that there is great danger for them. That if you do not do what I tell you, I and my friends will visit that place where you live. I personally will fuck your girl and your hag of a wife until they regret every jewel and expensive dress they have earned from your whoring with the West. When I and then my brothers have punished them in the way of Ibn Tumart, I will cut their throats and leave their carcasses on their beds. Then you will be next, and your death will be slow. Do you understand?'

'Yes, but how? I cannot withdraw from the tunnel. The difficult work is done. They will carry on without me. There are others ...'

'No, you must continue to give the impression of complicity. This is what you must do ...'

Faruq listens, numbed, for perhaps five minutes, before muttering agreement. 'In the name of God, sayyid. I will do as you say.'

'We will be watching, my friend, trusting you to serve God and your people. This is your opportunity to bring glory to your name. You have been a good man, a devout man, all your life. You have obeyed God's law. Let me tell you that if you help the kufr, when the Day of Awakening comes, your devout life will be of no account. When you walk the narrow bridge over the fires of hell, you will fall, while your wife and children walk on to Paradise. Is that the end you have longed for?'

'No, sayyid.' Faruq is mumbling now, staring at the tabletop, sick at heart, not hearing the final threats ... *Do not even think of calling the police, or bringing them here. We will be gone, and if you do so, you and your loved ones will be dead before the echoes of your voice ...*

Marika rarely dreams, and even when she does so, the images and sounds drain from memory within a moment of waking, leaving fragments of emotions — regret, wistfulness — or just a lingering half sadness that stays with her through breakfast, and occasionally beyond.

During the night at that palatial desert home, however, her mind takes her on a rollicking journey that jolts her awake more than once, riding on wings of spicy desert air, or choking on a fog of imaginary dust. Wearing jasmine-scented robes she roams a world peopled with the familiar yet unfamiliar, roles reversed and images altered subtly. Shadowy shapes of refugees fleeing from a rising ocean, running headlong into desert, dust, and starvation.

Marika dreams of the world she knows and has become a part of, where impartial media is just a memory and the public digests bias with the daily news without awareness, seeking out the entertainment factor beyond all else; where self-serving politicians no longer care about the public good and the forward march of nations, nor even civilisation itself in the endless thirst for personal power at the expense of morals. A world where, for a politician, there is only one justification for action and that is votes. A world that fears the end of the age of fossil fuels, the drying up of oil, more than rising seas and the burning sun.

Finally, she dreams of the acacia hut. The pouring rain, the mud dissolving in runnels towards the river. The cries as the man and the woman encourage each other in their efforts to resist what becomes inevitable. At how just a few neighbours come to help, how most stay inside their own huts. At how only more hands will save it now, more hands …

The pounding on the door comes when it is still dark. Marika starts awake, ripped from her nocturnal wanderings. The sheets fall away from her chest as she sits up. She clutches at them as if for protection.

'Who is it?'

'Sabah wanaqsan, madam. It is Ghedi.' She recognises the voice, muffled by the door. 'Aaba wants you to attend him.'

'Now?'

'It is five thirty in the morning, madam, Aàba has been at his desk for some time.'

'Can I have a shower first?'

'Yes. I will inform Aàba.'

Marika steps from the bed, aware of a vague hangoverish feeling that leadens her limbs. Her mouth tastes sour. She showers and dresses, again using the toothbrush placed there for her. Finally, stepping out into the corridor, she almost collides with Ghedi, who, it seems, has been waiting for her.

Marika feels a touch of apprehension. The night before, Ghedi seemed, on the whole, subservient and disinterested. Now she notices a sardonic twist to his lips; a half-amused expression. She wonders if Dalmar Asad has told his servant about their deal. Or has the man been looking at the feed from the camera in her room? Watching her dress, watching her sleep. She shudders and follows him down the stairs, feeling revulsion for the largesse of the previous night, most of all for the bargain she has struck. In the cold light of morning it seems so childish, pointless — dirty. No, she decides, Dalmar Asad can have something else — money, kudos — but not her. *This little Aussie is not for sale*, she says to herself, repeating it several times like a mantra.

At the foot of the stairs, Ghedi does not lead her towards the bar and dining room but down a wide, carpeted corridor. Closed doors lead off at intervals, and they pass through a courtyard, a skylight two floors high illuminating the space. Here Ghedi pauses at a door and knocks, turning the handle without waiting for an invitation from inside.

The room's interior is bright yet disorganised, an oddity after the clinical tidiness of the rest of the house. The first thing Marika notices is books — and not all in neat ordered shelves, either, but stacked on chairs and on the floor. A desk the size of a billiards table dominates one end of the room, and on the wall behind it are maps pinned so closely together that they overlay each other. Even from a distance it is obvious that Dalmar Asad's interest in geography is not confined to Somalia, but includes Europe, and the Americas. This man, she decides, is one with wide interests — or ambitions.

His voice reverberates through the room, but it is not until she has penetrated well inside that she sees him — down a side alcove, next to a window that overlooks a desert landscape tinged with the coming dawn. He glances across, yet his face registers no emotion.

Even when he ends the call, walking towards her, still holding the slim cordless phone in one hand, his voice is brisk. 'Sabah wanaqsan, I trust you slept well.'

Marika returns the greeting. 'Yes, very, thank you.'

'I'm pleased.' Turning to a tray he pours a hot, aromatic liquid into a tea cup and passes it to her. 'Cha,' he explains. 'You will find it tasty, and while you drink I have some news for you.'

Marika takes a sip. 'Your men have found her already?'

'Yes and no. Sufia Haweeya is not here in the local area — nor even in her native village where I expected her to be.'

'No?'

'Come with me.' Dalmar Asad leads her back into the main part of the office, standing in front of a map. 'This is our location, here. You can see to the west of us a mountain range called the Hamman, deep in the Ogaden Desert, near our border with Ethiopia. It is a place of dust and sandstorms and dry wastelands, the hangout of shifta and outcasts — there is no law there, and even my own men will not enter the area unless in force. The woman you seek is hiding there, under the protection of a family group of nomads. That makes her, I am sad to say, rather inaccessible.'

Marika nods. 'Even so, I have to make the attempt — there isn't much time left.'

'That is already taken care of. I have prepared a ten-man patrol in three vehicles to move into the area and bring her out.'

'I will go with them.'

'There is no need. You may stay here as my guest, and my men will bring the woman back.'

Ghedi interrupts, bringing two bowls of milky porridge, and placing them on the table.

'Ugali,' Dalmar Asad explains. 'Maize meal with coconut milk. Very nutritious.'

Marika picks up her bowl and eats several spoonfuls. The gruel-like preparation is bland and starchy, but not unpleasant; a step up from the version she consumed in the prison. 'I insist on accompanying them. My presence might be crucial — I do not want her to come in under duress. Not unless it is necessary. Do you understand?'

'Of course I do. You will be well protected and quite safe. The shifta are like dogs — ready always to attack the unprotected and unwary, but will run to their pathetic hiding places when the victim turns to bite. They will not take on a well-protected patrol, not one with heavy machine guns. I would accompany the venture also but I

have already been away for several days, and I have much
to attend to.'

Marika shivers, wrapping her arms around her middle
as if to warm her body. The success of her mission now
rests in this man's hands. Looking down at the ground so
he cannot see her face, she wonders if, once again, she
has misplaced her trust.

Simon dreams of Isabella so often that at times he wakes
with the feeling that they are still together, and he has
to feel across the bed to be certain she isn't there. Other
times, these nocturnal visions turn to a darker side.

This is when his mind conjures the most terrifying
spectre he can imagine: *the other man*, naked and as male
as a bull, muscled torso straining against Isabella. He
dreams all the detail in the manner of the most graphic
pornography. The man has the face of terror: bearded, eyes
filled with hatred, eyes that have seen and orchestrated
violent death many times.

The image jolts him awake. At first he has the
unpleasant feeling of not knowing where he is, hearing the
dull thump of the diesels, conscious of the forward motion
of the boat, slicing into the back of a swell, stalling for a
moment, then racing as the energy of the wave carries her
along. Blinking, he sits up, and sees Ishmael at the end of
the bed, staring with an unusual, hazed expression, eyes
narrowed to slits.

The cabin has long been used as a storage room and
every available space is filled with boxes, ropes, fenders,
polystyrene buoys and even stacked books so that there is
no room for two to stand. Ishmael, for this reason, is half

out the door, half in. Simon's anger flares at the Yemeni seaman walking in without knocking.

'What are you doing in here?'

'Lubayd told me to wake you.'

'You could have knocked.'

'I am sorry.'

'Are we almost there?'

'Two hours, but my brother thought you might like to eat and be refreshed before our arrival.'

'Thank you.'

Simon sits on the edge of the bunk, reaching down to pull on crusty, dry socks, then his shoes. Standing, he is still so drowsy from sleep that he needs to clutch at the doorway as he leaves the cabin.

In the saloon Lubayd is at the dinette, busy with an archaic Toshiba laptop computer and open books. The helm is controlled by the autopilot, the wheel moving as if of its own accord. There is no sign of the old woman. The strange burnt smell Simon noted the previous day is stronger now, and he recognises it now — hashish smoke. The realisation explains Ishmael's eyes and behaviour.

'You slept well?' Lubayd asks.

Simon studies the older brother. There is no sign of drug use in his eyes or manner. 'Yes, thank you.'

'Forgive my books. I am studying a Bachelor of Economics degree by correspondence.'

'Most commendable.'

'King Saud University.' He pauses as if waiting for a comment, then, 'Ishmael will prepare your breakfast.'

'How far away are we?' Simon looks across at the plotter screen, seeing the first islands marked ahead, little more than outcrops in the sea.

'Not far. Soon we will have to reduce speed, for there are uncharted shoals here, and many other dangers. Would you like to shower? There is sufficient time and we have a full tank of fresh water.'

'I would appreciate that.'

'I also advise you not to land on Socotra in Western attire. You will be a curiosity there and draw much attention. I will give you suitable clothes — I have many spares. They are loose, so will fit you.'

Lubayd hurries below, returning with an armful of clothes that smell of naphthalene. Thirty minutes later, Simon looks in the mirror and cannot believe his own reflection — paler skinned than many Arabs yet, with his dark brows and hair, the shemagh on his head and a loose-fitting kandoura, he would not stand out in any Arab city.

In the saloon he finds that Lubayd has abandoned his studies and is huddled over the radar set with Ishmael. In his hand he holds a compact USB memory stick, fiddling with the cap.

'What is it?'

The older brother turns. 'We have received a distress call from a vessel near a stone outcrop called al-Kahf. You can see them on the radar.'

Standing between them now, Simon sees the blip on the screen, so close to the stronger return off the outcrop that the two are almost indistinguishable. The VHF radio speaker crackles into life, a desperate voice: 'Mayday, Mayday. Out of fuel and drifting towards rocks. Any vessel able to render assistance please acknowledge.'

'Ask her to identify herself.' Simon feels the thud of his heartbeat pulsing down into the deck under his feet.

Lubayd speaks into the microphone and a voice from the ether responds. The name of the vessel is clear in the stutter of rapid, frightened dialogue.

'The *Sa-baah*. That's her,' Simon shouts.

'What if it's a trap, a lure?'

'We have to take that chance. How far away is she?'

'Twenty-five nautical miles, but there is a head sea. One hour's steaming at fast cruise. These are dangerous waters. I will not risk my boat.'

Simon walks to the chart table, wrenches open the drawer and reaches for the gun he noticed there earlier. His hand grips the butt and drags it out, aiming the muzzle at Lubayd's head.

'The gun is not cocked,' the elder brother says, seemingly unafraid.

One of the many training courses Simon has had to attend over the years involved weapons that might be encountered in a hijack attempt. This particular handgun is familiar to him — the name he does not remember, but he recalls enough to grip the slide between his thumb and the knuckle of his first finger and pull it back, watching a brass cartridge slide into place. 'Thank you. It is cocked now. I am a desperate man. Change course and radio that you intend to render assistance. Hurry.'

The two brothers look at each other. Lubayd spreads his arms in supplication. 'This is not the way of a civilised man, Simon. You are making a mistake. Put the gun down.'

Simon glares back, saying nothing, but his forefinger tightens on the trigger.

'OK, OK, we will do it.' Lubayd disengages the autopilot and makes exaggerated movements of the wheel. 'We are changing course. Look at the chartplotter if you don't believe me.' He jabs a thumb at the screen.

Simon relaxes but does not lower the gun, merely allowing his elbow to drop down onto his chest to take the weight.

Lubayd goes on, 'All I was trying to say was that we are not set up to help when we get there. This is a pleasure boat.' He shrugs. 'What can we do?'

'There is no point me going to the main island when the ship I am looking for is foundering out here. Can you go faster?'

'Not against this sea, I am sorry.'

Simon walks closer to the helm where he has a good view of the plotter, the ship represented by a dark triangle, their course a trailing dotted line. The abrupt change in course shows as a clear dogleg. On the top left-hand corner of the screen is a series of pale circles, the rocky island in question marked in red. At the bottom of the screen the speed readout flickers around twenty-four knots.

Looking down at the gun, Simon feels embarrassed, wanting to explain. *Hey, I don't normally do this kind of thing, very sorry, it's just that there's these terrorists and they're holding my children, and I'm pretty sure they're on that boat ...*

Day 4, 11:00

The technicals line up in the yard, machine guns pointed skywards — Russian DShK 12.7mm, Marika decides. Serious firepower. The weapons look well maintained, with oiled rags wrapped around the breechblock and mere traces of rust where the original blue has worn through.

Waiting while the men load the trucks, she adjusts the fatigues that Dalmar Asad ordered to be issued from the stores. Most of the men, however, wear a conglomerate of clothes: part camo, part jeans and T-shirts.

One of Asad's men gives her a cardboard box that contains her handgun, and the CVCID. The screen is cracked through and nothing happens when she presses the power button. This is a real setback, and she glares up at Dalmar Asad, who shrugs, 'I am sorry, but my men are like children with electronic gadgets.'

Still scowling, wondering what she is going to do without communications, she unclips the magazine on the Glock, dropping it into her hands and checking that it still contains eight 9mm parabellum cartridges before sliding it back into the butt, surprised but pleased that Dalmar Asad hadn't ordered the gun to be unloaded before giving it back. Next she straps the holster on over her clothes and delves back into the box, removing a folded square of black cloth.

'Thank you,' she says, 'but what is this?'

'It is a hijab — head scarf. Some of the villages you will pass through are very traditional. You might cause offence if your head is exposed. Please put it on if my men advise it.'

Marika finds that the cloth fits into one of the cargo pockets of her camouflage trousers. 'Thank you,' she says, 'yet now I have one more favour to ask.'

'Yes?'

'I would like to speak to the man called Madoowbe. The one your men beat up and tortured.' No matter who or what he was, they came in together and she would have to account for him.

'I'm afraid that is not possible.'

Marika feels a chill. 'Why not?'

'Because he escaped from his cell during the night. The man must be as strong as a bull *and* a contortionist — he managed to bend a bar and squeeze through a space that I doubt *you* would get through. He will not get away so easily if we meet again. Come, the patrol is ready to leave. Please do not be afraid of my men — they will treat you well in every way. Under threat of death.'

Marika opens one of the rear doors, sliding across the ripped and worn upholstery of the bench seat. The remainder of the men clamber aboard. The air explodes with sound as the man on the heavy machine gun not two metres away fires a burst into the air. Brass cartridges clatter down into the vehicle tray and the earth below. The act is a mere punctuation yet, to Marika, it smacks of ill-discipline and waste. She turns to Dalmar Asad, who stands beside the vehicle, unperturbed. 'I'm surprised you let them waste ammunition like that.'

'Not at all. I provide meals, accommodation and qat. They, however, pay for their own cartridges. It is my way of preventing them from shooting things all day. My boys love to shoot their guns.'

A man walks from the office building towards the vehicles, carrying a Nam-style green pack in one hand and an assault rifle in the other. Marika recognises the fine moustache and lean frame, the memory of pain and fear raising the gooseflesh on her arms.

Dalmar Asad sees the direction of her eyes. 'Yes, Wanami will command the patrol. I am sure you will put your previous differences aside. He is a good man. I trust him more than most of the others.'

Marika takes a deep breath. *Good man? Previous differences? The bastard beat the shit out of me; connected a truck battery to my nose.*

Captain Wanami, at a soft order from Dalmar Asad, pauses beside them, listening while the warlord issues a stern-sounding stream of Somali.

'I just warned him that you are important to me,' Asad says, 'that he will answer for your life, with his own.'

Wanami answers with a nod, but his eyes never leave Marika's. The moment is soon over, and she watches him move to the lead technical, open the door and slide into the passenger seat. Wheels spin, gravel flies and her head snaps back against the seat as they accelerate out the driveway.

Simon rues that wasted hour, staring out through the armoured glass screen at the bows, shining stainless steel windlass and a hank of chain draped across it, the swells marching across in soldierly lines. Now and then another desperate plea from the stricken ship crackles out from the VHF. Twice they steam past tiny islands — lonely fragmented sentinels with white smudges of spray at the base.

The old woman appears from below, moving to the galley where she prepares a half-slice of flat bread smeared with cream-coloured yoghurt from a plastic tub. If she notices the gun in Simon's hand she gives no sign, moving to her usual place at the dinette table.

'How far now?' Simon asks.

Lubayd fiddles with the set before announcing, 'Four nautical miles — ten minutes at this speed.' His eyes drop to the gun. 'Put it away, please. You have my word that I will continue on this course.'

Simon lowers the barrel but makes no attempt to part with the weapon. 'Sorry, but I think I'll just hang onto it. Makes me feel better.'

Lubayd shrugs, as if he does not care, and turns back to the helm.

Across the world, regardless of time zone, latitude, longitude, and electoral fortitude, governments meet and deliberate, discussing the terrorists' demands. Many of the necessary actions have been on the drawing board for some time, lacking only determination and electoral consensus. Some politicians privately see the Rabi al-Salah ultimatums as an opportunity to fast track legislation that might have taken years.

The debilitating effects of climate change have coincided with a critical point in the downward spiral of the major Western economies. Every responsible leader knows that the borrowing can't continue. That expenses must be reined in. Yet austerity budgets lead to public outrage, rioting, and electoral oblivion. Greece, a country technically in default of its repayment obligations as early as 2011, suffers general strikes, and violent confrontations on a scale not seen there for more than half a century.

Finance Minister Evangelos Venizolos attempts to salvage some national pride by accusing the EU of making his country a scapegoat for the crisis, when other states like Italy, Spain, Ireland and Portugal are also spiralling towards bankruptcy. Despite a last-ditch referendum, the country cannot fight what Albert Einstein once described as the most powerful force in the universe — compound interest.

Responsible world leaders understand that carbon emissions must be stopped, and fast, if only to prevent the most expensive natural disaster in history. Plant nurseries gear up to output fifty billion new trees, a production run to rival any wartime munitions program. The late Professor Wangari Maathai's Green Belt movement mobilises a generation of Kenyan women into tree planters. The Great Green Wall project on the same continent works towards a fifteen-kilometre wide corridor of trees, eight thousand kilometres long, across the southern Sahara from Senegal to Djibouti.

Alternative methods of reducing carbon, including blasting sulphates into the atmosphere to reflect sunlight, stashing concentrated CO_2 underground and pumping it into outer space all have their advocates and adversaries. None offer hope of more than token reductions.

Responding to the Rabi al-Salah crisis, the United States Congress meets in an all-night, record session that sees tempers flare and insults thrown. A dawn statement from the Vice President goes live to air.

'I have been instructed by Congress to inform the people of America that, while condemning the methods of the terrorists at Rabi al-Salah, we will begin an assessment of the logistics and ramifications of withdrawing all US troops from the locations named in the militants' demands. As a sign of good faith we will evacuate four major bases in the region ...'

In Australia, the Government threatens a double-dissolution election when the Opposition at first refuse to support a full withdrawal of troops. In the end, however, three key independent MPs and the Greens side with the Government, giving them the numbers.

Pakistan, fighting to control an internal conflict that borders on civil war, issues a statement that all demands will be complied with.

The Israeli Knesset sees some of its most emotional and passionate speeches in living memory. The Yesha Council and Almagor threaten to take matters into their own hands. The ruling Kadima party attempts to broker a compromise position between these parties and the political left — the People's Voice and the Peace Camp. The result? Stand off.

The most populous Muslim country in the world, Indonesia, offers tentative support to the Rabi al-Salah terrorists, daring to issue a statement along these lines, surmising that the United States and her allies are too preoccupied to cause a diplomatic fuss. This lead is followed by Bangladesh, Northern Sudan, Algeria, Malaysia, Niger, Senegal, Guinea, and Sierra Leone. The Sunni majority Maldives, a country that will soon lose half its land area to a rising Indian Ocean, offers the 'freedom fighters of Rabi al-Salah' sanctuary should it become necessary.

The left-wing magazine *New Day*, a journal that has seen a phenomenal growth in circulation over its three years of existence, makes the case that the terrorist attack on Rabi al-Salah was made inevitable by the policies of the self-centred democracies of the West. That America and Europe have proved themselves to be the fat sows of humanity, lying in a bog-hole of their own filth, polluting the world until it is too late; responsible for bringing the terror of rising sea levels and unprecedented storms to the Third World. China's role in this disaster rates no mention.

The article argues that when a handful of men from the affected countries fight back in the only way they can, they should not be labelled terrorists: *Western civilisation is putrescent. There must be something new, something better. A way to embrace the natural world. Something that will let us exist on this planet for millions of years, not just a few centuries as technological beings. The long-term survival of our species is at risk and no price can be too great to ensure the common good. Only a plague species does not have the intelligence to know that its very fecundity threatens its survival. Our never-ceasing hunger — for food, for possessions, for money, for luxury — has brought us to the brink.*

The so-called developed nations have not brought peace, but war and weapons on a scale never imagined. They have armed the majority world, in particular the bottom billion — the most disadvantaged people on earth. They have bombed and maimed civilians as they jostle for influence. They have forced the dispossessed to use distasteful methods of war, for they are powerless without them. They have driven the world to a physical crisis from which it may never recover. Let them learn, let them accept that there must be change; dramatic social and economic change. Let them act, at last. Now that it is all but too late.

The article, attributed to a freelance journalist attached to *The Guardian*, Yanis Moussa, runs for an unprecedented fifteen pages, and ends with a cartoon of Uncle Sam kneeling down for beheading by a stylised Islamic warrior and his scimitar.

Media organisations continue their blanket coverage of the situation, with endless opinions from experts in any field related to the drama. Few outlets find time to report a significant weather event in the Indian Ocean, forming south of the Bay of Bengal and threatening the Andaman Islands. India's meteorological department tags the developing storm as Tropical Cyclone Zahir, yet it remains of local interest only.

Day 4, 13:00

Ali Khalid Abukar holds his hand to his eyes, staggering with vertigo. Fatigue is a black wall that looms from all sides. In the last seventy hours he has slept for just an instant at a time, leaning or sitting, allowing the blackness to settle into his psyche before he fights it away.

The headaches began a day earlier, an internal hammer that throbs with each heartbeat — one of the side effects of the drug Modafinil. Ali, like the others, carries a package of capsules, printed in Indian script with the trade name Modalert.

Unlike more archaic stimulants — amphetamines such as Benzedrine — Modafinil, apparently, has few side effects with normal use. The user, however, requires increasing doses to stay alert, and now headaches have come, along with an anxiousness that lurks under the surface, never quite morphing into real panic. He descends into a kind of half sleep. A trance. Dreaming of the Islamic State that he has created in his mind, the salafist society like that of Mohammed's Medina, and of the twelfth century al-Muwahhidun.

There is food for all; just laws; work for every adult man. For women too there is a fulfilling society behind the closed doors of the home. When he pictures the woman of that home it is Sufia. The pain of their separation is a deep thrust, yet he allows her image to distract his thoughts for just a moment.

Twelve months earlier he travelled into the Shabeellaha Hoose region of southern Somalia, occupied by the Islamist group Shabaab al-Mujahedin, now infiltrated and strengthened by al-Muwahhidun and Hizb al-Islam. Despite their constant attacks on what they call 'apostate' forces in Mogadishu and beyond, there is a side to their struggle that demonstrates to Ali just what is possible under the Sharia.

At dusk one day beside a field near the coastal village of Baraawe, an imam explained to him the simplicity and beauty of the new order he had helped bring to the region. 'This,' he said, 'is the political system God ordained for His people. All men know the law, for it is explained in the Qur'an. Each knows his place. The children are respectful. The elderly have dignity.'

Yes, the women were hidden, seen in public swathed in niqab and abaya, but the imam explained that even these wraiths had a rich and interesting life behind closed doors, with visitors of their own sex and a sense of joy that they lived their lives in the way described by the Prophet, may peace be upon Him.

Ali closes his eyes and prays with all his heart.

The convoy follows a dusty track, vehicles skidding and sliding around corners, as if the act of driving fast relieves boredom for the drivers. The technical's roof provides welcome shade from the sun, but there is no air-conditioning, just the stifling desert air rushing in through open windows. Marika stares out at occasional small villages as the patrol stabs through, scattering people and livestock without regard for their safety. Now and then her eyes settle on the erect figure of Captain Wanami in the lead jeep, and she is glad she wasn't forced to travel in the same vehicle as him.

Listening to the conversation around her, Marika learns a few basic words of Somali by studying the gestures attached to a word. *Ha* means yes, often emphasised with a double: *ha, ha. Mia*, similarly used, means no. *Ghaba* means something along the lines of bitch, and *whas* appears to translate to 'fucking'. The latter is their favourite word, used often and with emphasis. Since the start of the journey they have called her the *whas ghaba*. The fucking bitch. The nickname gives her the first and only belly laugh of the trip.

On the outside, however, there is little to laugh about. Here Marika sees poverty more dire than any in her experience — men, women, and children with desperate, hungry eyes. Most live in dome shaped tukul huts made of acacia branches and thatch, or cast off iron sheets. Poor crops, drooping corn and wilted root vegetables stand in fields fenced with thorn to keep out goats that have long ago been eaten. There are cattle, but few in number, as skeletal as the villagers who protect them with guns. The starving beasts stand with mournful eyes, an oxpecker bird on a flank or bony shoulder.

Marika finds it strange how men and women alike sometimes hold hands while walking together. This affectation seems at odds with the guns. Men and boys down to the ages of nine or ten carry AK47 rifles in the same way as Australian males carry surfboards or cricket bats. Marika remembers reading somewhere that Somalia has sixty thousand armed boys, who have no trade but war, fending for themselves by force of arms, living and dying in a cycle of violence that seems unstoppable.

It is hard not to make comparisons with teenagers back home — their world of hairstyles, smartphones, iPods and iPads, desperate to obtain the most recent designer electronics before their peers, and where the natural world, life, and death appear through the interpretation of writers, editors, programmers, and news directors.

Many of these young people, aware of the basic injustice of society, even of their own relative affluence, joined the 'Occupy' protests that began with Wall Street then quickly spread to nine hundred cities world-wide. This was a grass roots reaction to injustice and inequality, and as such deserved respect, even applause. It also, in Marika's opinion, brought about a feeling of connectness between the youth of the world. A feeling that young people in Cairo have the same overall goals as those in Melbourne, or Beirut, or Paris, even if the circumstances are vastly different.

Some of the protesters, however, acted without understanding that they were part of the problem. That the smartphone in their jeans pocket or handbag, was, ultimately, purchased with the blood and sweat of the developing world, and with money borrowed from the future.

Braver individuals from the ceaseless stream of refugees beg as they go past, falling to their knees, displaying children with rib cages like tree branches, and sunken eyes and cheeks. The local villagers, however, are afraid of Dalmar Asad's men, hurrying away at the convoy's approach, taking to the shadows and tukul huts. Even those with weapons avoid aggressive stares or postures. In this world of violence, Marika reasons, there is always someone stronger to be afraid of.

They reach the first massive refugee camp, an informal collection of fifty thousand or more souls, most without shade or shelter. Charcoal and dung fires create a miasma that hangs over the dry valley. Near the roadway, men with AK47s operate a shop of sorts, rows of trestle tables loaded with bags of rice, cigarettes, tinned food. Plastic bottles of drinking water in one, five and twenty litre sizes sit beside the tables. The scarcity of customers suggests the exorbitance of the prices. As they pass, a tall woman, dressed in a lime green kikoi, one child at her hip and another clutching her leg, haggles over what appears to be a ring in her hand. The older child turns to look at the passing vehicles, head too big for the rack thin body, eyes like brown moons seeking out Marika, who wants to tell the driver to stop the car, to give the woman what she wants. To feed them all, for God's sake — though of course there is not enough, will never be enough.

The driver of the lead vehicle slows, and Captain Wanami stands, half out the door, half in. One of the armed men at the stall comes across and talks. Marika sees that they are dressed and armed in the same manner as her guards. These too must be Dalmar Asad's men, and she does not have to guess where the profits from this and many other such places flow — all to maintain one man in a palace while a million others starve.

The tall woman at the stall hands over her ring and takes a small cardboard box of foodstuffs and water in return. Marika clenches her fists. To take the last item of jewellery from a destitute woman in return for a meal or two infuriates her.

Again she compares this woman with those of her own suburb, many if not most preoccupied with tennis, gardens and the latest handicraft; raffia hats; decoupage; scrapbooking; stained-glass windows — beautifully made up faces; trying on outfits at Myer, preening in a mirror while a less fortunate woman, no less intelligent or capable, carries a twenty-litre water can five kilometres from a well.

Marika tries to rise, reaching across for the door handle, but the man next to her reacts, shouting, '*Mia. Mia.*' To emphasise his point, he slides a Tokarev pistol from his holster and holds it to her temple, continuing to do so until she settles back into the seat. The conversation at the front vehicle concludes and the technical surges forwards, past another kilometre of the massive camp, then a cemetery, thousands of crosses among the whistling thorn. Marika feels hollow. Empathetic yet helpless.

They pass an abandoned airstrip with a single derelict building and the hulking wreck of a Russian Antonov AN-70 transport plane lying skewed beside an overgrown runway. Even from the road Marika can see the three remaining propfans, and the holes small arms fire has drilled into the fuselage. A blackened gash near the tail wing gives a clue to the aircraft's demise.

Soon, she knows, she will have to ask them to stop so she can relieve the pressure of her full bladder. In the meantime she crosses her legs, closes her eyes and dreams of other times, other places.

Day 4, 14:00

Socotra. Dvipa Sukhadhara, the Island of Bliss in Sanskrit, officially part of Yemen but in actuality something more distant, more ancient, appearing first in recorded history as Dioskouridou, in *The Periplus of the Erythraean Sea*, a seafarers' guide written back when the stone at the entrance to Jesus' tomb was still warm from repeated rollings back and forth.

An archipelago of four major islands and innumerable rocky outcrops, the landscape is more akin to that of Jupiter's moons than of earth. Trees that weep blood, giant succulents, and bizarre flowers grow in the arid earth. Grosbeak birds and reptiles found nowhere else on earth roam arid mountains and plains. The unique fauna of Socotra has seen scientists tag it the Galapagos of the Indian Ocean.

The islanders were Nestorian Christians when Marco Polo dropped by, but their religion was mingled with bizarre magic rituals that dated back to the days of the Oldawan stone age culture. The Mahra sultans conquered the islands in the sixteenth century and brought the inhabitants into Islam.

To soar with the wings of an eagle over the islands is to swoop down stone cliff faces and over vegetation that looks like nothing else on earth. To visit Socotra is to understand that the world is not all known and familiar, that there are cubby holes of strangeness and mystery beyond the ordinary. A niche tourist industry in the first decade of this century ended with the capture and ransom of eighteen foreign nationals, eleven of whom were murdered before ransom money could be delivered. Since then the islands have slipped deeper into anarchy, a haven for pirates, extremists, and criminals.

The *Sa-baah*, when it comes into view, is a toy in the heavy seas pounding against red and guano-streaked cliffs, rising three or four hundred metres with the regularity of cut crystal from the turquoise sea. Not trusting his vision through the screen, Simon stands on the side deck, wind in his face, gripping the rail and staring. The vessel sports a single heavy stack, low to the water, waves breaking against the beam as she drifts out of control towards the rock. Simon has seen old tugs like her rusting away in ports all over England. The last coat of paint, a lusty red, has all but flaked away, victim of corrosion from within.

My girls, Simon says to himself, *my darling girls are in that death trap. What are they thinking? How are they feeling? Have they been fed? Allowed to wash?* There are darker questions he does not dare articulate. *Is there still breath in their lungs? Are they living still?* He ducks back inside. 'Have you raised them on the radio again?'

'Not yet, but I am trying.'

'Try harder, for God's sake.'

Unable to let the vessel out of his sight, as if he were keeping it off the rocks by sheer force of will, he stares out through the screen. A garbled stream of Farsi comes through the radio, and he turns. The frightened voice is as clear as if the speaker stood beside them: 'We have no power, and are drifting out of control. The rocks are just four hundred metres off the bow. Mayday. Mayday.'

Lubayd looks at Simon. 'I am sorry, but there is nothing we can do but ask them to abandon ship. We will then try to pick up what survivors we can. It is too rough to go alongside — too dangerous.'

Simon hesitates, aware of how difficult a rescue mission will be. 'Ask them if they can abandon ship safely.'

Lubayd does as he is asked, and a reply comes through, even more confused than before. The truth dawns on Simon. They have no lifeboats. No floatation devices. He grips Lubayd's arm. 'We have to take them in tow.'

'That is not possible. I am sorry, Simon, but we can do nothing. We do not have the power, nor even a tow cable.'

'The anchor chain, use that ... and you have done nothing but boast about the power of this vessel since I first climbed aboard.'

'How will we pass a line across?'

'You *must* have some cord we can use as a messenger rope. I will swim it across and then we'll use it to drag the chain.' He uses the gun as a pointer. 'You are a sea captain. You are obliged to render assistance. You have no choice.'

Ishmael crosses his arms. 'I say that we sail away. It is dangerous.'

Lubayd purses his lips. 'We will give it one try, out of respect to the rules of the sea. Just one. Insha'Allah, it will be enough.'

'Well for Christ's sake let's hurry then.' Simon looks down at the gun. 'I'm going to have to trust you.'

'Of course. You have my word that I will try once.'

Simon walks out onto the side deck and throws the gun underarm, like a bowling ball, out into the sea.

'Rope,' he calls, 'and hurry.'

Up close the cliffs tower over them like seaborne skyscrapers, raucous colonies of birds on the many faces — terns, petrels and gulls — some roosting, others leaving and arriving, wheeling and arguing. The ammonia smell of guano mingles with salt spray. The waves appear to sense the barrier ahead, gathering strength for the confrontation, rearing higher and curling.

The old tug wallows like an animal carcass. Even to Simon's lubberly eyes she is obviously taking water. Men scream for help from the deck as they steam closer.

Lubayd picks up the radio handset, and announces, 'We are attempting to swim a messenger line over, please have men standing by to haul.'

As Simon strips to his underwear, the *Jameela* turns in a wide arc, bows facing the seas, presenting her stern to the tug. Ishmael appears with a long coil of rope around his neck — ten or twelve millimetre white nylon cord. Simon takes one end, passing it twice around his bare waist. 'Just feed it out as I go,' he says, 'and that way we should avoid tangles.' Looking into the other man's eyes he sees malevolence, but puts it from his mind. *You cannot put a gun to a man's head and expect him to like you.*

This thought echoing in his mind, Simon climbs over the rail. The boat's twin propellers churn the sea to froth as Lubayd fights to keep the vessel straight. Gathering himself, coiling the muscles of his thighs and knees, Simon dives far out into the water.

The sensation is initially pleasant coolness on his skin, but as his head surfaces and he begins to strike forwards, that feeling disappears, replaced by a terrible fear that has him stroking in a mad panic for the tug, still fifty metres away. These waters are infamous for sharks. He pictures them in his mind, looming below, dark and hungry.

The rope tied to his waist catches for a moment and the shock jolts him, before it continues to stream away. Already the muscles of his arms and shoulders are tiring, and he swallows air with each stroke.

The tug looms up quickly — the strong current helping — but when he raises his head he sees that the island is now so close that breaking waves are a continuous thunder. Men on the side decks and cockpit mill around; arms reaching down like sea anemone tendrils to grab him as he surges along with the swell then drops down into the trough.

He makes contact with one outstretched hand, but loses grip at the last moment. Tries for another. A firm hold this time. Clambering aboard, half dragged, a dozen voices talk at once in three different tongues. Many of the crew are bare chested, brown skinned, and scarred. Some wear turbans, one a hooded thoub. Others sport wild hair matted from salt air and a paucity of bathing.

Standing there, chest heaving, leaning over to untie the line from his belly, he looks back towards the *Jameela*, Ishmael in the cockpit, chain in his hands.

'Haul,' Simon bellows. Naked backs and arms take the strain. With a wrap of cord around his hands he joins in, turning to see that the towering island is just a stone's throw away now, the tug surging with the waves, fragile as glass against the dangerous black rocks. The smell of shaded, drenched earth mingles with that of bird dung, kelp, and dead sea creatures.

Simon realises that they might have lost the battle already — the chain is impossibly heavy, even for a dozen hands. A swell picks up the vessel and drags her sideways, rope slipping, men falling all over each other. One jumps out into the foaming sea, and attempts to splash his way towards the rock.

'No,' Simon cries, seeing the man disappear beneath the surface, 'don't give up, for God's sake! Pull.'

The chain comes closer, heavier with every metre as the coil of rope on the rusted iron deck grows. When the first links appear, Simon loops a metre or two of chain over his shoulder and heaves; a wave hits the stern, drenching them, yet that pulse of power adding to his strength. He removes the chain from his shoulder and wraps the links in and around the massive port-side cleat.

'Chain secured,' he shouts across at Ishmael. 'Pull us off.'

Even over the surging ocean he hears the *Jameela*'s engines, then the metallic snick as the chain comes taut. The tension almost pulls the chain clear of the water, all but for the peaks of waves. Simon clutches for balance, the rocks so close now that he can identify each barnacle. Brown-yellow kelp strands wave like hands in the shallows.

The sea is too strong, and he watches as the *Jameela* is pulled sideways by the force of the waves. But for that tow, however, the tug would already be on the rocks, pounded into scrap metal by the surf. In the cockpit he sees Ishmael, at first staring back at them, then moving forwards and rummaging in a locker, returning to the bow with an axe. They are going to sever the tow, Simon realises — abandoning them, leaving them to certain disaster. Brute force is necessary to sever a chain under such enormous pressure as this one.

'No,' he screams, climbing to the gunwale and diving over the side, stroking overhand to reach the other boat.

Now, however, both the swell and surge are against him. His progress is slow, like walking up a steep slope of loose pebbles, every metre gained an exhausting struggle. Raising his head once, he sees Ishmael taking his stance at the bow, where the chain loops around the stainless steel cleat, the only place where he can strike without damaging the hull.

Swimming up-current, sobbing with effort, eyes stinging from the salt, Simon strikes something hard and unyielding and realises that it is the chain itself, rigid as an iron bar. Reaching out with both arms he uses it to drag his body towards the *Jameela*, close now, seeing the world through a lens of water and spray. Ishmael raises the axe, brings it down, the blade landing awkwardly and his face contorting in annoyance.

Simon feels his strength ebb away, but somehow his arms still thrash through the water. It is as if his physical being no longer matters, only the irrepressible will inside. Finally the boarding platform is close and he grips a rail, swinging himself aboard just as Ishmael's axe reaches the apex of its swing. Seeing Simon coming he alters the stroke at the last minute, aiming for him, killing rage on his face. A hashish-misted murderous rage fills his eyes.

Simon seizes the axe behind the iron head and pulls, sending Ishmael off balance. He throws the heavy implement overboard and takes hold of the other man's neck. Even as his thumbs push against the windpipe some small part of him cries, *What kind of man have I become?*

'No. Mercy, please,' Ishmael gasps. 'We must cut the tow or we will all be killed.'

Simon relaxes his grip, moving his hands to the loose cloth of the younger brother's robe, using it as leverage to push and shove him into the saloon. He shouts at Lubayd, 'We had a deal! Your brother was about to sever the tow.'

'No deal includes risking my boat.'

'There's only one way out of here — drag the *Sa-baah* off. Do it now.'

'It is not good for the engines to exceed four thousand revolutions.'

'I don't care what is good or not. Give it every ounce of power or I'll throw your brother overboard.'

Lubayd says nothing, but his hand drops to the throttle lever and eases it forwards. The engines build to a steady whine, hull vibration quickening. The vessel straightens. Simon's eyes drop to the chartplotter, speed over the ground reading, 0.1 knots, then 0.0.

'We're still not moving,' Lubayd said. 'It is no use, you see — we cannot do anything. That is full power. We have no choice but to stop the tow — stand off and hope we can pick up survivors.'

'There won't be any survivors after she hits those rocks. My girls are on board. Locked up in some dirty iron cabin. That boat will sink like a stone. Put her out of gear for a moment while I take the chain off the cleat. Get ready to engage the winch.'

Lubayd shrieks, 'No. It will just drag us closer to her. It is too dangerous.'

'We have no choice. It is the last chance.'

'You know nothing about boats,' Lubayd says. 'It is very hard to tow a boat by the stern.'

'Why didn't you tell me that before?'

'Because you just hurry, hurry, do not give me a chance to say anything.'

'Then get on the radio and tell them to move the chain forwards. I'll give them some slack.'

Simon walks out onto the side deck, then aft to where the chain is wrapped over the cleat. The straining engines die and the chain goes limp. The place where Ishmael struck with the axe is visible, one of the links severed almost through on one side.

'Hold, you bastard of a thing, please,' Simon whispers. In a single twist the chain is free, and he begins to pay it out as the men on the other boat move the tow, waving when it is done. He turns back towards the bridge and shouts, 'Now — take her off.'

Again the engine revolutions build to a roar, the deck vibrating. The chain begins to move as the anchor winch engages. Looking back at the tug, he sees the huddled, frightened faces, almost disappearing as yet another wave engulfs the stern.

Now, however, the chain tightens and the tug begins to spin. Simon sees how sensible this approach is: already the crew of the other boat are protected by the raised bow. Now Simon feels real movement in the hull.

Ishmael appears, his face sullen and dark. 'My brother told me to tell you that we are making better than one knot over the ground.'

Simon sees just the faintest curl of water against the other vessel's bow and hears subdued cheering. 'Thank you.'

'So, Englishman,' Ishmael goes on, 'what do we do now? We have rescued a boat load of fanatics — what do we do with them?'

Simon turns and grins. 'As soon as we are away from this damn rock I will go aboard and get my daughters, after that the rest of them can drown in the sea as far as I care.'

Two nautical miles from al-Kahf, the two hulls rafted up, fenders squeezing with the compressive force of the sea like fat sausages. The crew lines the rail, seven strong, the most unlikely terrorists Simon has ever seen: bedraggled and confused, yet happy to be alive. He is first aboard the *Sa-baah*, clambering over the gunwales, accepting thanks and tears, men bowing and embracing him as their rescuer.

The captain, better dressed than the others, has a hint of the Orient in his eyes, a maroon turban tied low and decorated with a cut-glass ornament.

Simon greets him with a handshake. 'I am looking for two girls. Where are they?'

The captain looks confused and raises three fingers. 'Three, but one is much older than the others.'

Kelly, of course. *How might she have fared at the hands of her captors? After all, she is a very pretty young lady.* Simon's anger returns in an impatient wave. 'Where are they?'

'Gone.'

'Gone where?'

A shrug of the shoulders, then a long explanation that they are mere hired crew, and do not know who they are working for — only that the owners have a ready supply of cash and carry weapons. All wear long beards. The crew were unaware that the three females were captives, having seen them on deck for short, supervised intervals.

A fast boat, a large kind of inflatable called a RIB, Simon gathers, met with the *Sa-baah* in darkness the previous night, removing the three females and all the owners. Before they left, someone opened the diesel tank drain cocks and left the vessel without fuel and therefore power, as well as damaging the radios. Though the long-range HF set had proved impossible to repair, the engineer had managed to patch up the VHF and send out the Mayday.

Simon bends almost double to navigate the narrow corridors below the tug's deck, careful of pipes and bunched wires. He thinks of how Hannah, particularly, must have hated it here — she of the bright open spaces and sunshine. An iron door creaks open to reveal a cabin that consists of four walls with a pair of portholes, firmly closed. On the floor lie three filthy foam mattresses and a mess of sheets and blankets.

Simon sinks to his knees on the scattered bedding, flaring his nostrils as if he might detect the scent of innocent girlhood beneath the harsher scents of rusted metal, engine oil, and bilgewater. Frustration builds in him. Frances and Hannah have been here, slept here — wept here. He falls to his knees and begins to search. There is nothing obvious, nothing in the open.

Hannah and Gretel. Hannah and Gretel. Clever girl. Where did you hide it?

Under the filthy blankets, and into the dark corner. Running his hand over the greasy flaked steel plate. Something sharp butts into the heel of his hand. He holds it up to the light.

Another charm, this one the grisly visage of a skull. He remembers how Isabella did not want Hannah to buy it, calling it macabre. The child, however, prevailed, and it was hers. Simon lifts it to his lips and kisses the cold surface.

Day 4, 19:00

Dusk. Travelling at speed on a smooth section of road, head lolling with the curves, the crackle of automatic gunfire jolts Marika awake. Sitting up, she sees two or three brilliant muzzle flashes from broken cover on the left-hand side of the road. The technical ahead lurches and stops, steam jetting from under the bonnet. Her own vehicle swerves to avoid the other, losing grip and sliding for one terrifying moment before scudding to a halt.

Someone swears, already returning fire, the DShK machine gun stuttering from above, seeming to rob the air of oxygen. Bullets thud into the doors and chassis of their vehicle. Marika hears shouted instructions. One of the men grabs her arm, dragging her out of the vehicle into the swirling dust and smoke outside.

Even as she follows the crouching gunman across the road, Marika studies the mechanics of the ambush. As far as she can see there must be only a handful of attackers, yet they show signs of training, conserving ammunition and preventing their weapons from overheating by firing short, controlled bursts.

Behind a small hillock, Marika's guard urges her to the ground, his rifle held flat. Her breath comes hard, even though they have run just a short distance, and she knows that this is one of the debilitating effects of being under fire, what some of her instructors called the adrenalin factor — a feeling that cannot be simulated under training conditions.

One vehicle has been destroyed, decimating their complement and perhaps compromising their ability to win through to the mountains. Her hand curls in annoyance, reaching down to press against her aching bladder. Just a short time ago things were proceeding well. Turning to the guard, who has a rudimentary grasp of English, she asks, 'Who are they?'

'Shifta. They ... after the guns, may God ... curse them.'

Marika thinks back on Dalmar Asad's conviction that the shifta would not dare attack them. *Maybe they're not such bloody cowards after all.*

The wooden stock of a rifle appears out of the darkness, swinging in a wide arc as if of its own volition, smacking into the side of the guard's head with the crack of a breaking tree branch. He utters no sound, falling almost gently to the earth.

Already she is responding, reaching for her sidearm, rolling onto her back to clear her field of fire. She brings her gun hand up, staring at the killer, expecting him to attack her before she can get the shot away.

'Stop, do not shoot! It's me.'

Marika blinks, as if to clear a vision. 'Bloody hell! Madoowbe, is that you?'

'Yes, now hurry. Follow me.'

'What in Christ's name do you think you're doing?' She struggles for breath, indignation building.

'Nothing in Christ's name. I do not act in the name of religion.'

'Good for you. I had a freaking escort ten minutes ago in case you didn't notice what they were doing before you decided to kill half of them.'

'Leave it. We must hurry — already they are regrouping.'

Marika, seeing no alternative, follows, her voice louder now, muffled by the firefight occurring around the vehicles. 'By morning I would have had her, you interfering idiot.'

Madoowbe turns, and she sees that one eye is still swollen, the socket dark with bruises. 'What should I have done — stopped your friends and asked them? How was I to know that they were not taking you out to kill you?'

Marika is about to offer a reply when she sees the outline of a motorcycle under the tangled canopy of a thorn tree. 'You want us both to travel on that?'

'It is all I have.' He hurries to the machine, straddles it and kicks the starter several times before the engine fires.

'You weren't alone back there,' Marika observes, crossing her arms and making no move to follow him. 'Your friends — where the hell did you find them?'

'After I saw your column leave the compound I went to a cafe in Bacaadweyn. I made a deal with some bandits. They want the guns and vehicles. If they can get them.' He lifts his head and appears to listen, even over the rattle of the motorcycle engine. 'They have stopped fighting; we had better hurry. Get on.'

Shaking her head at her own bad fortune, Marika sits on the hard and narrow pillion, tense with anger, bladder pain, and the after effects of being shot at. 'Jesus Christ, I hate you.'

'Will you please stop saying that?'

'Only if you stop being such a pain in the arse.'

'Put your arms around my waist, and hurry.'

'Do I have to?'

'If you do not want to fall off, yes.'

As soon as her fingers link together the machine roars off over the sand, overloaded and unsafe, it seems to Marika. 'Next time you want to rescue someone, ask them first, for God's sake,' she says into his ear. The road looms ahead, and the bike crests a hillock on the verge before gathering pace on the loose dust of the road surface. A pale crescent moon is out, along with a multitude of stars in an otherwise jet black sky.

'Next time I will not bother.'

They ride in silence for a minute or so before she speaks again. 'Where did you get this piece of shit from, anyway?'

'I stole it.'

'Where from?'

'Out the back of a repair shop.'

'That's stupid — how do you know it's not totally stuffed?'

'She is running, is she not? And has started every time. Eventually.'

As Madoowbe increases speed, Marika looks back, noting the vehicle headlights not far behind. 'Bugger. Looks like they're back on the road.'

Marika wonders if Captain Wanami will have the stomach to return and tell his boss that they have lost her. No, he will do everything in his power to get her back. This thought is shattered by a burst of heavy machine-gun fire as the technical accelerates.

'Don't just sit there,' Madoowbe cries. 'You have your gun. Shoot them.'

Unclipping the Glock from the holster she pulls back the slide to push a round into the chamber, then turns to aim at the pursuing vehicle. When she pulls the trigger there is a click as the mechanism slides through, but no discharge. She tries again. Nothing.

'Damn it!' Bringing the gun back she works the action and tries again. Still nothing.

'What's wrong?' Madoowbe shouts.

'My gun,' she cries. 'Dalmar Asad must have taken out the firing pin. Damn the bastard.'

With an angry flick of her arm, Marika throws the useless weapon out into the night.

'The rifle on my back,' Madoowbe urges. 'Unstrap it.'

'How am I supposed to do that?'

The back wheel of the bike hits a powderpuff of dust and wriggles across the track. Recovering from the momentary lack of balance, Marika lifts the weapon over Madoowbe's shoulders, gripping the machine with both knees like a rodeo rider while she does so. 'Lift your arm, for God's sake, it's in my way,' she calls, risking a glance back, seeing the headlights of the technical gaining, another behind it. A burst from the MG sees tracer rounds arc towards them through the darkness.

Now the weapon is free, however, and even as it comes into her hands Marika recognises the familiar balance, the user-friendly feel of the most popular small arm in the world. Designed by Mikhail Kalashnikov, and designated the AK47, for seventy years it has been beloved of terrorists, mercenaries, Third World armies, reactionaries and screenwriters the world over. This one is well worn, with a wooden stock polished from constant handling over many years. Someone has carved words in Arabic on the stock, like school children might on a desk.

Drawing back the charging handle, she feels a round click into the chamber, then moves the selector to the lowest position, knowing that there is no point spraying rounds all over the place. Turning, bracing herself against Madoowbe's back, she lifts the weapon to her shoulder and lines up the peep, attempting to focus on the windscreen.

Both vehicles move so erratically it is possible only to draw a bead in the general direction and wait for the target to bounce into view. About to pull the trigger, she stops, lowering the weapon.

'Hold on,' she says, 'these guys were helping me not long ago ...'

'Trust me, we have no choice. Do you really think Dalmar Asad is going to hand Sufia Haweeya over to you? No, he will use her as a bargaining chip with the West. That is how he operates — I have found out much about him. Besides, these three technicals would never have got you through the mountains. People hate Dalmar Asad. By tomorrow you would be dead.'

'Even so, I don't know. If we surrender now, I'm pretty sure they wouldn't kill me.'

'No,' Madoowbe cries, 'but they will kill *me*. Worse. They will roast my testicles before my eyes. I am fond of my testicles. Shoot, and hurry, before it is too late.'

Machine-gun fire stitches its way across the road ahead of them. Passing bullets whip through the air.

'Hurry.'

Marika raises the rifle again, first settling the peep on the driver, and then the man beside him, waiting for the aim to come true. It seems to her that the passenger must be Captain Wanami — surely he would have changed vehicles and this is where he prefers to sit. Her finger tightens on the trigger. This is a cruel man, one who hurt her physically more than once. Surely he deserves to die?

Still she cannot bring herself to kill him, switching her aim to the front passenger-side tyre. She fires twice. The reaction is immediate — the vehicle swerves towards the road verge, where it stops. The other vehicle pauses beside it for a moment, then continues on, now staying back a respectful distance.

'Good shooting,' Madoowbe shouts.

'Thank you, just one of my many talents. You know … a modern girl and all that.' In an effort to mould her body to the fast moving bike she feels her ankle contact red-hot metal and stifles a yelp of pain.

'Are you OK?'

'Yeah, just the exhaust pipe. They're gaining on us. Can't this thing go any faster?'

'I'm trying. Stop chattering and let me concentrate.'

The motor, however, is erratic, racing one moment and dawdling the next. The remaining vehicle surges closer, and Marika takes the opportunity to lift the rifle to her shoulder. She fires two short bursts, aiming at the engine block, a much clearer target at a distance than tyres. Despite seeing sparks as bullets strike in the correct area, her efforts seem not to impede the vehicle's progress.

'You were just now boasting about your marksmanship,' Madoowbe complains.

'Shut up, damn you. If it wasn't for you I'd be half asleep, on my way to pick up our target.'

'If it wasn't for me you would be dead on the side of the road when Dalmar Asad's thugs decided they didn't like where they were going.'

'That's your opinion. Anyway, you're the big SAS man. Why don't you stop and shoot them yourself?'

'What I told you about being in the SAS was not strictly true,' he grunts. 'I was in the infantry for a time, but I have never been SAS.'

'You lied to me?'

'Yes. I wanted to come with you.'

'Have you ever parachuted before?'

'Never.'

'You seemed to know what you were doing.'

'I Googled how to do it before we left. There is a Wikipedia article that goes into great detail ...'

'Shit. There's three billion men in the world and I had to get lumped with *you*.' Marika lifts the assault rifle and fires again, this time rewarded with a plume of white steam from the vehicle's radiator.

'That's better,' Madoowbe offers, 'but it does not seem to be slowing them down.'

'No? Look.'

The vehicle appears to falter, but remains on their tail, spewing steam like a fountain.

'It can't last — they'll overheat, surely.'

As if in response to that observation, the machine begins to fall back. Marika's last glimpse is of men tumbling from the vehicle, one lighting a cigarette, another gesticulating wildly.

Marika needs all her self-control to wait until they have put the technical several kilometres behind them. 'Stop the bike now, please,' she says.

'Why? We should travel as far as we can while we have the opportunity ...'

'Shut up, Madoowbe. If you don't stop you're gonna get a wet arse, and I'm going to need a change of underwear. Get it?'

The Somali says nothing, but swings the bike over to the verge. Marika steps off and, hobbling like a cripple, ducks behind the nearest bush, just managing to get her trousers off in time to enjoy the most beautiful relief she can remember.

Lubayd agrees to pump two hundred litres of diesel into the other boat's tanks — enough for them to reach the Somali port of Raas Binne — only when Simon offers to pay for it. The refuelling process requires a long black hose snaking between the two vessels, thirty minutes of intense manoeuvring and men standing by with boat hooks. Finally, the *Sa-baah* steams away, manned by a somewhat more cheerful crew. When they have gone, Simon sits in the saloon, head in his hands, knowing that now, on the cusp of finding Hannah and Frances, the search has become more difficult than ever.

Ishmael disappears into his cabin, and when he returns the smell of hashish smoke wafts up behind him. Eyes red and pupils tiny as pinpricks, lips puffy and motionless, he broods over a mug of mint tea for some minutes before lifting his head to speak to Lubayd as if Simon is not present. 'At last, that foolishness is over. I say we drop the Englishman on the main island as was the original plan. We owe a man who pulls a gun on us nothing.'

Lubayd, ignoring his brother, fixes his eyes on Simon. 'You heard the crew of that tug. Your daughters' captors took a fast boat. There are many islands — we cannot search them all. They could have met a float plane, a tanker. Anything.'

'No. If they were going to rendezvous with another vessel or aircraft, why would they have sailed so far? It doesn't make sense.'

'Lubayd! Think straight!' Ishmael cries. 'Do not listen to his clever fabrications. Take the money now and set him ashore. Anywhere. There has been nothing but risk for us since we brought him aboard. Let that be the end of it.'

Lubayd's face is a picture of concentration. 'You are right, Ishmael. And this time I will listen.' His eyebrows knit together as he stares at Simon. 'We will now make for Socotra, where you will pay us and leave this boat. That is our bargain. What you do from there is not our concern.'

'If my girls are not on Socotra, then there is no point going there. Help me for just one day, that's all I ask. Cruise past some of these islands; let us see if there is a boat such as they described moored there.'

Ishmael pushes his face so close that hashish and garlic fumes assault Simon's senses. 'You are not so tough without a gun in your hand.'

Simon ignores him, instead fixing his eyes on the older brother. 'Please, help me. Just for one day.'

Lubayd lifts one hand. 'No argument. That is the end of it.'

Simon remains at the dinette table, staring into space. The old crone who has said nothing for so long extends one long, bony hand and covers his. Staring into his eyes she speaks in archaic Arabic.

'You must not weep,' she says. 'You cannot hold on to what you love forever.'

Day 4, 21:00

In the port city of Umm Qasr, Southern Iraq, in a base that does not officially exist, twenty-two men burdened with packs and assault rifles file out from a C130 transport plane and towards a Unimog truck that will take them to temporary barracks. This is the port that once protected a bridge linking Saddam Hussein's regime to Kuwait, famously compared with Southampton by Geoff Hoon, defence secretary during the Second Gulf War, to which a British soldier quipped back: 'There's no beer, no prostitutes and people are shooting at us. It's more like Portsmouth.'

Each man in the line carries rations for three days, five hundred rounds of NATO standard 7.62mm ammunition, and one hundred of 9mm. They also carry three grenades — two phosphorus and one high explosive.

In addition, each individual has the tools peculiar to his trade — sniper rifles, long-distance listening equipment, or communications. Each squad is equipped with a packaged, folding watercraft and diving equipment. Each man was hand-picked for his strength, stamina, and competence. He can run a hundred metres in under twelve seconds and swim ten miles in a cold sea.

First in line walks PJ Johnson. Point men get in the habit of leading, and also in the habit of watchfulness. His eyes never stop moving, flicking ahead as if he is already in a combat zone. He climbs into the open back of the truck and onto the bench, leaning forward, resting his weight on the stock of his Heckler and Koch assault rifle. The men settling into their places opposite him show signs that they share his own nervousness.

PJ turns and looks out the acrylic windows; dust blows in a constant stream from the ground, obscuring the hangars and workshops of the airfield and the high fences beyond. He closes his eyes, thinking back to when all he wanted was to be a soldier; a tough guy like the GI Joe action figures he pitted against one another. Toy tanks shooting it out, dust flying and children crying.

A childhood moving from city to city. Norwich, Ipswich, Colchester. Another school, new faces, yet always the snide remarks on the first day, comments about his ears, or the stained and torn jacket three sizes too small. Sometimes a knowing slur on matters beyond his control.

'My dad says that his dad is a drunk,' someone would announce. 'Can't hold down a job anywhere. My dad says that his dad has been in Brixton.'

It was true. PJ remembers the long year when the old man was inside, and they visited him every Saturday afternoon. Brought chocolate and cartons of Player cigarettes, watching him sit with his muscled, tattooed arms on the table, listening to the monosyllabic news of a man who had nothing to talk about, nothing to share of interest to an eight-year-old boy.

His mum insisted that they went. 'Some families won't visit their dad in jail — too ashamed. I won't be like that. Not one of us will be. A man needs to see his family, no matter what mistakes he's made.'

'See if the little fucker can fight,' someone said after school one day. They circled him with their bikes and catcalled until one slid off his seat, turned him round, and hit him on the lip. PJ always tried to fight back but they were bigger, and if he managed to overcome one tormentor there was always another ready to step in.

PJ's growth spurt came late, and by his senior years he had friends of his own. Not many, but they were true friends, ready to stand at his side when the chips were down. The bullies moved on to easier prey, especially since PJ now stood as tall as most, and had thickened around the shoulders and arms.

After school he joined the army, determined to make his mark, yet he remained quiet and retiring. Singled out for Special Forces training, he was taught to fight, yet learned restraint, and he came to understand what his tormentors would never know — that humanity is the most important quality of all.

PJ looks up as the truck rumbles to a halt outside a hangar. Beside it is a Sea King chopper on twenty-four-hour standby. From now they will be on a five-minute state of preparedness, able to deploy anywhere in the Middle East.

The sea journey seems to take an age. More than once Lubayd has to work his way around a coral reef lurking black and murderous just below the surface, unmarked on the charts yet betrayed by a flash of disturbed white water under the moon.

Relieved to rid himself of the bulky wad of money, Simon sits at the saloon table and negotiates an extension on Lubayd's fee for the dramatic rescue off al-Kahf. After this he packs his few belongings into his flight bag, ignoring the occasional poisonous glance from Ishmael.

The darkness is a blanket over a sea that has calmed somewhat through the previous hours. No time remains to go down to the cabin and sleep, and Simon is anxious not to put himself in Ishmael's power, sure that the younger brother would love to plunge a knife in his back, especially since he again disappears below to smoke hashish, returning to the saloon in a catatonic state, dozing in the helm chair, head lolling like that of a marionette.

Simon does not notice his own drift into semi-unconsciousness until Lubayd's sudden shout has him standing, grasping at the chair frame for balance. 'Wake up. There is a vessel coming up fast on the port beam.'

Simon strains his eyes, looking out into the night, seeing the masthead and running lights of a substantial ship, moving with the speed of a hunting panther across the dark plain of the sea. 'Who is it? What kind of boat?'

'I don't know yet. But you had better hope they are not Somali pirates, because they are very fast.'

'So what do we do?' Simon asks.

'As the Americans would say, we put the hammer down.'

Simon watches Lubayd push down the throttles. The *Jameela* leaps forward, engines rising in tone to a high-pitched hum. The radar shows how that burst of speed takes them well ahead of the other vehicle's path. The pleasure at this, however, is short-lived, for the other vessel turns towards them and begins to give chase.

'There is no doubt,' Lubayd says, 'they have us on radar — they are in pursuit.' Again he ups the throttles, and though the engines now have a note of strain, there is just an incremental increase in the speed — thirty-two knots according to the plotter. The deck vibrates, and the glasses in the galley tinkle against each other with a distracting rattle. 'We'll see if they can stay with us now. There are few boats on this ocean who can match us.'

Sweating now, Simon watches the radar. At first it seems that Lubayd is right, and they will easily outdistance the other vessel. Then the other craft begins to gain on them.

'This is impossible,' Lubayd says. 'We can go no faster, yet they are still with us.'

Ishmael, coming out of a drug-induced torpor, stands and points a wavering arm at Simon. 'It is the Englishman's fault. I rue the hour he came aboard — there has been nothing but trouble since I heard his name. Now that we have his money we should throw him over the side and let the sharks feast on his flesh.'

'There is no advantage in that, brother.'

'Is there anything we can do?' Simon asks, feeling a new solidarity with Lubayd.

'Nothing but prayer will help us now. If they are pirates, and they catch us, we are all dead. They will soon find that we are no good for ransom.' He glances at Simon. 'Except perhaps for you.'

Simon looks away. Everyone he loves is in the hands of extremists. No one else would care enough to pay an extravagant ransom.

Ishmael cries, 'Set the autopilot and let us take the life raft!'

Lubayd shakes his head. 'I cannot leave my beautiful boat. Not even to save our lives.'

Simon looks down at the blip of the other vessel, closing fast.

'A few minutes,' Lubayd whispers, 'and they will be on us.'

Ishmael disappears below, returning with an archaic shoulder-fired rocket launcher, a single missile lodged in the scratched, green-painted tube. The faded script on the side identifies it as Soviet-era Russian.

'I will give them something to think about,' Ishmael mutters. 'I will set fire to their stinking buttocks.' He charges out into the cockpit. Simon follows, staring into the darkness where the pursuing ship is now close. A floodlight beam turns the intervening sea to daylight, and pains the eyes.

Ishmael now has the launcher at his shoulder, one hand on the rail to steady himself, the other on the launcher's grip. 'Come closer, thing of the night,' he whispers, 'and may God guide the fire of my rage into your heart.'

The ship grows in stature as she steams closer, and Simon recognises her at last — a British Navy destroyer, D93 painted on the hull in black letters. She has a low profile for a warship, yet with high, flared bows. A rounded gun turret seems to aim directly at them. Further aft rises a network of grey iron, surmounted by more domed turrets and twin masts bristling with communications aerials and surrealistic spheres.

Ishmael mutters, 'I will destroy you, ship of the darkness, enemy of God. Closer, come closer and you will feel the death I send forth across the night.'

A klaxon blares as the destroyer looms close enough to blot out the night sky, the superstructure towering towards the heavens. Simon cringes back from the light, even as Ishmael leans forwards, ready to absorb the recoil.

'Die, evil thing,' he shrieks.

Loudspeakers blare: 'Heave to, heave to. This is Royal Navy destroyer HMS *Durham* …'

Simon sees Ishmael's hand curl on the trigger of the weapon. 'No,' he shouts, 'it's one of ours. Are you trying to get us killed?' The words have no effect. He charges across the deck.

Ishmael must be waiting for him, for his hand leaves the weapon and connects with the side of Simon's chin, sending him staggering across the deck.

'Go back, go back. This is God's work.'

Gathering himself, again Simon goes for the half-crazed Yemeni, knowing that he is too late, connecting with the man's shoulder just as he pulls the trigger. A tongue of flame leaps from the rear of the tube and a long flash of orange and blue fire shoots up to an impossible height in a fraction of a second before fading into darkness.

The turret gun on the destroyer fires a single round over the *Jameela*, lighting up the sky and sea in a brilliant flash that pains the eyes. The concussion of sound follows an instant later, setting off a ringing in Simon's ears. The loudspeaker comes to life again: 'Any further aggressive act and we will fire upon you. Heave to, and stand with hands on heads.'

The *Jameela*'s engine hum dies away to nothing, and silence descends. It is a strange feeling, Simon thinks to himself as he raises his arms, to want the safety offered by that giant ship, yet aware that it might also mean the end of freedom.

THE FIFTH DAY

And God said, Let the water teem with living creatures, and let birds fly above the earth across the expanse of the sky. So God created the creatures of the sea and every living and moving thing with which the water teems, according to their kinds, and every winged bird according to its kind. God blessed them and said, Be fruitful and increase in number and fill the water in the seas, and let the birds increase on the earth.

But man cages the birds and fences the animals so he does not need to hunt, and he breeds the birds to be fat, and the animals to grow fat and be docile. He cages them closely, and feeds them by-products from the bodies of their own species. Birds caged to lay eggs are so confined that they cannot learn to walk.

The birds and animals become diseased. The wild creatures disappear before a relentless passion for building and clearing. When the men and women of the earth begin to realise what they have done, it is too late to bring back what is gone.

And there was evening, and there was morning. The fifth day.

Day 5, 02:00

Zhyogal's eyes reflect the orchestration of a hundred deaths over twenty years, and there is a glimpse of Satan in a cloak of pure faith. Blackness hides behind each footfall, and in the hiss of words that issue from a throat that scrapes the raw tissue of lies and false belief. It is the middle of the night but the lights have not dimmed. No one sleeps.

'All functionaries of Jewish and imperialist governments who sign a confession of their crimes will be released from this room,' Zhyogal announces. In his hand he holds a sheaf of paper. 'It is necessary only to read the words on this page, admitting to the guilt of which you are surely aware.'

The conference room is tense and silent, men and women alike staring back at the Algerian, hands immobile on arm rests, not one making eye contact with another.

'Yes,' he shouts, 'I give my word. Sign the confession and we will arrange for the door to open and all those who sign can leave. Think upon it! In just hours you will be reunited with your loved ones — your husbands, wives, children. All you must do in return is read the confession aloud and sign your name before the cameras. Stand up now all those who will do so. All those who desire freedom. Stand now and soon it will be so.'

The silence deepens, broken only by an uncomfortable cough out there in the darkness. Not one person stands, but there is a feeling that if someone would do so, more would follow.

'Not one among you wishes to be free?' Zhyogal shouts. 'Do you fear the consequences? Do you worry that the world's media might vilify and mock you?' His voice becomes a wolf-like howl of menace. 'What does it matter when you are going to die here?' He takes a step, pointing at a young man in the third row, dishevelled in his rolled sleeves and half-unbuttoned shirt. 'You,' he shouts, 'do you not want to live?'

At first the delegate does not respond, but then slowly, wilting under the stare, he nods slowly.

'Of course you do. You have a girlfriend. You want to live to father her children. To grow rich perhaps. To live your life.' Zhyogal's voice softens. 'Step down here now, read the confession and sign. Then you can go free. You have my word.'

'No.' The young man's voice is tremulous, whisper soft, but it can be heard in every corner of that room, with a power stronger than all the histrionics of the Algerian.

That answer sends Zhyogal into a rage. 'What if I execute ten men and women every hour? If we see a lake of blood beneath your feet. Then you will sign my papers, I can guarantee it.' His eyes move around the room, finally meeting those of Isabella Thompson. He points with one arm.

'That one,' he shrieks. 'Bring her to me.'

Isabella has not moved for some time, held rigid to her seat as if by a magnet. Now, as Zhyogal's arm swings to identify her, she sags as if there is no strength left. The nightmare takes the form of a whirlpool, spinning, dragging her deeper.

The mujahedin come from both sides, gripping her arms and dragging, fingers digging in to the bone. They force her to walk with them, half stumbling down the rows past dull, staring faces, hair falling in front of her face so that she cannot see.

On the dais they knock her down, and she does not try to rise, allowing her legs to fold underneath her. Zhyogal grips a fist full of her hair and lifts her. Until that moment she would not have believed such a feat possible. The pain is so sharp she can do nothing, scarcely even breathe as he does it. Then she is looking into his eyes, just as she had a week earlier in a moment of passion, when she had believed in him, imagined that he was attracted to her, helping to find and piece together the shattered porcelain of her heart.

Now his eyes are red rimmed and raw from lack of sleep, and there is madness in him. 'You,' he cries, 'you will sign.'

'No,' she sobs, 'I won't do it.'

He holds the paper in front of her face, still half supporting her with the hand in her hair. 'You *will* sign. If you do not I will make a simple phone call and two beautiful girls will die. I promise you.'

'Oh Jesus, *no*. I hate you, I hate you!' She tries to rake down his face with one hand but he moves deftly out of the way, changing his grip on her.

'Come now, sit and begin reading. Hurry, I am losing patience.' He pulls the cell phone from his suit pocket and switches it on.

'Stop. I'll sign. I'll do anything.'

There is a table prepared, a pen on the synthetic top. Isabella sits, pulling her hair back so she can see, avoiding the staring eyes of the people in the rows, knowing their contempt for her weakness. The words on the page are a blur as she picks up the pen and seeks the line reserved for a signature. Just two paces away one of the mujahedin has a tiny digital video camera trained on her.

'No!' Zhyogal shouts. 'Read it first. You must read it aloud. The camera is rolling. They must see you do it.'

Crying again, Isabella picks up the sheet, trying to focus on the words. They come haltingly. *'I now recognise that I represent a corrupt government; that they have initiated a crusade against the ...'* Isabella stops, looking up at the people around the room. There is sympathy there, and understanding, yet ...

Now the words come in a flood, like a hurdler who has reached the final straight. *'... the government which I represent is a farce and ... lies to the world ... I have been personally responsible for the death and persecution of ...'* Again she looks out. These are good people. Not all, but in the main. Some have clutched at power above all else, but in her experience the majority want the best for their country, their people, and there is no misplaced higher purpose beyond that. Not religion. Not power for its own sake. She studies the next line. *I have been the tool and puppet of the Jewish overlords ...* There is no truth there, not one sand grain in a beach of lies. There has to be a point, she realises, where truth carries more weight than any other consideration. That her life, even those of her children, no longer matter.

She takes a deep breath. 'I'm sorry, but I will read no more. I will not sign.'

Zhyogal lashes out with an open hand, and the blow lands like a whip, stinging her skin and knocking her head sideways. He does this repeatedly, one side then the other, knocking her from the chair and to the carpet where she lies sobbing.

Stepping back from her he takes the phone from his pocket and taps out a number. A short conversation in Arabic follows. When it is done he stands over her. 'My colleague is on his way to the place where your daughters are held. He has assured me that he will execute them in the name of God. You have made your choice. Go back to your seat.'

Isabella cannot hear through the roar of pain and helplessness in her head.

Madoowbe purchases fuel in a village that comprises no more than a collection of hide tents, with camels tethered next to abandoned motor vehicles. It is still so dark that the only light emanates from a kerosene lantern belonging to the local mullah.

There are no more refugees now. Nothing to see. Marika dozes off for short periods. Waking, on one occasion, she feels dreamily content, the desert bathed in tawny beauty, and the bike continuing its steady drone.

Arms around his waist, she asks, 'How much further?'

'Soon we will reach the Wells of Wahbadi. That is the beginning of the mountains.'

The landscape here is flat and empty, with few villages but for the occasional semi-nomadic camp, ten or less tukul covered in thatch, or hide and potato sacks sewn together. Rarely is there any sign of a serious attempt at cultivation. Camels and stoic, staring goats are the only livestock.

The wells loom out of this wasteland, first marked by the crumbled walls of some ancient fortress, yellow stone blocks in rows, chimneys stark against the sky, and the

fallen ramparts that must once have been ten paces thick.
Marika wonders what defenders manned those walls, who
they must have faced. Whether they won, or if time was the
only victor here.

Many of the wells have fallen into disuse and the most
recent tracks lead to just one — a circular, earthen pit, a
long stone's throw across, a foot trail winding down to a
muddy pool at the bottom. Camels must have often been
tethered to the thorn trees nearby, for their dung lies in
scattered piles on the sand.

Marika waits while Madoowbe kicks down the bike
stand in the shade, seeing, for the first time in daylight, the
fading bruised and puffy patches around one eye and both
cheeks from the beating Dalmar Asad's men gave him.

'You need attention for that cut under your eye,' she
says. 'I can bathe it if you like.'

'There is no need. I am a man, not a child.'

'Suit yourself, but if it gets infected, don't blame me.'

They walk the path down towards the muddy water.

'How long do you think these wells might have been
in use?' she asks.

'Oh five hundred years, perhaps a thousand or more.'

The thought makes Marika smile; five hundred years of
feet, and camels led in single file down that narrow track.
Five hundred years of warriors, lovers, quarrelling spouses
and questioning children. 'Do they ever dry up?'

'Every few hundred years or so a new one might be
dug.'

'How did your ancestors find them?'

'They say that elephants began most of the wells, but
no elephants have been seen in these parts for many
years.'

'Where have they gone?'

'As you have seen, this is a country where every man owns an AK47 assault rifle.'

Marika is incredulous. 'They kill elephants with a 7.62mm round?'

'Ammunition is cheap compared to the price of ivory. It might take fifty bullets, but they fall in the end.'

The descent takes longer than Marika expects. The well floor is as wide as a tennis court. The water is inches deep in places, and nonexistent in others. It smells of urine and earth. Here and there people have dug deeper with their hands to improve access.

Marika watches Madoowbe sink to his knees and suck the cool water by making a straw with pursed lips. She, however, squats at the edge and uses cupped hands to raise water to her lips. As soon as she does so, however, sediment stains the surface, making the area filthy.

Madoowbe grins at her. 'Drink as I did.'

'Yeah, yeah, a bit of dirt never hurt anyone.'

Again she cups her hand, ignoring the rank taste, drinking until she feels satiated. She splashes her face and hair, enjoying the feel of it on her skin, watching Madoowbe fill the canvas water bag that hangs from the bike pillion.

They sit down together on the shady, cool earth, resting. Madoowbe at first seems content to sit in silence, until finally he says, 'You have lived all your life in the West. What do you think of Somalia?'

Marika hesitates, resisting the temptation to throw out a dismissive, empty comment. A basket case. A lost cause. Yet the truth is so much sadder than that. 'I think that Somalia embodies where we have gone wrong as a species.'

'As a Westerner, you accept the blame?'

Marika shrugs. 'Not personally, but I have lived in a system that let this happen.'

'Unfortunately,' he says, 'you are right. Somalia is full of guns, refugees, and feuding clans, but it is not us who will destroy the earth, but the West. The world cannot afford to give up its bounty indefinitely. Oil is running out now, the age of the internal combustion engine is almost over; plastics too are petroleum by-products. Next the iron ore will go. The planet will be exhausted. Every creature that outstrips its natural resources must die out. That is what plague species do. We will be the same. The meeting in Dubai is a farce.'

Marika looks sideways at him. 'Careful — I'll start to wonder whose side you're on. Again.'

'It is not a matter of sides. These guns you see everywhere in my country, we did not make them ourselves. They come from Russia, China, Pakistan, Korea, and America. This arming of the poorer nations of the world is not right. Militant Islam is not right either, but how can you blame a man who has seen his family starve, or be killed by American bombs, for picking up a gun? How can you blame him for hating? Your leaders can label him as evil, vilify and caricature him, yet you cannot, in all truth, blame him for standing up to what *he* sees as evil, in a direct and terrible way.'

'Oh yes, I can.' Marika thrusts out her chin. 'Western culture is good as well as bad. Rabi al-Salah is our chance to turn things around. The Almohad have taken it over and will exploit it for their own ends. They do not care about the welfare of their people, only their God and what they see as *His* desires. How can you defend *them*?'

'No.' He looks down at the earth. 'I do not defend them. They are misguided. But still, they have reasons for being what they are.'

Marika stands, reversing her palms to slap dust from her buttocks. 'Anyhow, this is all a little deep for this time of the morning. Especially when I've spent the whole night on a rattly old motorbike. Let's just say that I am not concerned with Dr Abukar's ideology — just his methods.'

'Wait,' Madoowbe says. 'You are an Australian. Let us compare Australia's history with that of Africa for a moment. Africa is, of course, much larger, and more densely populated, but there are similarities. Both are resource rich, and both were seen as unpopulated by sophisticated European nations.

'Africa's downfall was its close proximity to the fast-developing West. The European colonialists wanted a piece of it, and the land grab proceeded. First Portugal, then Holland, the British, Belgians, Italians, French, and Germans. They all grabbed a slice of territory. They all exploited it. They removed generations of young people and shipped them overseas as slaves. Australia's remoteness was its saviour, because it allowed for it to be settled by just one nation. That nation was able to eliminate the indigenous inhabitants as a political and military force, giving it a central and stable government. Now Australia seeks a voice on the world stage, yet will never be independent of the greater powers because it lies in a vulnerable, isolated position geographically. Look how close Japan came to making it the jewel in the Emperor's crown in World War Two.'

Marika starts to walk away, but Madoowbe has not finished, walking after her and taking her hand, turning her around.

'Look at you,' he says. 'You have never missed a meal in your life. You are beautiful and confident, almost arrogantly so. That comes from a lifetime of privilege.'

'I wouldn't say that … and I am not arrogant.'

'I do not mean to insult you, but that is how you seem to me.'

Marika screws up her eyes. 'So. You have all the answers. Do you think an Islamic state is the best thing for Somalia?'

'Not at all. I am no Muslim, Miss Hartmann. I was once, but now I am what you Westerners would call godless. I believe that we are dust. We belong to the earth and we will return to it. That is the only truth worth knowing.'

'You don't believe in any god at all?'

'Oh, I believe in them. I just think they are rotten. All of them and without exception. Gods pain me. I hate them. They enslave their followers and bring warfare and pain. The worst atrocities are committed with the name of some deity or another on the perpetrator's lips. Religion is the most dangerous concept of all, because it infuses people with self-belief far beyond what is warranted.'

'I don't think you are right. Not in all cases. Think of Mother Teresa. Joan of Arc. Mary Mackillop.'

'We were just talking about the Almohad a minute ago. They believe that God has authorised them to use evil to defeat His enemies. Would they be so violent and bloodthirsty without that belief?'

Marika crosses her arms. 'OK, but religion has also brought out the best of human nature.'

'I will take the middle ground without the peaks and valleys, thank you.' Now it is his turn to walk away.

Marika follows him towards the surface, not sure whether to feel insulted. *Arrogant? Perhaps we are all like that, only we don't know because no one has ever told us.*

On the way to the bike, Madoowbe pauses at a bush and breaks off several twigs, passing one to her. She rolls the stick between thumb and forefinger.

'What's this for?'

He grins. 'This is mswaki, the toothbrush tree. Everyone in Somalia uses it.'

'That's probably why everyone in Somalia has rotten teeth.'

'Even so, it is better than nothing.'

Marika follows his lead, using the twig like a toothpick, finding that it has a subtle but pleasant taste. The process is fast and painless and she places a few more sticks in her top pocket for later use before following him back to the bike.

Madoowbe pours the last few litres from the petrol tin into the motorcycle's tank then ties it back onto the luggage rack. Straddling the machine, he strokes the starter with his right foot. The engine coughs in response, then dies.

'Hell,' he curses, and tries again. No response. Ten, fifteen times he kicks the starter before the motor catches and settles into a steady rhythm. He grins back at her, sweat streaming down his face from the growing heat and exertion. 'I have the knack. Climb on.'

Simon has only once before set foot on a warship, at the Maritime Museum across from the Isle of Dogs in Greenwich. They went one May Day holiday, before the crowds, with Hannah and Frances skipping ahead, peering into cramped cabins and cosy mess rooms, while the tour guide regurgitated tonnages, complements, names, and dates. This one, however, is a working ship, with cooking smells, diesel fumes and humming electronics.

Having spent his professional life aboard aircraft, Simon appreciates the thoughtful layout and efficiency. The personnel who move down iron corridors under bundled pipes and cables do so purposefully, each knowing their job, relying on their shipmates to do the same.

The captain, a man of around forty-five, is not what Simon might have expected, with dark, tightly curled hair, what people politely call a Roman nose and laughter lines around his lips. A couple of old tattoos show through the hair of his forearms. That he is good at his job, however, is not in doubt — that is obvious in the spotless efficiency of the ship. Everything from the shining signal lamps to the freshly painted bulkheads indicates a high degree of care.

'Fantastic ship,' Simon points out. They are on the bridge, looking out through the downward-sloping toughened glass windows of the foredeck. The officer of the watch occupies a central chair, radar operators to either side. At the rear is a Perspex-covered navigation table and beside it the sonar sets. Forward and below are the Sea Dart missile launchers, beyond that the rounded gun turrets, the jackstaff, and the dark sea. Instruments glow eerily, illuminating the faces and arms of the men and women who man them. 'Must be, what,' he muses, picturing a rugby field in his head, 'a hundred and fifty metres long?'

'Close. One-forty-one to be exact. Type 42 destroyer, Manchester class, 5200 tonnes.'

Simon nods; he has heard of the Type 42 ships. And something about those Sea Dart missiles — hadn't one done something newsworthy way back in the Second Gulf War? He tries to recall but it doesn't come. 'These ships have been around for a while, haven't they?'

Marshall smiles. 'Oh yes, she's an old girl. Upstaged some years ago by the Type 48 tubs. That's why we're poking around the Indian Ocean. Bloody navy's too embarrassed to put us where someone might see us. Oh well, at least we're in the right place at the right time. We picked up that rusty old tug — the *Sa-baah* — three hours ago. The crew gave us your bearing and told us what you did for them; thank you.'

'It wasn't just me — the two brothers helped.' Deflecting praise was a habit with Simon, and besides, despite the problems with Ishmael, he and Lubayd *had* helped.

'A pair of ratbags,' Marshall grunts.

Simon smiles back. The captain did not detain them, but insisted that they leave the area and return with their mother to the port of Aden immediately. He was pleased about that; neither of them meant any harm, and he wouldn't be here without them.

'The question is,' Marshall rests one foot on a sill, and holds his dimpled chin between thumb and forefinger, 'what the hell do we do with you? I've had orders from the top to bring you in.'

'I want to find my daughters. End of story.'

'How old are they?'

'Hannah is eleven; Frances, fourteen.' On impulse he takes out his wallet and passes across the photo. 'Hannah's being a bit silly — always hamming it up. She's like that.'

Marshall studies the print before handing it back. 'I started young. I've got three. One still in high school, the other two have careers of their own now. One in the navy.' He sniffs. 'Expecting my first grandchild in December. Not bad going, eh?'

'Then you know how I feel.'

'Yes, but look, my orders are to keep you under lock and key, but that doesn't sit right with me — you're doing what any man would do for his children. Besides, it might be a few days before your SIS pals pick you up. If I let you remain at large, will you promise not to interfere?'

'You have my word. If that changes, I'll tell you.'

'OK.' Marshall clears his throat and reaches for a bottle of spring water, air escaping rhythmically as he drinks. Finished, he wipes his lips, and screws the plastic cap back on. 'There's been satellite imagery of some suspicious activity around Khateer Island. Thirty nautical miles north of here. It's a long shot, but I've been ordered to do some discreet surveillance, so we're steaming that way. Now, how about a guided tour? Plenty of young lads laying around who need something to do.'

Simon suspects that this is a ploy to get him out of the captain's way for a while, but this, he decides, is understandable. 'OK. I'd like that.'

Marshall runs his eyes over Simon's Middle Eastern garb. 'Have a shower while you're at it, and I'll arrange some proper clothes. That is, unless you'd prefer to run around like that?'

Simon smiles. 'No, some clothes would be great.'

Marshall touches his shoulder and leads the way out onto the signal deck. 'We'll let these gentlemen do their jobs, shall we?'

Taking a last look through the glass screens, Simon decides that it is a fine feeling to be out on a warship, towering over the darkened sea, the breeze raising the hair on his forearms, knowing that there is nothing out there to fear. Not even the best armed Somali pirates would mess with a warship like this one.

A pair of ladders take them down to the side decks, the awning above stacked with white canisters labelled as twenty-man lifeboats. Midships, Marshall stops in front of a notice board, studying what appears to be a roster sheet. 'I'll find someone to give you the grand tour.' After a moment's thought he picks up a handset and issues an order.

The guide is a radar operator called Matt Wyman, a twenty-something Leading Seaman with rosy red cheeks and a perpetual smile. Simon is delighted to discover that he hails from Guildford, the county town of Surrey, on the River Wey. The revelation is like a breath of fresh air.

'Guildford, Jesus, we used to play cricket against you blokes. Before your time, of course. What school did you go to?'

'St Peters.'

'A Catholic, then. I won't hold it against you, of course.'

'Thank Christ for that.' Matt rubs his hands together as if with controlled excitement. 'Now, let's start right down the arse end, will we? Work our way along?'

'Whatever you like.' Simon smiles to himself. *Guildford, eh? Small world.*

Apart from a cramped quarterdeck, the flight deck is the most aft section of the ship. 'Normally we've got a

Lynx or a Sea King chopper there but they took it away after the last tour. We only get one now on a needs basis.'

'Budget cutbacks?'

'Something like that. That's what happens when you work for a government that's flat stony broke. I don't think the brass have too high an expectation of us doing anything too useful. Waiting to sell us off for scrap.'

They amble along the walkway for the length of the ship, while Matt points out the various turret guns, the quick-firing Oerlikons, up high on the B gun deck for the best field of fire.

'I'd tread softly here if I were you,' Matt warns.

'Why?'

'Because the ammo room's down beneath us.'

Simon's face falls. 'Could it actually — '

'Nah, just messing with you.'

Simon struggles to remember the name and purpose of each radar array, antenna, and item of weaponry. Each has an official designation, and a nickname. 'What's that one that looks like a screen?'

'Oh, that's the Early Warning Navigation System, but we call it the flycatcher.'

'Those spheres, what are they for?'

'Radcoms,' Matt explains, 'gunnery control. Look cool, don't they?'

The most intriguing are the rounded radomes over protruding gun barrels that resemble futuristic armed robots. 'Yeah, we call that one R2D2,' Matt explains. 'The Phalanx weapon system. You know those Gatling guns they have on choppers?'

'Yeah.'

'Well, same thing, but this one fires 20mm cannon

rounds, radar guided. Spits out four and a half thousand rounds per minute.'

'Hell.'

'It'll destroy an incoming missile in midair, or take out a small boat in the blink of an eye.'

Once they have covered the exterior, Matt takes him inside, moving fore to aft this time. 'You've already been on the bridge so we won't worry about that.' They climb down an iron companionway. 'The captain's cabin is that way, but I won't take you there. Place is always a bloody mess anyway. These are the officers' quarters, along the corridor here.' He drops his voice. 'If you listen closely you'll hear them wanking from here.'

Simon is still laughing to himself as they descend another level. The hum of the engines grows louder, vibrating through the wall. 'How do people sleep with that going on?'

'Oh, you get used to it. One of those things, you know.' Matt opens a door, showing a cabin with three bunks, one of which is occupied by a man, blanket pulled up and face jammed against the bulkhead. Matt makes no effort to moderate the volume of his voice. 'This is my cabin. You're staying in here too. That bottom bunk is empty. It's yours while you're on board.'

There is a neat stack of long-sleeved workwear, along with a towel on the bed. His flight case sits on the deck.

'There's your number eights,' Matt says. 'You're to have a shower and change. The captain says that you're making everyone nervous getting around like Lawrence of Arabia.'

'I'd be happy to.' Simon continues to study the cabin. A poster of Miss June or her equivalent, bare breasted, pouts from pride of place on the wall.

'That's Elsie — I hope she doesn't offend you,' Matt said.

'Not at all. Er, she's very nice.'

A quarter-hour later, inconspicuously dressed, his face bright red from the hottest water he has encountered for some time, Simon's tour continues. Mess rooms; kitchen; laundry. Always the crew are polite and friendly, almost as many women as men, looking up from their tasks to smile and say hello.

Even so, Simon is pleased to reach deck level once more, feeling as if he's just spent half an hour down a mine shaft. Before he has adjusted, however, Matt leads him back down, through a wardroom and into the ops room.

'This is the heart of the ship, or the brain, more like. It's where I work. Pretend to, anyway.'

This room, lit by red overhead lights, is crowded with personnel and equipment. Marshall occupies a central seat much like the officer of the watch on the bridge. Beside him stands a man Matt describes as a principal warfare officer, on board to discuss possible strategic courses of action with the captain.

A plotting table dominates the foremost quarter of the room, used for marking known positions of other ships, aircraft and land masses in the area. Radar displays occupy the corners of the room, with circular screens mounted on giant hinges so they can be moved to suit the viewing angle. A large LCD screen is mounted above the plotting table, showing a scrolling text of operational updates.

With a word to the operator, whose blonde hair is braided close to the back of her head, Matt takes over one of the radar units for a moment. 'This one is my baby, the surface scanner. Have a look.'

Simon does so, struggling to interpret the greenish tinges on the screen.

'The captain authorised me to tell you that we have orders to check out a particular island,' Matt says.

'What for?' Simon feels the slow germination of excitement.

'Atypical activity is the official term.' He thrusts a long narrow forefinger at the screen. 'You can see the peaks, there, and the general outline. All this clutter here — they're seabirds.'

'You can pick up birds?'

'Sure we can — we can pick up a lolly wrapper blowing in the wind if we want to.'

Simon's mind races ahead. 'So what else can you tell about the island? Are there any boats?'

'Not that we can see — there's too much clutter down low. Maybe if there's something moving around we'd have a chance, but everything on screen is stationary, apart from them birds.' He points across at the other units. 'We have state-of-the-art long range capability, mainly for weather forecasting. For instance, we know that there is one hell of a hurricane a thousand miles east of here. Interesting one: started out in the South China Sea as a tropical storm, now in the Bay of Bengal. Ever seen one on a plotter?'

'Not for a while.'

'Come over and have a look.'

The cyclone has the typical spiral shape, with long tendrils of cloud reaching out hundreds of kilometres from the eye, occupying a chunk of sea between India and Pakistan. The image is overlaid by a trace of the southern Indian coastline and the Andaman Islands, an Indian possession on the south eastern quadrant of the Bay.

'Hit that area just a few hours ago,' the operator says. 'Getting quite a battering, by all reports.'

'Poor bastards,' Simon says, then follows Matt as he walks back out onto the deck.

The mountains begin with a beguiling rise, becoming a dramatic backdrop of silver and yellow. Few plants larger than the ubiquitous whistling thorn bushes grow here. Nothing green to soften the harshness of the landscape.

'Any trees would have been felled for firewood centuries ago,' Madoowbe explains, 'if ever there were any at all.'

'It looks stark — empty.'

By noon, despite the bike's slipstream, Marika is sweating from armpits to thighs. Heat dances in vaporous waves from the road. The mountains vary from plateaux to jagged passes surrounded on both sides with towering cliffs of stone. Generations of camels have nibbled the grasses down to a network of roots that scarcely bind the soil. Here and there are reminders of civilisation, such as a burned out car and even, once, the ruined shell of a battle tank, turret gun pointing westwards at some long gone enemy.

'From the war with Ethiopia,' Madoowbe comments, 'a long time ago.'

'Were you in it?'

'No. It was before my time. But some older men of my clan had burns and missing limbs. Others had lost fathers and brothers.'

Marika glares at the back of his head. 'You don't ever mention the women.'

'What do you mean?'

'You always talk about the men. What about the women? Didn't they lose husbands, sons, and brothers?'

Madoowbe looks at her as if she is crazy. 'Of course they did.'

'Well, why didn't you say so?'

'Because there is no need to state the obvious.' He shakes his head and concentrates on operating the bike. 'Why do you ask such pointless questions?'

'To me, and anyone who lives in the modern world, they are not pointless at all, but quite sensible. You come from a sexist society, and see no reason to change your views. Forgive me if I have the gall to challenge you on that.'

Madoowbe half turns and rolls his eyes as if to indicate that she is crazy, then concentrates rigorously on operating the machine, intent on avoiding conversation.

This silence remains unbroken until the mid-afternoon when, crossing a stony plain, the motorbike slows.

'We may be in for some trouble,' Madoowbe warns.

Peering ahead, slitting her eyes against the slipstream, Marika sees three figures on the road. Each is dressed in military-style clothing, most with a black shemagh wrapped tightly around the face. Dark sunglasses over the eyes. Each man also holds an AK47 with its long, curved magazine. Most have another mag taped upside down to the other — a trick used to facilitate a quick changeover. One individual, she notices, has a half-healed scar on his arms, pink and ugly.

Madoowbe's body tenses. 'I hope you've got a round in that chamber.'

In response she pumps the bolt and shifts the weapon so the butt rests on her thigh. 'Who are they?'

'Shifta — bandits.'

'Why are you stopping to talk to them?'

'Because if I don't they will kill us. Good enough reason?'

'I suppose. Can't you go around them?'

'They are not stupid. We are surrounded by a minefield. Probably left over from the war.'

Marika scans the roadsides, noting the rusted, mangled vehicle shells, blown apart by mines while attempting to skirt the ambush.

'A minefield? Jesus Christ.'

'Stop saying that please.'

'Sorry.'

'The road is clear, of course; we are safe provided we do not leave it. Now cover your face or you may upset them.'

Marika takes the hijab from her pocket and ties it around her head, letting it fall over her face and neck. As the motorbike slides to a stop all three of the shifta raise their weapons.

'Assalam alaikum. Peace be upon you,' the leader says.

'And upon *you* also be peace.'

Marika has to stifle a laugh — the shifta leader and his comrades are holding them up with automatic rifles while also wishing them peace.

The incongruity, it seems, has not struck the man, as he goes on, 'What is your clan?'

Madoowbe seems at ease as he first translates for Marika, then lifts his sunglasses, removes them and wipes the sweat from his eyes. 'My clan is the Leelkase of the Darod.'

The man narrows his eyelids in suspicion. 'You speak in an unusual manner for a Leelkase.'

'I have been abroad.'

'America?'

Madoowbe shakes his head vehemently. 'No. The Arab Emirates.'

'Dubai?'

'Yes.'

The man eases back on his hips and scratches his beard with his free hand. 'Ah. Where God's faithful are making the kufr leaders look like fools, and will butcher them like goats before the eyes of the world?'

'Yes.'

'Praise be to God that it is possible for a man to travel so far in this dangerous world. What is your name?'

Marika scarcely dares to breathe; the atmosphere remains tense. It will, she decides, be possible to take out one, perhaps two of the shifta. Surreptitiously she shifts the gun's selector from semi to full auto, before again squinting out at the bandits.

'Muyassar Namir Qutb.'

'So your father was Namir. Of what subclan?'

The third man is the problem, Marika decides — weapon held casually, yet his hand already curled on the grip, finger on the trigger … like so many of these men, he has a gun and wants to use it.

'My father is of the Fiqi Ismail subclan,' Madoowbe says, 'and *his* father Qutb was a well-known Sheikh.' In Somali culture, Marika knows from a briefing on the region, a Sheikh is not a political leader so much as a holy man, a healer and shaman.

The leading bandit lifts his weapon so fast it surprises Marika, and by the time she lowers her own barrel in response, ready to fire, she realises that the other man's rifle is not aimed at her. Instead he fires a long burst into the air. Confused, she stops short of pulling the trigger, watching as the bandit half empties his magazine skywards. 'You,' he cries, stepping forwards to clap Madoowbe on the shoulder, 'are my second cousin's cousin. Allahu akbar. Here, bring your motorcycle and woman. Break your journey with us.'

The shifta camp, two or three miles from the road, is hidden by a ravine, and must have once been a charming oasis. Here Marika sees the first real trees in a while — palms, acacias and moss-draped tree heather in clusters beside tents and lean-to shelters made of an eclectic variety of materials. The dwellings are enhanced by fireside chairs fashioned from seats taken from vehicles. Some have dark bloody stains on the upholstery.

Marika is still trying to make sense of the exchange with the shifta. 'Isn't your name Madoowbe?'

'Madoowbe is what we call a naanays, a nickname. I was telling him my full name. Now shush, they might hear us talk in English, and we do not want to alarm them.'

The group of twenty or more shifta travel ahead, discharging their weapons into the air to announce their arrival, just as troops from other cultures might blow bagpipes or bugles. Madoowbe slows the bike to walking pace, struggling to maintain a line on the sandy track, the front wheel wandering into ruts and dustbowls.

Women in hijab and kikoi scoop up running children as they pass. Older boys — bare chests, running noses — pause in their games and stare. Marika's heart melts at the round, brown eyes full of curiosity. A dozen or more mottled hens, undersized by Western standards, squabble out of the way while their rooster glares aggressively at the newcomers.

Madoowbe stops the engine and kicks the motorbike stand down beside tethered camels and vehicles in various stages of repair and disrepair, everything from quad bikes to an ancient Allison dozer with broken tracks lying like iron plates, half covered with sand. From here they proceed on foot, and the smells intensify, so many competing scents that Marika struggles to identify them all — spicy food; camel dung; firesmoke; human and animal excreta.

In a clearing below an inward-leaning cliff face they enter a busy compound with a rusted shipping container sitting drunkenly on the earth, a giant, faded logo painted in black on the side. Marika can only imagine the size of the truck they must have hijacked to get it. Up to now the encampment seemed almost friendly, yet she feels a heightened sense of danger, for all these men either carry weapons or have them leaning close at hand.

The bandit who met them on the road shouts his relationship to Madoowbe, but it is Marika who first captures the interest of the party, drawing hungry male stares — the lure of the unusual — for surely they must have noticed her light skin. Their thoughts are plain in their eyes: *Is she the same as my woman? What does she have underneath those clothes?*

'I don't like this,' she hisses at Madoowbe. 'We've gone from one lot of lowlifes to another. These ones are just a bit less sophisticated.'

'Be thankful that you are alive.'

'For the moment. Are you really related to this lot?'

'No, but please! You never know where you will find English speakers — at least to some degree.'

Marika feels a jolt of fear. 'You lied to them? What are they going to do to us if they work out the truth?'

'Quiet, please, unless you wish to find out.'

Marika bites her lip and turns her attention to a central hearth fire surrounded by more vehicle seats. A cast-iron cauldron hangs over the fire from a tripod that may have once been a gun mounting.

The emir, a squat, barrel-chested specimen with spiky whiskers and a whining voice, waves Madoowbe to a seat beside the fire. When Marika follows he shakes his head — *Mia, mia* — then leads her a short distance away to an iron bench.

'Sexual discrimination is alive and well in the wilderness,' she mutters to herself, watching as man after man comes to greet Madoowbe, offering long compliments and reminisces of childhood events — fights, droughts and milestones such as a particular individual completing the Hajj.

A woman appears, giving Marika a cup of hot cha and two cakes set on a bowl made of plastic sheet that she suspects might once have been a section of fender from a car. The woman says nothing, but moves away and out of sight. Marika eats hungrily while never taking her eyes off the shifta. The cakes are spicy with cinnamon, yet very dry, and the cha rougher and sweeter than that served by Dalmar Asad.

Almost as soon as she finishes she looks across at Madoowbe, trying to catch his eye. He smiles back as if in an effort to reassure her, then resumes his conversation.

Just as the afternoon seems as if it might stretch on forever without incident, the emir issues a shouted command, and the camp snaps to attention. A space is cleared beside the hearth, and a small team of men get to work, each to pre-arranged tasks.

At first Marika assumes that she is witnessing some quasi-religious ritual. Two men carry a wooden table into the cleared space. Two others disappear, then return with a portable generator, faded Chinese lettering on the sides. This machine they set up twenty or so metres away, then run a heavy-duty power lead across to the table.

Meanwhile, two others carry a battered cardboard box from the shipping container. The word SONY is printed on the sides. Watching them unpack the box Marika shakes her head in disbelief as first speakers, then the separate components of an archaic compact disc player and amplifier, are lifted onto the table and wired up.

The speakers are, with much discussion and pointed orders from the emir, placed on terra firma, facing out in Madoowbe's general direction. At a shouted order the generator splutters into life, and one of the crew, a beardless adolescent, obviously the outfit's technical wizard, walks from the container with a small stack of CDs. He powers up the machine, slips in a disc and the assemblage waits. A moment later, at a volume set to compete with occasional gunfire, the music begins.

Marika listens, bemused, the incongruity of the music making her laugh, taking her back to childhood, to her mother dancing around the kitchen to the husky male voice that now blares from the speakers.

Aw, aw baby, yeah, ooh yeah, huh, listen to this …

Marika smiles to herself. *Tom Jones*. Wonders if anyone has ever pointed out the meaning of the lyrics, doubting that they would please these strict Muslims.

The song ends, and after much discussion the CD is ejected and another slid in to replace it.

What next? Marika thinks.

A classical piece that Marika does not recognise follows, but the kettle drums echoing around the cliffs are strangely resonant. The music is warlike, martial in style, and appeals to the shifta, who stand throughout, eyes misty, as though recalling glorious battles and ambushes of long ago.

The recital lasts for around thirty minutes, at which point the emir barks an order. Someone presses the kill switch on the generator and the stereo system returns to the cardboard box. Everything is packed away in the shipping container and the door closes. Marika shares a glance with Madoowbe and does her best to communicate with her eyes. *These people are crazy. Let's get the hell out of here.*

Madoowbe appears to understand. He nods and looks away.

Before long, Marika dozes in the chair, waking to the occasional sound of gunfire. This, she realises, is an extension of the shifta's conversation — like a loud shout of pleasure. At one stage Madoowbe is led away — for a tour of the area, she imagines.

Returning half an hour later he is able to pause beside her for a moment.

'Have you found anything out?' she asks.

'Yes. These people know everything that passes through this land. Two of them made contact with a party of nomads a week ago. Apparently they learned that a woman who has been in America walks among them — a woman who wears clothes like a male.'

'Where?'

'Somewhere to the northwest, and not too far away. The same two men are out in the desert hunting dikdik, and will return before dark. I need to talk to them first, and perhaps they will lead us there.'

One of the shifta calls Madoowbe across. 'Hi, cousin, my friend Samih has come to hear your story of the two goats in the corn field. Can you tell it again?'

Marika shrugs, resigned to sitting there a little longer. 'Go on, keep them happy, but I want to be out of here by nightfall, OK?'

Day 5, 15:30

Twenty nautical miles out from the island, HMS *Durham* runs in with the Rolls Royce turbines barely ticking over, yet still making five knots over the ground. The ops room is lit from above with red fluorescent tubes, giving the appearance of a photographer's dark room. Captain Marshall stands at the front, in discussion with the PWO.

On duty, Matt is a different man altogether. His face shows a sheen of sweat, even in the air-conditioned room. 'Looks like we'll get a briefing, in a minute,' he says, 'and you might get an idea of what the hell is going on.'

'What if these people on the island have their own radar?' Simon asks. 'Won't they see us here?'

'The captain's already thought of that. There's an EA-18G Growler circling over us, forty thousand feet up, jamming them. They might suspect that something's amiss, but they won't know much.'

The main LCD screen now displays an image that resembles the civilian Google Earth, yet with superior resolution. The island is a dun-coloured sprawl, rocky and inhospitable, pounded by long lines of ocean rollers.

Marshall uses a pointer to mark out a group of crude structures above the cliffs. 'These are fishermen's huts, used occasionally — no one lives there. This image, however, is about a month old; the satellite has picked up at least one new dwelling since then, and signs of people moving around. There are two places where a boat can land on the island; one is the only protected anchorage, just below the huts. The other is a beach at the base of some rugged cliffs.'

The screen changes and the next image is a patchwork of colour. Marshall's eyes settle on Simon's. 'This is an infra-red exposure. Do you understand what that means?'

'Kind of.'

'The cameras pick up heat arrays rather than images. Human bodies, for example, stand out at night, because they are warmer than the surrounding ground. The coloured patches are humans, and the streaks indicate movement. There are at least ten people in and around the huts. Some haven't moved much in the period covered by the satellite pass. Some a little more.'

Simon leans back and sighs.

A signalman moves through the hatch, pausing beside the captain and saluting. 'Flash traffic from Fleet Headquarters, for CO's eyes only.'

Marshall smiles at Simon. 'This'll be it now.'

Simon watches Marshall unfold a yellow sheet of paper, scanning it with his eyes. His expression changes as he screws up the paper and slips it into his pocket. 'Bad news. We've been ordered back to base.'

'Why?'

'They didn't say. That's the way things work around here, I'm afraid. Obviously this little sideline is not important any more.'

Matt scoffs, 'It means that the brass don't think that the lives of two girls are enough to risk one warship. Even one as old and embarrassing as us.'

'Be careful what you say, young Wyman,' the captain warns.

Simon frowns. 'So we just have to pack up and go?'

'It seems that way, yes.'

'Can't you query the order?'

'I can, and I will. But I'll eat my hat if they change their minds.'

Simon grips a rail so tight it seems that his fingers might crack. 'Can I use the satphone, please?'

'Of course you can. If you think it'll do any good.'

Simon makes the call from the signal deck, looking down at the sea, helplessly watching the rapid and thorough preparations for departure. He dials the number from memory.

'Can I speak to Mr Thomas Mossel, please?'

'I'm sorry, sir, Mr Mossel is in a meeting.'

'Get him.'

'I'm sorry?'

'Are you fucking listening? Get him.' To Simon it sounds like someone else talking.

There is a shocked silence, then piped music as he is put on hold. A minute later, Tom Mossel's voice.

'Who is this?'

'It's Simon. Tom, I need your help.'

'OK, but you just upset my secretary.'

'Sorry about that. This is important.'

'Lots of things are important right now. What is it?'

'I think you probably know. *Durham* just got ordered back to base. They had a job to do and now it's changed. Why?'

'That's a navy decision. I can't interfere. More recent images have thrown doubt on earlier conclusions. Our analysts are now putting activity on the island down to a family group of fishermen.'

'Crap.'

'Listen, Simon, I'm in a link-up with the acting PM right now. That's important too. I can't interfere. I'm sorry, but I can't.'

Simon feels something cold and calm. 'I get it now,' he says, 'you wanted to find the girls because you thought they might lead you to this terrorist called Saif al-Din, didn't you? That's no longer the case. He's somewhere else and you don't care any more. Is that right?'

The sigh of expelled breath is audible across the line. 'If you must know, Saif al-Din was spotted yesterday in Dubai. Our operatives are busy looking for him there.'

'So finding my girls is no longer important?'

'Of course it's important, but just not a priority. Jesus, Simon, put yourself in my shoes. The world is turning to shit and we have to concentrate on the most critical problems. I'm sorry.'

'You gave me a spiel about my daughters being British

citizens, that they would not be abandoned. Was that just a speech? You're talking to the acting PM, surely she can do something.' He pauses, searching for the right words. 'You're my only hope.'

More silence. 'Simon, you're talking about men's lives. People getting killed maybe. Leave it with me, but for the moment, I don't have enough cause to interfere with RN orders.'

Simon ends the call and carries the handset back to the ops room, where he faces the captain. 'Take me up to the island,' he pleads, 'give me a small boat and a gun and I'll get them out myself.'

Marshall shakes his head. 'You know I can't do that.'

'If you turn and head for base my kids are dead. There's no one else.' Simon feels all the fight go out of him. There is nothing he can do now. Everything is in the hands of others, and they will never care the way he does.

Marshall drops one hand to his shoulder. 'Look, I've been thinking while you were out of the room. There is one other thing we could try.'

'What's that?'

'Stinger.'

'What the hell is that?'

'A micro air vehicle. Camera drone. Use it to check out the island. It won't take long, and it'll tell us one way or the other if there's something going on.' He turns and shouts to the executive officer. 'XO. Tell Comms to message Fleet. Tell them that we're going to do a flyover with Stinger before we go. They'll want to monitor it too.'

Simon lifts both hands and wipes a clammy sheen of sweat from his face, wondering how much more of this he can take.

* * *

Ali Khalid Abukar wipes his eyes and stares upwards. The newsreader has a dry, Eastern European voice with an American texture. Despite the red-painted lips and stylish clothing she seems as machine like and remote as a computer generated abstraction.

The Canadian Government today announced the withdrawal of more than one hundred military engineers from Afghanistan. They will also initiate urgent shipments of aid to East Africa, an initiative that may total five hundred thousand tonnes of grain.

The government of France has refused to cooperate with terrorism in any way.

There is a hiss of shock in the room and Ali watches the French President, seeing the fear in his eyes.

The United States Congress has agreed to the following ....

The government of Israel welcomes peace initiatives from Palestinian organisations but will not respond to demands made under duress, and rejects the methods used ...

The voice drones on: *Pakistan ... withdrawing troops ... ceasing hostilities ... Germany ... withdrawing armed forces personnel ...*

Ali leans over the dais, holding a pen at its fulcrum and swinging it like a toy, still watching the screen. The roll call of responses continues for at least ten minutes. He coughs, and stares out at the hostages. *His* hostages. They are restless, confused. Some countries have followed instructions, many haven't.

Hearing footsteps, he turns. Zhyogal is on his way to the dais, his face a mask of anger, his voice a cracking whip. 'Did I not tell you that there are countries who will treat us with contempt?'

'That is true, but ...'

Zhyogal slides the pistol from his holster. 'They are no longer afraid. We have not yet touched the greatest imperialists of all. They feel safe. Now is the time.'

Ali feels as light as air, panicking like a fish stranded on a beach, flopping in all directions yet still unable to breathe. 'So many are doing what we have asked. It is still a great success — even the United States. Will more violence not provoke them further?'

'Did you hear? They have committed nothing. Industrialised nations have plundered and exploited us for centuries. Their actions now bring ruination to us all. They must pay, and now is the time to show the world that we are serious.' Zhyogal takes the dais and shakes a fist. 'You do not understand the danger you are in. Many of your countries have chosen to insult their own leaders by showing bravado. It is time to bring down the biggest criminals of all. Starting from now, I will judge and execute the war criminals of the countries who regard themselves as the leaders of the West. I will begin with the French President.' He raises his voice: 'Bring Monsieur Bourque here. Let him be an example.'

Two of the mujahedin converge on the Frenchman. At the last moment he stands and tries to run, but they seize an arm each and drag him to the dais where they kick his legs out from underneath him.

'Kneel.'

The President of France is sobbing now, calling out obscenities in his own language.

Zhyogal shouts, 'The past governments of your country are the architects of nothing short of attempted genocide in Algeria. For two hundred years France has bled my country dry and I have grown from the womb hating you.'

'That was before my time — '

'Yes, but there has been no restitution. No responsibility taken. You, personally, have a long list of crimes to your credit. You, monsieur, were the minister of defence who initiated Operation Unicorn in the Ivory Coast. Paratroopers — masquerading as peacekeepers — slaughtered hundreds of innocent civilians *on your orders*. Your country hides many perpetrators of the genocide in Rwanda and fails to help bring them to justice. You are charged with murder in Libya, Iraq, and Afghanistan. You have treated the Muslim peoples of your own nation with contempt, used riot police to control their justifiable protest.'

Ali watches as Zhyogal holds the pistol an inch from the back of the desperate man's head, waits for the struggles to subside, and fires. The body slumps to the boards and a black stain spreads around it. Ringing silence fills the room.

Holstering the weapon, Zhyogal stands and addresses the cameras. 'If the world does not listen, I promise death. I promise to open the gates of Hell itself.'

The two hunters arrive in the evening, rifles slung on backs, the leader a hook-nosed giant of a man, yet lean of frame, black whiskers concentrated on the chin and upper lip.

'Who seeks Abdul Haq?' he asks.

'I do,' says Madoowbe.

'Why?'

'I have a message for him.'

'And who are you?'

'I am Muyassar Namir Qutb.'

Marika, watching from her place in the shade, has a deepening premonition of danger.

'No, you are not,' says Abdul Haq.

The silence is complete.

Madoowbe offers a little laugh. 'Of course I am.'

'No, you are not. Muyassar is my cousin. I saw him just six months ago, in Burtinle.'

Again Madoowbe laughs, yet the sound is hollow. These seconds, Marika knows, are the only ones she will get, for the hook-nosed man is in the process of unslinging his assault rifle. There on her bench, forgotten, she lifts her own weapon from where it leans beside her and fires from the hip. Warning shots would be futile, she decides — gunfire is more familiar than flatulence to these people. One bullet takes the man in the side of the chest and another in the head. He falls in a startled heap in the sand.

Marika starts running before the corpse stops kicking. Men move to block Madoowbe from joining her, but he is agile, and together they pound down the pathway towards the motorbike.

'Thanks for that,' he says. 'Rather timely, I might say.'

'Shut up and run.'

The first burst of gunfire follows them, but appears to have been aimed high, conscious of the danger to the women and children at the fires. Bullets zap and twang in the leaves and branches, some of which fall to earth.

Madoowbe, having started ahead of her, reaches the bike first and straddles it, kicking at the starter, face sheeted with sweat, swearing to encourage the machine to start.

'Damn it,' Marika cries. 'Hurry.' A horde of men attempts to reach them, hampered by their own numbers, weapons out and still firing. Her eyes blaze. 'Are you trying to get me killed on purpose? Is that your plan? If so you're doing one hell of a job.'

Five, six times Madoowbe's foot kicks at the starter, rewarded by not even the tiniest flutter.

'Leave it,' Marika cries, 'leave it and run.'

Madoowbe does as she asks, but stops at the nearest camel, a huge beast, adorned with multicoloured tassels along both neck and body, fur matted with dung below and around the tail. It drops to the ground with the same unwieldy grace as a building imploding.

'Climb on,' he exhorts.

Marika grips the beast's neck for balance, and straddles the hump, feeling Madoowbe get up behind her and lift the reins. The animal rises on long, knobbly legs, still in no hurry. After a solid kick from Madoowbe, to the accompaniment of shouts and gunfire, it breaks into a run. 'They will not risk killing this camel,' he says, 'he is a fine beast, and very valuable.'

'Then they will surely not allow us to get away with him either.'

'That is true,' he admits. 'They will follow.'

'So why did you have to tell more lies, back there, to the shifta? Why give them a false name?'

'Because if I hadn't we would both be dead.'

'That's always your excuse. Every bloody time. Who is this Muyassar whatever it is? Where did you get the name from?'

'I borrowed it from a man I met in the coffee shop yesterday — the one who told me all about Dalmar Asad. It was a risk, yes, but our only way through. I am not of this subclan and they would have killed us.'

Marika turns to see camels and riders lurch into pursuit. 'This is bloody hopeless, even if we find her — I've lost all my communications gear. What the hell are we going to do? Walk out of Somalia on foot? God damn you, Madoowbe, if you're not this Muyassar Namir Whatever, then who the hell are you? Can't you tell the truth for once? Just once?'

'Later perhaps,' he says, 'if they do not catch us, and if we do not ride into another minefield, then perhaps I will tell you.'

'More minefields?'

'Yes, of course. They are common in this area.'

'Where are we heading?'

'Northwest. She was last seen in that direction. We must look there.'

'How will we get away from the shifta?'

'There is one way: ride faster than they do.'

Marika is silent for a moment, conscious of the closeness of their position, his body pressed against her back, his arms extending from around her body to hold the reins. 'What if our camel is slower than theirs?'

'Getting away will not be possible.'

Stinger is constructed of four propfan equipped discs joined at the middle. The energy comes from a hydrogen fuel cell housed in the centre just above the camera. Sitting on a simple launch pad on the flight deck the entire gadget is assembled and prepared in just a few minutes.

At a command from the operator, who moonlights as a computer technician, the fans spin and the thing levitates from the deck, buzzing ominously. Controlled by a laptop computer, it swoops, dives, and hovers in a short sequence of operational tests. The device reminds Simon of the Golden Snitch from the Harry Potter films of his youth.

The buzz rises in pitch and in an instant, the machine is off and away, rising to an incredible height at which point the pale blue painted underside is no longer visible.

'That's the beauty of it,' Marshall says. 'At two thousand feet no one can see the damn thing from the ground. Can't hear it either. Come on, we'll get a better view on the screen in the ops room.'

The LED backlit screen shows a bird's-eye view of the ocean from what Simon judges to be around three thousand feet.

'Be handy for fishing,' someone says.

'Don't even joke about it,' Marshall warns. 'Before they pretty much wiped out the bluefin tuna, skippers were using these things to find the schools.' He turns to the technician in control of Stinger. 'How much flight time have we got?'

'Twenty-two minutes' power remaining. At this speed it should be plenty.'

'Change bearing eight degrees north.' Matt orders adjustments as he tracks Stinger's path towards the island.

'Course corrected.'

Simon can only guess the speed at which Stinger travels, but within five minutes the outline of the island appears ahead. He recognises the basic features from the flat topographical image that Marshall showed him earlier, but it looks very different. He finds himself praying. There is something dark and forbidding about the place. From a distance it looks uninhabited and drab, as if there is no vegetation at all.

Stinger moves closer, revealing steep cliffs, and waves rolling in, breaking on the rocks. Simon notes the small natural harbour, yet no real detail from that height.

'OK,' Marshall orders, 'put Stinger on a holding station there.'

Now Simon understands the design of the MAV better: the ability to hover, almost motionless, for long periods. The image slows and becomes better defined, focused on the huts above the natural harbour. Even at that height, they are visible. A smudge of smoke emanates from what must be a fire.

'Now. Zoom us in.'

Watching the screen gives Simon a feeling of vertigo; the unpleasant sensation of freefalling towards the earth at warp speed. The huts and surrounding landscape enlarge. Objects that were just specks become boulders, or human beings or bizarre trees that look like no other Simon has ever seen. The huts themselves are makeshift structures built of driftwood and flotsam, roofed with palm fronds.

'There's a group of men to the bottom left,' Marshall says. 'Enlarge them please.'

Simon scarcely dares to breathe as the camera zooms in. Are they merely fishermen, or something more sinister? The dress is certainly not military, but standard Arab garb that could mean anything.

'There,' someone shouts, 'that man has a weapon. You can see the muzzle.'

The vertical view makes positive identification difficult, but another of the men has his rifle slung, but levelled. 'That's a definite,' Marshall says, 'looks like an AK-style assault weapon.'

'That's it then,' Simon hisses, 'they wanted proof, and we've got it.'

Marshall shakes his head. 'Simon, just about everyone in this part of the world carries a gun.'

'Even fishermen?'

'Even Avon ladies.'

'Fourteen minutes' power remaining,' warns the technician.

'God, if only we could see inside those huts.'

Marshall takes a call on the sat phone and walks to the back of the room while Stinger covers every square metre of the encampment. The other item of interest is a tarpaulin-covered area to one side that might be a trench, possibly hiding more powerful weaponry.

Coming back, Marshall holds one hand over the phone. 'I've got Fleet on the line. They're still not convinced. Want us to have a look at the harbour. See what's there.'

The field of view drops back, giving Simon the uncomfortable feeling of rising through the air, and Stinger flies until it is centred over the harbour. Down again, camera zooming in until it focuses on what looks like a crude but solid dock, and another hut, this one more substantial than the ones above. Again there are men. Two of them, lounging in the shade. If they have weapons they are not carrying them. There is no boat in sight.

'Nine minutes' power remaining, sir. We'll need most of that to bring Stinger home.'

Marshall talks back into the phone, then. 'OK, bring her back. There's nothing else to see.' He looks across at Simon apologetically.

As the screen view changes, moving out over a white-capped sea, the general attention of the room wanders. The crew talk among themselves. Only Simon continues to stare.

Without warning, the view on the screen rocks as if shaken and Stinger turns somersault several times. Simon's first thought is that it has run out of fuel prematurely.

'What the hell?' someone blurts out.

Marshall's face displays a new tension. 'What's going on?'

'It's a plane, sir, just about cleaned Stinger up.'

'Get us a view of it, hurry.'

The camera scans from side to side until it picks up a fast-receding aircraft, floats visible below the fuselage. A faded blue stripe extends for the full length, and heavy struts support the wings.

'Hell, a float plane. Cessna 7045 by the look of her. What's it doing here?'

'They didn't even see Stinger.'

'She's going in to land.'

As the camera swivels back down to monitor the Cessna touching down, Simon sees the long white wake of a power boat on course to meet her.

'Six minutes' power remaining. We're going to lose Stinger.'

'Doesn't matter. I'll buy you another one for Christmas. Stay on station. Stay for as long as you can.'

* * *

The chartered float plane touches down on a ruffled sea, propeller buffeting in a crosswind as it turns. Saif al-Din sees the RIB waiting for him, ready for pick up, carving through the waves and wind chop.

Readying his few possessions, he waits at the door. There is no time to waste, not now, with Rabi al-Salah at such a critical stage. When the plane comes to rest, Saif watches the RIB motor closer. The man skippering the boat, a Pakistani called Inzaman, is a devout and reliable man, but still a relatively inexperienced seaman, and the hull bumps hard against the floats, prompting a bout of swearing and abuse from the pilot.

Saif waits for his opportunity, then steps across, almost losing his footing on the gunwale, gripping a rail hard as Ibrahim accelerates away. Settling into a seat, he focuses his mind on what he has come to do. Two tasks, both important. He had, in fact, been already on his way out here when the call came through for the kufr girls to be terminated. Saif would carry out the task without regret. If Zhyogal considered the death of the girls necessary then he would not flinch at the task.

The main reason for the journey to the island would not be so easy to resolve: two factions within the mujahedin here had developed a fitna, a division.

Although members of al-Muwahhidun, these men are drawn from different nations but also from different schools of Sunni thought. These schools are known as madh'hab, and each bring to Almohadism their own interpretation of the main principle of tawhid: the unity or oneness of God.

Most of the mujahedin were educated in the Maliki madh'hab, following the teachings of the scholar Malik ibn

Anas. This is the dominant African form of the religion, based on the practices and beliefs of the Salaf people of Medina, Mohammed's first kingdom.

Four men on the island, however, are of the Shafi'i school, followers of Muhammad Ibn Idris ash-Shafi'i, with its greater focus on the Sunnah, the collected observations of Mohammed's actions during his life. There are subtle differences in prayer and outlook between the two madh'habs.

While all regard themselves as al-Muwahhidun, above and beyond their madh'hab, this greater belief was interpreted with the eyes of one brought up in a particular madh'hab. Those of Shafi'i origin on the island see themselves as more devout than the Maliki, and this belief was pointed out to the others. A discussion came to blows. Mediation will be difficult.

As the RIB comes up on the plane and surges away across the surface of the ocean, Saif gives his approach to the matter serious thought. He must act first to solve the crisis. Then he will worry about the kufr girls.

Marshall stands. 'Gentlemen. We are in business. According to Fleet that man who just transferred from the float plane is none other than a terrorist wanted by law enforcement agencies across the world. We have new orders pending.' He turns to the bosun's mate. 'Pipe the crew to defence watches. Assume NBCD state. One condition Yankee.'

Simon cannot sit still. Stinger shadowed the RIB almost back to the island before it dropped into the sea. There is no doubt now. He gets up and touches the captain's shoulder. 'Do you mind if I make another call? It's very important.'

'Of course. Go for it.'

Simon carries the handset outside and punches in the number. Tom Mossel answers after a couple of rings.

'It's him, isn't it?' Simon breathes. 'That just got off that float plane. The terrorist you're after.'

'Yes.'

'Promise me you're not going to vaporise that island.'

There is a pause, then, 'You have my word. We're going to do this the old-fashioned way.'

The haboob storm comes from deep inside Ethiopia, howling and shrieking, collecting sand and dust as it rakes through the gullies and across the plains of the vast Ogaden Desert. Madoowbe shows Marika how to use the hijab for its original purpose — wrapping it tight around her face to keep the sand out, exposing just the lenses of her sunglasses.

'The haboob is both good and bad,' he says. 'The shifta will not find us, yet we will not find our band of nomads, either.'

'What do we do?'

'Keep heading north and west, and hope.'

'How do you know we are heading in the right direction?'

'If I keep the wind on my left hand, we are going the right away.'

'What if the wind changes?'

'Then we will go the wrong way.'

The air is so thick with particles that to open an unprotected mouth is to let it fill with dust, to expose an eye means temporary blindness. Only under protective layers of linen can Marika breathe, and only through the desert sense of the camel will they live. Above the moaning wind she hears the clatter of the wooden bell around the animal's neck.

Whether from exhaustion or the recent escape from extreme danger, Marika begins to feel relaxed. The blanketing sand is soothing, protecting them from any possible danger, for surely no enemy will find their way through it. Madoowbe's body is close against hers, and there are pressure points she can feel on her back.

Marika lets herself fall back against him perhaps another millimetre, enjoying the sensation, closing her eyes and letting the movement of the camel rock her away into a kind of half sleep. The darkness has been complete for some hours, and still the sand and wind continues. They ride on, together, into an endless darkness.

'You said you were going to tell me about yourself,' Marika prompts, snuggling back, closer still. His hands circle her abdomen, still holding the reins, fingers linked.

'Do you really want to know?'

'Of course I do. You're a fair old enigma, if ever I've seen one. For a start, tell me what Madoowbe, your nickname, means?'

'Madoowbe means black — my skin was very dark at birth. My full name is Libaan Khayre Istar — this is how Somali names work: Libaan is my own name; Khayre the name of my father; and Istar, the name of my grandfather. I saw each rarely, for my mother remarried twice.'

'So, Libaan — if that is honestly your name this time — why are you here? Why are you risking your life here with me?'

'I have to go back a long way to explain that.'

'We have plenty of time. I don't reckon this night will *ever* end.' The statement is heartfelt. To Marika, there is no east or west, and therefore no hope of sunrise or dusk. Just endless darkness.

Madoowbe appears to slow the camel down, as if he is thinking. Finally he starts talking, and at first Marika doesn't dare breathe in case he stops.

'When I was about twelve there was a drought. We wandered far in search of grazing, and rarely met other families. Now and then, however, we chanced a meeting with another family near a well or oasis. While the men pooled resources to dig through the sand for water, we boys were given responsibility for our few bony cattle. I remember how proud I was, on one occasion, when I found a hollow with some pasture and watched our beasts fill their rumens with sweet grass.'

Marika tries to picture the scene. 'So you were the hero?'

'Yes, until a boy from the other family, Raage, heard of my windfall and brought their cattle to the place. There was no question of sharing — we had to fight for it. The boy was older and stronger than I was.'

'What does Raage mean? It sounds like the English word for anger.'

'That naanays means delayed at birth. Anyway, work on the well stopped and the two families came to watch us fight — for above all things, a Somali loves to fight, and if he can't join in himself then watching others do so is a good second. Raage walked towards me with bunched fists, and my knees trembled. At the last moment I turned and ran all the way to where my mother stood. She shooed me away, shamed, as they all were.'

'You poor kid,' Marika says.

'My family left the place — no one would talk to me so I walked alone with one camel. When I went too close, Othman, my mother's husband, who had killed men for laughing at him, cuffed me on the ear.'

They cross a drift of sand, then descend into a deep gully where the dust flies less furiously. Madoowbe stops the camel and signals for it to kneel. Marika struggles to shift her weight sideways, finally dropping to the sand.

'What are we doing?'

'We have travelled a good distance. There is no point going further now that we have found a protected place. Here we will rest until the wind drops.'

In the deepest part of the gully is an overhanging stone ledge. After they have crawled inside, the camel drops at a signal from Madoowbe, creating a barrier between them and the storm, sitting so close that the animal smell is almost overpowering. Strangely, it lies with its head flat on the earth, turned in and away from the storm so that it appears to be watching them.

When they have settled Marika looks across at Madoowbe. 'So what happened — did your family forgive you for not fighting?'

Madoowbe appears not to have heard her at first, instead producing a sharp knife. She does not ask where he acquired it. Taking a tin mug from the saddlebag he incises a vein in the camel's leg and fills the vessel with blood.

'Drink,' he says.

'You've got to be kidding? Camel blood?'

'Your responsibility is to find this woman, Sufia, and you cannot do that if you die of thirst and hunger. This is not a matter of your preferences, of your likes and dislikes. You have a job to do — you must sustain yourself for the task. That is what a warrior does.'

Taking the mug, she drinks, finding the dark liquid sickly warm, but somewhat tasteless. When she has done so, Madoowbe refills the cup, drinks, presses his forefinger against the cut to stop the flow, then returns to the story.

'Within a few days I was able to bask in my mother's affection once more — she was a beautiful and imposing woman, around six feet tall, light brown, with a smile that drew stares from men wherever we passed. Our subclan suffered not their women to cover their faces. Othman, also, though he scowled, did not object to me taking my place with the others, and even allowed me a little dried meat from our meagre stores.'

'So how did you finally leave them? I take it you had no education at this point?'

'That is correct. We stopped at noon that following day and sat in the shade of the camels, while Othman argued with my mother about our direction. Many men would not deign to hear a woman's opinion, but my mother was a desirable, strong-willed woman, and had borne enough sons from three different fathers to have stature. My mother said that she had seen lightning far to the west the previous night. Rain might have fallen and, walking in that direction, there was a chance we might reach fresh pasture in a few days or a week. Othman disagreed, wanting to continue heading more to the south on the traditional route of the clans. His reasoning was that we had followed lightning many times before, only to be disappointed. The remaining cattle would not survive a long trek. Neither had convinced the other by the time we rested so we continued in a vague westerly heading that seemed as good as any other. In the late afternoon I spotted the dust of another family group in the distance, and our paths converged. Both groups stopped, and we looked at each other warily, trying to see if either recognised a member of the other. I remember that Othman took out his bilau, checking the edge with his thumb. He grinned and I caught his eye.

"'Come with me,' he said. I was frightened, but with Othman beside me I walked to within shouting distance of a delegation from the other party. Most of the time I liked Othman — once or twice he had even let me sit on his knee and stroke his beard — but he was very fierce and I was worried that there would be a fight.'

'Why didn't you run?'

'Because I was trying to prove that I was no coward. I counted just two camels but no cattle with the other group. They were poorer than us, but even so, unexpected encounters had to be undertaken cautiously while the two groups established their relationship to each other. A blood feud might exist, and those involved would either fight or avoid contact. Now and again a full-scale gun and knife battle would erupt with casualties on both sides.

"'My name is Othman Adam Arale," Othman shouted. "I am of the Darod people."

'The leader of the other group replied, "I am Mohammed Abdullah Mohammed. We are Marehan people, come for the promises of the great revolutionary leader of Somalia, Siad Barre, who will take us to a land where grass grows higher than a man's head."

'Othman frowned. The other group were interlopers, and now talked this crazy talk. We had heard of Siad

Barre. Somalis, no matter how remote, love politics and converse on the topic at every meeting. Barre and his men had started a revolution and taken over the country. In the normal course of events this would affect us nomads little.

'"You have not heard this news?" the Marehan asked us. It was a difficult situation for Othman, who could not admit ignorance, yet neither could he resist his natural curiosity. "I will come forward in peace and you will tell me more of this." While the women and younger children still looked at each other, the men came together and exchanged miraa.'

Marika nods understanding. 'Go on, please.'

'The marehan told of trucks gathering at the village of Sinadogo, to the south, taking all those who wanted to escape the drought to the coast, where grass grew so lush that cattle became too heavy to walk. I, for one, was ready to pack up and go that very moment, but Othman would never make a hasty decision.'

Marika was transported by these images of a harsh nomadic life, comparing it to her own. 'I just can't imagine it — owning only what you could load on a few camels. It must have been hard for you.'

'Yes, but we did not know it then.' He pauses. 'Shall I go on?'

'Of course, please do.'

'We did not share a fire with these newcomers for they had no blood relationship to us. Instead Othman pushed our group onwards, but I noticed a subtle shift in direction towards the village of Sinadogo. The marehan maintained a course parallel and a little behind. In the evening I took responsibility for the livestock and searched in vain for grazing. Here the land was flat beyond belief, with no trees to relieve the monotony. The sand was pale crimson, dotted with lighter rocks. I tried to imagine what this other, promised, landscape might be like, where grass grew as tall as a man — surely a place of such richness would support hundreds of cows and thousands of camels, and the beasts would breed with a will. Young livestock would thrive and a man would become wealthy. Going to the coast in Siad Barre's trucks was a good thing to do, I decided, and was determined to tell Othman what I thought, whether I got cuffed for the presumption or not.

'Days earlier my mother had traded a brass medallion for a small bag of rice. We ate it boiled in a cup of precious water — a handful of food each, unflavoured apart from a strip or two of dried camel meat. It was only enough to sharpen hunger, and the baby cried. In general Somali babies are not weaned until their third or fourth year but my mother lost her milk after six months, and camel milk and solid food had sustained the little girl since. I admit that I had little interest in the cloth-wrapped bundle.'

A change comes over Madoowbe, as if he has retreated into some kind of trance, his voice a monotone. 'The little girl was too young to play with, or to work. She stayed with my mother always. At the conclusion of supper I moved next to Othman and told him that I thought we should go in the trucks, or soon we would starve to death. It was true. Even if one day the drought ended it might well be too late. Besides, once we lost the livestock we were as good as dead — our animals provided almost every need: shelter, milk, meat, transport; my clan lived parasitically on them.

'No one spoke around the fire for a long time; even my mother was so wary of making an irreversible decision that she stayed silent. Othman unsheathed his bilau and whetted it on a stone, then stropped it on a leather. When he had finished he shaved a path of hair from his arm, grunted and sheathed the dagger. "We will walk to Sinadogo and find out more," he said.

'I was pleased with the decision. It was the sensible thing to do. But as I slept that night I thought of all the things we might find if we went to the coast — I had heard of the ocean and wanted to see it. I thought often of the pastures and fat cows. More than anything else, I wondered if there might be a school. I wanted to learn.

'When we reached Sinadogo we found that the trucks were real. Many other people were going also and when we sold our livestock they fetched little because everyone was trying to sell and no one had any money because of the drought. When we reached the coast we found no pasture, only camps full of people like us.'

Madoowbe's eyes become bright, and a smile touched his lips. 'Yet there was a school, and I went there. I learned to read, and before long I was one of the best students. My mother and Othman wanted to return to their tribal lands, but I would not go. They went with my baby sister and I stayed.'

Something occurs to Marika — that Madoowbe's story is perhaps more pertinent than it appears. In a moment of insight she understands why Sufia's photographed face seems familiar to her. 'Your baby sister,' she says finally, 'her name was Sufia, wasn't it?'

Madoowbe nods slowly. 'Yes, that was her name.'

'And that is the woman we seek? She is your sister?'

Madoowbe's head sags, and for some minutes he does not speak. 'I have followed her story over many years.

I took a position at Dubai assuming that she would be there, with her husband. I was wrong.' His voice drops. 'I only pray ... that she is safe. That we find her before something irreversible happens.'

Day 5, 21:00

The Special Forces troops arrive on the flight deck in a dusty green Sea King helicopter, squat and workmanlike, piloted by men who look almost alien in their flight suits and headgear. The aircraft hovers while an earthing tube is lifted from the flight deck to the aircraft in order to discharge static electricity before any part of the airframe touches the deck.

The new arrivals carry backpacks and dull black automatic rifles; quiet and calm, they stack their equipment in neat piles.

Simon walks down to B deck to watch, standing beneath the twin barrels of the Oerlikon guns. He turns to one of the crew. 'They're commandos, I guess?'

The lad looks at him as if he has just committed sacrilege. 'No way, mate, this is the Royal Navy. SBS. Special Boat Service. They eat commandos for breakfast.'

'Oh, of course. Forgive my ignorance.' Simon has heard of the SBS, but never seen them in the flesh. They look fit, and competent.

The chopper lifts off and turns into the northwest. The twenty-four SBS men spread out over the flight deck and quarterdeck, pumping air into black inflatable boats from a compressor hose. Each vessel has its own outboard motor that appears to be made of plastic. Assembling the vessels takes less than an hour, and afterwards the men sit in three circles and eat C-rations, talking among themselves. A davit is deployed to lift the boats down into the water, a process that draws a crowd of spectators. Soon after, the first of the SBS men descends the ladder and takes his place at the bow of one of the boats. The others follow with the same lack of fuss.

Simon stands at the edge of the flight deck to watch them go. He has a strange, knotted feeling in his belly, a shared anticipation of danger perhaps, admiration for men who are about to pit themselves against the sea and an unseen enemy.

One man walks up close. He is about Simon's height, yet broader across the shoulders. He wears a black skivvy, dark pants and a gun belt around his waist. His face is painted black with grease. In his arms he carries a submachine gun.

'The two girls,' he says, 'one of the lads was saying that they're yours. Is that right?'

'Yes, they're mine. Hannah and Frances.' He tries to smile, and not to let his voice crack. 'The nicest two kids you'll ever meet ...'

'We'll bring them back for you. If it's possible — we'll bring them back.'

With no fanfare, no announcement, the remainder of the group disappears over the side. The boats motor off, almost inaudible. Soon they are no longer visible. Simon turns to see that Captain Marshall has come up beside him, also staring at the blackness into which they are disappearing.

'It's a waiting game now,' Marshall says. 'Those fellows are controlled by their own base up at Poole — we've got nothing to do with it. Just do your best to relax.'

'OK, I'll try, anyway.'

Back in the ops room, Simon moves up next to Matt, who looks at him as if he is terminally ill. They all know, are all anxious for him, and the feeling warms his heart.

'Can we watch them on the radar?' Simon asks.

'No. They're invisible. Sorry.'

Simon runs a hand through his hair, surprised to find it sodden with sweat, wondering how he can get through a night such as this one.

Day 5, 22:30

Many things can invade and occupy a man's mind as he ploughs through an unfamiliar sea, particularly when he is heading towards events that might include his own death. PJ has several superstitions — routines that he has developed over the years. One is to empty the magazine of his SIG-Sauer handgun and reload the cartridges in reverse order, sometimes doing this several times before the trip is through. The other is to delve into his pockets and catalogue everything he finds there in his mind.

One packet odourless chewing gum, four pieces left. One rolled-up tissue. Swiss Army knife, genuine; present from Aunt Dianne. The knife, unlike the aunt, has since proved invaluable a thousand times.

Scanning ahead, the horizon seems darker than before, and PJ slips on his AN-PVS7 night-vision goggles. The island is dark and shadowy, with a lick of white spray at the base of the cliffs.

'There it is,' he whispers to himself, and focuses his mind on the mission at hand. Kill or capture Saif al-Din and bring back the three female hostages. Either task would be difficult enough, but the two, taken together, make the exercise much harder.

The engines are silent apart from water pushing through the telltale and steaming out into the sea. This silence accentuates the slap of water against the hull, and the muffled thump as the flat bottom hits the chop.

'Check bearing.' They are trained to take nothing at face value, to reconfirm everything.

'Check zero-two-five degrees.'

The dark cliffs loom ahead, and the roar of crashing surf grows louder. Just beyond the breakers, PJ waits for a set to pass through, picking the last roller in line and accelerating to hold position just behind the crest, hugging it all the way in, watching it break into a wall of white fury, riding on through among the boulders.

Something tugs at the hull, and he holds the grab handles with white-knuckled hands as the bottom of the boat nudges a bed of rounded rocks. A wave smashes into the transom, soaking them from behind. Tension and anticipation morphs into real physical fear. Even now, a man could die — drown; be pounded on the rocks. For all they know there are weapons trained on them from the shore. This is the moment of exposure, when there is no going back, no way of hiding.

The team disembarks together, leaping over the sides and dragging the hull up beyond the reach of the waves, into the deep darkness under the cliffs, securing the bow lines to the base of a palm, and turning to watch the others come through. The leading two boats manage the landing without incident, though Charlie section, coming up last, misjudges their set and are pounded by a bigger wave as they attempt to drag their inflatable clear. Members of the other two teams grasp the sides and lift the vessel beyond the tide.

Captain Pennington's blackened face moves close to PJ's, identifiable only from the voice. 'You ready, Johnson?'

'Yes, sir.'

'Then lead on.'

PJ turns and makes the universal symbol to move, the two men assigned to watch the boats glumly waiting — this is not a popular post.

Neither is PJ's. He is the point man — roving ahead of the others. He knows the statistics. The average life expectancy of a man in his position after contact with an enemy has been calculated at seven seconds. Sometimes he imagines, in detail, what those seven seconds will be like — wondering if he will hear the gunshot that kills him, or whether his senses will be already destroyed by the bullet that travels faster than sound through flesh and vital organs.

One of PJ's great skills is with maps — even as a child he pored over globes of the world and topographic charts of the English countryside. Every confluence of contour lines suggested a ridge or gully to explore and every stream an adventure — fallen trees to balance on; stones to hop across; tadpoles to collect.

Even though he had just thirty minutes to study the charts of the island, each rise and fall is stamped in his mind. Already he has picked out the safest and easiest route to the top of the cliffs, and is not surprised to find a track there, worn smooth over the centuries by the feet of fishermen and drifters. Tracks are always a risk, and as he moves on he studies the terrain, always with the barrel of the HK probing ahead of him.

Twenty metres up, he halts. Something has caught his attention, nothing he can put into words; an object too regular to be natural. Kneeling, he sees the trip wire through the night-vision goggles, stretching across the track and into a black plastic sensing device with a stub antenna.

The adrenalin in his blood, having subsided since the landing, surges again until he has to force his breathing back to a regular rhythm. The threat of upcoming conflict becomes a certainty. Pulling a compact aerosol can from a pouch at his side, he sprays the wire and surrounding earth with a fluorescent liquid that lights up through the infrared goggles, yet is invisible to the naked eye, even in daylight. Stepping over the wire he moves on up the slope.

At the summit he uses gorse-like foliage for cover while he scans the foreground. There is no room for error here — his life and those of his comrades rely on attention to detail. PJ uses eyes and ears in the search for anything unusual: voices; a muffled cough; the clink of steel, or the distinctive shape of a weapon.

Minutes pass. Every landscape has its peculiarities and it is important to understand them in order to recognise the unusual. A few minutes of briefing has prepared him for the plant life here, most notably the dragon's blood tree, with its bunched branches held high like a fist and the sap that runs red from both trunk and exposed roots.

The soil, pale pink, is studded with bulbous desert rose plants, some of which rise two metres from the ground. The landscape is surreal, unforgettable, so alien it might be Mars or Venus.

PJ comes back up to his knees, and waves the others on. Still alone, in front, he sets off across country, following the route he has chosen around the island's lone peak. There is a path, but the sensing device was a potent warning to avoid well-trafficked areas. The cross-country alternative is not difficult, and will make for a less hazardous journey.

A small animal scurries away in front of him, moving from left to right. PJ covers it, out of habit, with the HK, but it is soon gone. Again he waits, making sure that it was not spooked by a third party. After two or more patient minutes he moves off, stopping to scan unusual geography, likely sites for booby traps, or signs of men lying in wait.

The space between two twisted dragon's blood trees looks suspicious. PJ scans the area several times before his gaze falls on an unexpected series of spider web strands near the ground, seeming to hang in midair with nothing to hold them in place. He drops prone, and in that position sees the wire just a few inches from his eyes, having been used by the web-spinning spider to anchor the silk. He stops dead, eyes moving along the wire to the end, recognising the M18A1 Claymore anti-personnel mine.

Jesus Christ. I nearly laid down on the damn thing.

PJ knows just how effective the seven hundred steel balls propelled by C4 explosive would have been in tearing his legs and abdomen to shreds. Turning, he signals to the man behind to wait.

The tripwire is at ankle height, extending perhaps five metres across the clearing. PJ crawls along the length of it, to where it terminates at a twig embedded in the earth, then back again, settling on his haunches next to the mine, taking off the goggles and removing a tiny LED flashlight from a pouch. Dismantling a mine using night-vision goggles is not something he wants to try.

A dark shape comes up beside him. Don. 'What's up?'

'Claymore.'

'This is the real thing, then.'

'Yeah. Here, hold this.' PJ flicks on the torch and hands it across. 'Higher, hold it higher. Fucking hell, I hate these things.'

First, arm at full stretch, he disconnects the firing wire, then removes the blasting cap. Only then do the muscles in his arms, legs and face relax. Standing, he gathers the tripwire, bundles it up, and throws it away to one side.

Captain Pennington slithers up out of the darkness. 'What's going on?'

'Bloody mine. No more doubt though. They're here for sure.'

'We'll find some cover,' the officer says. 'You go on and check out the huts. And for God's sake, be careful.'

Taking a deep breath as if to dilute the fear, PJ sets off towards the peak of the hill, keeping to the heavier brush on one side. Moving through an unfamiliar landscape at night, alone, is difficult and frightening. The possibility of more mines makes it worse, never knowing if the next placement of a hand or foot will be the last act he makes on earth. PJ keeps low, moving from dragon's blood tree to hillock of earth. Always with stealth.

Over the peak at last, he sees the huts for the first time, nestled down towards the cliff tops. A roaring fire in the middle makes him safer, for few things ruin night vision like firelight, particularly on a night as dark as this one. He stays under cover, protected by a rise in the ground, studying the nearest hut. A facing window is covered by thin curtains yet once or twice he sees the shadow of someone standing behind.

He counts the men, five at first and then a sixth — taller than the others, casting long shadows as he moves to the fire. The huts are the key. There will be more men inside. *Closer*, he tells himself, *move closer*. He creeps down the slope, and even though he is at his most watchful he almost doesn't see them, hitting the earth as fast as he dares. Unusual shapes — yes, three heads in the darkness, and the telltale stub of a rifle. Ahead, in the darkness, is a fortified emplacement.

PJ swears under his breath, mouth dry as leather. Far from being unprotected, this is a fortress. A few moments ago, he was thinking of creeping close enough to peer through the windows. Now, with a sinking feeling, he knows that he is fortunate to have loomed so close without detection. No wonder the men around the fireplace are so casual.

As he waits there is a commotion near the huts and more men spill out from a doorway, carrying weapons, spreading out. The changing of the guard, PJ realises. Five more. He knows he should take the opportunity to get away while they are distracted, before their night vision kicks in. Instead he stays where he is. He has to see at least one of the targets, either the hostages or Saif al-Din, in the flesh, and yet many are dark skinned, and he has only seen a single photograph of the terrorist. He could be any one of those armed men down near the huts.

PJ studies everything, even the way they handle their weapons. One man checks the load of a machine gun, pulling back the firing handle as he takes charge. Voices fall away as the others disappear into the huts.

Silence descends, and PJ waits. Thirty minutes come and go. A call comes through on his earphone and he ignores it. More waiting, then the sound of voices. Three females exit the hut, followed by two men with rifles, obviously guards. The taller of the prisoners is in her twenties, willowy in figure, her voice raised in strident complaint.

'If you would just give us some dignity ... '

Her voice is educated British — middle class — cut off by a heavy slap to her face. She staggers backwards. PJ watches, transfixed, controlling the impulse to put a bullet through the man's brain, moving his eyes to the girls. The smaller one walks with her head held high. *Hannah, wasn't that her name?* The elder is less defiant, hands at her sides, eyes fixed on the ground.

PJ feels a surge of excitement. The hostages are still alive. All of them. And they are here, within spitting distance. The raid will go ahead. He has to subdue this adrenalin-fuelled restlessness and continue to study the camp.

The armed men lead the girls to a small building that must be an outhouse. The younger girl goes in first, followed by her sister, then the woman, who he guesses must be the nanny. After each girl has visited in turn, the men with guns prod them back towards the hut. PJ feels a pain in his chest so powerful he dares not give it a name.

Still he has not made a positive ID on the militant that they came to find, but the hostages are enough to initiate action. He turns away into the darkness, trying to subdue the heat that rises from his chest in waves. For the first two hundred metres he no more than crawls, then, out of sight, he rises to his feet, running hunched over like an animal.

* * *

Marika wakes in the night, so cold that her teeth are chattering. She sees nothing — the darkness is complete. Something moves out in the sand and she jumps and gives a little shriek, reaching out and grasping Madoowbe's shoulder.

'Sorry,' she says, 'I thought I heard something out there.'

'No, it was me moving my foot.'

'Where is our camel?'

'He must have got up and wandered off. Sorry, I was asleep.'

'Oh.' She makes no effort to let go of the warm hard muscle of his shoulder.

'Are you cold?' he asks.

'Yep, can't you tell?'

'If we still had our camel we could use him for warmth, but the best we can do is use each other.'

'I guess so.' Marika shifts closer, pressing against his back along her full length, her left arm flat beneath her and her right moving to his chest, amazed at the hardness and leanness of his body. As if in response, he snuggles back against her.

His hair is against her face and he smells of sun and the desert. There is something clean about him, something very different. In recent days her life has become entwined with three men of Somalia: one is willing to use violence to change the world; one has built an entire region into a kingdom; and the third is an enigma — a fighter, yet also one of the most thoughtful and gentle men she has ever met. *How can you think like that?* The voice in her head is shrill with indignation. *He betrayed you. Held a gun to your head.*

'You *are* nice and warm,' she says.

'Strange that you should say that — so are you.'

He has acted in my interests, even when it hasn't seemed so.

Marika squeezes him tighter, her fingers resting on his sternum, between the flat pads of muscle on his chest. Her breathing changes, body relaxing, hips pressing closer against him.

Besides, he is beautiful, and it is cold, and tomorrow I might be dead ...

Lifting her head she nestles into his neck so her mouth almost touches his skin. He turns in the circle of her arms, and a shiver of pleasure racks her body.

'Yes,' she groans, moving her hands to the back of his head, lolling back so that he can reach her, his lips inching their way up to hers.

Léon Benardt is fatigued beyond endurance, yet, sent back to his room on rotation to sleep, another need manifests itself. How nice it would be to share a bed with a woman! Just for an hour maybe. To drink good wine, then make wild, spontaneous love with a beautiful stranger.

On other occasions he has had great success at the Buddha Bar in the Dubai Marina. Music and dancing. A little loud for tonight. The idea of somewhere quieter appeals to him. A wine bar, perhaps?

After some thought Léon selects the Agency Bar at the Emirates Towers. This venue is over the other side of the city, but taxis are cheap here, and it is less trashy than other venues, without the loud music that can make it difficult to be heard. Besides, it sells excellent wine by the glass.

As the taxi carries him along Sheikh Zayed Road towards the Towers he finds himself, as always, blown away by the sheer exorbitance of Dubai at night. Seeing the speeding traffic — sprinkled with Ferraris, Porsches and Mercedes, and people out enjoying themselves — it is hard to remember just how dire the situation remains at Rabi al-Salah, and how deeply he is involved.

His working life has been an aimless drift into the military, then the Action Division of the DGSE. At times he is surprised to find himself a member of the multinational security force supporting the Dubai police.

His early years were innocuous enough, growing up in the village of Longueville, southeast of Paris. His career path appeared set, yet his leaving scores were insufficient to allow him to follow his father, the local tooth puller, into dentistry.

Instead he joined the infantry, seeing action in the Congo and the Antilles. After serving out his five years, he followed a colleague into a restricted course in military intelligence. From there, he was selected for an interview and found himself one of the handsome young men and women in suits who surround the president of the Republic of France — the man who now lies dead in one corner of the Rabi al-Salah conference room — as he travelled from one official engagement or other to the Palais Bourbon, from Paris to Berlin or Geneva.

The death of Martin Bourque has rocked Léon hard, underlining the dire situation that has developed and how powerless he, and men like him, have become. He wants to fight back, but for now he wants to forget, just for a few hours.

Léon enters the bar from the side entrance, pleased to see it full, the marble counter dotted with cocktail glasses. Most of the ladies are with male friends, but to one side, near the jazz band, a group of three women sit together, giggling, glasses in hand. One is plain, well dressed and heavily made up. The second is dark skinned, with ringlets of hair falling down to her shoulders, but there is an unattractive hardness to her lips. The third woman, thank God, is a beauty. Blonde and tall, with hair that swings back and forth as she laughs.

Léon places her at around thirty, a few years younger than he. He likes them that age — old enough to have lost the coyness of sexual inexperience. Old enough to get on top and shake their tits and squeeze a man. Old enough to like a little variety.

He does not make the mistake of staring overtly, but moves to the bar, pulling up a stool and waiting until the barman — a slim Filipino in a white shirt and bow tie — appears, taking his order for a lusty Cabernet, bringing it in a heavy, good quality glass.

'Those ladies over there,' Léon asks, 'have they been here long?'

'Yes, they came here after supper. Been drinking hard all night. Plenty bottles of wine.'

Léon ignores the man's knowing grin, instead sitting back and enjoying the aroma and taste of the wine, the way it burns with slow fire on the tongue, then all the way back into the throat, flowing into his brain like magma.

At the same time he flicks his eyes over the room, double-checking that he hasn't missed an easier prospect than the pretty blonde with her friends. Sometimes it is so easy there is almost no challenge in it — you can pick them a mile off, usually divorcees or at least the brokenhearted, travelling to try to kill the pain, only they can't, and they end up in a place like this, drinking alone, waiting for a handsome stranger to come along and give them what they need. Of course, it isn't what they need, even Léon knows that, but he gives it to them anyway, and leaves them in their rooms, sweating and worn out, his own member limp and spent.

Tonight, when such a simple target would be convenient, there is no one like that, only one lone female who must be in her fifties at least. She appears to be waiting for someone, judging by the frequency with which she consults her wristwatch.

His eyes flick back to the group of three, and just for an instant his eyes meet those of the blonde. Oh yes, she is a beauty indeed, and there is no mistaking the spark of interest there. At times it can be difficult to cut one out from a herd, but there is a chance, definitely a chance.

Still Léon does not make his move, continuing to study the room. Past the three young women is a table of men and their wives or girlfriends, all well on the way to inebriation. One of the men is so loud his voice carries across the room.

Léon wrinkles his nose in distaste. Loud drunkenness is obnoxious to him; such people miss the entire point of drinking. The cultured seriousness of it. The charm, the tradition. He looks away, back past the blonde, and again she looks up.

No doubt remains. She likes him. He feels that inner weightlessness that often comes in tandem with sexual excitement, and the tightening of his trousers across his crotch.

Surreptitiously he looks at his watch, allowing forty minutes for the seduction, one hour at her hotel room then back to his digs for sleep until dawn. It should be easy, but he will not rush too much. No. She is worth taking some time over. Time to stalk her heart with care. He knows from experience that once you have touched a woman's heart, you can touch her anywhere.

Lifting his glass he walks over to the table, gripping the back of a spare seat. When he speaks he makes no effort to hide his French accent, instead accentuating it. Women love it, he knows, especially American women, who are so starved of romance.

'Good evening, ladies. Forgive me, but an older woman over there that I am not enamoured of is making suggestive gestures. I wondered if sitting here might give her the idea that I am not available.'

The three young women dissolve into laughter, but the blonde speaks first, eyes twinkling with interest. 'Which one? Show us please.' Her voice is pure California. Sunshine and beaches. Hills and fast cars. Léon loves Californian girls. Hadn't they practically invented free love?

Léon sits down, places his glass on the woven raffia coaster, then folds his arms. 'It would not be gentlemanly for me to tell.' He smiles to himself. The rest will be fun.

The desperate brunette to the left clutches at his arm, all over him there in the bar. 'Oh please, which one?'

The blonde joins in. 'Yeah, spill the beans.'

Léon pretends to be swayed, twisting his lips one way then the other, letting his eyes dance as he does so. His eyes are one of his best features, he knows, so dark as to be almost black. 'Do not look, but there is one in a red cocktail dress sitting by herself. Reddish hair.'

The blonde laughs into her hand, and Léon smiles back. The third woman, younger than the other two, barely into her twenties and immature looking to boot, pipes up, 'Oh my God, she's so old, and if she's a natural redhead I'll run down Jumeirah Beach with my boobs out.'

'Doesn't she look like — who's that actress who got really fat?' The blonde gasps.

The other two dissolve into laughter and all the commotion attracts the woman's attention, for she stares back. As if in response the brunette half stands and slips an arm around Léon's shoulder. 'I'll save you, don't worry.'

He smiles and extends a hand, first to the blonde, making it plain that she is the one he is interested in. 'My name is Léon, what is yours?'

'I'm Cathy, this is June, and Elspeth.'

The third woman adds, 'Just about everyone calls me Ellie.'

He kisses their hands one by one, seeing them swoon as he does so. His forward progress is then interrupted by the nearby table of drunks, the male members launching into some kind of drunken rugby song. The English inflection is unmistakeable, and the sound is loud enough to forestall any further attempt at conversation.

When it is over, Léon continues his work. 'I suppose you three are old friends?'

'Not at all — we're on a tour. Only known each other for a few days.'

'Oh, OK.' That will make it easier.

'What about you?'

Léon stops for a moment; the conversation at the other table has turned to Rabi al-Salah, and he pricks up his ears. 'Fuckin' terrorists. Should all get fuckin' locked up ...' It is nothing, he decides, just drunken ranting. Soon, one of the doormen will hear and eject the man from the bar. The sooner the better, he decides, then realises that he is being asked a question.

'Sorry, what do you mean?'

The blonde brushes her hair back from her ears. 'Are you here on business or pleasure?'

'A little of both.' He smiles and gives his head that sexy little shake he knows women love. 'You know how it is. Work. Play.'

'What line of work are you in?'

'Ah, security.'

'Ooh, sounds exciting.'

And now it's like the other two aren't there. They fall silent, and the laughter stops, tension growing. Léon discovers that Cathy lectures at UCLA in Humanities, that she loves cats, and has taken a year off work to travel the world. Yes, she is going to Paris, and yes, it would be great if they met up there and he showed her around.

Again he finds himself distracted by the conversation across at the other table. Two of the men have been arm wrestling, but now that the contest is over the conversation returns to Rabi al-Salah.

'I could fuckin' fix that up in five minutes flat,' one of the men is saying. 'Shoot every one of those fuckers dead.'

'Yeah sure, how?'

'I just know, OK ...'

On cue, the brunette shoulders her handbag. 'Well. I'm off. Need my beauty sleep.' Elspeth stands also, excusing herself. Léon watches them go with a smile on his face. Now it's just him and Cathy, the blonde. He says nothing, just shifts in his seat until he is closer to her. 'Would you like another drink?'

'Not really, I think I've had enough.'

'Perhaps a walk then ...'

'OK, if you like.'

Léon feels his groin tighten further. It is so easy; a stroll outside around the massive curved exterior of the hotel, and then back to her room, almost certainly here at the Emirates Towers. He stands, but now his brow knits with concentration. The drunken man at the adjacent table is still talking.

'I done the fuckin' electrical work, see — worked for the main contractor. Supervised the whole job. When you put together a series of circuits you need to take into account maintenance in the future, and safety, see. Ya gotta have an override, a way of shutting down power so that future electricians can work in safety. So we had to have a way of both leaving the main door open, for access, and have power off to that circuit so that technicians can move in and out of the conference room, while working on the system without any risk of electrocution. That's how I could fix this up in five fuckin' minutes.'

Léon leans on the chair for balance, frozen to the spot.

The blonde reaches for his arm. 'What's wrong? Are we going?'

Ignoring her, Léon is already moving across the floor, reaching out for the drunken electrician, grabbing him by the collar. 'You installed an override that will do what you just said?'

The man tries to fight. 'Get away from me, fuck ya. Leave me alone.'

Léon grips his arm and twists it. 'Answer me.'

The contractor's jaw opens, panting. Tiny beads of sweat surround his lips. 'Yeah. There's a switchboard locker in the cleaner's storeroom on the southern wall of the conference room. It has a manual switch for the doors and the power.'

'You,' Léon says, 'are coming with me.' With a shove he propels the drunken man towards the door.

He does not even turn to farewell the blonde, who sinks back to her seat, watching him go.

Within thirty minutes the contractor, Robert Collins — Robbie to his mates — is showered and drinking coffee in an interview room, dazed and subdued. For an hour, Abdullah and Léon fire questions, establishing his bona fides, waking his employer from his London bed in a final check that he is who he says he is and not some red herring.

His authenticity established, it only remains to decide whether this new information is drunken fabrication or fact, and the level of detail provided soon points towards the latter. In the end, Abdullah sends him to the residential complex, under guard, to sleep off the alcohol.

When the door closes, the two men stand before the windows, curtain buffeting in the light sea breeze, staring out across the night. Léon cannot resist a flash of a smile at his own success in finding the electrician. The regret at not having the girl is a small thing in comparison. Perhaps when this thing is over ...

'Do you see the power station over there?' Abdullah asks.

It is impossible to miss the huge complex, with its rows of giant steel pylons carrying power to the most electricity hungry city on earth. Beyond are the tall funnels of the station itself, painted red and white in bands. 'Yes, sir.'

'As you know, there is a maintenance platform near the top of one of the funnels, and we have had men with optical equipment up there observing the conference room since the crisis began.'

'Yes, of course.' The conference room has just one window, and the power station funnel is the only point from which it is possible to see through it.

'Dr Abukar has taken to occupying a particular seat, for part of the day and most of the night. Zhyogal moves around almost constantly, but Dr Abukar does not.'

Léon is starting to smile. 'How far away from the conference room is your observation post at the power station?'

'Nine hundred and thirty metres. Out of accurate range of conventional small arms, but what about a fifty-calibre sniper rifle firing an armour-piercing projectile, sighted in for precisely that distance? It'll make short work of even cyrolon. One or two rounds punching straight through the window, followed a moment later by a high-explosive round, striking Dr Abukar in the head or upper body, not just killing, but obliterating him. At the same moment someone on the inside flicks a switch that makes the doors open and the lights go out. In come our troops. Sound interesting?'

'What if Dr Abukar presses the remote control before he dies?'

'He does not always have the trigger in his hand. Much of the time he carries it in his pocket. Our man will not shoot if he is holding it.' Abdullah says nothing further, just stares out at the power station smokestacks.

The shadow beneath the tree is a welcome sanctuary, so dark that Captain Pennington's blackened face is invisible without the goggles.

PJ moves in on his hands and knees, then rises to his haunches, feeling the relief in the strained muscles of his thighs, abdomen and back. 'They're in there. I saw them. Two girls and the nanny.'

'That fits with this.' Pennington opens his hand, displaying something that shines even in the shadows.

PJ takes the object from his hand, holding it close to his right eye. 'What the hell is it?'

'A tiny gold star. Jewellery perhaps. Deepak found it on a recce down to the harbour. How many guards are there?'

'Twelve at least, fifteen at most. Carrying AK47s, two heavy MGs.'

'Their positions?'

PJ describes what he has seen.

Pennington says nothing for a moment then, 'There's four or five more down at the harbour, guarding the boat.'

This information is sobering. At least twenty well-equipped militants, and these Almohad have proved in the past to be no pushover. These ones, moreover, occupy a strong defensive position. PJ's eyes lock on Pennington's, trying to gauge what he is thinking, knowing that it is going to be hard.

Dark shapes slither into the shadows under the tree.

Sitting up, waiting, the silence thick and heavy. The tension is palpable. No one likes entering a hostile zone full of adrenalin then being forced to wait.

Pennington's voice is clear and emotionless in the night. 'We're going to have to abort, I'm afraid.'

No one says anything for a moment, then PJ explodes, his voice still low, but thick with shock. 'Sir? The hostages are there, and they are being mistreated.'

'No. I can't see any way of taking out the terrorists without giving them an opportunity to slaughter the hostages. Therefore I have no choice.'

'Forgive me for saying so, captain, but there is a way.'

'How?'

'The Enniskillen Drill. We've practised it a hundred times.' The name Enniskillen referred to an unpublicised hostage rescue in Northern Ireland. 'Set Stewie and Dave up high with their rifles to take out the terrorists inside the hut with the girls, hit the guys around the fire with the rocket launcher. Disable the trench with grenades at the same time. We can be inside the hut in ten seconds.'

'That might be too long,' the captain points out.

PJ thinks of the girls, knowing that if he walks away their captors will kill them — as soon as they are of no further use those monsters will kill them. 'We have to take that chance. There is no other way.'

'What about the harbour? There are another five men down there, maybe more.'

'We have to leave it until after we've freed the hostages. We can't divide our forces.'

The silence stretches on for a long time, but finally: 'OK, we do it, but we do it my way. The Enniskillen Drill, but I want CS gas into the hostage hut.'

'Thank you, sir.'

'Does everyone understand what they have to do?'

Silence.

'Take the lead, Johnson, and good luck.'

PJ stands and takes the first step towards his enemy, and the girls, and the tall woman with so much spirit.

The drill is so well rehearsed and understood that men move to their positions without a sound. PJ's eyes stray often to his watch, for timing is critical. A few seconds either way might be catastrophic.

The positions of the team are also important, yet there is no way of determining these apart from sheer instinct. Training. Having decided on his location, PJ wriggles forwards another few metres before planting his elbows, eyes squinting through the low power telescopic sight, picking out a target. Forefinger drawing up the fractional slack in the trigger.

Again a glance at the watch. Thirty seconds. Long seconds only a fighter knows. First comes the dull primer pop of the launchers out to the right, and the canisters landing. Grenades thumping, the area exploding into angry light. A dozen automatic weapons open up. PJ is already shooting, weapon on semi auto, firing one round after another.

Saif al-Din, eating a hurried meal of dates and cheese washed down by tepid Pepsi cola from the cab, hears the first gunshot and freezes. The suspicion that he should never have travelled to this island becomes a certainty in his mind.

Upon his arrival, Saif first led the mujahedin in prayer, then prepared a meeting with the factions. Agreement could not be reached, and he had resorted to the satellite telephone he carried — that implement as essential to the modern terrorist as guns — calling for instructions before the issue was resolved.

Now the men of the camp appear to be working together again. For an hour they have been listening to MP3 recordings played via iPod connected to a portable stereo, of that most famous speech by the movement's founder, Yaqub Yusuf. Saif sees how their faces light up with new fervour.

Bravery is essential for our brotherhood to win through over the oppressors; those who defile God's earth. Death to America and her allies. Death to the Jews. If you do not fight one day our world will be ended, and there will be anarchy — your wives raped, your sisters raped.

The gunshot tells Saif that the kufr have found them and attacked without warning, failing to set off any of the booby traps that he was assured they would blunder through.

This turn of events, Saif knows, might threaten the success of the operation, as well as others in the future. The island has become both base and storehouse, and a secure anchorage. Down in the harbour sits the eight-metre RIB, a sturdy vessel with a sheltered wheelhouse and berth down below. The hardware of jihad — five hundred kilograms of explosives, a hundred assault rifles, handguns and ammunition — are piled in an ancient and solid fisherman's hut on the shore.

Besides that, there is unfinished business. The two kufr girls are still alive. This failure weighs upon him, yet the business of reconciling the mujahedin has taken precedence, and he had intended to remedy the matter after the evening meal.

Quick thinking as always, smelling the gas as the canisters detonate, he throws his head back, lifts the can of Pepsi and pours the bubbling fluid down over his face, saturating his closed eyelids. The properties of the soft drink in resisting the effects of tear gas are well known and understood by freedom fighters across the world.

Thus protected he drops the empty can and sprints back into the building to where the children are held. The kufr soldiers will be after the girls, of course, and taking one as a hostage might be the only way of ensuring his survival. The other, of course, must die now. The lights are off, but there is enough light from the outside fire and exploding munitions to see the hostages. His hand falls to the butt of his pistol, drawing it and aiming down at the larger of the two children, firing two rounds into her, watching her body jerk as the bullets strike before moving to the smaller child. Lifting and holding her against his chest, ignoring the sharp pain as the pressure of her body pushes the automatic pistol in its holster against his rib cage. The girl's cries and the beat of small hands against his chest are of no account.

Now he hears the crump of exploding gas canisters and realises that he has just seconds to vacate the building. He leaves through the back entrance at a run, where smoke is already thick from the grenades. Using this cover, he moves from the clearing into the sparse vegetation of the cliff tops, holding the girl tight to still her struggles. Gunfire comes from behind him, but he does not turn, just rips mighty lungfuls of air through his nostrils and expels them through his lips, taking leaping strides, almost tripping once but recovering his balance in time.

He enters the darkness away from the camp, and the concussion of gunfire loses its sharpness, the smell of phosphorus smoke fading, whipped away by the sea breeze that blows more briskly as they near the cliff, cool on his face after the claustrophobic hut.

Stopping at the edge of the cliff, he smells the sea now, hunting for a downwards path with his eyes. The girl in his arms struggles, cries out, a sound lost against the already withering firefight, but enough to alarm him. Freeing one hand he brings it down hard on the side of her face.

'Shut up, or die now.'

The warm bundle collapses in his arms and he tucks her back further, legs dangling like those of a chicken. He begins to run down the track towards the boat, heedless of the crumbling stony surface.

Men scramble from the huts — half dressed, guns in hands, coughing from the CS gas, cut down where they huddle and fall over each other in the rush to find safety, struggling to react to a wraith-like enemy that comes from all directions. The gas is a new variant of the old chlorobenzalmalononitrile formula, safer than previous versions yet, delivered as an aerosol, debilitating with the slightest contact.

Targets now scattered, PJ leaps to his feet, running. His feet hammer into the compound as if disconnected from his body. The retractable stock of the HK53 thumps against his shoulder. He views the world through the single-minded ferocity of the lens, focusing on the door. A bearded face appears and he follows it before squeezing the trigger, watching the man go down, following the fall, firing again before resuming the scan.

The hapless faces of the targets stream with tears and mucus. Most drop their weapons from the effects of the gas. PJ knows what it feels like. Once, during a drill, he was affected and he still remembers the nausea, disorientation, dulled senses. It is almost impossible to function in the conventional sense.

PJ primes a green phosphorus grenade at the door to signal that he is into the building. Time moves slowly as his eyes, empowered with the night-vision goggles, scan the interior.

A figure races for the door and PJ takes him with a three-round tap to the chest. Moving deeper into the room he sees two human shapes huddled on the floor. Another stands nearby, misty green through the goggles, an Uzi submachine gun directed at the hostages. On his face is a gas mask. The man takes on an inhuman aspect, the mask giving him an otherworldly shape that hardens PJ's resolve.

The field of fire behind the target is clear. PJ shoots him twice, watches him fall, then runs to where the oldest of the captives sits, weeping over the unmoving form of one of the girls.

Other men enter the hut now, checking, securing. PJ snaps, 'Help me get them out of here, for God's sake.' One leads the young woman towards the door while he moves to the girl, lifting her beneath her knees and shoulders, carrying her outside, past the prisoners kneeling near the central fire, setting her down at a safe distance where he assesses her quickly. She is conscious now, breathing heavily, her eyes wide with fear. He can see two wounds:

one in her shoulder and the other a nick on the side of her neck. He compresses the shoulder wound with his bare hand, stemming the flow of blood that has soaked the side of her shirt.

'Medic,' he calls, 'over here. Hurry.'

The girl's breathing changes and PJ realises that she is trying to speak, words interspersed with great racking sobs. 'He ... took her. Hannah. She's ... gone.'

'Who took her?'

'The black one ... The dark one ... When the ... shooting started ... Please get her back.'

'Where did he go?'

'Out there.'

PJ feels his throat squeeze tight. 'I'll get her, I promise.'

More promises. Hell. Blinding impatience, frustration, relief, subjugated by the realisation that the matter is not finished. He waits until the unit medic takes over her care, unpacking his field kit beside her, then moves across to where three bearded prisoners huddle around the fire. PJ grabs one by the hair and trains the HK on him. 'Where is the other girl?'

The upturned face stares up at him, then spits a single sentence that finishes with 'Allahu akbar'.

Someone touches PJ's shoulder. 'There's no point. He doesn't speak English.'

'The hell he doesn't.' PJ brings the muzzle of his weapon down to kiss against the man's temple. The smile widens, mouth dark and studded with yellow teeth. Strings of saliva join upper and lower jaws. 'Allahu akbar,' he croaks out.

'He's saying that God is Great. He wants you to pull the trigger. He wants you to martyr him.'

'Jesus Christ, how do you beat these bastards?' PJ shouts, shoving the man down, where he lies still, seemingly expecting a bullet.

PJ turns away. There are more of them down at the harbour. That is where she must be. The memory of the little girl being led across the compound fills his heart. He made a promise to a father, now to a sister, and it is not one that he intends to break.

Five men guard the storehouse, a stone hut tunnelled into the cliff, one of the original fishermen's huts that dot the stone outcrops of the archipelago. The boat sits adjacent to the timber jetty built of old teak logs brought unknown decades earlier from across the sea.

As Saif approaches he grunts out the password and the others crowd him, recognising him with relief. 'What is happening, sayyid? Please instruct us. Have the kufr attacked?'

'The kufr have overcome the camp. Help me carry explosives, let us fill the boat. Hurry! A battery, detonators, wires.'

Saif al-Din carries the girl into the boat, using a rope to lash her to a bulkhead, looping it around her chest, then winding several times around the wrists. His fingers are jumpy and nervous. He fumbles with the knots, and she starts to fight him, necessitating a swift blow to the side of the head. Again she falls limp.

Saif smiles down on her. She too will die; will be with him at the moment of detonation. But not until the last moment — then if the kufr chase him by boat he will have a hostage. Westerners are weak. They will not fire on him when she is aboard.

Now, lifting his head to listen to the sporadic gunfire, he climbs over the gunwale, loping back to the storehouse, where the mujahedin are unloading; the nervous, sweaty smell of them strong despite the breeze.

The storehouse is loaded with bags of nitrate fertiliser explosives, the remnants of a purchase made through Afriwide International suppliers in Nairobi, Kenya. Saif organised the consignment himself, using a fabricated NGO as a front, choosing the ammonium nitrate variety that he has used with success in the past.

The entire shipment was mixed with diesel fuel at the correct ratio here on the island and rebagged. Detonator systems were made up using 12-gauge shotgun cartridges, heat coils, plastic tube, and wire. Fifty kilograms of explosives went to make up the charges carried by Zhyogal and the others into the Rabi al-Salah Centre.

Now, Saif supervises the loading, packing explosives into the V-berth cabin of the RIB, the bags sitting in the curves and corners around the bunks. All the time Saif plans ahead — thinking of the next step. He knows that the kufr commandos must have come from somewhere. Out there in the sea is a ship, a big one. It would be a glorious act to send it to the bottom of the sea.

They carry across five more bags, enough to tear a hole in a battleship.

The mujahedin beg to be allowed to come with him and die also as martyrs.

'No,' he tells them, 'stay here, defend this storehouse, and when you are about to be overcome, detonate the rest of the explosives. Kill as many of the kufr as possible. I will see you in the green gardens of Jannah before the sun rises tomorrow.'

The twin Mercury outboards, tilted down on their hydraulic rams, start with just a pulse of the key. Saif throws off the lines while they warm up, water spitting out from the telltales and fizzing into the sea. Heedless of the hull bumping against the jetty, he pushes the throttles down hard, twisting the wheel, feeling the loaded RIB climb sluggishly onto the plane.

The entrance to the harbour is tricky, with sharp rocks lurking below the surface, and just a narrow channel. Negotiating it requires all his attention before he rounds the final cliffs, into the open sea at last.

Saif sets the boat on autopilot while he prepares the explosive charges. Not taking any chances he sets three detonators deep into the sacks then plays wire out into the cockpit. He cuts the ends with side cutters then strips insulation from both strands. These he sits next to the battery before moving back to the controls. There is no finesse to the preparations. The timing device he sets to the shortest possible delay. Thirty seconds. It is swift — uncomplicated and foolproof.

PJ is halfway down the cliff, clinging behind a hummock of earth on the trail when he sees the vessel as a blob of darkness passing through the sheltering arms of the harbour, just as the first burst of automatic fire comes out of the night, illuminating the storehouse below.

Captain Pennington settles down beside him. 'We could call in an artillery strike from the ship onto that storehouse.'

'What if the other girl is there? We can't take that risk.'

'Unlikely — surely she's on that boat?'

PJ turns, trying to keep the exasperation out of his voice. 'Beg your pardon, sir, but do you know that beyond any doubt? Do you know that I won't have to look a man in the eye and tell him we called in the four-inch HE round that blew his daughter into little pieces?'

'OK, OK. Take it easy. Let's have the benefit of your thoughts.'

PJ peers through the goggles. 'I can see three of them, no four. I'll go down and take them out.' The words come as disconnected grunts. What he is proposing is infinitely dangerous. Four, maybe five men against one at close quarters.

'That's your call. I'll stay here and keep firing as if they've got us pinned down. As soon as you engage we'll come down on them fast.'

PJ uses the officer's foot as a handhold as he goes over the edge, scrabbling for purchase on anything that comes to hand. Finally he is on his way down an almost sheer face, stones falling ahead of him and splashing into the sea.

Reaching the bottom, he is conscious of the sound of falling stones and rubble, trying to time his movements with outbreaks of shooting from above. The sea laps all the way to the base of the cliffs and he sloshes along in calf-deep water towards the jetty area, keeping his movements slow. Silence is vital now. Finally he stops altogether, using his eyes like weapons.

Three gunmen kneel close together, using the ruins of an old stone wall for cover. They shoot intermittently up at the SBS men on the path and it is tempting to take them out in one burst. Instead he moves as close as he dares, unclipping a grenade from his webbing, pulling the pin and lobbing it underhand into the midst of the group.

As if hearing the grenade land they hit the earth and roll fast, but the timer is set for just three seconds and they have little time to move. In the last of the flash PJ sees a fourth man run inside the door of the storehouse. He fires after him, and is just about to follow when he hears a shout from up on the track.

'PJ. No. Run!'

PJ does not even consider ignoring the warning — no SBS comrade would give it without dire need. He turns and tries to get away, pumping his arms like tie rods on a steam locomotive. Reaching the shallows near the jetty, salt water sprays up around his legs and to his thighs.

The blast, when it comes, picks him up and throws him face down into the water. The shockwave is pitiless, robbing him of air and strength. The heat sears and scorches exposed skin — the back of his neck and hands. He feels himself begin to drown.

Uncaring now, he lies face down. There is no longer any desire to breathe. Hands clutch at his shirt, and he feels himself lifted. Someone drags him to shore. He sits up, empties a stream of bile onto the bare earth. Recovering, he looks at Pennington, and then Don, who has come up beside him.

'Thank you,' he chokes out. He has lost his night-vision goggles, but not his weapon, still looped around his shoulder. He tries to focus on Captain Pennington.

'You,' he says, 'saved my bloody life.' He forces himself to his feet. It is not over yet. *They* still have one of the girls. No harm can come to her. Not when he has made a promise.

Saif hears the explosion and looks back to see the orange fireball ballooning high into the sky. He hugs himself with excitement, wondering how many of the infidel commandos have perished.

With that thought warm in his heart he turns and looks to where he tied the kufr girl against the bulkhead. He grunts in annoyance. The girl has gone, having somehow slipped out of the ropes. He opens the door into the cabin and switches on the interior light. It is filled with the sacks of explosive, surely leaving insufficient space for even a girl of that size to hide. He closes the door and moves back into the cockpit, then walks around the side decks once. There is no sign of her. Saif relaxes. She must have slipped overboard and, if so, the sharks will have her.

Soon there will be enough killing, he thinks to himself. A kufr warship, a thousand men perhaps, waiting out there in the night. Clear on the radar now. He thinks of the commandos trying to return to their ship, only to see an explosion lighting the heavens.

His preference would be to die in the act of destroying the enemy. To die shahid, the natural culmination of a life of piety. Years when he and other men spoke of martyrdom not just as a possible end of this life, but the most desirable one. There were times when it might have happened — conflicts against the security forces in

Nigeria; a police raid in Yemen. Now, however, his role is too important. There is much yet to be done to ensure the success of the Rabi al-Salah operation.

Making twenty knots into the open sea the boat begins to leap off each swell and crash into the next. Saif is no seaman and has to clutch at a rail with one hand to remain standing. The blip on the radar draws closer.

Holding on to the wheel with one hand, Saif gropes in a side pocket for a waterproof plastic container, manufactured in Ohio for the US military, sealed with a rubber gasket. In here he places the pocket edition of the Qur'an he always carries, the satellite telephone, and the roll of high denomination currency from his pocket. This case he shoves into the waistband of his military trousers.

Now, he gropes for a lifejacket; not finding one at hand where he had expected but having to leave the helm for a moment, feeling along the pockets until the cool vinyl crinkles under his fingers. He slips the Class 1 PFD over his head, tightening the belly strap and fastening the buckle. Saif al-Din is a man who knows his own limitations. He is not a strong swimmer. He is not afraid to use what he needs to achieve his aims.

Prepared at last, he sees the warship for the first time. To him the looming dark shape must be the pride of the fleet, a battleship, as huge as any ship can be. He knows that some are nuclear powered. Imagines triggering an explosion that will rock the earth. A shiver of ecstasy racks his body.

Simon hears Matt's voice and turns to see him peering over his display. 'Captain, we have a contact. Bearing two-

two-one. Range one thousand. Speed twenty-four knots. I don't know where the hell it's come from — just appeared out of the clutter.'

The ops room appears to close in and darken. General conversation ceases. Marshall's voice booms out. 'Sound action stations.'

The bosun's mate relays the instruction in what is meant to be a deadpan voice, yet it tremors with excitement. 'Hands to action stations. Assume NBCD state. One condition Zulu.'

The click-clack of locking dogs slamming home on a hundred hatches reverberates through the hull. Even the engine takes on a new, strained, urgency. Senior ratings move to their posts. The hair stands erect on Simon's arms as Matt's voice drones on. 'Small and low. Some kind of motor launch, sir.'

'Is it one of the SBS teams coming back?'

'No IFF, sir.'

'Shit!' Marshall turns to the radio operator. 'See if you can raise them on the VHF.'

'Will do. This is HMS *Durham*. Vessel on my port beam, identify.'

'I don't like this,' Marshall breathes. 'Acquire target.'

The radar operator blurts out, 'There's no response, sir.'

'Order them to divert, or we will fire on them.'

Another voice: 'Target acquired, Phalanx tracking and ready.'

The PWO, with his soft voice and serious eyes, says, 'Sir, under the rules of engagement we are not permitted to commence hostilities unless fired upon.'

'Damn the rules of engagement. Rules let them blow a bloody great gash in the USS *Cole* all those years ago.

They don't have rules, only we do. I am responsible for the lives of three hundred men — I will use any means at my disposal to protect them.'

Simon, unable to keep silent any longer, screams out, 'No, stop ... it might be them. My girls might be on board ...'

The gunnery officer's voice is shrill: 'Collision in thirty seconds.'

Simon's voice is pleading now. 'What if it is them? What if the girls are there?'

'My ship is in danger. I have no choice.' Marshall raises his voice. 'Commence firing. Destroy the target.'

Watching through the spray-spotted screen, Saif sees the dark, huddled shape move out of the tangle of ropes in the anchor locker. The girl. He had almost forgotten about her. He is so close, soon he will reach the kufr warship.

Pulling the handgun from its holster, he takes a shot at the poorly defined shape. He can no longer see her, and turns back to the helm unsure if the bullet found its mark, or if she is still on board, just as a wall of 20mm HE projectiles begin to 'walk' across the sea towards the boat.

The first armour-piercing 20mm rounds strike and the hull falters in the water, a fire breaks out, but the momentum of the craft, and the propellers push it on. The inherent buoyancy of the craft, however, helps keep it moving. A series of rounds go astray, churning the sea on the port beam to foam.

The warship rears ahead, a thing of utter repugnance to Saif al-Din, representative of all that he abhors. A military machine that has provoked his fellow believers into the most bitter fight since the crusades. He steadies the boat, aiming it into the centre of the kufr vessel, locking on the autopilot, then pressing the 'arm' button on the timer. Now he leaps onto the gunwale and jumps far out into the sea. Shrapnel tears into his leg, and then a needle like agony in his temple. He cannot prevent a shriek of pain.

He struggles to swim, his injured legs useless, watching the RIB disintegrating on its way to the warship. A shell finds the outboard engines before the range is too short even for the Phalanx system to bear. Saif feels a surge of triumph and excitement as he watches the RIB pass 'under the guns'. This is the moment of glory. He has succeeded.

The charges ignite and a blinding light fills his heart and soul.

There is only one God, and Mohammed is His Prophet ...

White heat sears through the windows of the bridge, and then the shockwave hits the ship. Simon goes down as if he has been punched. Durham tilts to an angle close to the tipping point.

Mingled with it all are shouts, shrieks, screams; unsecured items sliding across the deck. The floor is wet. Simon finds himself scrambling for purchase.

The hull rights itself. Someone is screaming, and there is a terrible, unfamiliar smell in the air.

Marshall is back on his feet and on the microphone. 'Damage reports.'

'Sir, flooding in compartments Echo, Foxtrot, and Golf. Fire in the engine room.'

Simon gropes his way out to the open deck. The sea is lit for a kilometre or more by flames leaping from the

side of the hull. A klaxon sounds, and men spill up from
below decks.

Fighting fires is the best-organised and most-practised
drill in the Royal Navy. The total crew on *Durham*
numbers almost three hundred, and each man and
woman has a station. Pumps clatter to life. Hose reels
turn. Automatic fire systems spit water and foam from
brass sprinklers.

Men in dreadnought suits hold long hoses that direct
streams of seawater onto the flames. Others produce
spray that cloaks the firefighters in billions of protective
droplets, shielding them from heat and flame.

Simon is conscious of being in the way, an errant
civilian with no purpose. He climbs to the signal deck.
From that vantage point he watches the flames lick higher,
feels the heat on his face, drying the tears to grainy salt.

To Simon, this is the end of the world. There now
seems no possibility of Hannah and Frances returning. If
the terrorists were in a position to attack the ship, then
what have they done to the SBS men? Their power seems
inexorable.

For perhaps thirty minutes, he is convinced that the
ship will sink, for she lists heavily. But the flames smother
under foam and water, and the list disappears as pumps
and damage control teams deal with the flooding. He gains
the courage to return to the bridge and ask the officer of
the watch, 'Will she be OK?'

'Yeah, I think we were lucky. They holed us, the
bastards, but just above the waterline and we're getting
the fires under control now. Once it cools down they'll

plug it up and we'll be operational again. This tub may be old, but she's solid.'

The smoke shrinks back to a black and stinking smudge that hangs over the ship like a blanket. The last of the fires dwindle to nothing, and the clean up process begins. Simon finds himself praying such as he has not prayed for many years. The darkness of the sky and the vast sea make him feel small — a mere thread on the tapestry the local vicar used to talk about. For most of his life he has rejected the strict Anglican faith of his childhood — did his time as a choirboy and in the youth group, and then turned his back on it all.

Psalm 23, so beloved of the faithful, comes back to him in all its majesty and beauty. His lips move silently.

The Lord is my shepherd; I shall not want.

He maketh me to lie down in green pastures: He leadeth me beside the still waters.

He restoreth my soul: He leadeth me in the paths of righteousness for His name's sake.

Over and over again he repeats those words, until he means them as he has never meant anything, believes in the sincerity of them; until his chest aches and his tears fall to his chest.

From out in the night he hears the soft hum of almost silent motors. From across the sea, three shapes blacker than the night itself appear, riding ahead of a greater darkness.

They come more swiftly than he might have imagined. Already he is craning forwards, seeing the shapes of heads in the boats. He hurries down a pair of ladders and onto the deck where crews are mopping up the mess remaining from the fire. First he tries to climb over the rail, then, realising the folly of that, stands, gripping a stanchion with one hand, waving his arms like a madman.

He runs aft, ignoring busy seamen, seeing a stretcher carried up from the sea, fighting his way to her side, seeing the bloody bandages, and the morphine calm of Frances's face. But he rejoices that she is alive. He kisses her lips and tears spill down his face.

They lead Kelly up, a blanket wrapped around her shoulders, and they embrace; he can feel her sobbing into his neck. Men form a silent circle around them, and Simon searches with his eyes for Hannah.

The SBS fighter who spoke to Simon earlier touches his shoulder, eyes dull. 'I'm sorry. We still haven't located her.'

Simon feels himself assaulted by an avalanche of feelings he cannot begin to control: despair; relief at having Frances back; worry at her wounds. An unfathomable abyss of hurt and thanksgiving.

THE SIXTH DAY

*God said, 'Let us make man in Our image, in Our likeness,
and let him rule over the fish of the sea and the birds of
the air, over the livestock, over all the earth, and over the
creatures that move along the ground.'*

*So God created man in His own image, in the image
of God He created him; male and female He created
them. God blessed them and said to them, 'Be fruitful and
increase in number; fill the earth and subdue it.'*

*So humankind was fruitful, and clever. Subduing
nature came easily to him. Very early he learned to fell
trees and bridge rivers, and devised sophisticated ways to
kill. Man invented science, and with science crafted the
world according to his wishes. If his house is cold he can
heat it. If there is rain he has a roof to defeat it. If his work
is difficult, he invents a machine to take his place.*

*And there was evening, and there was morning. The
sixth day.*

Day 6, 05:00

At dawn, Marika wakes to find the world changed. The
wind has stopped. Sand lies in drifts against the foot of the
hills and any other object that slows the torrent. Outside

their hiding place is a land without footsteps, devoid of any living thing other than thorn trees and vultures, already up and scouring the earth for carrion.

They rise together, and Marika senses a strangeness between them. On impulse she places a hand on Madoowbe's shoulder and leans up to kiss the wire-brush stubble on his cheeks. 'What do we do now?'

'We find our camel.'

Walking together, they circle the low hills, feet squeaking in the new layer of fine desert sand. Some distance away, they find their transport chewing the dried remnants of a bush. It pauses, still masticating, lifts its head and glares, yet allows Madoowbe to come close and grasp the halter.

Mounting the ungainly creature now seems as natural, to Marika, as climbing into a car.

'Sufia cannot be far away,' Madoowbe says.

Far, however, in the deserts of Africa, is a relative term. The landscape is an empty slate, yet to have the passage of man and animal imprinted upon it. The stillness is eerie, and Marika has to fight the numbing calmness that emanates from air and sand alike.

The landscape changes from sandy desert to vast clay steppe, where there seems to exist no life at all. Then, just as this emptiness promises to go on forever, they reach a surreal landscape that Madoowbe explains as petrified sand dunes. Once, as if to reassure her that animals do indeed live here, he points out the delicate tracks left behind by a tiny jerboa.

The seconds advance with dull momentum. *One and a half days*, Marika says to herself, *just thirty-odd hours to go. Barely enough time to find Sufia, and what then? Tell her that the man she loves is holding the world to ransom, that only she might have the power to change his mind? Will she listen to me, or to Madoowbe? He hasn't seen her since she was a baby. She probably doesn't even know that he exists.*

Marika's reasoning leads her to conclude that this is a useless excursion at the far end of the world, removed from the real action. It occurs to her that the whole thing could be over, even now — that a negotiator has convinced Dr Abukar to disarm himself, or the Special Forces troops she knows are standing by have forced their way in and shot the terrorists dead.

Swaying from side to side at the camel's progress, Marika continues this fantasy in her head, wishing she was at Rabi al-Salah still — that she could have been there at the end instead of riding a stolen camel into oblivion.

But then, what if … what if Sufia is the key? What if the lives of all those world leaders are truly in her hands? Why are they so important anyway? Why are they any more important than a woman of south India who has collected seeds for half a century and holds stores of pure species now forgotten in the world of monoculture? Why are presidents and prime ministers more important than a man who does nothing more than farm his land and feed his family?

The daydream ends with a feeling of hunger, not for Somali porridge and camel blood, but real food: roast lamb, baked potatoes, gravy; maybe a fresh snapper grilled on a barbecue, butter sizzling through the foil …

'Oi,' Madoowbe says, and while Marika drags herself back to reality, he slips to the ground before the camel has come to a halt, grabbing the halter and kneeling.

'What is it?' she asks.

'Tracks. A dozen men and women, some children. Camels.'

'Do you think it might be her?'

'I can read the signs on the earth but I am not a soothsayer. All we can do is follow, and hope. There is one thing for certain. A group passed here this morning, and may not be far ahead.'

Marika's eyes blaze. 'Well, you'd better climb back up here and get this animal moving.'

The camel, when persuaded with boot heels, is able to manage a reluctant trot, snorting in protest through oversized nostrils.

'Can't it go any faster?' Marika asks, voice shaking with the motion.

'Yes, but then he will falter within a mile. At this pace he can swallow the ground for an hour or more.'

The trail passes through a ravine between two dramatic stony peaks, sheathed and shelved with stone so weathered it might have been polished by some long gone river. There, in the shadows, the air cools, and Marika wishes they could stop. Perhaps find water. As if sensing this, Madoowbe turns. 'We can have a quick rest, if you like?'

'No, keep going. We might be close.'

Back out on the plain, Marika finds herself dozing, waking when the camel slows almost to a standstill. Madoowbe is gazing out at the horizon; she feels the change through her knees and her hands at his waist. 'What is it?'

'Look ahead.'

Marika squints into the distance, sees the tiny shapes wheeling in the still air, hearing the odd raucous cry. 'What are they?'

'White-backed vultures. Carrion birds.'

'Why are they here?'

Madoowbe shrugs, but she feels him kick back into the camel's flanks. The animal responds by gathering pace.

The vultures are further than Marika expects, but finally the cries sound close, the fat bellies and long, drooping beaks visible. Some are clustered on small brown hillocks. Not hillocks. Something else. Closer now, she sees the dark stains on the earth and twisted necks and limbs.

'Camels,' she breathes, 'dead camels. Why?'

Madoowbe says nothing, and then the first human bodies come into view. One is a child, who might have been running, robes billowed out under him. A bullet has torn a crater in his chest. One leg is twisted at an awkward angle beneath his body.

The camel stops to Madoowbe's command. Marika dismounts and kneels beside the dead child, trying to hold back tears. After remaining like this for some minutes she looks up at Madoowbe, who stands, one hand on the halter.

'Be careful,' he tells her, 'it is possible that whoever did this is still nearby.'

Marika comes back to her feet, walking around the dozen bodies that litter the area, most surrounding the still smouldering remnants of a camel dung fire, a small pot of spiced meat hanging from a cradle. All have been shot, some several times. Cartridge cases litter the earth.

Marika fights to control her emotions. She has been trained to deal with this kind of situation, yet still the anger and pain spills from her eyes. 'Who did this? The shifta?'

'No,' Madoowbe says, 'they would have taken the camels, not killed them.' He walks forwards ten paces and points to tracks in the dust. 'Four-wheel-drive vehicles. The killers were not shifta. And I have examined the female bodies — Sufia is not among them. Not unless she has changed a great deal from her photograph. They have taken her.'

'Who would have done such a thing?'

His tone remains expressionless. No trace of anger. 'The warlord Dalmar Asad, who else but he?'

Marika's heart feels as if it carries a tonne of ballast. 'Can we bury them?'

'There is no time. We have to follow.'

Marika's eyes blaze. 'Don't you feel this? Can't you show one shred of emotion?'

He shrugs. 'It is sad, but I did not know them.'

'Aren't you angry?'

Madoowbe's eyes are as cold as steel. 'I am not in the habit of displaying everything I feel. That is a peculiarity of Westerners.'

'Well maybe,' Marika says, 'that is at least *one* damn good thing about us. We don't feel the need to hide everything away.' Her voice softens and she touches his shoulder. 'It's OK to feel pain. Crying is not a betrayal.'

For a moment she thinks he might reply, but instead he orders the camel down so they can mount. 'There is no profit in standing around and talking. We need to find the people who did this, and we need to know if they have taken my sister Sufia.'

Marika nods. 'You are right. We don't have time for this now. But later, you cold bugger, I'm going to break through that shell of yours and see what's underneath. I had a sample and I like it. Got it?'

The smile on his face is a mere shadow.

* * *

Half a mile along, following the tracks of three vehicles, Madoowbe once again stops the camel.

'What are you doing?' Marika asks. 'You said yourself we need to hurry.'

Madoowbe points to a stand of umbrella thorn trees. Marika follows the direction of his pointing finger. Brown, stubbled legs and a patch of neck resolve into two camels, still with halter ropes attached. 'It looks like at least two of their mounts got away from the guns.'

Marika watches as Madoowbe dismounts and approaches the stray animals, talking under his breath. The camels lift their heads and watch him come, suspiciously, munching on their cud, molars grinding audibly.

Madoowbe's whispered words become a song: soft, melodic and sweet; distinctively Arabic with the extra quarter-tone notes. With each phrase he moves a step closer until he has the lead rope of first one camel and then the other in his hand.

'Upgraded transportation.' He grins, bringing them towards her.

'Well done. I'm impressed.'

'Perhaps there is something of the herdboy in me still. Which one do you want?'

Marika looks at the two camels — one is smaller than the other, and in camel terms, has a feminine, almost pretty face.

'I'll have her. She looks like she'll treat me well.'

'It's a him, actually.'

'Oh. I didn't see his, er — oh yeah, there it is. Him then.'

Having transferred their few belongings across, Madoowbe lets the other camel go free. They mount up. Marika senses the change — these new animals are well rested and trained to a higher standard than the ones belonging to the shifta.

'Still not as fast as a vehicle,' she says, thinking aloud.

'Not so much slower than you might think,' Madoowbe says. 'The men we follow are not careful drivers. They are more interested in bravado than safety. Does not your culture have a fable about a hare and a tortoise? There is an African version also.'

Marika does not ask him to explain further, but not far ahead they reach a plain of sharp stones where it becomes difficult to make out any trail at all. There are, however, occasional patches of sand where the wheels have left a bossed imprint. On the far side — a journey of almost an hour — they discover that the small convoy stopped to change a tyre on one of the vehicles.

'Fifteen minutes wasted, at least,' Madoowbe says, 'and it would have taken them almost as long as us to negotiate the stones. They are not far ahead now.'

Marika tries to smile, but her belly is as tight as a drum. 'I just wish I wasn't so damn hungry.'

'Both of us are hungry, but there will be time to eat later.' His face hardens. 'When we find Sufia and take her to safety.'

'I'm sorry, I forget sometimes that she is your sister. You must be so worried.'

'We cannot even be sure that they have her — that she was with that particular group. All we can do is hope that we will be in time, whoever they have taken.'

Marika says nothing. They both know that Sufia is there, and that Dalmar Asad has proved to be swifter and more ruthless than they imagined. Despite the heat, she shivers.

The man is a killer. A manipulator. Isn't this all my fault?

If she had never confessed her mission to him, the family might not have been slaughtered back there in the desert. But then, if that were the case, might she have been tortured and shot?

There is no right answer, she decides. No way to go back and find the right path — only the present, and the future.

For almost an hour, Isabella watches for an opportunity to check the phone for messages, but always the fat mujahedin, Jafar, stays close. Leering at her, lips parted, sometimes even adjusting his crotch when he knows she is watching. Ever since the death of the French President she has been edgy, the atmosphere in the room electric.

The constancy of death in this room is a reminder that these men operate outside the normal moral sphere. That the cell phone is a terrible risk. Still she waits. Zhyogal comes across to talk to the fat one and she is safe, for a moment, slipping the phone out from her underwear and turning it on. Two new messages.

Reading the first, unable to believe the words, stifling an exclamation of simultaneous joy and despair.

Frances injured but stable and with me. Kelly safe and well. All worried for you. Simon.

Each word is a tingling electric shock through her limbs, followed by a wave of relief and horror that flows like a tide in her bloodstream.

Where the hell is Hannah? Oh God. Hannah is still missing. But Frances is injured. Where? How badly? But she is alive …

Isabella is frozen. Stunned. For a moment she almost forgets to hide the handset, and it is only the approaching form of Jafar that has her dropping her hand into her skirt and slipping the phone back into its hiding place before he reaches her. As always his eyes seek her out, staring, lustful, and she knows that getting her emotions under control is not just desirable, but essential — to be caught is to die.

At last he passes on, and she leans towards the ground, hiding her face from view. Reading the second, unsigned message.

At three am do your best to distract the guard in your quadrant. It is important that he is not alert.

Isabella steels herself. *Oh God, but how can I breathe?*

This is a matter of importance. She, in a position of trust and responsibility, has betrayed her country. It is up to her to do her best to right the wrong, and work to her utmost ability to set the men and women in this room free.

The fat terrorist comes back into view. The plan is not hard to formulate. The difficulty will be to gather her self-control sufficiently not to spit in his face when she is close enough to do so.

Hannah, where are you? My darling. What happened to you?

Day 6, 12:00

The three SAR inflatables have searched since before dawn, starting from the island harbour and working their way out in planned sweeps, two hundred metre intervals between each one.

Simon huddles in the bow of one of the boats, alternately fighting tears and feeling thankful for the life of Frances, who now occupies an infirmary bed. Neither of her wounds is life threatening, but she is groggy and distressed.

The best present she could have, the most important boost to her health, Simon knows, is the return of Hannah, yet time is slipping away. His face is already sunburned, lips cracked, and he does not think to eat or drink unless one of the crew reminds him. They are all volunteers on this search; all conscientious and careful.

Now and then, he stops scanning the horizon, holds his head in his hands. He feels bruised, as if he has suffered the emotional equivalent of a beating with a baseball bat. He wonders if any further hurt can penetrate, any punishment break through the numbness.

All that remains is a kind of emotional flinching away; an attempt to fend off some final, massive blow that will end it all. The general opinion is that Hannah must have still been on board the launch at the time of the explosion, yet there is no evidence for this assumption. No human remains at all.

They eat lunch on the move — sandwiches and fruit — before resuming the search pattern. Occasionally the drone of two fixed-wing aircraft that have joined the search from their Saudi base, pass to the east or west.

By noon the day has become an ordeal, one that sees
Marika's thighs, already irritated, chafed almost raw from
the camel. Thirst and hunger combine into a cavernous
emptiness that extends from spine to stomach. Tired
of sand, sun and the endless desert, she begins to hate
Somalia as if it were human.

She feels the first flutter of despair. There is no sign
that they have gained on the vehicles, and they cannot
continue at this pace. She has named the camel that bears
her Sarah and offers encouragement as they ride.

'Sarah is a girl's name,' Madoowbe protests.

'I know, but he's a girly kind of camel. Look at those
eyelashes.'

The animal is, however, beginning to falter, exhausted
from the ceaseless trot across the landscape. Likewise,
Marika's body screams for rest, and often she looks across
at Madoowbe, pleading with her eyes, hoping he might
stop and say, *Let's rest, just for an hour — I have some food
and cold water I have been saving* ...

Just as the daydream develops into a fairy tale complete
with banquets, swimming pools and handsome young
barmen serving cold beer, Marika hears a gunshot ahead.
She pulls the camel up with firm pressure on the reins.
Madoowbe does the same. A second shot echoes across
the desert.

'Less than a mile away,' Madoowbe says.

'What do you think is happening?'

'I don't know. But I think we should find out. There is
a rise ahead — we'll leave the trail and see what we can
see.'

Leading the camels now, Marika follows Madoowbe
up the slope, the surface varying from soft, deep sand

to rubble. Everywhere is thorn bush and umbrella trees. Finally, near the summit, they leave the camels tied to an acacia branch and creep forwards on foot.

At the very lip, Madoowbe drops and crawls on all fours. Marika does the same, coming up beside him and looking out into a dry and desolate valley. Four technicals are drawn up in a circle, machine guns limp on their mountings, barrels facing skyward. Men stand near a fire in the centre of the camp. Others are in the process of finalising the pitching of a canvas tent the size of a small house, hammering in the last few pegs, guy ropes stretched tight.

'The patrol that brought you returned to Dalmar Asad,' Madoowbe whispers, 'and came back here with reinforcements.'

Marika knows it must be true. There are many of them now: more vehicles, more men.

Two of the militia drag the limp body of a man across the ground, moving him some distance away, dropping him, then walking back towards the camp. One man harangues the others in loud and strident tones.

'What's he saying?' Marika asks.

'It is Dalmar Asad himself. He is saying to let that man's death be an example to them — that men who are disobedient to him die.'

Marika studies the distant figure. Yes, of course it is him — the height and athletic stance are unmistakeable. 'What a bastard! I hate him. What did the dead guy do?'

Madoowbe's mouth takes on the stitched tightness of someone who has just tasted something too bitter to eat. 'I did not hear. It could have been anything — a slight disobedience perhaps.'

'Where is Sufia?'

'If she is there she must be inside the tent.'

'They might have killed her.'

'Yes, but we have seen no more bodies.'

Behind them, one of the camels wheezes. Marika looks back in that direction, staring for some moments before returning her attention to the camp in the valley. 'So what do we do? How do we get to her?'

'I am not yet sure.'

Even as her body relaxes, lying prone for the first time that day, Marika hears something that chills her blood. Weapons manufacturers take pains to ensure that safety catches and fire selectors operate silently. Even civilian users dislike spending ten minutes sneaking up on game then spooking the target with a click. Over time, however, metal parts wear and corrode. To Marika, the sound of this mechanism is instantly familiar, even though it comes from some twenty or more paces behind. Her reaction is instinctive — faster than anything she might have been able to prepare or analyse. The assault weapon in her arm becomes an extension of her body as she rolls, turning as she does so, the movement minimising the chance of being hit by enemy fire and allowing herself the chance to shoot back.

Now, however, she faces not one or two, but half-a-dozen men with automatic weapons — at least three have her covered. In the centre stands Captain Wanami, his sunglasses reflecting back the stunted desert landscape, gold earring shining in the sun.

With just a split second to respond, Marika turns to look at Madoowbe, who is a few paces further away from them. Their eyes meet, and even as she is ready to lower the assault rifle she remembers the dead men, women and children back on the trail. Anger at these killers blurs her vision. Anger at the arrogance of men who use guns as playthings. Her finger begins to squeeze the trigger.

'*Whas ghaba.*' Wanami hisses out the words, his AK steady, aimed so that she can see only the obscene black circle of the muzzle. Marika suspects that he would probably enjoy killing her — boast about it later to his cronies around the campfire.

Before she can make a decision, something moves on the periphery of her vision — Madoowbe. At first she does not understand what he is doing. He leaps to his feet and sprints away, jinking and sidestepping like a rugby fullback. The departure is so abrupt that for several moments no one reacts. Then, a burst of 7.62mm follows him through the scrub, bullets ripping and tearing at the undergrowth, breaking sticks and leaves. The smell of nitro fills the air.

Madoowbe, however, is soon out of sight and away. The gunmen, to her surprise, do not follow him. Instead she watches as the point men move out onto the flanks so she cannot escape.

Again her finger tightens on the trigger, furious now, ready to spray bullets into those arrogant faces. But there is no point in dying now. Not when Sufia is so close.

'Shit, shit, shit,' Marika says, dropping her assault rifle to the earth so hard she half expects it to discharge. She stands, raising her arms in reluctant surrender. 'OK, you bastards. You want another prisoner, you got one.'

They come forwards warily, as if expecting her to produce a hidden weapon. When this does not happen,

Captain Wanami steps up close, swinging one hand like a whip across her cheek.

Marika recovers slowly, still holding her cheek, glaring through her captor's sunglasses. His jaw never ceases moving, chewing qat like the others, one cheek bulging with leaf. 'Your breath stinks. Didn't your mother teach you not to breathe on people?'

Ignoring her now, he barks orders at two of his men, who take an arm each. A third follows, gun barrel jammed into the small of her back.

As they lead her away, Marika's nails bite into the sweating skin of her palms. Now she will face Dalmar Asad. The man who ordered the murder of the family of nomads — even the children. Some small part of her hopes that she might have the opportunity and the courage to kill him herself.

Captain Wanami leads the way through the compound, smoking a cigarette, shooting her the occasional look of pure, unadulterated hatred. Of course, losing her from the patrol would have led to not inconsiderable inconvenience. Dalmar Asad would have taken much of his rage out on the captain. Marika feels the chill in her heart reach the temperature of dry ice as the guards push her on, through a tent flap.

The interior of the tent belies the plain green canvas of the exterior: a cavernous space that incorporates several rooms, the first of which is more luxurious than Marika ever imagined a tent could be. The floor is a woven polyethylene sheet, covered with scattered Persian rugs. Folding chairs and tables in the centre of the main room are lit by a pair of hissing gas lanterns. The heat in here is intense — cloying and humid.

Dalmar Asad stands as she enters, dressed in a parody of a traditional English safari outfit, lacking only the pith hat. The albino stripes across one side of his face and neck appear more livid than last time she saw him. He wears an expression more of triumph than pleasure. 'You are here,' he says.

'Yes. Rather against my wishes.'

'Your Somali friend is a coward. He ran away.'

'Better by far to be a coward than a killer.'

'Killing is sometimes necessary for a man in my position to survive. As I have told you, my people respond only to fear.'

'The dead babies out in the desert — they were a threat to you? Is that right?'

'Babies grow into adults, and avenge their parents. Why create a problem for the future? Prudence dictates that they be killed now.'

'What had *any of them* ever done to you?'

Dalmar Asad's voice betrays a hint of irritation. 'It was necessary.'

A face appears at the door. The warlord confers with the man then returns, smiling. 'My soldiers caught up with your irascible friend. They executed him as per my orders.'

Marika reaches out to grip the top of a chair, fighting to keep her reaction from her face. *Madoowbe. Dead?* It seems incredible. At first she cannot speak, but then she stares, open mouthed. 'I've seen rats with more decency than you.'

Asad inclines his head, as if accepting a compliment. 'I dismissed the man as ineffectual once before. I gave him the opportunity to escape when I should have had him shot. He proved to be a thorn in my side. My mistake — now it has been rectified, and we have business to attend to.'

'What business?'

'You and I, my fair lady, have a deal. The highly sought after Sufia is in my care, and I am ready to pass her over to you. It remains only for you to fulfil your end of the bargain.'

'Never, you swine.'

Dalmar Asad spreads his hands. 'Of course, you may choose to renege on our bargain, in which case I will take my frustrations out on Sufia. When I am done my men can have her — women do not live long in their hands, especially not one with such rare beauty as she.'

Stall for time, Marika tells herself. 'Where is she? I want to see her.'

'She is very close, I assure you.'

'Prove it,' she says, folding her arms and locking her eyes on his until he relents and shouts an order.

In response, a guard leads Sufia into the room by one arm. Tall, regal and beautiful, Marika recognises her from the photos: her stateliness, the elegance that has seen several Somali women forge successful careers on the catwalks of Milan, New York, and Paris.

Dalmar Asad addresses Sufia, reaching out to take her hand. Her arm remains limp, falling back to her side when he releases it.

'This kufr woman is your saviour,' he says, 'should she choose to be. Do you understand?'

The woman does not flinch, nor acknowledge him in any way, yet moves her eyes to look at Marika.

Understanding passes between them in that moment, women of vastly disparate cultures, yet both strong and worldly in their own way.

Words are not necessary as Marika communicates with her eyes. *I will get you out of here, somehow.*

The reply is clear. *Thank you. I will be waiting.*

Marika sees something else too, behind the proud face. Worry that must eat at her soul like a disease. Worry for her husband and what he has done. What will happen to him? Is there a place in the sun for them some day? There is nothing reassuring worth saying. Much is at stake. The world for both women is changing. Ending. There is no guarantee of a new beginning.

'Take her away,' Dalmar Asad orders. A moment later the woman is gone.

Marika focuses her attention on the warlord. She wants to go at him with her fingernails, scratch out his eyes and smash his balls to pulp with her knee. 'You're like a medieval overlord — you suck the blood from your people to build your palace and equip your army. Now you are holding two innocent women so you can fulfil some pointless male desire. You kill a couple of families out in the desert. For what? Sex?'

'Fulfil your side of the bargain, and you and the woman may go — my men will not impede you. Fail to do so and I will hand you over to Wanami. He feels that you betrayed our trust, and looks forward to levelling the score.'

Marika swallows down the fear that rises up from her chest. What choice does she have? What if she *does* play the game, and Dalmar Asad keeps his promise? *What then?* What can she do in the middle of the desert with no means of communication?

'I will remind you again. We had a deal. I fulfilled my part of the bargain. You chose to abuse my trust, but as far as I am concerned the deal stands.'

'Really? Now? It's the middle of the day.'

'The time is immaterial to me.'

'OK,' her voice rises, 'let's get this over with. Where do you want to do it. Here? On the chair? Or just on the floor like animals — I guess it would be appropriate.'

The big man appears to relax. 'There is another room. Come with me.'

Marika follows him through a gap in the canvas, finding herself in a large space with a sleeping mat in the middle.

'Take off your clothes,' he says. 'I want to look at you.'

'No.'

'Take them off, or I will do it for you.'

Marika unbuttons her shirt, then reaches around to unclip her bra. His eyes have, so far, not left her face, but now she sees them flick down to her naked breasts — so white, tipped with rose.

'The rest,' he orders. 'Hurry.'

Dalmar Asad takes off his own clothes, underwear last. 'When I was a child,' he says, 'my brothers called my member Adh-Dhikh. The hyena.'

Marika sees the aptness of the description. Apart from the mottled colouring, the thing is huge and misshapen, enlarged behind the bulb in the shape of hunched shoulders.

Seeing her watching, he drops one massive hand and begins to manipulate it. Little happens apart from a slight thickening along its length. He steps forward so he is in front of her. 'Touch it.'

Hating him more, she drops one hand and feels the warm clamminess.

'Stroke it.'

She obeys.

'Lie down, woman.'

Marika stares back venomously as she obeys; squatting, sitting down and then stretching out on her back. A tear comes to her eye as she thinks of Madoowbe and what they did just the previous night. For comfort; lust, perhaps. For reasons infinitely better than this misbegotten deal. She has slept with men for love, sympathy — even to give in to the kind of relentless emotional pressure Australian men can exert. This, however, will be the first time she has been penetrated in pure, unadulterated hate.

Looking agitated, he lies down beside her. While his hand walks down her belly she pictures dead children on the desert sand. They died — for this. The thought makes her tense, clenching her thighs, locking them together.

'No,' he orders, 'move them apart.'

She complies, almost sobbing with shame and anger, but when he raises himself to his knees and swings Adh-Dhikh near her face she realises the truth. It remains flaccid. This giant of a man *cannot get it up*.

Feeling a repugnance and hatred that overwhelms her, Marika does something stupid. She laughs. Loud and cruel. Then she says, 'That's why you went to such lengths to have me. You thought maybe I could help you get a hard-on.'

Dalmar Asad's face changes, teeth coming together, lips curling up from his front teeth. Veins stand out in his forehead and his neck becomes a fibrous cable drawn taut. One hand is now a blade as straight and hard as a shovel, arm muscles bunching and compressing as he slaps the side of her face.

The slap rattles her brain in her skull and crushes her cheek against her back teeth. The shock robs her of the ability to breathe. She sees the hand change, bunching into a fist the size of a lunch box, coiling back to gather strength for the blow aimed squarely at her face. She realises her folly — that no man will suffer his sexual prowess being mocked. Her one chance, she decides, is to make him angrier still.

'Can't get it up, can you? The hyena can bark but not bite.'

Asad abandons the punch; breathes like an automaton, reaching for his trousers and the gun belt, fumbling with the holster and bringing out the nickel-plated automatic pistol.

Time seems to stand still, and Marika can do nothing but stare as he pulls back the slide, seeing the cartridges waiting their turn below the first one slipping into the chamber. As the barrel swings towards her she realises that he was always going to kill her, because that is the only way he can excite himself.

Closing her eyes, waiting, Marika is aware of two things: one is a sound similar to that of a zip being undone; the other is a grunt of surprise from Dalmar Asad.

Opening her eyes she sees the slim form of Madoowbe, very much alive, coming through a newly torn hole in the side of the tent, holding his bilau overhand. Dalmar Asad raises his arms to stop the blow, but the razor-sharp point strikes him at the temple, and, driven with all the strength of a desperate man's arm, flies on into the brain to just an inch shy of the hilt.

The body jerks and vibrates, before thumping backwards onto the floor, eyes staring at the canvas ceiling in apparent surprise.

Footsteps sound on the canvas outside the room. 'Are you OK, Aaba?'

Marika bites her lip, thinks for a moment, then simulates a soft cry of pleasure. 'Of course we are, leave us.'

The footsteps fade away. Marika dresses, then hugs her rescuer's arm. 'Sufia is here, in this tent. I saw her.'

'We must hurry. They are suspicious already.'

Marika goes to the body of Dalmar Asad, and extricates the handgun, still held by the sausage like fingers. It is a Colt Commander .45, heavy and powerful. *If ever a girl wanted a gun to shoot her way out of trouble*, she thinks, *this would be the one.* She looks back at Madoowbe, who sheaths the knife and unslings his AK47, checking the load with practised efficiency.

'I feel bad — I thought you were deserting me when you ran away into the bush.'

'I saw no point letting them catch both of us, and I was sure they would not kill you — not when you can be used as a bargaining chip.'

'I wonder why he told me you were dead.'

'Because he wanted you to despair.'

Marika grips his hand. 'Let's find Sufia and get out of here.' Walking to the door flap, she opens it a crack, holding the .45 on the other side of the canvas, out of view.

'You are wanted,' she calls.

A face appears.

Marika mimics the act of holding a water bottle and drinking, then uses the Arab word for bottle, boo-til, that she heard so often at Rabi al-Salah. Finally she holds up two fingers. 'Two,' she says, 'two boo-til.'

The man's eyebrows rise, surprised, it seems, at these orders issued from a woman.

Marika smiles and lowers her voice. 'Dalmar is exhausted, the poor man.'

The guard grins and moves away, returning moments later with two bottles of Kenyan packaged spring water. Marika waits until he is just a pace or two away before she fires, the roar of the discharge deafening. The heavy .45 slug takes him in the chest, his body collapsing. The recoil jars her wrist. Not looking at the body, not wanting to, she changes the gun to the other hand, shaking the pain away.

They leave the room and enter the next, meeting Sufia's guard coming to check on the commotion. Marika shoots him at point-blank range, then pushes aside another flap. The partitioned space inside is no larger than a closet, with a greasy woollen blanket in a rumpled heap on the floor.

Sufia stands. 'What is happening?'

'Hurry, you must come with us.'

'Who are you?'

'There'll be time for that later.' Marika turns to Madoowbe. 'The front entrance will be dangerous. Is there another way out?'

Madoowbe slits the tent wall and they step out into the sunlight. Running men converge across a canvas of grass and acacia trees. The gunshot has raised the alarm.

'To the vehicles,' Marika cries. 'Run with me.'

Gunfire arcs out towards them, the occasional tracer round stinging through the air like a phosphorescent bee. Marika is aware of Madoowbe turning, firing a long, searching burst, cut off by a misfire and jam.

The first of the vehicles looms ahead, a converted Ford pick-up. An F100, Marika decides. Her uncle once owned

one, a rusted heap that after thirty years showed no sign
of packing it in.

'You go for the gun,' she calls to Madoowbe, 'I'll drive,
and pray those stupid bastards left the keys in the ignition.'
She turns to look at Sufia, running beside her. 'You OK?'

'Yes. Confused but alive. That is a good start.'

'Go for the passenger side.'

Almost there, Marika turns and fires three shots from
the Colt, picking out running targets. One falls. The others
stop and go to ground. Return fire splits the air around
her. The slim figure of Captain Wanami remains upright.
Marika fires at him twice before he too takes cover.

Throwing open the driver's door, Marika gropes for the
key. The heat of the vehicle interior hits her like a sauna.
There are two AK47 assault rifles wedged between the
seats, long magazines curving up towards the ceiling.

'Damn,' she shouts, finding the ignition slot empty,
leaning down to feel the floor and finding nothing. Then,
raising one hand, she explores the upper side of the folded
sun visor and her hands close on a pair of keys on a ring.
'Bingo!'

Sufia dives in, slamming the door. The vehicle body
bounces as Madoowbe leaps onto the tray behind them.
The key slips into the slot and the engine fires. Starting the
big Ford in second gear, Marika eases off the clutch and
it shoots forwards, just as the heavy machine gun behind
them spews out the first burst, followed by the tinkle of
spent cartridge cases onto the metal tray.

The rear-vision mirror shows the flare of automatic
fire, and heavy lead projectiles thud into the vehicle body.
Marika flinches each time it happens. 'Oh shit,' she sighs,
'I think I've killed three men today.'

Sufia's voice remains level. 'Not three men. Three swine. A service to humanity.'

Marika forces a smile. 'They're not going to let us get away too easy, but I wonder if they know their master is dead?'

Sufia's eyes shine like pools. 'Who are you?'

'I am a friend, I assure you.'

'Is this about my husband?'

'You could say that. Do you know what he has done?'

'Ali is a good man; the best I have ever known. Whatever he has done is the right thing in the circumstances.'

Marika swears as the front offside wheel strikes a rock. 'A few billion people might disagree with you on that one, but we'll let it pass for the moment.'

Again the machine gun fires.

Sufia's voice is defiant: 'If you have come here to get me to divert Ali from the path he has chosen, then you have wasted your time. I believe in him, and I believe in what he has chosen to do — I have watched him grow in anger at the apathy, the political games of the West. I will not stop him.'

One of the pursuing vehicles closes on them, accelerating out onto the flank, heavy machine gun crackling. The flash of gunfire sears across the desert, a long flame lighting the area like a strobe light, or fireworks.

Marika swings the wheel with all the strength in her shoulders, feeling the vehicle begin to lose control, then shudder, as Madoowbe returns fire. 'Hell,' she says, 'this is no fun.' Looking across at Sufia she sees that she is calm, her face showing no sign of fear. *Nerves of steel*, Marika decides, *either that or just no bloody imagination*.

'Look out, ahead,' Sufia calls.

Marika turns just in time to see a hillside looming, wrenching the wheel hard in response. 'My mother always wanted me to be a hairdresser,' she says. 'I can tell you that curling hair looks like an attractive career option right now.' She hears healthy laughter, and glances across to see Sufia giggling into her hands.

'You are very funny, do you know that?'

'So are you if you can laugh while we've got a couple of truckloads of thugs on our tail.'

The vehicle skids out of control, slewing sideways before straightening, and as they accelerate, Madoowbe gets another burst away. Marika sees the flash of a petrol-fuelled explosion in the mirror as one of the technicals explodes. 'One down,' she cries, and her hands relax on the wheel. From what she can see there is still one other vehicle behind, but the driver is wary, keeping his distance, relying on short bursts that tell on the metal frame of the vehicle. It looks to her like Wanami sitting beside the driver, but the distance is great enough that she cannot be sure.

A drift of sand covers the track ahead, and Marika takes it at speed, the wheels spinning as she pours on the power, knowing that keeping up momentum is crucial. All the time the pursuing vehicle draws closer. The gun hammers.

'Take him out, for God's sake,' Marika encourages Madoowbe, shouting through the open window. One of the headlights shatters. 'Good shooting.'

Sufia opens the glove box and starts rummaging through.

'What are you doing?'

'Just seeing if there is anything useful in here.'

Marika glances across as Sufia takes out a dull, globular object the size of a cricket ball. 'Hell, that thing belongs in a museum.'

'It's heavy. What is it?'

'An old kind of grenade — a Mills bomb. First Gulf War vintage at least. You're taking your life into your hands just picking it up.'

'How do you use it?'

'See that lever at the side?'

'Yes.'

'Hold it in, then pull out the ring.'

There is a metallic snick as she does so.

'Keep holding that lever or it will go off.'

'How soon?'

'Five seconds, I think.'

'So if I drop it out the window it will go off in five seconds?'

'Yes, no — maybe. Give it a try and see what happens — just get the bloody thing out of here, it's making me nervous.'

Marika watches Sufia hold the grenade out the open window with one hand, releasing it a few moments later. The driver of the following vehicle must see it fall, for he swerves off the track.

The subsequent explosion rocks even the F100, and the effect on the pursuing technical is devastating, taking it out in a funnel of flame and dust. From what Marika can see through the mirror, the explosion tears through one side of the cab, tipping the vehicle onto its side. Men spill out into the sunlight.

'Well done,' Marika cries, 'that got the bastards off our backs.'

Abdullah is beyond nervous. There are so many things that can go wrong. The plan is simple, but years of experience have proved that simple plans are best. Turning off the corridor, he moves into a lunch room that has become a barracks. Inside, fourteen men clean rifles and side arms, strapping on Kevlar vests. The room smells of sweaty fear and tension. The chatter stops as he enters.

These are elite Dubai Special Forces troops, one of five platoons attached to the centre for preventative security. Dressed all in black, even the helmets with their shallow brim at the front, they carry FAMAS assault rifles, reliable and proven weapons, most with cut-down, folding stocks.

The men look up when he clears his throat, a few persisting with the nervous activity. 'I am sorry to interrupt your preparations, but I would like to speak, if I may.' Every eye locks onto his, and Abdullah knows the gravity of what he is about to tell them. 'There are no second chances. No back-up plans. This will either work or it will not. As you know, I could have had any elite team in the world brought in. I did not for two reasons. One is that the terrorists on the inside have eyes everywhere. A foreign task force would be too obvious if we tried to bring them into the centre. The militants would know something is happening and might behave unpredictably. The second reason is that I hand-picked you people because you are the equal of any soldiers in the world. You come from Dubai and I think that's fitting, because this is our problem, and the world is watching. Also, most of you are Muslim, and it is important for the world to see that we do not support the malignant legions that have misinterpreted the word of God and bring terror to our world.

'If that room goes up we cannot bring those people back. The plan is not difficult to understand. Our sniper takes out the man with the trigger unit. The door opens. In goes the tear gas. You men enter through the door and take out every militant in sight. On the positive side, they have had even less sleep than you, and won't know what's coming. They have ingested large doses of drugs to stay awake. The advantage of surprise is now ours. They will panic. You need to put them out of action before they recover.' Abdullah looks around the room. Every eye is locked on his. He feels a wave of something — admiration, even some envy. These men are about to put their lives on the line. They are trusting that things will happen the way he says they will. He goes on, 'At oh-two-thirty hours we'll move into position. At oh-three-hundred the operation will commence. Any questions?'

No one says a word, and Abdullah turns to leave. Surprisingly, before he goes, one of the men approaches him, touching him on the shoulder.

'Forgive my presumption, sayyid, but will you pray with us?'

'To do so will be an honour.'

Men put down their weapons and they kneel together on the carpet, their voices deep and harmonious. The prayer is short, taken from Surah 7:196. *My guardian is God, who has revealed the Book. He is the guardian of the righteous ...*

The prayer concludes with a round of embracing and handshakes. Abdullah walks back to his office, filled with a poignant mixture of pride and dread.

Once there, closing the door behind him, he moves to the window and stares out at the power station. There, in a platform little bigger than his prone body, waits Corporal Hani Nawaf, apparently the best rifle shot in the Dubai military, having won the prestigious Sheikh Salamah Musa'id Trophy for three consecutive years. On a tripod beside him is a Barrett M107 .50-calibre sniper rifle, possibly the most accurate long-range small armament in history.

The round in the chamber carries an armour-piercing projectile capable of smashing a hole through the armoured glass window of the complex. The next, following a fraction of a second later, will deliver a high explosive-tipped shell, designed to explode inside Dr Abukar's body, tearing organs and tissues apart, killing him instantly.

Abdullah goes to his seat and sits, head in his hand, thinking of his horses, two mares and a stallion, kept out of Dubai at the riding club. He realises just how frightened he feels. He thinks of his mother, missing her.

A shiver racks his body, and at that moment all he wants to do is ride away on the back of his stallion, into the desert, never to return.

They step out of the vehicle together, legs cramped from the drive and ears humming from the engine noise. They sit in the spidery late afternoon shade of a broad acacia tree. The sand here is impregnated with rubble; coarse and abrasive.

Sufia is almost motionless, uncannily fresh for a woman who has spent a day as a captive and a night as a fugitive. 'Thank you for coming to get me,' she says. 'Dalmar Asad is a bad man and I would have killed him myself if the opportunity had presented itself.' She turns to Madoowbe.

'We haven't been introduced as yet, but I owe you a debt of gratitude.'

'I'm sorry,' Marika says, eyeing each in turn. 'Sufia, this is Madoowbe.'

For the first time she sees the Somali woman lose her poise.

'Really? That is your naanays?'

Madoowbe nods.

'I once knew someone of that name. Are you of the Darod clan?'

Again he indicates assent.

'Your family name is not Libaan Khayre Istar?'

'It is indeed.'

'Then you are my older brother?'

'I believe that I am.'

This is not the first time Marika has been present for a reunion of family members long separated. Once, she helped a friend track down the mother who had adopted her out as a child, and agreed to be present at the reunion. Again she sees the slow awakening of joy, for, although she is young, Marika has learned that one's relationship with family is one of the few worthwhile pillars of this life.

The tall, regal Somali woman grips her brother's arm in both hands and weeps. His head falls to her shoulder as if to hide that same expression of emotion. Then, pressing their faces close, they rub noses, the gesture intimate and touching.

Marika, embarrassed, walks to the technical — removing and checking the two rifles, sitting them on the tray next to Madoowbe's weapon, half listening while she does so.

'As I grew,' Sufia says, 'you were like a ghost in the family — always there in our memories and dreams.

People would say, "Do you remember when Madoowbe did something or other?" Sometimes my father, Othman, would grow angry that you were gone. "He should be here to help us, not have abandoned us like he did."'

Madoowbe stares at the ground. 'What happened to them? What happened to my mother?'

'The warlord Mohammad Farrah Aidid shot them both. I was thirteen.'

Marika turns to look at Madoowbe. He lowers his face, but there are no tears. A wave of sympathy wells up from the pit of Marika's heart. *Cry, damn you. Cry!* she wants to shout. *There is no point hiding your feelings.* She wants to place her arm around his neck and soothe him. Instead she ducks back through the open front door of the technical, flicking the key to look at the clock.

Just twenty-four hours to the deadline. There is no time, not even for family reunions, yet what can they do? The technical has a radio, a short-range UHF set, useless for long-distance communication.

Marika walks back to the siblings. 'I hate to break up the party, but we have to make contact somehow. We're low on fuel. Any ideas?'

'American satellites pass over all the time,' Sufia points out. 'They use infrared photography. Light a signal they can recognise. Use gasoline — it will show up easily from the sky.'

'Good thinking — but what's something that might be clear to them? How will they know it is us?'

Madoowbe murmurs, 'Just the letters U and N? They should understand that.'

Marika thinks for a moment. 'Yep, we can do that.' Moving to the rear tray of the technical she drags out an empty orange plastic jerry can. 'Here, help me siphon some petrol into this.'

Once the vessel is full Marika moves out into a clear patch of desert, spilling the petrol in neat, even lines. When it is done she creates a trail back to a safe distance, then rifles through the vehicle's glove box, finding first a Zippo-style cigarette lighter with no fuel, then a yellow box of Kifaru matches from Kenya.

The first match fails to strike, but the second flares on the first try. When she drops it onto the sand, wet with petroleum, flames scorch down the trail. Reaching the main pattern, the heat forces her to step back. A heavy but brief cloud of black smoke rolls skyward.

Looking at the result with satisfaction, Marika smiles as she imagines the boffins sitting in their dark room studying this anomaly in the remote Ogaden Desert, scratching their unimaginative heads, arguing among themselves. This image alive and well in her mind, she walks back to where Madoowbe and Sufia stand close together, talking.

'That's the best we can do,' Marika says, 'now we need something to eat. What, I have no idea.'

Madoowbe grips the door handle. 'I'll go through the cab. There must be something.' Moments later he emerges with a canvas haversack, heavy with tins. 'These were behind the seat.'

Marika squats beside him and they go through the booty together. A box of 7.62mm ammunition, but then something far more desirable. 'You beauty! Beef and onions. Spaghetti and meatballs. Hell, I'm salivating.' Using a knife blade she cuts around the lid and levers it sideways, passing the first to Sufia, then another to Madoowbe.

'Are you going to heat it?'

'The second one, maybe,' Marika says. 'This one won't touch the sides.'

The next surprise is a warm aluminium can, much of the label bruised off from rattling against the other tins. Enough remains to reveal the contents as Keroro beer, brewed in Kenya. Marika pops the tab and takes a long swallow. 'I dunno if it will take off back home, but it sure tastes good now. Even as warm as toast it tastes like honey.'

She passes the can to Madoowbe, who shakes his head. Sufia also refuses.

'God, what a bunch of teetotallers! Looks like I'll have to finish it myself.' She eats three tins of food before sitting down, holding her belly in both hands. 'That's better. Pity there's nothing sweet. I could do with some sugar.' She grins at Sufia. 'Ice cream maybe.'

Sufia smiles back. 'Now that is one thing from America that I miss very much. Chocolate ice cream.'

'Mmm, choc ripple.' Marika sits back on the sand. There is no remnant of the flaming signal apart from the heat haze rising from the scorched sand.

'How long do you think it will take them to react?' Madoowbe asks.

'I have no idea. All we can do is wait.'

Standing, stretching, nerves on edge, Marika says, 'The flames barely lasted ten minutes; what if that was between satellite runs? How often will they pass over Somalia?' She turns back to look at the vehicle. 'If we're going to do this, let's do it properly. Let's get a real fire going.'

'There is nothing to burn but the spare tyres.'

'There's a lot at stake — we can't sit here until we rot. What if they take their pictures with normal film rather than infrared? Our flames might well be missed.

'It is not yet dark. A column of black smoke might be dangerous. Drawing attention to oneself can be fatal in the desert.'

'What choice have we got? Come on. Get the rest of the petrol out of the tank.'

Using a wheel brace from the tool box, Marika unbolts the spare wheels from their mounts and piles them fifty metres away from the camp.

'Can I help?' Sufia asks.

'You bet. Get everything you can find — oily rags, plastic bags — and stack 'em up. Anything that will burn or make smoke. We've got just one more chance at this; we might as well make it work.'

Madoowbe walks towards the pyre with the jerry can half full, bouncing against his leg as he walks. 'This is all there is left.'

'Pour it all on.'

Back at the vehicle Marika uses a knife to cut away the seat upholstery and pulls wads of stuffing from the inside. 'Light it now,' she calls, tossing the matches to Madoowbe. As she works at the seats there is a concussive thump as the pyre goes up. By the time she has gathered another armload of combustibles the flames lick six metres into the air. Clotted black smoke rolls skywards.

The heat is so intense they have to stockpile materials nearby and wait for the inferno to recede, standing back to watch as the flames peel the rubber from the tyres, releasing further dark vapours, exposing the radial layers beneath. Marika feels her anxiety increase. Now they have well and truly signposted their location.

'I'm probably now the biggest polluter in Somalia,' she says, half joking.

Madoowbe raises an eyebrow. 'The most visible one, in any case.'

'We'll be out of here before anyone catches up with us,' she says. 'Dalmar Asad's men will be on foot now. I doubt they will follow. They must all know that he is dead.'

Still searching for ideas, she uses the child's method of dragging a stick through the sand to form giant letters: RABI AL-SALAH PICK UP REQD.

'If that doesn't get them interested, nothing will,' Marika says, but her voice is high with strain. She paces backwards and forwards near the vehicle. Madoowbe never strays far from the heavy machine gun on the rear of the technical, stripping back the breech block and cleaning it until not a speck of dust remains on the metal, lubricating it with clean engine oil from the dregs of a plastic bottle of Castrol.

As the sky darkens, the fire is all but exhausted and, in a last effort, Marika takes the jack from behind the seat and they remove one wheel after another, adding the tyres to the fire, leaving the vehicle embedded in the sand like another war relic.

Marika stares at the renewed blaze. 'If this doesn't work we're too late — there's nowhere we can get to in reasonable time. We're buggered. All I can do is hope that Abdullah bin al-Rhoumi and his merry men found some other way.'

'You mean that perhaps he and the Americans have stormed the centre and shot my husband dead?'

Marika folds her arms in front of her chest. 'I didn't mean that.'

'It is the only other way.'

'Then I'm sorry. I shouldn't have said it.'

Sufia's eyes narrow. 'Marika, you are just beginning to see the things Ali has lived with for twenty years. The cries of the dispossessed and starving became a cacophony in his heart. The so-called leaders do not care, will do nothing to threaten their own comfort, their positions. Ali was always devout, but over the last five years he became obsessed, reading the Qur'an daily, finding solace there. I knew things had changed when he requested that I begin wearing hijab outside of the house — something I had never done.'

'He became extreme?'

Sufia nods. 'If you want to use that word. But it was born of a sickness at what was happening in the world. You can condemn the Almohad and, yes, their methods are vile, but they were born of a sincere belief that Muslims should live in autonomous states, ruled by God's law.'

'I've only been here for a few days but I can't bear it,' Marika says, 'the sight of the refugees, the starving villagers. When this is over, one way or another I'm going to make a difference for them.'

'What will you achieve, just one woman?'

'I don't know, but I have to try.'

Sufia offers her hand. 'I believe you. Count on me to help. It is time for strong women to join across cultures and continents. It is time to reverse the path that progress has taken us down.'

Marika takes a deep breath and tells her about the acacia hut. The rain. The mud. The impossibility of it all. 'I dream it almost every night.'

'You were meant to come here. You have a part to play, just as Ali does. He told me many times that he is sick of trying with all his heart to stem the tide, yet remaining unable to do so. Call him extreme if you want, but it is too small and sharp a word to describe the feelings that have built over the years. His deep compassion could not allow him, like the builders in your story, to cave in to exhaustion and frustration.'

'We need more hands,' Marika whispers.

'Yes. That is all. More hands.'

'You really do love Ali Khalid Abukar, don't you?'

Sufia's eyes burn like coals. 'Even as they lower my coffin into the earth I will love him.'

Marika looks down at her knees. *Wouldn't it be nice to be that sure about someone. To love a man like that.*

Sufia's face changes, eyes narrowing. 'Wait. I just saw something.'

'What do you mean?'

The Somali woman inclines her head towards the crest of a dune some distance to the east. 'Over there, I saw … a person, I think.'

Marika turns and studies the area, seeing nothing, hoping that the observation can be dismissed out of hand. Nothing reappears. 'Are you sure?'

Sufia shrugs. 'I wouldn't say anything if I was not sure.'

Marika hefts an assault rifle, and looks up at the darkening sky, hoping to see the insect speck and gathering sound of a helicopter. Nothing. 'I guess I'd better walk over and check it out,' she says.

'It might have been a couple of curious tribesmen — herdboys even,' Madoowbe joins in, 'but I think it would be a mistake for us to separate, and we'd best stay with the vehicle. The machine gun is too heavy to carry far, and that is the only thing that can guarantee our safety.'

Marika knows he is right. 'OK, but I don't like sitting here while someone peeks at us.'

'They cannot shoot us from behind that dune,' Madoowbe says, 'it is too far.'

'What if they're sighting in a mortar?'

'I did not think of that, but a mortar is not a common weapon out here. Only the warlords have such things and they are not very portable.'

'There,' Sufia cries, 'did you see him?'

Marika squints in concentration in case it happens again. A dark shape appears and disappears over the dune. 'Sorry, guys,' she says, 'but I'm not going to sit here and let whoever that is call in his cousins. No way. I'm going across for a look while there's still enough light to see.'

Madoowbe frowns. 'I will come with you.'

'No, don't leave Sufia alone. You are better off here, with the machine gun. Then at least if I have to run back you can cover me.'

The sun has disappeared below the horizon, and there is just enough light for safe navigation as the SAR inflatable planes back towards Durham. Simon's hands are clamped around his own chin, eyes gummed together from staring out at the glittering water, a dazzle that even polarised sunglasses can't eliminate. The setting sun comes as both a relief and an unbridled terror as any hope of finding Hannah alive fades.

'Flotsam off the port bow.' The shout comes from a man in the bow. The engine dies back in response, then throttles away on a tangent. Simon picks himself up, leaning both hands against the gunwales, hoping against hope, peering out at the water, wondering how the seaman's eyes were good enough to pick an object out from the darkening sea.

All day there has been endless blue, the occasional foamy white current lines tinged with reddish orange coral spawn. Once even a dead turtle, floating up high in the water, two or three small sharks worrying at the head and flippers, sharp grey shapes in the ice blue of the sea.

The outboard clicks back into idle. At first Simon can see nothing, even when he takes off the dark-tinted sunglasses. Then, something small and yellow that at first looks like the dead petal of some enormous flower.

A boathook, wielded by one of the crew, plucks the item from the water, lifting it, dripping, over the gunwale. A neoprene cap, one of the latest surf/street fashion must-have accessories. Simon lifts it from the boathook with his hand and stretches it out to read the writing on the front, advertising a boy band Hannah has been enamoured of for some months.

Simon almost staggers and falls, but instead sits back down onto the thwart seat. It is hers. But this is no charm, nothing purposeful, just a remnant; a floating relic. The fairy tale is over. He stares at Matt, who sits next to him on the thwart, with a strange expression in his eyes.

Simon grips his arm. 'Start circling the area. She might be here somewhere.'

'I'm sorry, but that's pretty much final,' Matt says. 'It's too dark now, anyway. The captain's gonna need me back on the job. We can't stay here forever.'

'Just for ten minutes. No more. That's all I ask.'

Matt cannot meet his eyes. 'OK. Ten minutes.' He nods at the helmsman, who shifts the outboard into gear, and sets off at a slow idle, the sea now black and impenetrable. No hope of seeing anything or anyone.

Simon cannot meet Matt's eyes, but weeps even as he stares out into the gloom, each sob a chunk torn from his heart.

Marika sets off with the assault rifle across her chest, eyes fixed not only on the horizon but also the left and right sides, her training compelling her to examine any hollow or ridge that might hide a human being.

The dune is further than she expects, and with every pace she relaxes, for the figure does not reappear. It could be an animal, she decides, or nothing. *Perhaps the jitters are getting the better of us.*

Glancing back at the camp, she sees how the smoke rises in a single, black, unbroken column, before seeming to hang in the stratosphere against the stars. Yes, it is visible, but why would such a thing attract people? The reality of life here is surely such that they have better things to do than chase fires. She sees the dark figure of Sufia beside the technical, and Madoowbe manning the gun.

Nearing the ridge, despite her rumination on the unlikelihood of finding anything, her footsteps slow, and her finger tightens on the trigger. Instead of climbing the dune she skirts the sides, soon moving into the dip behind it.

The animal she sees sniffing through the sand is no taller than her knees, with an elongated nose and pig ears. She can see how the creature might be mistaken for a human head. She stops and draws a deep breath, just as it looks up, sees her, and trots away.

'You're a little pest,' she says, 'but cute. I guess I'll have to forgive you.'

The unusual creature disappears behind the next dune and she continues to walk along the dip, thinking how in a moment she will climb the dune and wave to Madoowbe and Sufia to let them know that there is nothing here — that there is no threat, unless a bundle of fur, teeth and claws that weighs about twenty kilos at the outside could be described as a threat.

Relaxed now, Marika rounds a bend in the valley of sand. Ahead, in a clearing, stand ten or more men in a group, talking urgently, as if discussing a matter of importance. Each carries a rifle or carbine. Tethered to one side are half-a-dozen camels, accompanied by a couple of adolescent boys.

Marika's appearance has a dramatic effect. The boys run. The men in the group scramble for cover and for clear ground in which to take a shot. She, however, fires first, jerking her finger back from the first joint and emptying the magazine in a sustained burst that does little but disrupt the air above their heads.

Having wasted her ammunition she turns and runs, ascending the dune in long-legged bounds. The first bullets spit after her before she reaches the top, striking the sand, raising angry powder puffs. Reaching the crest she runs towards the reassuring figure of Madoowbe and the machine gun.

As she reaches the foot of the dune the men she surprised appear behind her and resume shooting. Again bullets zip through the air around her.

'Shoot them,' she screams to Madoowbe, seeing the muzzle flash from the gun on the technical before she hears the discharge. The gunfire behind her dries up, and when she turns again, halfway across the plain, the crest is empty.

The return seems to take much longer than the initial journey, but finally she lopes past the fire, leaning the gun up against the vehicle, hands at her hips to help her lungs find breath.

Madoowbe jumps down from the tray. 'Are you hit?'

Marika shakes her head, fighting for breath to speak. 'No.'

'Who are they? Who shot at you?'

The words came in breathless bursts. ' ... a strange animal ... small ... with a trunk ... then I saw them ... men with guns ... a dozen of them.'

'Shifta?'

'Yes, the same gang we stole the camels from ... I recognised one or two from the camp. God, I'd forgotten about them. If they want their camel back then ... surely they can see that we don't have him any more.'

'It's gone beyond that. They are angry. Now they've seen that we have a machine gun and a vehicle, they will want both, along with revenge. How many did you say there were?'

'A dozen, plus a couple of boys.'

'Then they will have sent a boy back to bring more. They are waiting for reinforcements.'

Marika's chest heaves. 'Just what we need. You were right about the black smoke — it brought trouble, didn't it? You can say I told you so if you like.'

Madoowbe looks up at the sky as if contemplating their predicament before uttering a single, seemingly inexplicable word: 'Kukukifuku.'

'I beg your pardon?'

'The animal you saw. We call it the kukukifuku. Ant bear. The shifta must have disturbed him.'

'Kukuki-what? That's a *silly* name for an animal.'

He frowns back. 'Silly? Westerners call it an aardvark. That's not much better.'

'That was an aardvark? Shit. I always wanted to see an aardvark.' Marika laughs again and, still chuckling, picks up her assault rifle, pops out the magazine and begins reloading it from a box in the technical. She looks at Sufia. 'There are spares in the technical. Do you know how to fill 'em up?'

The other woman narrows her eyes and tosses her head, reacting in the same way a Bondi matron might have when asked if she could boil an egg. 'I learned to reload a rifle when I was three years old.'

'Sorry, just asking.'

They work together in the shade while Madoowbe procures more scraps for the fire. Marika turns away when Sufia notices her looking at him.

'You and my brother are lovers, aren't you?'

Marika finds herself blushing, and her fingers fumble, dropping a golden 7.62mm cartridge to the sand. 'Yes. But only once.'

'I'm not surprised — you are both attractive human beings.'

Marika wants to spill her guts to Sufia — wants to tell her how the sandstorm and the tiny cave made the act special. Unforgettable. Instead, as if to hide her thoughts, she slams the magazine home and aims the gun at the distant ridge. 'Now just let those fuckers come down here.'

Day 6, 19:00

Zhyogal calls them to Salat-ul-'isha, the night prayer, with a whispered, haunting voice.

Allah is most great,

I bear witness that there is no God but Allah,

I bear witness that Mohammed is the Messenger of Allah,

Come to prayer,

Come to the good,

Allah is most great …

After the qa'dah, Zhyogal bades them linger with a commanding gesture. 'It is apt,' he says, 'to consider our souls on this night, on the eve of martyrdom, to reaffirm our faith in God, and in the word of the Prophet, may his name be forever praised. You are fortunate, for to die shahid is to confirm your place in Paradise. Let me remind you of what it will be like for us.'

Ali closes his eyes, tears of shame and anger boiling below the surface. The sight of death and murder is taking its toll on his faith. He tries to hide his weeping. He wants to shout at Zhyogal that their martyrdom is not yet assured, that there is still time for the West to comply with all demands. Is that not a more important outcome? He looks around at the others. Some have already begun their preparations for martyrdom: shaving body and facial hair and cleaning the skin.

As Zhyogal speaks, Ali finds himself relaxing, falling under the spell of those words. Drinking them in, shivering with religious fervour that is as potent as any drug, as sweet as love and as beautiful as sunrise.

'In Paradise are rivers of water, whose taste and colour never change, never running turbid after flood, nor rank in drought. The taste is of honey, sweet and wholesome. There, basking in God's favour, we will recline each to a throne, with shady trees shielding us from sun, bountiful fruit of all kinds hanging low where no effort is required to pluck whatever one requires. Adorned with silken robes we shall drink from goblets of crystal, served by young men of perpetual youth. In Paradise, each tree has a trunk of gold, and there are palaces beyond imagination. There are virgins, yes, for the taking, and we who die shahid will sit beside our God, with jewelled thrones and the choicest fruit of all. Since the death of the first martyr, Sumayyah bint Khabbab, at the hands of the polytheists of Maccah, many thousands of our Muslim brothers have joined God in Jannah, to live a life of ecstasy, remembering always that God has promised pleasures and rewards that are beyond comprehension.'

Ali tries to visualise such rewards, but all he can imagine is a blinding light and oblivion. Other men weep with longing.

Zhyogal smiles back at them. 'Remember the founder of al-Muwahhidun, Ibn Tumart, so long ago, and his vision of an empire of Muslim states across North Africa, Arabia, and Europe. Let it be so. Let us make it so, seeded with our own blood and that of our enemies.' He glares around the small group, as if daring contradiction or comment. Then: 'Now, there is more work to be done. The greatest war criminal of all. It is time for him to die.'

The President of the United States of America has been on the dais for six days. Forced to kneel for much of that time, his knees are rubbed raw from contact with the carpet. When he has been able to sleep it has been curled up into a foetus-like ball.

Fear has kept the shrinking line of those around him silent, and he has not had a meaningful conversation for many days. There are bruises on his body where the mujahedin have kicked him as they pass, and one of his ears bled after one such attack.

All this time he has watched the so-called trials of the leaders of other nations, and has flinched each time the executioner's bullet found its target. Now, hearing his own name called, he understands that it is his turn to die, that no matter what might befall the world from here, this is his own ending.

From the time of his election as congressman for Missouri's District Three fifteen years earlier, he has understood, in an abstract kind of way, that the population of a large proportion of the world does not love America. That they see a brutal military machine, and the cinema world of apple pie, blonde cheerleaders, sorority parties, free sex, and drug dealers. They do not understand how America has improved the quality of life for so many, powering the technological revolution through vast investment in research and development. Organisations devoted to knowledge: the Battelle Institute; the Glenn Research Center; the Carnegie Building; the Jackson Lab; the Enrico Fermi Institute. Purcell could have listed a dozen more off the top of his head. Americans, he knows, have a Grecian zeal for, and belief in, democracy and science.

Yet even Edward Purcell did not understand until five days earlier just how much he and his country are hated.

Pure, consuming hatred. He did not understand that attempts by his country to seek out and destroy threats to world peace are not appreciated by the victims. That somehow belief in democracy can go too far. Combined with religion, it can become an imperialistic fervour that was so effective in building the British Empire a few centuries earlier.

Hands reach down for his arms and he reacts angrily. 'Let go of me,' he shouts. 'I will stand on my own, damn you.' The innate political instinct that took him to the highest office in the land tells him that the best thing he can do now is die well.

The faces of the mujahedin are as haggard and tired as his own, the eyes red moons of drug-enforced wakefulness. Indecision shows on their faces and they leave him for long enough that he finds his way to his feet, staggering yet determined, moving with them over to where Zhyogal waits.

'You are charged with the mass murder of untold thousands of Muslim civilians, you are charged with sending missiles raining down upon husbands and wives, sons and daughters. You are charged with policies that have brought chaos and division to the world.

'In the year of the Hijra 1424 by our reckoning — 2003 in your calendar — the weaponry of America turned on the people of Iraq. Sources within your own puppet organisation, the United Nations, estimate that more than one million Muslims died, and five times that number were left without homes. Just as your predecessors tore apart Korea and Vietnam, your legacy to the world was the slaughter of hapless villagers and the urban poor of Baghdad, Kirkuk, and Basrah. This you followed up with strikes on the Muslim people of the Middle East. Libya. Iran. Yemen. Somalia.'

Purcell stands firm. They got smarter after Iraq and Afghanistan. No more large-scale invasions, no GI body counts for the press to get in a froth about, just targeted UAV missions, missiles, and precision bombing raids.

Zhyogal went on: 'You supported the Zionist state in its blockade of Gaza, a policy that led to famine and death. You stand judged before God, may praise be upon Him. How do you plead?'

Edward Purcell lowers his chin. 'I plead guilty of attempting to protect the people who chose me to represent them. I plead guilty of seeking to destroy the forces of terror wherever they exist in the world, and I plead guilty of attempting to build a better life for those who placed their trust in me.'

Zhyogal stamps one foot, and the President remembers an eighty-year-old newsreel showing Adolf Hitler doing the same thing. The same incapacity to see that what he did was wrong. The same rage when others did not click their heels and say 'Jawohl, mein Führer'.

The President finds himself pondering the nature of evil. It is a word he has used often — a word that probably helped him pluck the presidency from a field of hopefuls. Was Hitler wholly evil? He was ultimately responsible for the deaths of thirty or forty million people, yet he loved and cared for his Alsatian dog, Blondi, had a taste for music, painted, enjoyed cinema, and played practical jokes on his staff. Bashar al-Assad, the tyrant of Syria, was a trained eye surgeon.

The President sees the gun come up and even the trigger finger moving. He does not see his body falling to the carpet and Zhyogal firing the gun over and over again, long after his heart has been shattered into a bloody mess of tissue.

Marika picks up her assault rifle and stands, staring out at the night horizon. Neither the shifta nor the aardvark have reappeared, the only sign of life being a horned viper that wriggles across the sand near the acacia, burying itself in leaf litter near the base.

'What will their tactics be?' she asks Madoowbe when he comes up beside her.

'They will sneak up close and try to take us out one by one, if they can. Chances are that we won't even see them come.'

Marika shivers, not just from the growing cold. 'Great.'

'They are afraid of one thing: the machine gun. We need to stay close to it.'

'Up on the tray?'

There is a pause. 'Too exposed.'

'Can we get the gun down, and the mount? Is it too heavy, do you think?'

'We can try. There is a stony rise just over there. More defensible than here.'

They stand together, almost close enough to touch. Impulsively she reaches up to kiss him on the lips. His eyes glow like bulbs, staring back at her in shock, as if what happened between them is a secret to be kept, never mentioned.

'Do you regret what happened between us,' she asks, 'on the night of the sandstorm?'

'Is such a question necessary?'

'I know I'm a crazy Westerner, who wears her heart on her sleeve, but I want to know what you think.'

His eyes narrow, and for a few seconds he rests his chin on his palm. 'No. I do not regret it. Do you?'

Marika thinks for a moment. Even on the most basic level, it was a special moment, a special night. 'I'll remember it for the rest of my life.'

Now Madoowbe does something incomprehensible. He touches her face, whispers a soft and melodic sentence in Arabic, then appears to blow dust from the palm of his hand into her eyes.

Marika stares as he completes the strange ritual. 'What are you doing?'

'It is an ancient charm from the Qur'an that will make you invisible to your enemies. To protect you.'

'I thought you didn't believe in that kind of thing?'

'You misunderstood my words. There are some things I will never stop believing.'

The Somali seems pleased with himself, for when he walks away a smile touches his lips.

Manhandling the heavy gun down from its mount is more difficult than Marika expects. Mounting screws have corroded in place, holding the heavy flat base to the tray floor. Madoowbe uses a hammer to smash the bolt heads off and together they lug the heavy weapon, then the boxes of ammunition to the rise. Marika begins to dig, using a folding shovel from the vehicle. 'My granddad was an infantry officer in Vietnam — when I joined up he gave me some damn good advice: If in doubt, run. If you can't run, dig.'

'Here, let me help,' Sufia says, and, taking turns with the tool, they work until the trench is deep enough to squat in, and thereby shield their bodies to the neck. On the earth ahead of the trench Madoowbe sets up the gun, sliding back the action and chambering a round, the long belt of cartridges drooping into the ammunition box.

For the hundredth time that day, Marika raises her eyes skyward. 'Where are they? For God's sake.'

An hour later the shifta come, moving with the stealth of clouds.

'I'd give a thousand bucks for an infrared scope,' Marika says, then changes position, checking the load on her assault rifle, selecting semi automatic and lying prone, gun butt against her shoulder. Turning to Madoowbe, she whispers, 'Don't shoot unless they come this way, OK? They might think we've gone.'

The noncommittal grunt communicates what he thinks of this advice. Marika grins to herself. *How could anyone disappear across the desert with a ninety-kilo gun and its mount?*

The shadows are many in number, and Marika sees that reinforcements have arrived. These are men born in the desert, hardened to the business of killing to survive. Their rifles are extensions of their bodies, as familiar as a limb. There are many of them, thirty perhaps, and despite the machine gun, Marika knows that her chances of surviving the night are slim.

They still don't know where we are, she says to herself, watching them make for the technical and the smouldering rubber pyre nearby. The grip of the assault rifle becomes sweaty in her hand and she snugs the butt into her shoulder, lowering her head so she can see through the sights, taking one dark head in the ring and resting the pip high in the chest, moving the weapon to follow the man's erratic movement. How many can they kill if they open fire now? Maybe four or five before the others fall flat on the sand. Not enough.

Minutes pass before the leading members of the party reach the technical. Now she hears voices, sharp angry words, indecipherable. It becomes difficult to discern who is where, for they start to disperse.

'Get down,' Madoowbe hisses, 'they're looking for us. Whatever you do, don't lift your head.'

Marika turns to look at Sufia, crouching between them, still giving no indication of fear, and she experiences a strong feeling of protectiveness. In a short time this tall, proud woman has come to trust her. Dr Abukar, Sufia's husband, the one who holds the remote control that might mean death for hundreds of human beings, is a man to take seriously. Marika senses that this woman would not have given herself lightly. Looking out into the night, she reaffirms to herself her commitment to protect Sufia and take her to safety, not just because it is her duty to do so, but because people like her are important to the world.

As the shadows disperse across the night, Marika's unease deepens, and she feels again a conviction that these minutes might be her last on earth. She finds that she is not afraid, but saddened for the feelings of those she will leave behind. Family, friends. Then there are things. Places. The cobalt blue Pacific Ocean, the mountain ranges of eastern Australia. Gum trees. Her flat in Pimlico, London. Even her Macbook.

Finally, there is the god of the church that figured so strongly in her early life. No prayer comes to her lips. No last-minute reconciliation. Only nothing. The realisation that her destiny is in her own hands. That life and death are so closely intertwined that one cannot be without the other.

The shifta no longer move predictably, but have scattered, searching. Someone kicks a pebble out to the rear, yet when she turns she sees nothing. Still she scans, using the night-vision enhancing method of moving her head from side to side, looking out from the corner of her eyes as she does so.

'Three men, coming this way,' Sufia says, 'dead ahead. Can you see them?'

The hammer of the machine gun adds to the ringing blankness of Marika's hearing, and despite the flash suppressor, a tongue of flame two or three metres long sears out from the muzzle, lighting the area as if with floodlights.

Marika sees men drop to the ground. She lifts her assault rifle to her shoulder, trying to pick them up in the sights but mainly firing by feel at the area, squeezing the trigger several times in succession. She turns to Sufia. 'Can you keep an eye on our rear? Call out if you see anything.'

Silence follows, broken by the pop-like discharge of Sufia's rifle. 'There was just one,' she says, 'and I think I hit him — he's down anyway.'

'Good work.'

The machine gun fires again, but this time there is nothing visible in the lit area. 'Sorry,' Madoowbe says, 'I'm getting jittery.'

'Where are they? Do you think they might have run?'

'I doubt it. These men live on their reputations for bravery and savagery. They know there are just three of us, and won't stop until they have us.' He pauses. 'I don't need to tell you that we must resist being taken alive. It would be bad for me, but worse … for women. If it comes to that, please let us make sure …'

'I understand,' Marika says.

'Have you still got that pistol?'

'Nah,' she murmurs, 'no ammo. I left it in the vehicle.'

Time stretches on, silent but for muffled voices out across the desert.

'What are they doing?'

'Having a conference, deciding how to take us — puffing up their courage, accusing each other of cowardice, discussing what they're going to do to us when it is over. Some of these men have just lost a brother or a friend, and will be pleading to be allowed to lead the attack.'

Marika again looks up at the sky, seeing a light moving low down near the northern horizon. 'Look — what's that?'

'Probably a commercial airliner,' Madoowbe says.

'Do they fly across Somali airspace?'

'They would not be silly enough to do so at low altitudes, but at forty thousand feet, yes. There is not a plane or missile in the country capable of flying to those heights.'

Still watching the light, Marika prays for it to come closer and morph into something that will take them away. Instead it recedes into nothing.

'The shifta are attacking again,' Madoowbe hisses. 'Get ready. They will be more determined now.'

This time the shifta creep from mound to stone with such stealth that when Marika closes her eyes she feels as if she can will them away. Then comes the roar of the machine gun, and in the muzzle flash a number of the enemy are revealed as closer than she believed possible. Panicking, jamming her forefinger back on the trigger, she watches one man drop, then another. Return fire comes in, from two or more men using a boulder for shelter. The heavy machine gun seeks them out, stone chips flying and the air filling with the metallic smell of shattered stone.

A cry fills the night, and the machine-gun fire illuminates a single shifta, firing a carbine as he runs, screaming indecipherable words of rage. The single-minded charge must have unnerved Madoowbe; his first burst flies wide. Marika also misses, the pin clicking down on an empty chamber as she exhausts the magazine. She has no more spares and has to unclip it and press in loose cartridges from her pocket. She looks up in time to watch the machine-gun bullets chew the suicide charger to pieces.

'That was a distraction,' Sufia cries. 'They've come up on all sides. They are going to overwhelm us.'

Again the machine gun fills the night with a long shuddering roar, then falls silent.

Marika fires again, twice. 'What's wrong?' she calls.

'The gun has jammed.'

'Leave it. Run.'

Bullets fly as they take to their heels, away past the vehicle and the smouldering, stinking pyre of burning rubber. Running, knowing how close behind death pursues them. On impulse Marika reaches out, taking Madoowbe's hand, feeling him return the pressure.

As they reach the lower slopes of a sand dune, a sound drifts across the desert that can only be the heavy beat of a chopper. 'Do you hear it?' she cries. 'It's them. They're coming for us.' Her feet struggle through the soft sand to the summit. 'Stop running. They'll be able to see us here.' She has them visually now, three choppers: all Sikorsky Blackhawks, the UH-60M variant with the glass cockpit and wide chord rotor blades, distinctive to a trained ear.

The shifta, too, have seen the aircraft come, but rather than melting back into the desert, they continue to come, the fusillade of bullets intensifying now.

'They know they'll be safest right on top of us,' Marika says, 'and that the choppers won't pick us up under heavy fire.'

'I'll stay here and hold them off,' Madoowbe hisses, 'you keep going with Sufia. Get to a safe distance so they can pick you up.'

'No! I won't leave you.'

His hand grips hers. 'Listen. This is not a matter of your preferences. You have a job to do — now do it. Go!' He takes his hand away, lifts his weapon to his shoulder and fires twice. 'Do it. Hurry. Make it worthwhile.'

'Hell,' Marika sobs out, 'don't do this to me, Madoowbe.'

'Don't say anything,' he shouts back, 'just go.'

Marika feels her heart breaking as she bends and kisses him on the cheek. 'You are the bravest of men,' she says, 'and I will carry you always in my heart.'

The two women, so different, from such disparate backgrounds, run down the soft slope of the dune, no words necessary. The ground is firmer in the valley between two dunes as they run headlong between patches of thorn bush scarcely discernible in the darkness.

'The next dune,' Marika says between deep breaths, 'they can pick us up from there.' Turning back she sees the lights brighten as the choppers continue to move closer. Tracer rounds arc up to meet them, and the chain guns hammer back in response, shooting flame ten or more metres towards the ground.

Sufia does not reply, but Marika hears her footfalls behind her. The dune is close now, the first slopes made up of dry sand that clings to feet and ankles, doubling the effort. It all seems too much, but still there is the sound of fighting and yelling behind. Gunshots that make her wince each time they come.

The words *this heroism must not be in vain* becomes a mantra in her head. Over and over to the rhythm of their flight and the gunshots behind.

The sound of following footfalls stops and Marika turns to encourage Sufia along, eyes falling on the shadow that has appeared from nowhere; the glint of a knife and skin in the lights that pour from the choppers. The knife moves to Sufia's throat, behind it teeth bared in a savage and triumphant grin.

At first Marika thinks this must be one of the shifta who has somehow edged his way around the firefight on the dune. Then, however, she sees the desert fatigues and the thin moustache. She sees also fresh burns covering one side of his face and the glint of an earring.

Somehow, despite what appear to be terrible injuries, Captain Wanami has followed them across the desert, and now he holds the power of death over the one woman in the world who might help prevent disaster at Rabi al-Salah. From his lips comes a stream of Somali, which Marika has no hope of translating, yet the venom and hatred is unmistakeable.

Holding the assault rifle by the barrel, she swings it like a baseball bat, the stroke growing in power as she brings her shoulders to bear, until the heavy wood stock strikes Wanami in the side of the head with a sickening thud. He goes down, dropping the knife, and Sufia is free.

Marika reaches for the other woman's hand, hearing her frightened sobs. 'Run,' she screams. They take flight together, but when Marika turns she sees that Wanami is back on his feet, dazed, taking first one step and then another after them. Still holding Sufia's left hand in her right, she doubles her speed, half pulling the dazed Somali woman after her.

The soft sand is impossibly unstable. Their feet slide back one pace for every two forward, and the ascent becomes a real physical ordeal, even for Marika who once thought herself as fit as — fitter than — any young woman of her age.

'Not far now,' she grunts, 'hurry.'

Finally, the sand shelves into the flattish peak of the dune, and Marika glances back. Wanami is no longer in sight, and her eyes move to the firefight just a few hundred metres away, the choppers hovering overhead, out of range.

'Shit,' Marika cries. 'If we don't do something they won't even know we're here — they'll fly out again.'

Unbuttoning her shirt, and slipping it from her shoulders she lights a match from the box in her pocket and holds it out while the shirt catches fire, the flames flaring high. She waves the burning garment backwards and forwards, keeping on until her hands scorch from the heat.

Even as she drops the last of the burning fabric she watches the gunships loom closer, like giant predatory insects. Standing in the floodlights, clad in camo trousers and white bra, Marika is conscious of the tears flooding down her face. Watching, relieved, as the nearest craft stops, hovers, and begins to descend. An arm extends from the open side door, helping Sufia inside, with Marika pushing her up. Glancing back she sees Wanami running over the edge of the dune, hunched over like an animal. A killing madness is evident in those glaring, rounded eyes.

Marika places both hands on the door sill of the chopper and tries to boost herself up, but Wanami reaches out one arm and grips at her ankle with a strength no living man should possess.

Marika shrieks, kicking at him with her free foot, feeling it strike something but there is no lessening of the grip. Her eyes plead with the men inside the machine. 'Help me, for God's sake,' she implores, and someone leans down beside her with an automatic pistol in his hand. A blast of sound as it fires once, twice.

Still the hand holds on, and the chopper starts to rise. Again she tries to kick Wanami away, looking down and seeing that bullets have pulped half the dome of his head, but the hand still grips her, dragging her down. Now she screams, unable to escape the foul thing that defies logic and the natural order.

Someone fixes a bayonet to a carbine and leans down beside her, slashing at the tendons in the dead man's wrist until, finally, the hand opens and the corpse falls back to the desert sand. The chopper crew pull her inwards, safe inside the machine.

Someone passes her a blanket but she ignores it, holding a grab rail against the motion of the rocking, rising craft. 'There's one more,' she cries, resisting the crew's efforts to make her sit. 'He's holding them off on that dune there. We have to help him.'

As she watches, however, the shifta in the floodlights continue to shoot back up at the choppers. A burst of fire from the chain guns does not put them to flight, but sees them loom closer to the top of the hill.

One the men shouts, 'We can't risk it. Sorry.'

Madoowbe's tall figure is visible in the floodlights. She sees him stand, throwing the empty assault rifle away and beginning to run. Despite a fusillade from the chopper's armaments the shifta are on him in seconds. Marika watches him fall and men swarm over him.

'Jesus. No,' she screams. Hands grip her shoulders.

Before she gives herself to grief she turns to Sufia and understanding passes between them. Madoowbe has laid down his life for them, just as they were coming to know him.

Day 6, 21:00

Durham's infirmary is the size of a household living room decked out with double bunks and a screened operating theatre at one end. There is scarcely enough floor space to stand. Pipes and conduit run in bunches along the ceiling so low that Simon has to constantly duck.

Frances is asleep in a lower bunk, her face white, one side of her neck covered with a pink dressing, and her shoulder bandaged. Simon kisses her on the forehead and rests one hand on the soft blonde hair of her head, before walking across to where Kelly is sitting up in bed, tapping away on a borrowed tablet, catching up on all the electronic smokescreens and mirrors people use to feel that they are still part of a community in this modern world.

'Good night,' Simon says, placing one hand on her shoulder.

Kelly stops typing and looks at him, trying to smile, but he can see the pain inside. The pain they all feel. There is a fragility to her face now, her hair in a pony-tail like a little girl, yet her eyes are much older. 'I can't help thinking that this is all my fault. If I had shouted at the airport — attracted attention — they wouldn't have ...'

'They would have killed you, and taken the girls regardless. There was nothing you could do. Trust me. OK?'

Kelly nods. 'Yeah, sure. I'll try.'

Returning to Frances's bed to pull up the blankets he sits beside her for a moment. With a final kiss on the forehead he leaves the cabin, to find Captain Marshall walking down to meet him. Simon shakes the older man's hand, and the gesture becomes more than that, a lingering attempt to communicate something for which words will always fail.

Marshall drops his eyes. 'Are you OK?'

'Not really.'

'You have no idea how bad I feel — giving the order to open fire on that launch.'

'Why? It was rigged to explode anyway, and we don't even know if she was aboard.'

'I know, but ...'

Simon shakes his head. 'No guilt, please. None of this is your fault. Put that out of your mind, for God's sake.'

'Thank you, I'll try.' A pause, then, 'Look, Simon, the reason I came to find you is that my Ops Officer assures me that there is no further terrorist activity in the area. There's nothing on the radar and the satellite assessment is clear. I've made the decision to relax the ship's readiness state to allow all non-essential duty personnel to muster on the flight deck at twenty-one-thirty. A lot of the blokes were emotionally involved with this search. I think they need some kind of closure before we steam home. Is that OK with you?'

'Of course it is.'

'I've also ordered the ship's engines be brought down to slow ahead for a short time so as we can all enjoy a beer issue. Would you join us?'

'That sounds like just what I need.'

The flight deck is a wide clear space, painted with the usual white helipad 'H', the safety rails extended horizontally so as not to interfere with the landing and takeoff of the Lynx and Sea King choppers. Tonight, with an array of stars brighter than any Simon has ever seen, and in the soft glow of a dozen different lights, the deck seems almost magical — far removed from a ship of war.

The hangar is half full of the SBS troop's equipment, along with the ship's Zodiac inflatable. Like everywhere else on *Durham*, all is ship shape — everything in its place with a place for everything.

A hundred or so enlisted men and women are already there with beers in hand standing in groups, dressed in their number eights. The mood is sombre. Simon notices how the conversation hushes as he arrives. He moves closer to where a group of leading hands are opening and distributing beer cans from cardboard cartons under the watchful eyes of the duty coxswain.

The latter calls out to Simon, 'Lager or bitter, sir?'

'Bitter, please.'

The coxswain rips open the ring pull with a practised flick of his wrist. 'Would you like a glass for that, sir?'

'Thanks, but the can will do fine.'

Simon carries his drink towards the rail, and most of the crew greet him as he goes; some clap him respectfully on the shoulder and others shake his hand. Many of them have been part of the SAR effort and Simon knows how much they wanted to find Hannah.

Toying with his beer, Simon does the rounds, talking to men and women alike as they pay their respects — genuine, heartfelt commiserations that he accepts in the spirit in which they are given.

The crowd quietens as the XO calls for silence, and hands over to the captain, who begins with ordering a minute's silence.

'I won't say much,' he says afterwards, 'cause this isn't a time for words. Let's just say that we have a man here who has lost one of the most important people in his life. His own daughter. Let's give her a send-off in our own way.'

Each person drains their can in a single long swallow. Simon hesitates, then seeing the eyes turn to him, follows suit, feeling the beer slip through his lips and down his throat, cool and slightly bitter. A sudden headache comes from drinking the beer quickly, but that cannot explain the moistness of his eyes. Rather, he is touched very deeply by the warmth of feeling on that deck, overseen by the stars that glow on forever, that have shone down on so many other lives before his, and will do so for many more.

Someone brings Simon another can, and he is happy
to drink it, while realising that no amount of beer will
take the pain away. He has lost something far more
important than a limb, something that no man can learn
to live without. The frail aluminium of the can crushes in
his hand until he has to consciously stop squeezing it. He
turns to see that Matt has arrived beside him; the look in
his eyes mirrors his own feelings.

Yet Matt can get no more than a few words out. A
signalman comes aft from the bridge deck at a run,
catching the attention of Simon and most of the crowd.
The man is pale but excited as he stops and looks in all
directions for the captain, locates him, then strides towards
the captain.

'Sir, the yeoman requests that you come to the Comms
Centre immediately.'

There is a silence, for this is unusual — normally a
message would be brought to the captain on paper,
anywhere in the ship.

'Of course, I'm on my way.'

The messenger turns to Simon. 'Begging your pardon,
Mister Thompson. The yeoman asked that I should tell
you to come too. As quick as you can.'

Simon catches Matt's eye and sees the uncertain shrug
before he sets off behind the captain.

The huddle around the radio set parts to let Simon
through. He stands next to the captain, who places a hand
on his shoulder.

The voices emanating from the short-range UHF speak
Arabic, yet with local variations that make it difficult for

Simon to understand. Reference to a local seafood known as kawa-kawa makes it clear that they are fishermen, then there is a laugh and the word zaara, meaning white rose; along with the Arabic word for girl: bent.

Simon stiffens.

'*When white rose grows breasts I might marry her myself,*' one says. '*She will make a good bedfellow.*'

'*Unless Sameer takes her for himself. He is the richest man on al-Akhawain.*'

'*Ah, but it was I who plucked her from the water ...*'

Simon turns to Marshall, his voice strident. 'Where is al-Akhawain?'

'I don't know, but I'm about to find out.'

'White rose,' Simon muses. He looks up, seeing how the captain's eyes are shining like stars. 'It's her. It's got to be her.'

'Let's not jump to conclusions but there's a chance ... you can count on me to pursue it. Bosun?'

'Yes, sir?'

'Get those lazy bastards on the flight deck back to work. We're going hunting.'

THE SEVENTH DAY

Thus the heavens and the earth were completed in all their vast array. God finished the work, so on the seventh day He rested. And God blessed the seventh day and made it holy, because on it He rested from all the work of creating that He had done.

After the seventh day men multiplied in number. Those who believed in one god did not always like the devotees of another, and some gods were jealous gods, and some gods were rotten gods.

Strangely, a single god could be good and kind to one man and rotten to another. Sometimes wars were fought between believers who worshipped in different ways. There were catastrophes that men called pogroms, and inquisitions, where men and women were tortured for the manner in which they believed.

In Gaza, a squadron of Israeli battle tanks kills five civilians. In retaliation Hamas sends a wave of suicide bombers to blow up teenagers at a cafe and lovers at a cinema.

In North Sudan, a Christian militiaman, fighting back against decades of oppression, holds a Janjaweed baby by her ankles and throws her into a fire.

In West Papua, an Indonesian military patrol burns a

village harbouring suspected members of the Organisasi Papua Merdeka. A mother and her infant daughter are unable to escape the flames. A grief stricken husband is shot and killed.

In Magdalena, Columbia, a gang belonging to the Marxist Revolutionary Armed Forces kidnaps three US backpackers. When ransom demands are ignored the group hangs all three from a sandbox tree branch by their ankles, posting video of their death struggles on the internet.

In Baghdad, a Sunni suicide bomber explodes a van packed with explosives outside a Shia mosque, killing and wounding fifty-three. One is nineteen-year-old Farrah Asara, due to be married the following day to Rahim Zaid, a corporal in the US-trained security services.

In Somali territorial waters off Eyl, Nugaal Region, four skiffs are launched from an eight hundred ton mother ship, surrounding the Esther Marie, *an English motor yacht that lost engine power and drifted west from her intended route to the Red Sea and Suez Canal. The crew, along with two security contractors, are armed, but after a short firefight, three of the five are left in bloody pools on the deck, and the master, his wife and one child, are transferred to the mother ship. Ransom demands will be made within an hour.*

Also in Somalia, amidst famine and civil war, the terror organisations al-Shabaab, local elements of the Almohad and Hizb al-Islam merge into a united force to fight the kufr. The leader of the latter group, Shaykh Ali Ran, issues the statement, 'We have unified our might, unsheathed our swords, loaded our bullets and equipped ourselves for war.'

In Balochistan, two agents of Pakistan's ISI, the secret police, wait for Kachkol Tahir outside the school at which he teaches politics and economics, bundle him up and drag him into a black SUV. Three days later his body is found on a hill outside the city of Quetta. The fingernails of both hands have been torn out, and only two teeth remain in his skull. His crime? Ethnicity and intellectual activity leading him to be branded a potential activist. Ninety-nine per cent of the world's population have not heard of his people, the Baloch, and their struggle for freedom that has lasted for more than half a century.

All night Raghavendra Adhir of Kadamtala watches the sky, a strong feeling of dread in his belly. The moon is full, with a double ring surrounding the white, pockmarked orb. Two stars lie within the ring, dull in that brilliance. Raghavendra ignores his wife when she calls him to bed, squatting outside until dawn, face turned upwards.

Now the sky is brilliant, deep red, confirming his suspicions. He wakes his wife and three children and says, 'There will be a typhoon. A bad one. It will blow for three days and it will destroy our home. Carry everything to the hollow and wait for me there. I will trade for as much food as I can carry and join you there soon.'

There they waited, and soon the storm came.

While God rested and admired his work, something deep and dark inside the souls of men was already stirring. Intolerance. Anger. Jealousy. With the day of creation came the seed of Armageddon.

Day 7, 02:30

The squad comes through in twos and threes, internal couriers with trolleys carrying long arms, covered to avoid comment. By 0240 they are ready, and Abdullah is close to his emotional limits, running over the plan in his mind, knowing the risks, yet unable to ignore the possibility that in thirty minutes it will all be over. The political landscape of the world might change forever. Important men and women of two hundred nationalities will not sleep tonight.

With eleven minutes to go he begins chewing his lips, and consoles himself, *If this doesn't work we've still got Benardt's tunnel.* No. *If this doesn't work, most of the leaders of the world, good and bad, will be dead. Dear God. It's not too late to call it off.*

He walks into his office and closes the door, running his hands through his hair and across his face.

At five minutes to three, Jafar walks close, eyes staring boldly out from his fleshy face. For almost an hour Isabella has teased the man with her eyes and lips, with her cleavage and legs. She has seen enough cinema to know what a woman consumed with lust and longing should look like — lips parted; eyes misted and unfocused.

This time she unclasps one more button on her blouse. Jafar saunters by again, staring as he passes. Isabella gives him everything, widening her eyes; doe-like admiration. Certain compliance. The expression on his face changes from surprise to certainty.

Oh yes, you arrogant bastard. You really are stupid enough to believe that I'm getting turned on — here in a

*room full of stinking, sweating people — turned on enough
to want to fuck one of the men who arranged the kidnap of
my daughters.*

For some moments she thinks of Hannah; can no
longer concentrate. But, she tells herself, this is important.
Her task is to distract Jafar. This is the beginning of
her restitution. Again she widens her eyes and feigns a
passionate swoon as he walks past.

*You really believe that all Western women are whores,
you believe your own pointless rhetoric ... dreamed up by
ten generations of sexually repressed misfits like you ...*

Isabella waits until he has passed, then slips the phone
out of her underwear and back in her bag. She looks
down at her watch. Two minutes to go. She touches her
lips with the tip of her tongue, then stands and walks
towards the bathrooms, turning once to be sure that he
has seen her go.

Heart beating like a drum, she closes the door behind
her, glancing at her watch one last time. Thirty seconds to
bluster through. Then what will happen? She has no idea.
An explosion perhaps — a hole in the wall through which
Special Forces soldiers will pour. Gas, maybe. Hadn't they
once tried that in Russia and killed sixty or seventy hostages?

Her feet scarcely touch the tiled floor of the bathroom
before he comes through the door behind her. There are
no preliminaries. One hand grabs her shoulders, the other
brushes her hair away from her neck. His lips press wetly
against her skin. The smell of him, the feel of him makes
her shudder with revulsion.

Isabella counts the seconds in her head as he continues
to nuzzle at her, hands gripping her shoulders, sliding
downwards so the base of his palms graze her breasts.

Surely, now, please. Happen. Something. From the outside there is only silence.

His face engorges with blood as he continues to work at her. Something has gone wrong. Nothing is going to happen and now she is stuck with this ... hand delving up under her skirt. His lips nuzzle her ear.

Isabella feels his hand tear at her underwear and his full weight force her up against the wall. Panic begins deep in the pit of her belly. Rape has been, until that moment, something that happens to *other* women ...

Zhyogal has not slept for more than a few hours in six days, and little in the week prior to that. Still he is alert, pacing the conference room, staring, assessing. Looking down at his body, he knows that he has lost five or more kilograms. The toll of these days has been heavy. In spite of this, his gaze is always outwards, looking for any threat to the success of this chapter of the jihad he has devoted his life to fighting.

A sixth sense — a biological antenna fine-tuned over a dozen missions — tells him that something is afoot. The building is too quiet, and the kufr security people have ceased their regular and pointless requests for him to release hostages. Looking around the room he checks that his men are at their stations and awake. One is not to be seen, and he walks in that direction.

From the beginning he recognised Jafar Zartosht as, morally, the weakest of the mujahedin. Not just because he is not African, nor an original member of the group that fought in Algeria and Nigeria. There are other signs. Even his excess weight indicates a man who overindulges, in defiance of the Prophet's strictures against gluttony. There has been no sign of unreliability from the man, but now, at this crucial time, he is not at his post — possibly off in some nook, sleeping.

As Zhyogal moves around a row of chairs he sees one of the delegates stand, look around, then move down to the end of the row. At first he assumes that the man is moving to the bathrooms, but there is something self-conscious about the way he walks, as though he is frightened of discovery.

Ducking his head behind the cover of some seats, Zhyogal waits, then follows as the dark figure slips through to the end of the row and on towards the wall. Now, sure that the man is a threat in some way, he eases the safety catch off the Norinco 9mm in his right hand.

Ahead is a cleaner's room. The man opens the door and moves inside. A few paces behind, Zhyogal moves quickly. Running now, gripping the handle. The interior light is on, and an electrical locker wide open. He feels a flash of fear. He had not thought of this.

The frightened face of the man turns towards him, arm extended to the switchboard. Zhyogal recognises him now — one of the Brazilian delegation. Zhyogal pulls the trigger twice, aiming for the centre of the chest, watching the man slump against the wall and slide down to the floor in a pool of his own blood.

Isabella knows that the only way to avoid what seems inevitable is to fight.

'No,' she shrieks, pushing Jafar away with one hand in the middle of his chest. He staggers back, face twisting

with surprise. Seconds pass as she tries to brush past him
to the door but finds her neck held in a vice grip between
his thumb and forefinger, as hard and strong as steel. His
face is close to hers, eyes screwed into dark slits.

'Bitch,' he hisses. 'Slut.'

The gunshots register on the monitors, and Abdullah feels
an icy fear. He turns to the others. 'What has happened?'

'Gunshot, from the eastern side.'

'Our man is discovered?'

'It must be so.'

Abdullah depresses the trigger of the microphone.
'Abort, abort,' he cries, with a desperation born of the
knowledge that less than a kilometre away, a young
sharpshooter has Dr Abukar in his sights, and killing him
now will achieve nothing but the slaughter of hostages in
retaliation and the ability of another terrorist to detonate
the charges.

'Ta-maam — OK,' come the replies, one after the
other.

Abdullah turns to the assembled control room. 'I am
sorry to say that the operation has been cancelled.'

No man or woman in that room can hold his eyes.

Isabella fights the Iranian with every muscle. Kicking and
punching. Forcing him to hold her.

His face is close to hers, red with fury and desire. 'You
were looking at me. You want me.'

'You misunderstood.'

'No.'

His hand resumes its movement. In response she jams her thighs together but he uses his finger like a crowbar. Isabella cries out in pain. His mouth closes on her neck.

Again he forces her up against the wall. His hands are at his own clothing, and now, even more certain that she is about to be raped, she redoubles her efforts. He slams her head against the tiled wall.

The door opens, and Isabella watches over Jafar's shoulder as Zhyogal enters the room. His shirt is splattered with droplets of fresh blood and she smells the stink of a recently discharged handgun.

'Jafar,' he snaps, 'you neglect your duty. An attempt was made in your area to access an electrical panel. The consequences might have been disastrous.' Only then does the leader seem to understand what he is seeing — the dishevelled, open clothing. 'You insult God. If I did not need you I would put a bullet in your skull now.'

Jafar's reaction is immediate. Turning, babbling his apologies in Arabic, he lets Isabella slump to the tiled floor where she lies, sobbing with disgust and loathing.

From 07:30 onwards, local time, the Rabi al-Salah crisis is drop-kicked from the headlines by breaking news from Bangladesh and the West Bengal region of India, where Tropical Cyclone Zahir has struck, bringing winds up to 285 kilometres per hour. A storm surge combines with the already high water levels along the Ganges Delta, where river tendrils run down to the sea from multiple mouths, held at bay by sandbags and home-made earthworks. It is clear, even in the early stages, that a disaster of biblical proportions is underway.

The BBC World Service begins its broadcast with a heartfelt oration from the newsreader.

'There are times when the world stops. The 9/11 attacks; the Boxing Day Tsunami of 2004; the Haiti earthquake; the Pakistan floods of 2010; and the Japanese earthquake and tsunami of 2011. Now, on the heels of the disaster of Rabi al-Salah, Cyclone Zahir has broken levees, already straining to hold back the sea, and all the clever silt works have come to nothing in the face of a devastation that defies belief. The meteorological station at Chittagong measured wind gusts of two hundred and sixty-eight kilometres per hour before the equipment failed. What was not blown away is now under water. An inland sea has turned much of Bangladesh and West Bengal into a new Atlantis. A land that may never see human feet again.'

Both Indian and Bangladeshi meteorological offices issued a series of warnings yet most of the population chose to stay and trust the levees that their governments had assured them would stand up to rising sea levels. Those who did attempt to leave overwhelmed the available transport and found themselves trapped.

SKY News has a chopper in the region, showing footage from a dawn flight over Tazumuddin where a ten-metre-high storm surge has filled fifteen thousand square miles of land like a bathtub, apparently within hours. The cameras focus on human bodies washed with other flood debris against the tops of drowned trees. Once the levees were breached there was no going back.

Across the Ganges Delta the result is similar. The UN's Bangladesh agency reports that up to five million villagers may have perished. Eighteen million more are on the march, streaming towards high ground.

India closes its borders, lining the barbed-wire fence with men with machine guns and armoured personnel carriers. Tensions mount. The United States announces Operation Sea Angel II, despatching a full amphibious task force, pledging an initial one hundred million dollars in aid. Other nations follow suit.

The world mourns. Archbishops, cardinals, and ministers pray. Financial markets plumb unexplored depths. Speculators leap from windows. Boards of public corporations meet to discuss 'strategies' and 'harm minimisation', in the face of this latest threat to stability and profits.

Marika is not sure how long she has been asleep, but remembers at least one refuelling stop, in some Saudi base, where she lifted her head to the sound of men carrying hoses and shouting all those minor operational commands that ensure protocol is followed even in the most difficult conditions. Hours of silence before they took to the air once more, but she was content to sleep — a state where she no longer needed to think, to feel, to care.

Waking now, she looks at the gas fires far below, burned off from the oil wells. The flames have a beauty that is both temporary and ethereal. Flames that will soon pass from the earth as the brief, dangerous, Age of Oil draws to a close. An age of carbon monoxide, lead, gridlock, and deep-water oil wells pumping poison into a sea already dying a slow death from overfishing, storm water runoff, and neglect.

Something new is coming, something that might be an ending or a beginning for a world predicted to bulge under the strain of population growth that threatens to see the equivalent of two more Chinas walk the planet, two and a half billion more people by 2050.

Marika reaches out to take Sufia's hand. 'Hello.'

Sufia turns. 'Good morning.'

'Do you know where we are?'

'Yes. We have passed the oasis of Liwa, and are now over the region of Ramlat al-Hamra. Soon we will be there.'

'Thank you. Have you slept?'

'Not yet. There will be time for sleep later. Something terrible has happened, the pilot came to tell me. In Bangladesh a cyclone has flooded the Ganges Delta. The sea has risen over the levees. Many millions might have died.'

Marika takes her hand away. A tear drips down her cheek. More lives. More nameless men, women, and children on the march to oblivion, praying and doing their best and trusting that somewhere, someone cares.

'Madoowbe is dead,' she says, 'but he is just one of millions.'

In the darkness of that aircraft, Marika confronts a question she has avoided through the past days. Something that goes deep into the dark kitchen dresser shelves of her soul, where memories are stacked like delicate china plates.

Where the hell is God in all this?

God. The Creator. The God of Saint Anne's Catholic Church, Mitchell Street, Bondi. The God of morning tea with trestle tables in the hall laid with scones with jam and cream, and instant coffee in foam cups, and Irina Marquez showing off her three-month-old baby. The God of incense burners, collection plates, paschal candles, and Father Murphy's veined, red face and white hair. The God of sunshine on the sea after Mass and the twinkling multifaceted diamond stabs of light on the eyes accustomed to the darkness inside. The dark side of the church. Sexual abuse. Where is God when a priest rapes a child? Why would He send our species out into the world so perfectly evolved physically, yet so flawed in our minds and emotions?

Where the hell is He now? Is Madoowbe right — are they all rotten?

In Africa, more people will die. Millions more. And if Zhyogal and his cohorts succeed, a hundred million souls will live under the heel of another god sick with arrogance and jealousy.

There, in the rocking aircraft, Marika thinks of Madoowbe. The unusual beauty of his face. With all her heart she wishes she could see him again. Just one more time.

'Are you thinking about him?' Sufia asks.

'Yes. He was a special person, but it took a while for me to understand that.'

'I think so too. I would have liked to get to know him.'

'You had a hard life,' Marika says. 'Madoowbe told me all of it — how you fled drought and famine for the coast in trucks sent by Siad Barre.'

To her surprise, Sufia throws back her head and laughs.

Marika lets go her hand and frowns. 'What's so funny?'

'You know I told you that my family often mentioned Madoowbe after he left us?'

'Yes?'

'He was most remembered for one thing — his stories. Always he made things up to entertain his friends and family. We did not escape famine in trucks — never went near the coast. Our father was a trader in Bacaadweyn. He sold nails and saws. Ali went to live with my uncle in Somaliland when he was eight or nine so he could go to school.'

'Then Madoowbe was not a herdboy?'

'Not that I am aware of.'

Marika shakes her head and smiles also. Thinking of him, she watches out the window as desert gives way to coast. The lights of Abu Dhabi loom below, then Jebel Ali, and, as dawn turns the Persian Gulf to glistening silver, Dubai itself.

The first officer calls back more breaking news — a dozen delegates at Rabi al-Salah have agreed to sign confessions and will be released at noon today, well ahead of the deadline. There is a faint feeling of sickness and pity as Marika turns back to the window, and the impossible shining glory of one of the most extravagant agglomerations of modern architecture on earth.

The city seems false, as if the tactile world is out in the open spaces and desert sands of Africa, and the flooded Ganges Delta. Dubai is not real — the wealth that created it was an illusion that sucked badly needed resources from the entire region — brought untold thousands of a mostly male workforce from the subcontinent to labour in the hot sun from dawn to dusk, building, cleaning, even dusting the leaves of outdoor plants in the city's showpiece locations. Indentured labourers treated with contempt and exploited, trying to scrape together money to send home, yet many not able to afford a return fare, trapped in the workers' slums of Dubai, trapped with the debt they incurred just to get over there.

'Almost there,' she says to Sufia. She pauses and swallows. 'Will you do what we discussed now — will you talk to your husband?'

'Yes, I will talk to him.'

'He is wrong to do what he plans to do. The others will not let him act with honour. They want martyrdom and death.'

Sufia's eyes lock on hers. They are a perfect brown. No flecks, no variation. 'Perhaps you are right.'

'I know I am. Please, don't let Madoowbe suffer in vain. Will you help?'

'I will talk to my husband, and then I will try to sway him.'

'Do you mind if I call ahead and tell them that, so they are ready?'

'No, of course not. Go ahead.'

Not long after she makes the call on the aircraft communications equipment, the first officer warns them, 'We're going down. Make sure you're strapped in, OK?'

The chopper settles to the earth, rocking like an impatient horse, and Marika grips the seat hard, staring out the window at the Rabi al-Salah Centre below, the helipad's blue tarmac surrounded by lawn and landscaped garden. She has always hated landing in these things — it just seems so bloody unnatural. Besides, every minute, every second, counts now.

The twin skids touch the deck. Rotors slow and doors open. Marika understands just how tired she is as the world swims around her and the early sun blinds her. The men who greet them she recognises as other members of the Rabi al-Salah security force. They look so damned *clean*, after the people of the desert. They fuss over her and Sufia like roosters over a pair of hens.

Inside the complex, after the degrading searches and scans, Marika feels a sense of unreality as they walk the corridors again — the last few days seem like a lifetime of experience. The shining glass is no attraction, just a distraction from the real business of life that she found in the drought- and famine-ravaged landscape of East Africa.

Abdullah bin al-Rhoumi meets them in the corridor, looking like he has aged fifteen years. He greets them sagely, and Marika is disappointed at the impersonality of it, considering the rapport she thought she had built up with him. *What did you expect*, she asks herself, *a marching band? A medal?*

Marika introduces the tall Somali woman, a touch of hurt pride in her voice. *You might not appreciate what I did, but I went through hell to bring her back.* 'This is Sufia.'

He bows from the shoulders only; a perfunctory gesture. 'Very pleased to meet you. We have a room set up where you can talk to your husband.'

Marika smiles encouragingly at her.

The room they are shown to has a monitor and camera on a tripod. A seat has been placed near the opposite wall. As Sufia enters, a slim technician rises, smiling. This, Marika realises, is his moment in the sun. Perhaps the only time in his life he will be near the centre of world affairs. He wears grey suit trousers and a white pinstriped business shirt. Thin brown arms extend through the rolled cuffs like drinking straws. His moustache is neatly trimmed, his eyes small and brown.

'You're Sufia? Good, good. Now, what we're going to do is sit you down here and cross you live into the conference room. From there you can deliver your plea to your husband to surrender and let us open the doors. Is that clear?'

Marika watches Sufia. She has a strange tilt to her chin, yet is smiling. 'I suppose,' she says, 'the signal will go out live to the news networks?'

'Of course. What a moment! Your face will be beamed around the world.'

Sufia nods again, but Marika sees that she makes no move to sit down.

The technician hurries around to the back of the chair and holds it ready for her. 'We have the networks coming on in fifteen seconds, if you would please sit ...'

Sufia shakes her head. 'No.'

Abdullah bin al-Rhoumi steps forwards from the doorway. 'What do you mean, no?' He points at Marika. 'That young woman risked her life to bring you in here. You have the chance to save almost a thousand very important people, including your husband.'

Sufia's voice is as lifeless as flint. 'I will not perform like a monkey. I said I will talk to my husband, but I will do it face to face.'

Abdullah explodes. 'Face to face? How? In case you haven't noticed, your husband has locked himself in the most secure room in the history of the world.'

'I have been told that the door will be opened at noon today to let people out. Those who have signed confessions. I will enter the conference room at that point.'

'A thousand times no. How do we know we're not letting another terrorist in?'

Marika breaks in, 'She is not a terrorist. I will vouch for her.'

Abdullah's eyes are like brown lasers. 'Quiet. One unreasonable woman is enough.'

Sufia crosses her arms over her chest. 'I will talk to him face to face. No other way.'

Abdullah pushes his face close to hers. 'The militants will blow the room at the time of maghrib — sunset — today. According to the *al-Alam* newspaper, the sun will set at 19:06. That will not give you much time.'

'I cannot promise that I will sway him, only that I will try.'

'Then I insist that you wear a wire so that we can follow what is happening. Your life might depend on it.'

'In what way?'

'If we know that you are making progress in talking your husband out of carrying out his threats then we won't send troops in to put a bullet in his head.'

'Is that likely?'

'We're working on something. Of course we are. Unless you can reason with him then we have nothing to lose by trying.'

'I have no choice, do I?'

Abdullah shrugs. 'You can put it that way if you like.'

Day 7, 09:00

Ali Khalid Abukar is tired beyond endurance. Closing his eyes means drifting off into sleep and his legs are leaden weights. Now he is taking Modafinil at ten times the safe dosage. The conversation in the room is a blur of noise. He wants silence — somewhere to sleep. Forever perhaps.

There is blood on the floor from a dozen new executions, all in retaliation for the attempt on the switchboard. The Brazilian delegation slaughtered, including a twenty-two-year-old aide whose fear manifested itself in a flood of urine down her legs when the first of the men died.

Out on the dais there is a pathetic but growing line of human beings — twenty or more now — each of whom have agreed to read the confession and sign it in front of the cameras. There is no anger in the room for them, only sympathy. The slaughter has been too much for the delegates; the reality of blood and death. Every few minutes a new volunteer slinks down from the rows and joins the line.

I now recognise that I represent a corrupt government, that they have initiated a crusade against the ...

'At noon today, the time of dhuhr, those who have signed will leave this room and go to the arms of their loved ones,' Zhyogal announces. 'It is that simple. Tell the world of your crimes, admit the bastardry of your governments and your part in the murder of Islamic peoples, and you will be spared the carnage that will descend in this place when the sun sets.'

Ali is scarcely listening. A light blinks on the panel ahead of him. He presses a button and picks up the telephone handset. 'Yes?'

Abdullah bin al-Rhoumi's voice, different this time. Triumphant perhaps, as if he has something up his sleeve. 'Does the name Sufia Haweeya mean anything to you?'

Ali staggers as if he has been king-hit. Only his grip on the lectern keeps him upright. *Sufia. Here? How and why has this happened? She is safe. Out of reach of the modern world. Is it a trick? Is it true?*

Somehow he manages to keep his voice calm and level. 'You wouldn't be asking if you didn't know.'

'Sufia Haweeya is here beside me, and she wants to come inside when we open the doors at noon.'

'Wait,' Ali says, then turns to Zhyogal, who ceases his diatribe and circles in close like a shark with the scent of blood. 'They have my wife, and she wants to come in at noon when the kufr who have signed the confession go out.'

'No. It will be a trick.'

Ali feels his anger rise. 'I insist.'

'You would compromise the success of this operation, after having come so far, for a woman.'

'Not any woman, but the one that I love.'

'Love,' Zhyogal spits. 'You use words that are weak — Western words.'

'I will tell them to let her in.'

'Then you do not have the strength I had hoped you possessed.' Zhyogal snatches the phone from his hand. 'Let the woman in, but if anyone else tries to enter the consequences will be catastrophic. Do you understand?'

Day 7, 09:30

The RIB crashes through the surf at the beach, surging around an outcrop of coral and into a channel. Simon grips the rope in his hands and braces himself, catching a burst of spray that tastes of salt on his lips and stings his eyes. The outboard whines as the helmsman guns the throttle, and they shoot into the calm waters of a lagoon so clear they might be floating on air, dappled with scarlet highlights from the sky.

On the beach, wooden fishing boats are drawn up on the sand above the tide. Two men stop their work of untangling a net, then run for a scattering of makuti thatched huts atop a dune, where men and women are already looking out from doorless openings. Simon feels a new slipperiness in his hands. He sees that the rope has cut into his skin from the force of his grip, and blood coats his wrists.

The RIB hits the beach and a pair of seamen leap over the gunwales, dragging the hull high with the help of a surge as a wave floods the lagoon. Simon follows, not caring that the warm water laps over his ankles, winding the legs of his trousers around his calves. The SBS men move up the beach at his side, three of them, weapons looped over their back. Together they walk past the boats with their stinking sea-catch smell, to the huts, where a central fire burns, water boiling in a battered white enamel kettle. There is no sign of life now, the people having retreated indoors.

Simon stops. 'We come in peace,' he calls in Arabic, 'don't be afraid.'

No answer, just the tinsel soft roll of water on the beach and the crackle of the fire. Durham is a dark and imposing shape, anchored out in the depths beyond the lagoon.

Simon clears his throat. 'I have heard of a girl who was bravely rescued from the water. You have called her the white rose. This girl is my daughter. The love of my life, the pearl of my heart.'

Still no answer.

Feeling foolish now, as if he is baring his soul to the dragon's blood trees and spindly palms, he goes on: 'I have come to reward those who saved my daughter with cash. A quantity of Euros that can be used to purchase anything, anywhere in the world.'

A face appears in the doorway of one of the huts. Then another. A man steps from behind a palm trunk, tall and wrinkled though he could scarcely be of middle age.

'It was I,' he says, 'who rescued her from the sea. With my own two hands I picked her up and trickled fresh water between her lips ...'

Simon has stopped listening, for Hannah, her hand gripped by a giant of a woman, emerges from the nearest hut.

'Daddy,' she screams, breaking away from the woman and running into his arms.

He scoops her up and presses her against him.

'You,' he says at last, 'are the cleverest little girl in the world, and I love you.'

Her face is wet and hot on his neck.

Faruq is accustomed to work, putting in long hours to meet deadlines and contract dates. Al-Moler is an expensive lump of machinery, and idle time is lost income. Even so, never before has he laboured so hard as this. For twelve hours he has been at the controls. Inch by inch, hour by hour, the machine's cutting discs have eaten their way through earth and rock to precise coordinates below the Rabi al-Salah Centre.

As the moment nears, Faruq begins to grow nervous, decreasing engine revolutions in order to negate the possibility of someone hearing the noise from above. He looks at his watch, noting the time, then brings the machine off automatic control, taking over manually.

He massages the levers until the tracker image aligns with the target. Twenty metres above where he now sits, Faruq knows, is the concrete-reinforced bunker designed to keep the delegates safe from even a nuclear blast.

Following the orders given by the Almohad, he has built the tunnel to the location the kufr requested, but many metres too deep. When he thinks back to Saif al-Din, and his burning eyes, when he thinks of the threat to his family, he knows that he is right to take this course.

With the engine barely ticking over, Faruq initiates a series of control changes that will terminate the spinning discs and reverse the hydraulic 'legs'. The machine's vibration changes, and Faruq feels the backwards motion. He relaxes. The thing is done. He is on his way out, soul and body intact.

Even at maximum speed an hour passes before al-Moler nudges its way out into the pit and the open air. Surprised faces appear over the lip, the conversation developing into a commotion. Faruq barrels out the side door, already shouting orders, sending men scurrying to fetch trucks and equipment. They are pulling out. He has a contract to finish, and will be damned if he will let sleep stand in the way of getting al-Moler back to work.

Near the entrance he sees the Frenchman and his underlings waiting. *You will not get through there*, he says to himself, *not through my tunnel*.

The massive low loader is back beside the pit and the crane rumbles into position before Benardt appears, face red with anger.

'You stopped the machine too deep, way too deep.'

Faruq nods. 'I am aware of that.'

'You can get your brown arse back in the tunnel and do what we agreed.'

'No.' Faruq trembles with anger at the racism in the insult, but then, he remembers, the French are well known for bigotry and intolerance.

The Frenchman's palms are drawn back ambivalently, halfway between supplication and aggression. 'We have a contract. Why will you not honour it?'

'I made an agreement to dig your tunnel to a precise coordinate beneath the Rabi al-Salah Centre. I will do no more.'

'How are we supposed to get through twenty metres of earth and then reinforced concrete?'

'That is not my problem.'

'You won't see a cent from this, I promise you.'

'Money is not as important as a man's soul.'

The Frenchman takes a pistol from inside his coat and points it at Faruq's chest. The thing is a revolver, like some cowboy gun from a movie. 'I order you to return to your machine and finish the work. You have no idea of the authority I can summon.'

'No power on earth will make me change my mind. I am happy if you pull the trigger. There you are. You have my invitation. Shoot, and be damned.'

Faruq watches the Frenchman's face as he lowers the gun, slides it back in the holster and strides away, muttering as he goes.

Ever since the assault on the island stronghold, PJ has felt something warm in his chest. Something that makes him look at the world in a new light. Now that the second of the girls has been found he is inordinately pleased with himself.

PJ smiles when he thinks of them. Hannah and Frances — now sitting up in bed — the darlings of the ship. With more chocolate, sweets, ice cream, gifts and visitors than a pair of genuine princesses.

Finding a congenial place on the signal deck, he sits with his legs and lower body in the shade, face in the sun, watching the seabirds work over bait schools. The grey iron is cool, and he idly scratches at some flaking paint with a fingernail. There is another layer below, then another and another. *Durham* has, of course, been painted dozens of times over the years.

He wonders if perhaps he should enrol in officer training. That perhaps he can be a real leader of men. The others had wanted to follow him, back there on the island — had recognised his as the correct view. Shouldn't he develop that? Might he again one day save a life, and perhaps ensure the triumph of right over wrong?

Or, on the other hand, aren't there other ways to help? Better ways even. Ways that don't always involve shooting and killing. He tucks the idea away, to be investigated further, just as he hears footsteps on the ladder. Captain Pennington's head appears, then his shoulders and body. PJ looks up, unafraid, yet with resignation. Sooner or later they will have to sort this out. 'Are you going to give me a bollocking for questioning orders?'

'No. I'm going to give you a job.'

PJ stares back suspiciously.

Pennington stays on the ladder, leaning on the deck with both hands. 'We just had a flash message from

CINCFLEET. We need someone for the task force the security forces are preparing to take on the terrorists. They have a plan, apparently. I'm volunteering you.'

'Why one of us? Isn't it up to the DRFS boys, and the Dubai Special Forces. Wouldn't have thought they'd want to give us a shot at it.'

'We went up against this same group of militants and came out winners. Our mission has been a great morale booster. Front page headlines and all. They think that one of us might bring some know-how on the way these Almohad fuckers operate.'

'Why me?'

'Because you're the best of us, me included. God, I wish I could move like you.'

PJ watches in amazement as Pennington finishes climbing the ladder then slides to his rump beside him on the thick steel plate. 'Really?'

'You have no idea how challenging it is for a young officer to come in and command blokes like you. Frightens the living shit out of a man.'

PJ looks down and chuckles. 'Well that's the strangest thing I've heard in a long time.'

'Back there on the island. I was scared — I wanted to put it off, come back with more men, let someone else make the decisions. You forced me to stand up and do what I should have done in the first place.'

PJ sticks out his hand. 'I misjudged you, sir. I thought you hated my guts.'

Pennington smiles and shakes the outstretched hand. 'Maybe I did, just a little bit. Now, you better get your skates on. Chopper will be here at ten-hundred. You've got twelve minutes to get your shit together.'

* * *

By the time he has his kit in one hand, the HK looped over his back, a crowd has gathered on the flight deck. PJ shakes hands with the ship's captain, then Simon Thompson, brushing aside the thanks and praise of a man filled with gratitude for the return of his children. Finally he pauses in front of Kelly, the nanny, no longer the same young woman he first saw in the firelight of the militant camp. She has showered, and although her face is free of make-up, a healthy glow has returned to her skin. Jesus, she is pretty. Brown hair to just above her shoulders. Body just right — not too skinny.

Not only that, but Kelly has class written all over her — she is something special, far removed from the usual young specimen out for a good time at the Bricklayers Arms back in Poole. He suspects that she wouldn't be seen dead in the place. This makes her somewhat unreachable — unapproachable.

She kisses him lightly — not on the cheek, but the lips — a momentary contact, but enough to stir him. When she speaks, it seems loud, but he guesses that the approaching chopper will drown out the words from the others.

'If you ever want to look me up, I won't mind,' she says.

PJ doesn't have time, or the wits, to reply at first, for the chopper settles down, and a man in the back waves him inside.

He turns once, halfway across the helipad and shouts, 'I will. You can count on it.'

Day 7, 11:45

Hair-thin wires pass from the mike on the inside of Sufia's lapel to a tiny pack on her waist. Abdullah marvels at how things have changed from the bulky devices he used thirty years earlier. This modern bug will be undetectable without someone running their hands underneath Sufia's clothing, unlikely in the crowded conference room.

'Are you ready?' Abdullah asks.

'Yes.'

'I apologise for my earlier comments. You are brave to go in there.'

'No.' She shakes her head. 'Not brave; just a woman in love.'

Zhyogal's voice crackles through the speakers.

No one must stand within twenty metres of the opening, or ten hostages will be shot. Any attempt to rush the door by armed men will result in the immediate detonation of the explosive devices in this room.'

Marika walks Sufia to within the stipulated distance and smiles up at her. 'Madoowbe did not die without reason.'

'No. He did not.' Sufia lays a hand on each of Marika's shoulders and kisses her on the cheek. 'Thank you.'

'What for? Bringing you here, to the most dangerous spot on the face of the globe?'

'No, for risking your life for coming to get me. Whatever happens, my place is beside him. Even if we must die hand in hand.'

Feeling herself close to tears, Marika reaches out and grips Sufia's arm. 'You deserve the chance to be together.'

She again has the feeling that there is something special about the Somali woman. The word noble springs to mind.

The door opens and a heavy, filthy smell wafts out. The smell of fear, captivity and, worse, the smell of putrescent human corpses. Marika almost gags, seeing the mujahedin on the other side, flanking the pathetic line of men and women, shouting, urging them through, some of the hostages stumbling, attempting to run.

Marika has a sudden and deep understanding of the bravery of those who remain inside, yet she can feel nothing but sorrow for these desperates who did what they had to do to survive. The line is long, now forty or more in total, and only after the last is through does Sufia walk towards the entrance. Marika can see her fear in the trembling of her legs, watches the Almohad stop her and pat her down, looking for weapons, still shouting and brandishing rifles and pistols.

Even after the main door closes Marika stares, knowing that she has done something momentous in finding that woman and bringing her here. Who else in the world would have the courage to walk into that room?

With a strange feeling of emptiness, she climbs the steps towards the control room. Faces look up at her as she enters and slumps into a seat, staring at the blank monitors, so physically tired, yet more awake than she has ever been, wishing she could see what is happening inside.

Abdullah comes out of his office and takes a seat opposite her. Content at first to simply share the space with her, searching for words perhaps. Someone is reading a news item from a screen out loud, in halting English — an Op-ed predicting an Asian food crisis after Cyclone Zahir has devastated up to one fifth of the world's rice production.

This seems likely — Thai floods a few years earlier showed how vulnerable the sector was to natural disaster.

'You have done well, Marika Hartmann,' Abdullah says. 'For what it is worth, I thank you.'

His words mean more to her than she might have imagined. This man's approval is important to her.

'Your part in this is over,' he continues. 'Go to your room. Shower. Then you may leave. They will begin evacuating the centre at around three this afternoon in any case.'

Marika shakes her head. 'I'm not going anywhere until this is over.'

Abdullah smiles back at her. 'I knew you would say that. Let us face the end together. Whatever it may be.'

Ali's heart seems to pause, mid-beat, to look at Sufia, knowing now that it was a mistake to let her in here. Grasping her arm, he leads her to where they can find some privacy. He had not expected to see her again before death takes him, but it is a pleasure laced with despair.

Knowing there is a cubicle where a group of shorthand clerks once took details and messages, sent faxes, gossiped, and filed their nails, Ali leads her there, turning, placing a hand on each of her shoulders and staring into her eyes. He has not forgotten how beautiful she is, but her time in the desert seems to have heightened that beauty. Her skin glows with health and vitality. Maybe it is just the sallowness of those in the room that makes her seem that way.

First they embrace for what seems like minutes. Strange how he wants to weep for sheer joy, and at how memories pass before his eyes as if he is already dying.

'You do not have to do this,' she says. 'It is not too late.'

'Nothing will change my mind now. Perhaps this day will be remembered when other men sit down to make what they call policies, when greed rules over sense.'

'I have always admired you,' Sufia says, 'most of all for your humanity. This is not the right way. It is not the way of the man I love.'

Ali breaks away, unable to meet her eyes. 'For so long I agonised, and now I believe that this is the only way. If I save ten thousand lives, it is worth it.'

'Saving by killing? Isn't that an argument that others have used before you? My dear Ali, they are using you. They do not want to save the world like you do, but to create it in their image — cold, savage and harsh. They do not care about floods and refugees, or a changing world. They just want power in the name of God. They want to repress the people of Africa. From there they will spread their ideology outwards. Ideology that is more than a thousand years old. They are wrong. They have no place in the kind of world we need to build. There is just one way to change the world — people of goodwill coming together and working for peace, equitability and justice.'

Ali reaches out to her, embracing her, eyes closed, one hand on the small of her back, wondering if he can press the switch with Sufia here, allow high explosives to wrench her limbs apart and blast shrapnel into her heart. 'You cannot persuade me against the course I have chosen. Instead, I ask one thing of you.'

'Yes?'

'Get out of here. Let me arrange for you to leave the way you came.'

'I will not. Instead I ask you to stand up before the world, show compassion, and disarm the weapon you carry. To murder the people in this room you must murder me as well.'

Breath trickles from his lips. 'I cannot change my mind.'

'You must! You have made your point. Nothing can be achieved.' She points out towards the tiered rows. 'Look at them, each one. Their lives have a validity and worth of their own. They may be wrong, much of the time, and they must change, but this is not the way to bring change about.'

Tears spill from his eyes. 'No, I am sorry, but it is too late.'

Day 7, 12:30

Abdullah has just managed a cat nap — two or three minutes swaying on the chair with his eyes closed, dozing into a distant and fitful state so hypnotically sweet that the sound of the cell phone in his pocket scarcely cuts through at first.

Even when it does, his first instinct is to turn it off like some wayward alarm clock. With consciousness, however, comes memory, and the meaning of the excited chatter at the other end.

'No,' he breathes, 'that is not possible. We had an agreement for him to finish the tunnel.'

More from the other end. Excuses. A plea for orders. Léon Benardt wants to know how to save the situation. How to salvage the work of days. To stop the bastards from winning. To stop them sending the whole conference room as martyrs to a God who must already be shrieking with delight at blood so thick that it will run off His hands into a river.

'I'll tell you what you must do. Get every pick and shovel you can find, and put one in the hands of every man and woman who can hold one, including you. Finish the tunnel.'

'I don't know anything about such work.'

'Find someone who does. Appeal to the public. Anything.'

'What about the floor of the bunker? Picks and shovels don't work on concrete.'

'As I said. Get some advice. It can be blown. Just start digging.'

Abdullah leans back on the chair, hands behind his head in a parody of relaxation, staring at the letter-sized photographs pinned to the board. Each depicts one of the Islamists inside the centre. Dr Abukar, the enigma. Jafar, the Iranian. He focuses on Zhyogal, however.

You don't give a shit about the demands, you son of a bitch. You don't care what concessions we make. You just want that room to blow, and now that the Americans are giving over Africa your comrades will move in. You want to dominate a continent. A new empire. You're using Dr Abukar, aren't you?

Abdullah wipes his eyes then lifts a pen from the wooden holder, tapping it on the desk. There is no time. In a few hours they will all have to leave. At sunset the room will explode, and no one knows if the building will collapse or not. No one can take that chance.

* * *

If Léon Benardt, in all his years of training, had imagined himself leading a dozen young men out of a truck, with a sledgehammer in his hand, about to attack the locked front door of a Dubai hardware store, he might have suspected that he was insane.

Already his eyes are red with strain and he feels more stressed than at any other time in his life. The failure of the planned attack on the centre hurt him personally, since it was he who found the electrician who precipitated the plan. Now this tunnel alternative seems, likewise, to be failing before his eyes.

Somehow, through a series of urgent television and radio announcements they located Alan Kruger, a South African mining consultant who cut his teeth on the Witwatersrand goldfields, holidaying with a new young wife at the Burj al-Arab hotel on Jumeirah Beach. He appears to be a real find: bullheaded and knowledgeable. Kruger's first act was to order five thousand empty sandbags. These they tracked down to an emergency supply organisation. Then he requested huge quantities of hardwood shoring timbers and reo bar. Now they need hand tools, the fastest way possible.

The ten-pound iron head of the sledgehammer, swung with all the strength of Léon's arms and shoulders, connects with the lock and shatters it. Another blow and the left side of the door sags in on its hinges, glass shards tinkling to the pavement. An alarm wails.

Kruger, whose nose looks like it has been broken with a pick handle, says, 'Good shot, man.'

Illuminated by the store security lights they forge past shelves of homemaker items towards the hand tools hanging in neat rows, painted in businesslike green and black.

Léon turns to Kruger. 'You're the expert. What do we need?'

'Short-handled spades will be better in a confined space. Here.'

A dozen hands reach out to take them.

'And these mattocks. We'll need barrows to take the material out. Get the ones with galvanised iron trays, they're stronger.'

By the time an impromptu chain of men is busy emptying the section of tools, Léon has made his way back out to the truck. The Dubai police are just arriving, lights flashing over the blue paintwork and yellow lion insignia of the cars.

Léon feels like a thief, but watches as a deputation of GDOIS division police sent by Abdullah bin al-Rhoumi arrives to take the heat off them. He climbs into the passenger seat and waits while the last of the booty clatters into the back.

'Go,' he shouts to the driver. The big diesel rumbles to life.

The tunnel is eerie and strange, reeking of disturbed earth, roots, and underground creatures. Here and there are patches of damp, but mostly the floor is dry earth. The walls and ceiling are smooth, slurry dried hard, perfectly shaped by the passage of al-Moler. Léon is astounded afresh at how efficiently the machine has done its work.

Those who walk behind carry an assortment of lights — headlamps, flashlights, even fluorescent camping lights. Many have 'borrowed' hard hats from the hardware store and others wear military steel helmets, surely uncomfortable in the heat and humidity of the tunnel.

Léon turns to Kruger. 'What are the chances of a cave-in?'

'Very slim: a TBM compacts as it goes. Having said that, it is always best to tread softly underground.'

Ahead they see the wall of earth where al-Moler stopped digging. This area is not so smooth. Heavy clumps of dirt and a few stones litter the floor area.

Léon feels a twinge of claustrophobia, along with confusion. A hand-built tunnel sounded simple back on the surface. Here, it is difficult to know where to start. The bunker complex is directly above. He knows from images on the computers at the control centre how it is laid out. Where to begin? Surely they cannot just start digging into the ceiling?

He watches Kruger circle the area, studying the walls, picking out samples of soil from here and there and squeezing them in his fingers. He stops, appearing to make a decision, then glances at Léon. 'Can you bring everyone in?'

They come, faces shining in the artificial light, standing in an anxious circle. This is a foreign environment for all of them, Léon realises. They are a mixed bunch; all those who were available on site. Some are Dubai police, others security contractors or labourers. Many are Pakistani, others local, and there is little talk among them. All understand the gravity and difficulty of the task ahead.

Kruger points at the end wall of the tunnel. 'We go in there, from the side, and zigzag our way up. Just five men will dig at a time, five on the barrows, five filling and stacking sandbags and five resting. Swap every ten minutes. Do you understand?'

The affirmative is a low mutter, punctuated by scuffing feet and silent nods.

'I'll mark the beginning. Pace yourself, don't go crazy. Who wants to start at the face?'

Léon is full of pride at this underground command. 'I'll begin,' he says, yet with some trepidation. He can run ten miles in fifty-three minutes, and bench press ninety kilograms, but swinging an agricultural implement? Hadn't he assisted his aunt Noelle to hoe the turnip patch? Last year? Maybe the year before.

Within ten minutes his shoulders ache, sweat pours down his face, and blisters form on the pads of his hands. The soil is hard in places, and though his mattock bites deep, he sees with some chagrin that the other men in the tunnel are making better progress than he.

Only weaklings give in to blisters, to pain, he says to himself, then tightens his grip and attacks the face with renewed vigour.

Day 7, 16:30

It is hard for PJ to shake off the schoolyard fear of unknown personalities as he comes off the chopper and into a canvas-covered Unimog with twenty-seven men he has never seen before. Little by little, however, they chat and introduce themselves, say things that sound mindless, but carry fears and terrors — hidden undercurrents that only other men in this situation would recognise.

The man alongside PJ offers a few squares of army-issue chocolate. He accepts, grateful to break the ice. These are all men like him, he realises, from different countries and cultures and experiences. They are not in the Special Forces because they are violent types, but because they value peace and are ready to accept the burden of protecting it. Most would be scrupulous about physical fitness. Many have young families of their own. All have acknowledged that their community and culture are worth preserving, even at the cost of their own lives.

Yes, PJ decides, these will be good men to work with. Good men to fight with, and if it comes to it, good men to die with.

The new tunnel cleaves at a fifty-degree angle into soils that Kruger describes as calcareous sand, proceeding in that direction for five or more dark metres before, on the South African's advice, Léon orders forward work to cease, and for a larger cavity to be hacked out. From here the tunnel beams back in the opposite direction, at the same angle.

'Like a New York fire escape,' a wiry American volunteer suggests.

Léon grunts at the aptness of the description. 'Change shifts.' His voice rings clearly, yet not too loud, for already they are conscious of the proximity of the conference room above. He passes the mattock into a pair of willing hands and staggers a few yards down the tunnel to the sandbag detail.

Here, under Kruger's direction, barrow loads of what he calls spoil — the material dug from the tunnel face — is poured into the sandbags and secured with drawstring closures. These are stacked in overlapping, brick-like rows along each wall of the new tunnel, pierced by spears of reinforcing bar hammered deep into the earth. At full height, the hardwood shoring timbers are laid across the top, making an immensely strong structure that also solves the problem of what to do with much of the soil they have excavated.

'Are you OK?' Kruger asks.

Léon covers his face with both hands and wipes the sweat away. 'I am fine. How far to go now?'

'Three hours at this pace, maybe a little more.'

Léon checks his watch. 'That is not quick enough. We have two and a half hours until the deadline. Then it is too late for all of us. We have no choice but to dig faster.'

The images fill the small screens on the benches and larger ones scattered around the room. First one procrastinating politician, then the next. It does not seem to matter — the demands will not be met, can never be met. The world has become a nightmare of darkness and there is nothing Isabella can do to change it.

'... the British Government has made the following further concessions ...'

'The United States Congress has agreed to ...'

'Australia's acting Prime Minister has announced that ...'

Isabella is transfixed by the horror of Jafar, the man she is forced to watch all her waking hours, patrolling, eyes hating and wanting her all at once. Then there is Zhyogal, to whom she gave herself willingly, fooled by a performance that was more convincing than that of any trained actor.

She has come to the realisation that her chances of leaving this room alive are slim. The knowledge that she will never see them again — Simon and Frances — is a sick weight in her belly, along with the desperate need to know what has happened to Hannah — if she is truly gone.

In her hands she holds the iPhone, shielded by her legs and the folds of her jacket. By now her SMS activities have become routine. First she looks around to identify where each of the terrorists is standing, then slips the handset from its hiding place and switches it on. Once she turns to see that the same man as always, the American, is watching her. They share a smile, as they have on other occasions.

There is a faint vibration as the unit powers up, a text message from Simon. Disregarding her own safety she thumbs through, reading the black LCD words that mean so much to her and she sees the word Hannah, and strings it together with the others. *'Hannah safe with me. All well. Praying for you …'*

Oh thank you, Simon, you prince among men who loves your family more than any mother has the right to expect. Oh please take me back … I'm so sorry for everything … I will love you forever, love you until my arms ache if only I can leave this death trap and breathe free air just once more …

'Stop.'

The voice comes from behind her. Jafar has moved fast, faster than she can credit. It is already too late. He has seen her.

'Bitch,' he shrieks, racing in with his pistol held like a club.

Isabella drops the phone, lifting both hands to protect her head. The heavy butt strikes her wrist and then, coming down again, the side of her head. Pain. Numbing, blinding shock.

Even as she begins to fall the curly-haired American who has watched her so many times jumps to his feet. 'The phone is mine,' he shouts. 'I asked her to hold it.'

Isabella looks up at the tall stranger, eyes watering with pain, body shaking as if she were cold. 'No, he's got nothing to do with it.'

The Iranian's face comes into focus, grimacing with anger, red and contorted. She watches him swivel the handgun and shoot the American man in the chest; watches him fall back against the seats, a dark stain spreading across his chest, body sprawled, people crying out in shock around him.

Oh dear God. The discharge is so loud that her ears feel like they have been plugged with wax, and shock steals the strength from her limbs and the processing power from her mind. *How is it possible that a tiny lump of copper and lead can steal a life so irrevocably?*

Pincer-like fingers grip her bicep, pulling her to her feet so that she shrieks with pain and her legs struggle to support her.

'The penalty for disobedience is death. To send messages is to die.'

Isabella feels the gun barrel against her temple. Now she is sobbing, waiting for the crash of sound and the end; no longer struggling, paralysed by fear stronger than words. Time telescopes into precious moments and images. She knows how much he wants to kill her. That to do so is the only way for him to expunge his guilt at what he feels for her. What he almost did to her.

'I kill her now,' Jafar Zartosht screams to the room, 'and soon all of us will die together, a glorious offering to God.'

* * *

Léon brings the incoming team together and warns them, 'You must be silent now. No sound at all … not even a fart. OK?'

The work becomes silent and intense. The cursing and banter stops. Léon takes his turn at the mattock handle, hands wrapped in rags to protect his blisters, knowing that he is ineffective, yet wanting to see this through to the end, determined not to shirk. Even when the rags soak through with blood he does not stop, but continues the slow thud of the blade into the earth.

When his arms feel like they will fall from their sockets and his hands have fused into claws, Kruger calls him across. Léon stands, chest heaving, while the South African directs their efforts to the ceiling of the excavation.

'Softly, slowly,' he hisses, 'it is close. Very close.'

Minutes pass before there is an imperceptible click as one of the men on Léon's right strikes reinforced concrete.

'That's it, take it easy now.'

Across three metres of shaft the undersurface of the slab comes into view, encased in plastic sheet in most places, rough mottled concrete in others. They finish off with their hands, attacking the work with new vigour, despite blisters and exhaustion.

When a section of the slab is clear Léon confers with the South African, then announces, 'Get the men out of the tunnel, bring up the explosives.' He stays and watches while the charges are set, unable to tear himself away from an operation that he understands might be the most important few hours of his life. The powder monkeys — thin, nervous types with an obvious close rapport —

unpack their bricks of plastic explosive and set their detonators.

'Ready to go?' Léon asks.

The ranking expert shows a black box with a Perspex-encased switch. 'Once I press this, that slab will be history.'

Léon waits until they are done and turns back down the tunnel to where the Special Forces team waits in grim double ranks, an officer passing through, sharing a few words with each man, shaking their hands like tennis players before a tournament.

Walking past, Léon says, 'Best of luck,' to the nearest of the men. It is good to feel like an equal with these machine-like troops. Some look up and nod, some remain silent, others talk softly to each other.

Léon tries to imagine what it will be like for them — he knows from his training that this is the most difficult of all hostage situations, and not just from the point of view of personal danger. There is a real possibility that mistakes will be made, that in a few minutes not just the terrorists might be dead, but the innocent, killed by an accidental bullet — someone's mother, someone's brother, or even someone's president. There is also a strong chance that the entire room will go up — that these elite troops will find nothing but pulped flesh and spot fires, disembodied limbs and screaming survivors. Some will be dead themselves within a minute or two. He stops beside the officer. Serious and tall, as broad shouldered as the others, yet bowed a little, as if with the extra weight of responsibility.

'Good luck, captain.'

'Thanks. You better get out of here. We're moving up now and as soon as the charges go,' he slaps a fist into a hand like a truck hitting a rabbit, 'we're through.'

Léon turns away, more than a small part of him wishing he could go in also.

PJ faces what might be just two or three minutes of intense action, a time when milliseconds could be more important than weeks of normal life — when the decision to squeeze a trigger might have ramifications for his career, his future, and even the world's political landscape.

Looking down, his kit is unfamiliar to him — a desert camo pattern instead of dull grey. The weapons are his. The HK53 and the SIG Sauer automatic at his waist. Already he has changed the sequence of cartridges twice, and resists the temptation to do so for a third time.

The ranking officer addresses them, and there is soothing authority in his voice and bearing. 'You all know what to do. Time is critical. We have three minutes until the terrorists detonate their explosives. Follow me, and good luck.'

The reply is heartfelt. They are dependent on each other to a degree impossible in any other situation.

PJ does not know who determined the safe distance they should wait from the explosion, but it seems close. The tunnel ends only metres ahead before heading up to the shelter above. A drop of sweat rolls down his forehead.

'Down,' someone orders.

PJ does as he is told, making sure the protective ear muffs are tight over his ears.

Day 7, Maghrib – Sunset

When the explosion comes PJ feels rather than hears it — an oncoming rush of dust and air and the earth itself shaking as if in a signal that things will never be the same again. That the old world order is crumbling.

There is no shouted command, just the ranks of men moving off at a run, onwards and through the shattered, broken blocks of reinforced concrete — into the unknown.

Ali Khalid Abukar watches Zhyogal take up the microphone for what might be the last time. So many countries have not gone far enough, paying lip service to the demands. A thrill goes through him, of pleasure and revulsion and atavistic terror.

Zhyogal's voice echoes with triumph. 'I am sorry to announce that the response has been inadequate. In two minutes, at the expiration of the deadline, we will destroy this room and everyone in it.' Then with a final shout he exclaims, 'Allahu akbar.'

Yes, Ali decides, *now I am truly bringing glory to God.* Something akin to ecstasy begins to course through his veins as he walks away from the dais and to Sufia. It is time to say goodbye.

Again they go to the cubicle. He takes her in his arms. His breath comes fast. He wants to live, yes. He does not want it to end. But are there not more important things than life? He hears footsteps, and turns to see Zhyogal walk into the area, scowling.

'Ah, the bitch continues to work her poison.'

Ali shakes his head. 'Leave us, I am entitled to some privacy.'

'No. The Americans and their puppets in the GDOIS have sent her here. I told you, she is with them.'

'That is a lie.'

Before Ali can stop him Zhyogal takes two quick steps forwards, grips Sufia's collar and rips it open, revealing the fine microphone with its wires against the clear dark skin of her chest and white underclothing.

'See? See that she is the tool of the kufr.' Zhyogal slips the handgun from his holster and passes it across, pulling back the slide. 'Kill her yourself, brother. Prove to me that you will not falter. Remember how we talked of the glorious world when Islam outshines the insanity of Christ followers and the Zionists?'

Ali's gaze settles on Sufia. Yet even now there is no begging in her eyes. 'You wore a wire in here?'

'I agreed so they would know if you planned to disarm yourself. So that when the soldiers come they will spare you.'

'They are coming?'

'Yes.'

Zhyogal speaks through gritted teeth. 'She is a liar. She is a tool of the capitalist machine that you and I must destroy. Kill her.'

Ali focuses his eyes on Zhyogal and passes the handgun back. Taking Sufia's arm, he leads her from the cubicle, while the deadline comes with the inexorability that is unique to time — never stopping, never slowing or speeding, despite sometimes giving the impression that it might.

Twenty seconds.

In Paradise are rivers of water ...

Ali looks at Sufia, now as close to despair as he has ever seen her. The delegates too are restless now that the time is close. The weaker souls are gone. All that remain had the courage not to sell their honour for freedom.

One man stands up, shouting, 'Murderers.'

Ali's body shakes as if from a physical blow. Never has he imagined that such a word might apply to him. He hears snatches of prayer, as the delegates prepare themselves.

Hail Mary, full of Grace …

The sound of the explosion down below is muffled, yet unmistakeable. Ali turns and locks eyes with Zhyogal. Both know what is happening. *They* are coming; the Special Forces troops are on their way. Ali feels a treacherous but profound relief.

Zhyogal, however, wears a sudden and terrifying expression on his face: fear that someone might snatch the moment of glory away from him.

Ali tries to turn but already Zhyogal is coming for him. With a thrust of outstretched hands he attempts to push him away but the Algerian is too strong. At first Ali thinks that the other man is trying to hurt him, but instead the focus of Zhyogal's strength and determination is the carbon fibre trigger that Ali takes from his pocket and holds in his hand.

'Push the switch,' Zhyogal shouts. 'Let it end the way God wills it to end for us.'

Ali knows now that he cannot kill the woman he loves. Cannot allow her beautiful face to feel shrapnel and pain. Here in this room are other men and women who love also. *This is not the way*, he wants to shout. *I was wrong.*

The strength of the other man, however, is too much — his fingers have the power of pliers and he uses them to prise away Ali's grip on the switch, a knee on his chest. Now Ali knows that he is seconds from death, and his wonderful, beautiful Sufia …

* * *

PJ moves through the opening, familiarising himself with the darkness — finding himself close to the front as they take the bunker staircase three steps at a time, reaching a small alcove and two doors beyond it. A single guard waits for them, getting a round or two away before his chest is torn apart by concentrated fire.

Two men swing a ram and the door smashes open. CS gas grenades arc into the space beyond. People scream. Pandemonium.

He enters the room, seeking targets, hearing the man ahead of him fire twice in quick succession. Someone goes down. PJ is no longer nervous, but is instead filled with a feeling of invulnerability, of abnormal strength. Over to the right he sees a militant running, grasping for bodies to use as human shields. Even as he fires, another rifle discharges behind him and the man dies where he stands.

The tear gas is disabling people now, forcing eyes closed, some vomiting and retching. Leaning over, hands covering faces. More than a few crawl on the floor towards the entrance, trying to get below the toxic cloud, anxious to be among the first to leave when and if the doors open.

PJ comes off the dais and turns the corner to see two men struggling on the floor. Almost a second — a long time in this kind of operation — passes before he realises that the man on the ground is Dr Abukar, and Zhyogal pinning him down.

He would have already fired but the Algerian has just wrested something from his adversary's hand. PJ recognises it as the trigger that will detonate the explosives.

'I have it,' shouts Zhyogal. 'Die! Feel the wrath of God.' He is on his knees, swaying in religious ecstasy. 'There is no God but Allah and Mohammed is His Prophet.'

PJ knows that there is no one else beside him — they have dispersed throughout the room hunting down the militants one by one. He knows that he has just microseconds to act — to do something. To do nothing and die, or act and die also.

Isabella looks up from the floor at Jafar, looming over her with the gun in hand, the barrel on her neck. The explosion has changed everything. Fear fills his eyes at first, and then a strange kind of determination. Lifting her by both hands he crushes her against his chest. She tries to struggle but his grip is like iron.

The Special Forces men are everywhere now, like alien creatures in their gas masks, rifles levelled. Impersonal and strange.

'Get back!' Jafar cries. 'You cannot shoot me without killing her also.'

His grip shifts so that the crook of his elbow is underneath her chin. In this position he begins to back away, pulling her with him. At first she lets her legs drag but he frees a hand to slap her face hard, and the shock is enough to force her into moving her feet, supporting her own weight, drawing her deeper into a nightmare. The gas makes her eyes water. Nausea builds in her throat.

'Let me go,' she croaks.

'Silence.'

She can tell by the timbre of his voice that he too is affected by the gas, yet somehow is still functioning. It occurs to her that perhaps some people are more resistant than others.

Shadowed by three soldiers, the terrorist backs towards the wall, adroitly using her body to shield him all the way. Reaching the bathroom door he pushes backwards through it, shouting to the men who follow: 'If you try to enter here I will kill her.'

He closes the door behind him, locking it, shoving her to the ground as he does so, withdrawing his pistol from his belt. 'It was you,' he shrieks, 'who brought this upon us, with your cell phone. Move, across the room.'

These are the men's toilets, and they pass a row of porcelain urinals, half screened from each other, then the cubicles. The air in here is free of the debilitating gas. Her eyes and nose stream less.

The terrorist stops before the window with its view out to the sea. He reverses his handgun and raps at the glass. It makes no impression. Again, harder, he smashes the butt against the glass and nothing happens.

'In the name of God,' he swears.

Isabella has only to look out the window to see that they are at least twenty metres from the ground. What does he expect to do? Climb down in full view and make a miraculous getaway?

Now he stands back and fires at the glass. The sound is shocking, numbing, in that confined space. Isabella feels tiny shards strike her face, and raises both hands to find her skin slippery with blood. She screams, but again he fires.

When the smoke clears it is obvious that there is no way through. The surface is chipped but not cracked. Isabella gathers herself to try to run while the terrorist stands facing the glass, chest heaving.

Realising her intention, he turns and is on her within a few paces. 'Bitch,' he cries, and with a grip on the back of her shirt, drags her down to the floor. Her head slams against the tiles and he is climbing onto her, his breath on her face. 'Damn you.'

His face is filled with a thousand sleepless nights of sexual confusion and desire. The war in his mind between passion and religious law. Isabella senses his need to expunge his own guilt with her blood.

'Whore!'

Stunned from the knock on her head she cannot move a muscle as he smashes his hand against the side of her face.

'Prostitute,' he grunts. 'Western pig.' Hatred fills his eyes and now she is more afraid than she has ever been in her life.

For a moment she stares, her mouth open as if it might let the grief escape rather than build. 'No. God. No, please ...'

Her vision comes back into focus. Summoning reserves from deep in her subconscious she tries to fight. Her brother Peter, long ago, as a fifteen-year-old tough, taught her the rudiments of street fighting, and the tactics come back to her in a rush.

She tilts her head with the suddenness of lightning, forehead butting into the soft flesh and gristle of his nose, breaking it so blood pours from both nostrils. He grunts in pain.

Still off balance he tries to raise himself. Isabella brings up her knee, catching his genitals. He rolls off her, moaning and writhing in pain. She expects him to come for her again with his hands, but instead he kneels, slips a knife from a hidden sheath. She sees his fury as he raises the weapon then brings the blade down; the sting as it enters her chest, brutally hard, rising again, plunging inside, cracking against a rib this time before sliding free.

At that moment Isabella understands that he is not merely killing her, but is killing everything he is afraid of and cannot understand, killing her as a way of killing the things inside him that he cannot control. Killing the gods of the others. The rotten and the good. All those things that nothing this side of death can explain.

The blood floods from her chest, and she scarcely hears the ram on the door, heavy-booted footsteps. Isabella's eyes register three men, alien in their gas masks and fatigues. Muzzle flashes. Gunshots.

Isabella Thompson stares with unseeing eyes as her rescuers fill the room. Soon someone lays a blanket over her body and face. On the tiled floor her blood mingles with that of Jafar Zartosht, a man whose primary battle has always been within his own soul.

PJ sees himself from outside, elevated as if through some hidden camera as he makes the decision to fire. There is no other choice. He will die no matter what, but this is the only way of saving hundreds of lives.

Taking careful aim, he shoots Zhyogal in the cheek, seeing the neat round hole appear just below the left eye. The second round catches him in the temple.

At the moment of violent death, human muscles can behave in either of two ways: to grip, or release. After the passage of a bullet through the frontal lobe, a man is not capable of thought — is brain dead at that moment —

but still there are tricks the body can play before all functioning and movement ceases.

Dropping his weapon, PJ lunges across the intervening ground, reaching out for the terrorist's hand as it swings through the air — the hand that holds the plunger, seeing the gripping reflex of the fingers, wondering just how far the trigger has to fall before contact is made.

PJ's hand closes around the fingers, dragging them off the trigger. As he recovers his balance he brings his other hand to bear also, hearing the terrorist's dead fingers snap under the force of his grip.

Coming to his knees, breathless with relief, he sees one of the SAS troopers bring up his rifle. A single shot catches Dr Abukar in the back of the head, spinning him around.

A woman's shriek. The tall, regal Somali woman goes to her husband, kneeling over the body, cradling him like a child.

Other men reach PJ. Congratulatory thumps on the back or a gentle touch on the shoulder or arm. Yes, somehow, they have done it. It is over.

'Felix on the way,' someone says, using the British army nickname for a bomb disposal expert.

More men arrive, and with the explosives in the process of being neutralised, PJ watches the tall woman weep over the body of Dr Ali Khalid Abukar. The love in her dark brown eyes is plain to see.

The main door now open, Marika comes in behind the second wave, with the medic and relief teams, who focus on the delegates huddling in their shocked circles, hanging blankets on their shoulders and leading them out in silent, shattered groups.

Sufia is on her knees and it is the end of the world; just one of a thousand small deaths that will make up the whole. When the medics come she stands and lets them cover his body and face. Then, her voice carrying to every corner of the room, she begins to speak. Footage, recorded on cell phone cameras, will later be beamed across the world.

'Ali Khalid Abukar is dead,' she says, 'and some of you will call him a terrorist. My husband was seduced by the radical extreme of his religion. But it happened because the leaders of the world have stopped listening. Political posturing has become more important than right. People are starving, people are dying, we are making our planet uninhabitable, and still our leaders are more ready to send men with guns than food. Power is not inherent in one person, just the illusion of it. Power resides in the will of the people. Please, I beg you, listen to his voice, now lost to us. Listen to the voice of a gentle man called to extremism and violence.'

There is some murmuring, and the room might have erupted but for one man who has not yet left, having regained his place at the front of the room, staring out at the exodus of delegates as if imagining what might have been. Marika watches him stand, and the voices that follow Sufia's outburst fall silent. The Secretary General of the United Nations has the face of a man who has stared over the precipice into another Dark Age, into something no sane individual can contemplate.

His voice carries across the room: 'Terrible things have happened here. Perhaps the world will never be the same;

perhaps we have been made to see things we have not seen until now. We cannot let this chance pass by. Time is running out for all of us.'

The room becomes still. Even medics sliding bodies into black, zippered bags stop to listen.

'The planet earth is a most beautiful place. Unique in all the universe. We have the intelligence and means to be wise caretakers. Instead we have indulged in an orgy of want, of waste, and destruction. We are faced with decisions that cannot wait. In spite of what has happened, the conference will reconvene in the morning, and hard decisions *will* be made. *Must* be made before it is too late. Too late for all of us.'

The clapping starts from a group of delegates, grey army blankets wrapped around their shoulders, being shepherded from the room. A new feeling permeates the room.

Yes, there is much to be done. It is time for the hands of the world to join.

Aftermath

The sun is just nudging the horizon when Marika climbs the last ridge, rewarded with a glade coloured with rock-cress and protea flowers. Beyond is a sweeping mountain panorama, surmounted by the peaks of Batian and Nelion and deep, mist-filled valleys between, cut through by the Liki River. One whole side of the sky is filled with grey and black thunderheads stacked high in the firmament. Thunder rumbles constantly. Lightning flickers and flashes across the sky.

Knowing that she should be finding a campsite, pitching her tent and gathering sticks for a fire, she instead sits down on a shelf of syenite rock and watches the view. The immensity and grandeur of it all. The feeling of wonder is strong within her. Of privilege to be who she is, where she is.

After four weeks at home, healing the aches and pains, she couldn't resist the urge to travel again. This time to the mountain trails of Kenya; not ready to return to Somalia, yet wanting to be close.

The Rabi al-Salah conference, reconvening the day after the terrorists were killed, has been hailed as a breakthrough. The people of the West face inconvenience and perhaps a level of want many have never before experienced, but there is a chance that the tide of change can be checked, if not stopped. The stockpiles of the West will be opened to feed the world. Carbon emissions slashed.

Marika feels part of something new — that her role in this new world has not yet ended. Perhaps just beginning.

One thousand kilometres away, Saif al-Din squats beside a group of men. All carry assault rifles of various makes and models. None smile. They have just finished praying together. They remember those who have fallen. They talk of death and life, of purpose and mission. These eight men from three continents are the remaining members of al-Jama'a al-Ashara, the council of the Almohad, united with a common purpose.

'This is a setback,' Saif tells them, 'not an ending. We must deal more harshly with the kufr. Zhyogal was weak: he should have destroyed the head of the snake when he had the chance. We will not make that mistake again.'

He looks down at the fresh, livid scars on his lower legs, where shrapnel tore through to the bone, remembering his terror as he swam four miles to an island, bleeding from limbs, body and head, making contact there with Sana'a, via satellite telephone. There is another scar on his temple, yet no doctor has yet cut for the sliver of steel inside.

Saif al-Din is certain now that God spared him for a reason. There is no doubt in his mind that he has a part yet to play in bringing glory to Him.

* * *

Eyes closed, Marika hears the first heavy rain drops, thinking of the mob at the gates of Dalmar Asad's compound. A scene that will be repeated across the world. The clamour of the people of this earth, yet to be heard in full voice. Freedom. Dignity. An environment free of pollutants and danger. Eight billion voices. Marika remembers the acacia hut. She remembers what it is like to cry.

The sun dips below the mountains, the moon becoming defined with the passing of a greater light. She stands, brushes off her khaki shorts, then slips her pack over her shoulders, adjusts the straps so the weight is distributed evenly and turns away.

Her feet leave prints in the dust behind her, only to be washed away by the coming storm.

Acknowledgements

'Thanks to:

Brian Cook, my agent, who saw something worth nurturing and stuck with me through the lean years. Your loyalty and faith are returned in full measure. To editor and publisher Anna Valdinger without whom this book would not exist. Shona Martyn, Sue Brockhoff, Christine Farmer, Jane Finemore, Kylie Mason, Kathy Hassett, Mark Higginson, Sarah Haines and Michael White. Matt Stanton for his incredible cover design. My wife and best friend, Catriona, Faye and Bob Barron (such endlessly supportive parents must surely be rare), Leanne, Maree, David and Fiona. All the extended family. My sons Daly and James, you make fatherhood such a rich experience. Readers: Bert Hingley for an honest and searching appraisal, Mark Daffey (thanks for sharing your deep knowledge and experience of the Middle East), Rob West, Sam West, Melina and Justin Murphy, Lisa Hall, David Hall, Steven Smith, Lucy Shepherd, Mark Shepherd for sharing a wealth of knowledge and personal experience on navigation and naval matters, as well as a good eye for a story. Steve and Nicky Russell, Margaret and Ron, Ged Clohesy, Lisa Heenan. Paul Daffey who has been such an inspiring friend and a great example of how to write. The staff at Eungai over the years; Lyn, Jenny, Ruth, Ashlee, Tony, Bev,

Fiona, Brett and Kylie. Steven Horne, a great writer, and such a wonderful host in Dubai. To all the authors who gave me so much pleasure and inspired me to write. To Bruce without whom I would surely have been lost on that long and magical trek across Arnhem Land! And to any others who have helped me through the ups and downs over the years. You know who you are.

Finally, to all those who risk life and limb to inform the world, this book would not have been possible without your work: hundreds of non-fiction books, thousands of websites, Twitter posts, blogs, newspaper and magazine articles. Thank you, I stand on your shoulders.

Reading Group Questions

1. Madoowbe could be described as a shape shifter. He can never be relied on to tell the whole truth, though he is good in a crisis. If he could write his own epitaph on a tombstone, what would it be?

2. Dalmar Asad has an unusual skin pigmentation. This might be construed as a symbol for competing European/African elements in his persona. We learn that he has had a poor background. Money, it seems, is not enough. What does Dalmar Asad really want? What does he strive for?

3. *Rotten Gods* presents the story from several viewpoints, attempting to explain the circumstances of each character's lives. Why do you think the author took this approach?

4. Isabella makes a choice at the critical moment. Is this selfless act enough to redeem her earlier actions?

5. What do you think Ali Khalid Abukar decides to do at the end of the book? Does he press the trigger?

6. Gods in their various guises become almost synonymous with violence in this book, or at least a very important causative factor. Both Christian and Muslim gods are, however, described by their followers as symbols of peace and unity. Are violent extremists merely psychopaths using religion as an excuse?

8. The man and woman building their hut in the rain is a powerful symbol in Marika's mind. What does it mean and why does it resonate so strongly with her?

9. *Rotten Gods* offers a vision of the future. Do you think the picture the book paints is realistic?

Interview with Greg Barron

Rotten Gods deals with the significant themes of religion and politics. Did you set out to write about these and does the novel in any way reflect your own personal philosophy?

Religion is, as the title suggests, a central platform for the book. I find it fascinating how religion is so often used as a reason for terror and violence, and also to justify a disproportionate response to such acts.

I am concerned that Muslim people can be tarred with the same brush, and wanted to present a number of different characters, spread out along the spectrum from quiet and law abiding, to those in positions of power actively working with Western governments to contain militant Salafism, a movement seen by many observers as the new Taliban.

My personal philosophy is that people have the right to believe whatever they want to believe, so long as it does not cause them to be violent or intolerant to others. Blind, unquestioning religious faith that becomes an excuse for war and terror is unacceptable. These, to me, are the Rotten Gods of the book.

You recently studied terrorism through the University of St Andrews, Scotland. What was your motivation for this and can you tell us a bit about the course?

To me, the object of fiction is not to present stereotypes or clichés, but to help understand the motivations and viewpoints of all the characters I present in my stories. This is only possible through knowledge, and St Andrews offers a Certificate in Terrorism Studies, designed primarily for people working in security forces active in terrorism hotspots across the world.

The section of the course that I have, at time of writing, completed — Key Issues in International Terrorism — offers a thorough understanding of terrorist ideologies, how they use fear as a weapon, how they are financed, organised and armed. Importantly, it delves into how terrorists are radicalised in the first place — motivated enough to kill in order to bring about change.

Generalisations are useless when dealing with terrorist groups. All are different: some aim simply to change just one or two aspects of government policy in their country, (e.g. extreme animal liberationists); others demand independence, or statehood for a specific group of people, (e.g. Hamas); and others have a regional or global agenda, such as the dozens of Islamist organisations that the media likes to call 'al-Qa'ida linked'.

One of the central characters in the novel, a strong young Australian woman who likes to bushwalk, seems a somewhat unlikely hero in the context of a terrorist situation. Can you explain your choice and what the character of Marika represents?

Marika was one of the first characters that came to me, and I never had any sense of creating her. To me she is a 'real' person with a past and a future. If you delve into the files of any international security force you might find a farm girl from Iowa, a Canadian law school dropout, a former Parisian street tough. Why not an Aussie chick who likes beer, with a mania for fitness and the wilderness?

In many ways she represents what is good about Western society, bearing in mind that she has had advantages many people haven't — good school, stable family and society — yet many readers will be able to relate to these same circumstances. It is how she acts when confronted with disadvantaged people that is the key to her character.

In *Rotten Gods* you are scathing of Western consumerism, debt levels and inaction on climate change. Why do you see these as important?
Rotten Gods is set a few years in the future. While climate change is already making itself felt now, by then things will be far worse. The natural disasters we are seeing now will be far more common. The drought in the Horn of Africa will never really go away. It may come and go, but there are permanent changes happening now. The cyclones and super tides. Famines and mass relocations of refugees are features of this new world that we will have to learn to address.

Consumerism? The concept of producing at least half a billion plastic containers a day, and throwing them into (mainly) landfill after a single use would have been regarded with disbelief and horror fifty years ago. We are so used to our own profligate waste that we don't even see it clearly any more. How many working CRT TV and computer screens were thrown into council clean-up piles when LCD and plasma screens became affordable? Why are electronic devices made redundant every year or two when new models come along? The planet cannot afford this level of waste.

Rotten Gods is a story, not a manifesto, but the concerns are real. It presents a vision of the future that may or may not come to pass in exactly that way.

The novel attempts to present both 'sides' of the situation. How were you able to present a sense of authenticity in your depiction of both the terrorists and security forces?

I do hate shallow, simplistic fictional representations of Muslim fundamentalists as 'evil.' What a stupid word! Their methods, I believe, are very wrong, but they don't think that. They see themselves as oppressed, and that they have the right to fight back in all ways and means at their disposal. They did not invent terror, nor the strategy of targeting civilians. Politically and militarily weak minorities have been doing this since the Sicarii initiated a reign of terror on occupying Romans in ancient Judea.

However despicable some of their acts are, it is important to understand why they do what they do, and this is something I have attempted in the writing of *Rotten Gods*. One of the conclusions drawn must be that this jihad would not be occurring without religion, so the image of a bloodthirsty God becomes a leitmotif throughout the book.

You grew up, and currently live, in country NSW and yet your novel has a distinctly international feel. How were you able to create this?

I seem to have a knack for blending in with my surroundings, and have travelled fairly widely. I lived in North America as a teenager and visited every international location used in the book that was feasible, and safe to reach. Besides, I no longer feel that Australia is a back woods location. Sydney is just 13 hours on an Airbus from Dubai, and Perth even closer.

The Department of Foreign Affairs and Trade (DFAT)'s voice has been growing on the international scene for many years, and we have cemented a position as a regional leader. Australians have risen to prominence in many UN agencies, and have little fear of remote and dangerous posts.

I think it is time that writers based in Australia are recognised as having a part to play in global popular fiction.

In contrast to the violence and the bleak view of humanity presented in the novel you also develop a number of loving relationships, such as that between Dr Abukar and Sufia, Marika and Madoowbe and Simon and his daughters. This is an effective way to develop their humanity. Can you explain how you dealt with these situations as you wrote *Rotten Gods*.

Readers, I think, enjoy romance, and of course a touch of sexual tension always spices up a plot. Generally I don't work out relationships in advance, letting them develop as I write, almost going through the stages of falling in love myself as I do so! I find sex scenes very difficult to write, as it is hard to know how much to reveal, and what to keep hidden. Generally I find a compromise, and am usually startled to read extremely graphic sex in popular fiction, particularly if it seems gratuitous.

The love of a father for his children was an easy one for me, being the proud dad of two boys. I believe that even a person who is generally mild, even cowardly, would lay down their lives for their children. Simon is a very bright man, yet uncomplicated in some ways. I think his love shines through the book. Nothing tricky, no hidden twists. To me he symbolises much of what is good about Western society, amongst the many, many faults.

There is a contrast between the terrorists and their unswerving faith, and the Westerners, such as Marika, who put their faith in themselves. Can there be a way to find a compromise between these two views?
Not all Westerners think this way, but I believe generally that people working in security organisations have to be self reliant. Faith in a greater power is a complication to obedience of superiors, the ability/need to kill when necessary and break other religious laws. That is not to say none believe in God, but there is a difference between believing in a deity and being intolerant of all others, and slavishly following rules and precepts that were in many cases developed one or two thousand years ago.

Popular fiction springs, at its source, from Greek myth, and the cult of the hero. Our fiction, which portrays the strong individual hero who fights for good against evil, can sometimes be misguided, but he/she acts from altruism and an innate sense of justice. That sense of right and wrong does not derive from a set of scriptures, but from something older. Something we don't, perhaps, understand ...

Rotten Gods is not the first novel you have written, but it is the first to be published. Can you tell us something about your journey to publication?

I wrote a number of novels before *Rotten Gods*. But I could never quite work out what kind of writer I wanted to be. I attempted literary and historical fiction. My first thriller landed me a hard working agent, Brian Cook, and under his guidance I rewrote that book several times, then another, before I finished *Rotten Gods*. On the first round of submissions HarperCollins offered me a contract.

You travelled widely as part of your research for Rotten Gods, in some of the more troubled areas of the world. Were you, at any time, in fear for the safety of yourself or your family?

Before travelling into the Horn of Africa, I was given a warning by a friend, an ex-military man who now provides armed security for journalists and corporations in the world's worst trouble spots. He said: 'Ask no questions, and do not, under any circumstances tell anyone that you are a writer or you will be targeted.'

Heeding this advice, I kept very quiet about my fact finding mission, particularly close to the Somali border.

Even so, while we were staying in Lamu, Frenchwoman Marie Dedieu was kidnapped from just across the channel by Somali gunmen. This was the second violent kidnapping in the area in two weeks. At first we did not know what was happening, as Kenya Rangers, armed with AK47s arrived at the waterfront in truckloads, and planes evacuated French and American nationals from the airstrip on Manda Island.

As a result of this we felt quite exposed and vulnerable. Most of the white tourists had already been evacuated and we stood out everywhere we went. Apart from cancelling a planned dhow trip north along the coast, however, we did not let this interfere too much with our enjoyment of this extremely special part of the world. Watch for more about this region in my next book.

Most African cities can be confronting at times, and you need a thick skin in dealing with touts, and people begging, who can be quite aggressive. Many approaches can be friendly, but persistent. Being firm but kind at the same time is an art form that regular travellers develop.

Finally, you are a voracious reader as well as a writer. What books have influenced you the most?
I once read an interview with a musician who was asked if he was influenced by other songwriters. He replied that he doesn't listen to a great song and think, 'I want to write a song like that.' He rather thinks, 'I want to write a song that makes people feel like that.'

I know where he's coming from. Great fiction gets under your skin and into your brain and resonates with all the experiences that are on offer. It recalls the great moments of your life and those you haven't yet experienced. I grew up in the seventies and eighties reading the big thriller writers of the day: Wilbur Smith and Jack Higgins, James Clavell, Alistair MacLean and John le Carré. Then there was Peter Carey, Thomas Keneally, Jon Cleary and a love affair with F. Scott Fitzgerald, John Steinbeck, Larry McMurtry and those giant doorstoppers by James A. Michener.

Living on a remote property on the Northern Territory with no TV, I read every book in my English teacher wife's collection. Everything from Thucydides to Stephen King, Gabriel Garcia Marquez to Somerset Maugham. When I'd read them once I read them again.

Somehow along the way I guess I must have learned what works and what doesn't; learned what is trite; learned to recognise what keeps the light on way past midnight, and the pages turning. Sometimes I even get it right. Watch this space. There's more to come.

SAVAGE TIDE

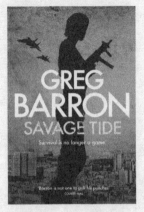

**'The Hourglass brings death
wherever he goes. That is his business.
He leaves a trail of corpses ...'**

Marika Hartmann, an intelligence officer for a shadowy subdivision of MI6, captures an extremist foot-soldier guilty of a massacre of school children and aid workers in Southern Somalia. Renditioned to a CIA 'black site' in Djibouti, the prisoner hints at a devastating terror plot in the making, led by a ruthless doctor known as The Hourglass.

Marika and her ex-Special Forces colleague PJ Johnson team up to investigate, uncovering a cold-blooded conspiracy to decimate the cities of the West. But the enemy is always one step ahead – is there a traitor at the very heart of MI6?

From the refugee camps of East Africa to the azure waters off the Iranian coast, the marshes of Iraq to Syria's parched eastern desert, *Savage Tide* is a manhunt, a quest for truth, and a desperate search for the legacy of a cruel regime bent on dominating the world.